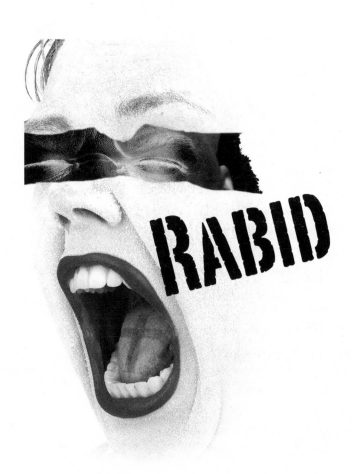

"Kenyon is definitely a keeper."
Booklist

STARRED ★ REVIEW

"A priest, a professor, the professor's wife, and his mistress—it sounds like the set-up for a dirty joke, but debut novelist Kenyon isn't fooling around. What begins as a riff on Peyton Place (salacious small-town intrigue) smoothly metamorphoses into a philosophical battle between science and religion. You would think that in attempting to deal with so many different themes—shady clergy, top-secret scientific research, marital infidelity, lust, love, honor, faith—Kenyon would run the risk of overwhelming readers. But, and this is why Kenyon is definitely an author to watch, she juggles all of her story's elements without dropping any of them—and, let's not forget, creates four very subtle and intriguing central characters. This is a novel quite unlike most standard commercial fare, a genre-bending story—part thriller, part literary slapdown with dialogue as the weapon of choice (think Who's Afraid of Virginia Woolf)—that makes us laugh, wince, and reflect all at the same time. Kenyon is definitely a keeper." ■ David Pitt/*Booklist*

"RABID is a solid good read by first time novelist TK Kenyon, a gifted writer who has crafted a book of such mystery that you find yourself, at midnight, on the edge of your seat, asking, 'What's next? What's next?'" ■ **Thom Jones**, author of *The Pugilist at Rest* (National Book Award), *Cold Snap, Sonny Liston was a Friend of Mine*

"RABID is a biopsy of our heated emotions and troublesome philosophies." ■ **J.C. Hallman**, author of *The Chess Artist*

A NOVEL

T K KENYON

KÜNATI

DEDICATION

To my Family:
Tom and Juleen Kenyon, my parents,
George and Kay Hossack,
and Frank and Evelyn Kenyon, my grandparents,
and Mahesh Krishnan, my husband.

Chapter One: Bev

Pink?

Under the stale khaki pants and blue shirts in her husband's suitcase, Bev glimpsed *pink*, and her fingers gathered the soft fabric. *Pink* slithered soft and silky like crawling smoke out of the suitcase and hung in the air in front of her.

Pink panties.

Not her own.

Her skull burned white-hot under her skin. A caged ape rattled her ribs and her stomach snapped like an angry bull shark surging through chum. Bev lunged into the bathroom and hung over the open toilet but wasn't sick and pressed her temple against the cool yellow wall, pulled back and let her head fall against the wall again, then harder.

She dangled the underwear over the gaping toilet. The panties, *someone else's* pink silk panties and horrid, matching camisole, swung above the gaping porcelain and water. Bloody vomit hemorrhaged inside her and clung in her guts, corroding. Her fingers loosened and the panties slipped but she grabbed them again, slammed the toilet lid down, and sat. She threw the damned panties against the wall with a strong right-handed whip that should have embedded the silk in the plaster like tornado-torpedoed straw through a telephone pole but the underwear slid to the floor. Her heart slammed so hard that her temples bulged and her carotid arteries hurt in her neck, threatening a stroke like a smiting by God. She drummed her head against the wall in fast time with her hammering pulse.

The bastard. The goddamn, cheating bastard.

Her skull smacked the wall and she rattled inside. Again. Harder.

She wanted a drink but there was no liquor in the house. She wanted to drink herself unconscious to stop the sight of those pink panties in her eyes and stop the gushing vomit in her throat and stop her mind from hating him. She knew that drinking would make everything worse, but she wanted a drink.

On his way from the airport to work, Conroy had dropped off his suitcase at home. That other woman might be a secretary, or a student, or a nurse, or one of the other scientists, or it might have been a real whore, a prostitute he'd bought while he was in Washington.

Bev was stupid. She was a stupid doormat. She slammed her stupid head against the wall.

If Bev told her friends, they'd know that she was a stupid doormat, and they'd tell her to leave him, and she couldn't. If she cried all over Conroy, he'd say she was being manipulative like his mother and he'd get mad. God, she was so stupid and she didn't want anyone to know how stupid she was, not Lydia and Laura and Mary, not Conroy.

Bev's temples pounded. Her fingertips throbbed like she was ripping out the whore's pulsing throat. Her palms burned from the heat of a match setting the whore on fire. Her arms strained with the effort of shooting or strangling or bashing the whore.

Or stabbing. A strong knife that slipped in at the right angle with the force of a good golf swing that made crisp contact, and the whore would gush blood.

It was sin again to dwell on those terrible images. She had sinned again. The bathroom and the house and the world echoed with the absence of God. She was a sinner, everyone was a sinner, but she was disgusting and horrible to God.

Confessing the violence to Father Nicolai would make the thoughts go away. She was so alone, and those evil, sinful thoughts had driven away even God, and she was lost to hell and surrounded by demons.

Chapter Two

Conroy juiced the accelerator, and the antique black Porsche jumped. The blue Infiniti speeding in the inside lane fell behind. Testosterone or adrenaline or an opiate neurotransmitter crackled in his spine, riding ionic potentials cresting down axons like surfing the Bonzai pipeline.

The sleek black dashboard curved away from the steering wheel and over Leila's long legs. The Porsche was six years older than she was. Her black hair spilled over the seat like the silk and leather thing she had worn a couple of weeks ago. Pale pink lipstick smudged her upper lip.

He sped along Woolf Road, which led to the University hospital and health science district. "Got much to do at the lab?"

"Too much." She scrunched up her coat sleeve and consulted her watch.

Ah, the grousing of the overworked, underpaid grad student, the lament voiced by all those who sacrifice to raise themselves, to chase fame and the betterment of humanity. Her complaining warmed the barnacles on Conroy's heart. Yes, barnacles, not cockles. A cockle is too small a shellfish to describe Conroy's arterial deposits. Barnacles encrusted his cardiac system, sessile barnacles and other crustaceans, a whole, flashy coral reef. Even his cholesterol plaques dreamed big. His genes had preprogrammed him for a hull-scraping before the age of sixty, less than a decade away.

"Finished that mutant virus yet?"

Leila's trim eyebrow dipped. "Almost." Her mouth firmed into a scowl.

"What's wrong?"

"Nothing." Her glance was an acidic glare. She drummed her fingers on the Porsche's black armrest. Outside the car, dark university buildings sped backwards.

He slid the car to a stop. Snow-dandruffed gargoyles clung to the stone walls of Medical Laboratories. His lab's windows, halfway up, were dark.

Leila unlatched her un-retracting seatbelt and opened the door. Black-ice January air swarmed into the car. She toed the asphalt outside like an unsteady foal. "See you tomorrow, Dr. S." She slammed the car door, hesitated with a glance behind the car, and swiped her keycard through the card-reader by the building's door without looking back.

Tomorrow, they would be student and P.I. again, just the way she said she liked it, just the way he said he liked it: a professional relationship in the lab and a casual fuck on the side.

He jammed the Porsche into first, ground the gears, tried again, found them, and drove home angry, blazing through yellow lights and swerving around crawling cars that shouldn't even be on the god-damned road.

THE PORSCHE'S icy door handle needled Leila's hand through her glove. Headlights crept out of the dark. Someone might see her emerging from Conroy's ostentatious Porsche, and the department gossip grapevine would rumble and grow fat. "See you tomorrow, Dr. S." She slammed the car door and hurried, holding her half-buttoned coat around her.

The Porsche's gears grated and the tires screeched, leaving her alone in the night. Dead bushes of bundled sticks lined the sidewalk. Usually when she worked late, she slipped her handgun into her purse, but Conroy hadn't turned his back so she could grab it.

Headlight glare caught her against the brick wall. Her chilled fingers fumbled with her badge in the card reader's slot. The door clicked, unlocking. She hustled. Dangerous types scurry in the night around deserted buildings.

This casual fuck with Conroy was getting dangerous. She should break it off and live celibately, chastely, like a nun, or a priest.

Revolting.

DRIVING UP to the MedLabs building, Malcolm saw a low, red stripe of taillight wheeling away and that slinky Leila Faris walking in the building door.

"Oy! Leila!" he hollered into the cold night, but she didn't stop.

Months later, Malcolm might have testified that Leila had emerged from that red, horizontal taillight slash, so obviously Dr. Sloan's Porsche, into the January dark, but he had forgotten.

Murder trials are never about the dead person anyway. Strong Scot fatalism would have kept his testimony just the same: that Leila and Conroy were but grad student and mentor, and that if anyone was to blame, it was the wife herself or that Papist priest.

BEV'S HANDS, finger-knotted and pink-knuckled, pressed the confessional's latticework, and she rapped on the wood. A priest grunted on the other side. Father Nicolai should be in there. His timid laugh flopped his piebald hair, like the calm, clean guy introducing puppet shows. The confessional smelled humid, like sex.

The priest slid open his shutter and mumbled the benediction, "In the name of the Father, and of the Son, and of the Holy Ghost, Amen." The voice wasn't Father Nicolai's.

Her skirt hem, tucked under her kneecaps, chafed. "Bless me, Father. I have sinned. It's been two weeks since my last confession."

"Yes?" The priest shadow rubbed his face.

Her breath stuck in the hollow at the base of her throat. Not making a good confession would leave her unreconciled, and with a mortal sin on her conscience she couldn't take communion because her soul offended God by dwelling on her hands strangling a redheaded whore, then a gun shooting a blonde bitch, then a knife slashing tanned, firm, young flesh.

The priest sighed. "You only need to confess-ah the mortal sins."

"I know that," and she stopped. The priest's young voice was not Father

Samual's gravelly bass or Father Nicolai's timid grumble. His accent was Spanish or something, and wrong. Suspicion fused with panic. "Who are you?"

The man said in that odd accent, "The reason for the antique confessional is the anonymity."

His words were slurred, drunk. Her frantic energy refocused. "You're not a priest. I've heard about people who sneak in and sit on the priest's side of the confessional."

His smooth, young voice strengthened. "Madam, I am a priest."

"We Catholics have to confess to a priest!" She rattled the fragile latticework. "Why would you trick someone?"

The door clicked and she thought she had driven away the imposter, but the curtain on her side jerked back.

The man there, with curling hair framing a face almost familiar in its beauty, like a painting of a wrathful angel holding a flaming sword, said, "Madam, come with me."

His hand slipped under her palm and her fingers slid out of the lattice.

Black sleeve, black whirling cassock, and he pulled Bev past her daughters' seed pearl–teethed open mouths and shocked eyes, through the echoing cathedral.

IN A LONG PEW outside the confessional, Dinah turned to Christine and said, "Wow, I wonder what Mom did."

Christine, the older, worried child, shrugged and composed her own sins in bloodless, effete terms that would not provoke the strange priest to haul her away.

MONSIGNOR DANTE PETROCCHI-BIANCHI gripped the woman's arm and led her through the dollhouse cathedral punctuated by narrow stained-glass windows to the library. His head throbbed with jetlag and spun from the plane's miniscule whiskey bottles. This parish was supposed to be a university environment, not a small, parochial town where people shied at a new priest and had crow-barred open an antique, claustrophobic, moldy confessional.

In the library, books on mismatched bookcases hemmed in three chairs. Dante's Italian accent, despite his efforts, broadened, "You can-ah see that I am indeed the priest."

He certainly looked the part of a Roman priest in his long, black, Jesuit cassock and gold pectoral cross. Wearing the cassock was common among conservative Jesuits and *de rigueur* in the Vatican, especially because Dante's previous boss, then-Cardinal Ratzinger, made it a point to wear the humble, conservative, traditional clerical garment.

Tears ran glycerin tracks from her wild, brown eyes down her cheeks. "*Who* are you?"

His hand rose and he palpated his temple. Alcohol had abraded the skin over his cheekbones and orbitals. "I am Father Dante. I was sent to replace Father Nicolai."

The woman glanced around, frantic, as if the bookcases might pounce. "Where is he?"

Questions already. "He was reassigned."

"Why didn't he tell me?" Her hands, the nail polish oddly chipped off, climbed over each other as if each were drowning, pulling the other down.

Dante refocused his grimy eyes. This distraught woman was in her mid-thirties, near his own age. The confessional's latticework had piecemealed her and shown him only a brown eye gathering skin and sun damage spots on her throat. "I'm sorry, madam. And you are?"

She sniffed and wiped her cheek with the back of her hand, dragging a lank of pale brown hair out of the band that gathered it at her neck.

"Bev Sloan."

"Mrs. Sloan, please, sit." He gestured toward an armchair and hunted among the dusty, musty books for tissues. "What do you want to confess?"

Her eyes teared again. "I keep having terrible thoughts."

Dante found a slim box of paper tissues stashed between two books and extended it to her. She plucked one and wiped her eyes. He sat and laid the box of tissues on the table between them. The possibility that she was possessed by a demon occurred to him, but he discarded it. Suspecting demons behind every normal neurosis was paranoid. Sometimes, Dante suspected that the Adversary was trying to make him paranoid, but the notion that Dante warranted Satan's attention was itself paranoid. Being an exorcist had its workplace liabilities. "The thought is?"

Mrs. Sloan's hand-clawing intensified. "Hurting someone."

He rubbed his stubbled jaw line, trying to massage away the teeth-grinding tension. He'd seen demons incite murder. "Who?"

"Some woman, somewhere. I found pink women's underwear in my husband's suitcase." She wiped her eyes.

Ah, provoked. Always, people told him their secrets if given sufficient time. Dante pinched a fresh tissue, pulled it out of the box, and waited.

She said, "He went to Washington. I'm sorry. I'm sorry," she sobbed.

She reached for another tissue, and he touched her suspended hand gently, in a priestly way, he hoped, then held her fingers. He was just a priest, a muzzled, leashed, caged priest, and no threat to a woman, no matter what paced in the cage, what lunged on the leash, or what snapped inside the muzzle.

Tears wobbled in her wide brown eyes. She reached with her other hand for the tissue and pressed it to the lower half of her face, covering her mouth and nose, stifling herself. Her eyes, still too wide, glanced at his hand, but she didn't tug. She said, "He's having an affair."

"Oh, yes." Dante covered their clasped hands with his other hand. The move was priestly, not predatory, he hoped. "You have talked to him about this?"

"No, he just dropped off the suitcase and went to the hospital. He's a neurologist."

It was a monstrous thing, disregarding a spouse, committing adultery, and especially within the ken of doctors. University and medical school, those crucibles of memorization, indulged thoughtless excess. "You need the marital counseling. You know a counselor?"

She shook her head. "Everybody knows everybody at the hospital. People would talk."

"Father Samual, then."

She glanced at their warm hands clasped on the table. "He's such a gossip." Her hand squeezed his within their Gordian knot of fingers. "You could counsel us."

His pants chafed his groin, and he shifted. "I will be here only for few months."

Mrs. Sloan nodded. "That'll be long enough to know if we're going to stay together."

Stay together, she meant *divorce*.

He shouldn't counsel them. "The girls, sitting outside the confessional. They are your daughters?"

"Yes. Christine and Dinah."

Her daughters, they were so small. He removed his covering hand from their grasping fingers. Mrs. Sloan held onto his other hand. "*Si*, yes. I do it."

"Can we come tomorrow?"

So soon. "Six and a half o'clock. For a moment, to meet." Her hand still clamped his hand to the table between them. "How old, your daughters?"

"Eight and ten. Why?"

"Some things about the school, I should like to ask them about." Dante loosened his grip on her fingers and flinched, to suggest she release his hand. His palm was sweaty, encased in that morass of hand flesh and fingernails. He liked it too much, so he needed to let go.

Mrs. Sloan fluttered her eyes. "All right." She touched her eyes with the tissue and untangled her small hand from the raw meat of his paw.

They prayed the Act of Contrition together and Mrs. Sloan rose to leave. She smeared another wet streak from her eyelashes to the pale brown hair at her temple. "We'll see you tomorrow, Father Dante."

It was odd, the English *Father* instead of *Padre* or *Monsignor* or *Professor*. He was so far from Roma, but he had volunteered for this. Rooting out an evil as ancient as the Adversary itself was more important than his creature comforts and routine of Roma. He could shout above a screaming demon-possessed man or dodge flying chairs, but this assignment in New Hamilton—his primary assignment, not this tangential marital counseling—required delicacy and empathy, which were qualities he did not exercise as an exorcist.

She smeared another blossoming tear from her eye to her hair.

Her tears infused the library with suffocating humidity. Dante said, "Mrs. Sloan, the sex, to men, it is nothing. It is animal instinct. Friction. It is appetite or domination or an attempt at their own damnation, for a man, but it is never love."

CONROY OPENED the door from the wintry garage to the house. As his face broke into the warm air, browning meat scent lingered in his nose and traveled the neurons to his brain. Ah, the olfactory bulb, a source of stem cells that migrated from the hippocampus and, when damaged, caused olfactory hallucinations, phantom scents. "Hello, ladies!" he called.

Dinah, his younger daughter, clattered over the tile. "Daddy!" She flung herself at him.

Beverly hadn't hollered hello. "Dinah, where's your mom?"

"Making supper. It's late 'cause we went to confession. The new priest took her away."

New priest? "Beverly!" he yelled. "You here?" He walked into the house. Priests were twisted creatures, repressed by a sick corporate structure that wrung them into castrated caricatures of men.

BEV HEARD CONROY HOLLER. She stirred the gravy, scraping browned bits. The rich scent of reducing gravy rose through the yellow kitchen and ascended with her soul, seeking God. She had to get Conroy to counseling. She had to do this right. A fragment of the Rosary hovered in her head, *pray for us sinners now and at the hour of our death.*

Footsteps clacked on the tile. Conroy's arm slipped around Bev's waist and he kissed her ear with a smacking sound. "Beverly," he whispered.

Bev's angry spine wound tight at the touch of his body, still slimy from Washingtonian sex. *Now and at the hour of our deaths.* "Hello, Conroy."

"Sorry I had to run this afternoon." He moved away and her spine, no longer touching his defiled body, unkinked. "Did you see your friend Mary at church?"

"No." She tossed the vegetables. Parti-colored bits showered down into the pan. Not Mary, but Father Dante. He had seemed kind when he took her hand, but he was so young. Priests should be older, aged men with the manliness in them burned away so that they were beyond gender, beyond handsomeness, robe-wrapped emissaries of God. There was no reason a priest shouldn't hold her hand when she was distraught. He belonged to God. It was as if God were holding her hand. Her stomach giggled a little at the thought of him holding her hand, but he was a priest, and beyond her. She needed strength now, not odd thoughts about priests.

"I'll herd the girls to the table." Conroy walked out of her kitchen.

Bev was a swamp of revenge and spite. She breathed deep into her soul and created space for God and the Blessed Virgin to fill her with peace, but they didn't. Anger whirled faster behind her smarting eyes as she finished cooking and plated four suppers.

She settled into her place at the end of the dining room table, opposite Conroy. The glass chandelier reflected in the glass tabletop and twinkled in the silver structure below. Christine and Dinah sat between them on the long sides of the table.

Conroy sat with his back to the bay window. He flapped open his paper napkin and said, "Study section was interesting. The usual assortment of solid work and this one wild, off-the-wall submission."

Wild, off the wall, against the wall, was he still talking about grants? Bev ate a carrot and chewed slowly to avoid grinding her teeth.

"He thinks he can vaccinate against cholesterol. It's not even a peptide."

Bev ate something. "Insane, thinking he could fool you like that."

"Yes," Conroy said. "Dr. Lindh made some interesting comments."

Dr. Lindh. Bev couldn't remember him or her. "I'm sure *he* did."

"Valerie Lindh. *She* did."

Bev knifed her beef. "Such talk about business. Didn't you do anything fun?" and she couldn't believe she'd said that. *Mary, be with us now and at the hour of our deaths.*

"No. Didn't even go out for dinner. Just ate in the hotel." Conroy smiled at Christine. He asked, "Did you score this weekend, honey?"

Conroy had certainly *scored.* Bev tried to breathe slowly.

Christine said, "No, but I stopped the other team from scoring twice."

Dinah swung her legs, bouncing in her chair. "Mommy, can I have some more potatoes?"

On Dinah's plate, the vegetables and meat huddled, trying to look small and eaten.

Bev turned to Christine. "Honey, would you help Dinah dish up some potatoes?"

Christine mumbled, "Yes," and folded her napkin.

"Thank you, dear. Just one spoonful."

Christine held Dinah's hand as they went to the kitchen.

Bev turned back to Conroy and whispered, "I found *panties* in your suitcase. Pink ones. Whose are they?" Her harsh stage whisper carried through the dining room, bounced off the modest chandelier, and reflected back to her in fragments. *Found. Pink. Whose.*

Conroy leaned back in his chair, his palms pressed against the table. "I don't know what you're talking about."

"You know what I'm talking about. *Do you love her?*"

Conroy blinked, his gray lashes and crumpled eyelids flapping over his fluorescent blue eyes. "What are you going to do?"

Bev leaned back. Her fork clattered onto her plate. "We need counseling."

Conroy launched into the old routine. "We know everyone."

From the kitchen, a spoon clinked and potatoes splatted on a plate. Dinah said, "More."

Bev said. "There's a new priest down at the Church."

Conroy rolled his eyes. "Priests aren't doctors. They're not even *married.*"

Her voice dropped. "Our first appointment with Father Dante is tomorrow at 6:30."

"*Dante*, for our own private trip to Hell, that's appropriate."

"I mean it. We'll get counseling, *or else* I'll take the girls and walk out right now."

"You can't take the girls." He picked up his fork and held it in his fist.

Bev leaned forward. "I will."

His hands balled into fists and shuddered in the air like a baby preparing to wail. He said calmly, "People will talk."

"That's right," Bev said. "Everyone will know, all your friends, the administration, the committee."

"You wouldn't." His hands dropped below the table. Through the white twinkles in the glass tabletop, she could see his fingers curling around the cushion on the metal chair seat. "You wouldn't do that to me."

"I thought you would never do this to *me*."

Conroy's jaw clenched hard. He looked away and whispered, "Fine."

"And you will break it off with whoever she is."

The skin over his nose and cheekbones reddened. "Obviously."

Bev sat back in her chair. From the kitchen, again there was a spoon clinking and the splatting of potatoes. Dinah said, "More."

Bev called over her shoulder, "Girls, that's enough." To Conroy, "Then it's settled."

Conroy smiled tightly at the girls coming back in. Potatoes covered Dinah's plate and were puddled with three gravy pools.

CONROY WAS HIDING in his home office, reading scientific papers. In the kitchen, Beverly splashed and clanked. In the *Journal of Virology*, an article detailed a glowing green virus that traced nerve connections from a pig's eye to its brain. The virus was named pseudorabies virus because PRV causes symptoms similar to rabies—foaming, hallucinations, psychosis, photophobia, encroaching paralysis—but so did a host of other neurotropic viruses, including mad cow prions. Conroy had been particularly interested in rabies and other neuropathological viruses lately. One could, perhaps, use them to understand and even induce hallucinations. He made a couple of notes in the margin about the fusogenic action of the viral glycoprotein.

A clank in the kitchen, and the dishwasher growled and whooshed.

Lingerie in his suitcase after a weekend trip was damning. Idiot. He should have checked.

He wandered out of his den. In the kitchen, Beverly was washing pots. She swiped a suds-covered hand at her ash-brown hair, inhaled a shuddering breath, and began scrubbing again.

He didn't want his wife to cry. Poor Beverly. No wonder she'd gone to the Church.

Perhaps he was lucky that she'd gone to a priest. Priests were supposed to keep secrets. If Beverly had confided in Laura or Mary, he might have found an empty house and divorce papers. The department would have gossiped until, like a water buffalo in a piranha-infested river, they reduced him to skeletal remains. "Beverly?"

She didn't look at him. If anything, she scrubbed harder. "Yes?"

"I wanted to say," and she stopped scrubbing, "we'll work through this."

Beverly's shoulders slumped, but she still didn't look at him. "I think so, too."

Conroy retreated to his office and read papers on RNA viruses, neurovirulent viruses, herpesviruses and rabies. He didn't go to bed until he thought Beverly was asleep.

BEV LAY IN THE DARK BED under the covers, her fists clenched against her breastbone. Conroy's clothes shushed against his polluted skin as he undressed on the other side of the bed. He lifted the covers. Chill air sucked her toes.

In the morning, things might not look so bleak. Problems expanded in the sun's absence. Darkness pressed her, weakening her knees like vodka, so she lay in the bed beside that bastard.

She dreamed that smoke filled the air, and her two girls, unfathomably both two-year-old toddlers, rested on her hips. She could hardly walk under their weight and she flowed with the crowd away from the smoke and the screaming and falling debris. Another fireball lit the sky behind her and its heat scorched her neck.

Ahead of her, Conroy jogged easily with the crowd.

Plaster and concrete dust rushed through the air and closed off the path between them. The whiteout parted and a man's hand, swathed in black, reached out to her. She took the warm, comforting hand and held on. She flew, and Father Dante carried her.

The Daily Hamiltonian:

STILL NO MED HEAD

By Kirin Oberoi

After interviewing several candidates, the selection committee is still looking for a new Dean of the Medical College. "All the candidates were well qualified, but none had that spark of enthusiasm for the University of New Hamilton," said Dr. Stan Lugar, a committee member.

The committee is interviewing more candidates, including an unnamed UNH candidate, before their February 15 meeting. The selection committee will base its decision on career milestones such as awards, grants, publications, community connections, and career potential.

LEILA SCANNED THE PAGES crowded with wordless jumbles of letters, and her finger stopped on a short sequence of As, Cs, Ts, and Gs. Her tongue licked her upper lip. That short DNA sequence was the reason that her mutant virus kept dying.

A key scraped the lock in the lab's door.

She sat at her desk, the binder propped up on her knees, reading the DNA sequence in the fluorescent light. She bit her finger and stared at the page. Finding it was exhilarating, like a downhill sprint after a six-mile run against a staunch wind.

Conroy opened the lab door, said, "You're early," and jiggled his keys to extricate them from the jimmied lock.

She kept her right hand on the block of DNA code and typed it into the computer with her left.

Conroy set his coffee on the lab bench beside the PCR machine and shifted his bundled papers and journals to his other arm. "I found an interesting paper. PRV neurovirulence."

"Pig herpes. No one works with herpesviruses. You might catch something in the lab."

"Just read the article." He flapped the journal onto the desk.

Leila said, "The kinase and the late glycoprotein are on a bicistronic mRNA."

Conroy sat at the other computer and checked his email. "Bicistronic. Sounds kinky."

She folded her arms across her chest and waited.

Conroy's head clicked to the left. "Jesus. Why are you sitting here? Go make that mutant. You have other experiments going?"

"None to speak of. You?"

Conroy chuckled, a bit of bitter in a single cluck. "None to speak of."

Anyone else, postdocs or grads or undergrads or techs, would have stopped. She said, "Your writing is on eight flasks of cells. You have five cages of mice."

Conroy's skin surged into his wry smirk. "Don't play with them."

"Your technique is sloppy. I had to bleach the incubator and hoods."

He laughed his usual bass rumble. "It's preliminary work. Nothing special." His hand covered hers. "When can I see you?"

Leila pulled her hand away, and his palm slid on her skin. "Don't do that in the lab."

His hand slipped over her hip. A thrill slithered up her spine at the same leisurely pace as when she'd panther-crawled onto Conroy yesterday in her bed surrounded by gauzy curtains under the Persian red, gold-spangled canopy. Persian Empire harem women, though sequestered, had expressed the range and depth of their sexuality, before the Abrahamic religions had twisted women into the male ideal: monogamous, unimaginative, repressed.

"Dinner, tonight?" he asked.

"No." She walked out of the computer room.

As a rule, sleeping with married men creeped her out, so she rarely indulged. Conroy was one of the very few exceptions. Marriage reeked of religion and other perversions.

Chapter Three

Conroy was editing his R01 grant proposal on the outrageously expensive, oversized computer monitor he'd bought so he wouldn't need to wear reading glasses. He'd kept at least one R01 grant for twenty years. First grants are easy. Many associate professors don't receive tenure because they don't get their *second* grant, which should be based on results since the first grant, and then they can't hire techs or accept new grad students to produce data, and they can't publish papers, and thus they cannot apply for grants.

He wanted this new R01 grant under review, preferably with an encouraging rumor floating, before the department chair selection committee meeting, Monday, February fifteenth, the Ides of February, almost a month hence. On his desktop calendar, carboniferous pencil ringed the date.

But this renewal, these results and this particular grant were problematic. His hesitant typing bounced staccato off the crammed-full bookshelves and cold windowpane.

His office door was closed. A poster detailing cartooned cellular apoptosis pathways covered even the arrow-slit window. Apoptosis, that most orderly, regulated death, was Conroy's secret interest, though he toed the party line that apoptosis in brain cells was absent or aberrant. Even an infected neuron is better than no neuron. On the poster, cartoon arrows representing intracellular pathways bulged or diminished, and the whole poster suggested a global map of WWII armies surging, clashing, retreating, re-supplying, running amok, traveling on their bellies, flanking, fighting, and overrunning.

Ah, crap. He'd forgotten about Bev's counseling appointment that night.

He wrote *Coun c Beverly @ OLPH* on the month-at-a-glance calendar on his desk, then opened his office door and leaned out.

Leila stood beyond Joe and Danna, the young grad student who bound her electrically frizzed hair in a ponytail. Danna sucked on the end of an eighteen-inch pipette. Colorless buffer, lightly salted water, shot up the glass straw. Her undergrad P.I. had taught her to mouth-pipette and Conroy hadn't broken her of the dangerous habit yet. Danna maintained that her mouth was cleaner than the gunk-filled pipette bulbs that littered the bench like beached pufferfish.

Conroy scowled at Danna's mouth-pipetting and she goggled at him over the pipette as if she were sucking thick milkshake through a straw as Conroy called "Leila?"

Leila turned. A scratched Plexiglas shield reflected white lines of fluorescent light over her exotic face. She held a micropipetter in one blue-gloved hand and a tiny tube in the other. Her tie-dyed rainbow lab coat enveloped her slim, black clothes.

"Do you have a moment? Computer problem."

She said, "I'm elbow-deep in ethidium. One minute?"

Ethidium bromide is a DNA stain. The dye molecules slide between DNA bases. Things that intercalate into DNA are strong, strong mutagens. One sip, and you've got two years before your body dissolves in tumors.

IN THE SLOAN LAB, Danna sidled up to Joe while he bent over, loading blue-dyed glycoprotein into a gelatinous slab. "O'Malley's graduation party is tonight. You going?"

O'Malley rode a black motorcycle, had a beer-dispensing vending machine rigged to accept A.A. keychain tokens, and thought he was the wildest player on the planet. Fate had granted him the name of a cartoon alley cat. Everyone talked about him.

Danna's father was the Lutheran minister in a small Iowa town and her mother was a teacher, and the gossip in the molecular biology department shocked *her*. The hardy stock of gossip grapevine tendrilled the university buildings in lieu of more prestigious ivy.

Joe click-ejected a tip into the waste bucket. "Is Leila going?" Joe asked.

"I don't know. Dr. S. just called her into his office again. Is she dating anyone?"

Joe stabbed the tip box with the steak knife–sized micropipetter. After he and Leila had stopped sleeping together last year, he hadn't seen her leave the bar with anyone, but Leila was secretive to the point of subterfuge. "I don't know who she's dating these days."

"Do you think she'll go to O'Malley's party?"

"What, are you looking for herd immunity?" Joe filled a well with glycoprotein.

"I don't want to be there alone with O'Malley and his rugby friends."

"I'll go. I'll bet Leila will. She gets on well with O'Malley. Did you hear about that guy at Berkeley who got Herpes B?"

She smoothed her hair. "Macaques are all latently infected with Herpes B, green monkeypox, and everything else. I'm grossed out that it peed in his eye. I'm glad we work with mice."

"He's got to take four *grams* of acyclovir every day for the rest of his life, otherwise the encephalitis will kill him." Joe shook his head. "Herpes encephalitis. That's a bad way to go."

LEILA PERFUNCTORILY KNOCKED ON Conroy's open office door and walked in. She'd de-gloved and pulled off her lab coat. Stripped down to street clothes, the air cooled her arms and hands. She kicked the door closed. The chair opposite his desk crackled as she sat on it. "Howdy, Dr. S. What's up?"

His face was tight around his eyes, *stricken*. "I'm afraid I have to cancel dinner tonight."

"We weren't on for dinner. Are you all right, Conroy?"

If anything, his eyes drooped further. "Yeah. Fine."

He was hiding something as obviously as the morning after she'd first seduced him, when he'd stuttered like Humbert Humbert confronted with a nymphet. This time, something had snake-bitten him. She blurted, "Are you HIV-positive?"

Conroy blinked and a small, dismissive smile curved his lip. "No."

Leila's hand, clutching the front of Conroy's desk, cramped. Everyone in the lab lurked just outside the door, and her voice dropped in case someone walked by. "So what's wrong?"

"Nothing." He scowled.

"Fine, then. Let's take a break from the casual fucking."

He slapped the desk. "Are you threatening me?"

He was acting as if they had a *relationship*. Jesus, he might end up stalking her, and she might have to grab her gun and shoot him when he broke into her apartment in the dead of night and she woke up to him masturbating over her. She stood and leaned on the desk. "Get a hold of yourself."

Conroy stared at his computer screen. "I don't want to take a break."

"Fine." Leila tapped his monitor. He looked up. His eyes were startlingly, vibrantly blue, like an empty cable television channel. "Do you actually need anything for the grant?"

"It was a pretext."

"Fine, then." Leila opened the office door. "I'll email you that gel," she said as she left.

At her bench, Leila donned her tie-dyed lab coat and struggled into sticky nitrile gloves the color of Conroy's bright blue eyes. O'Malley's graduation party started at ten. She should toss her handcuffs into her purse. They'd broken O'Malley's pair.

THAT EVENING, DANTE PACED. Books, magazines, and papers packed the mismatched library bookshelves: rococo teak, oak veneer, bowing metal, and raw lumber stacked with slump block.

A knock creaked open the door. Mrs. Sloan called, "Father Dante?"

"*Si?* Yes?" Mrs. Sloan walked in with a man. Moderate lines creased the man's middle-fifties face. Dante ventured, "Mr. Sloan?"

"*Dr.* Sloan."

His pompous attempt to establish authority annoyed Dante. "Father Dante Petrocchi-Bianchi. Pleased to meet you." Dante opened his hand toward the two plush chairs. "Sit down, please?"

Mrs. Sloan sat and stared at her clenched hands in her lap. Dante had worried that she might be smug because she had initiated the counseling, but she seemed despondent.

Her husband crossed his legs and twitched his foot. "This'll have to be short. I have some work to finish. I'm a doctor and a professor." Sloan drew himself up in his chair. "I work on neurodegenerative diseases like Parkinson's and Alzheimer's. Synucleopathies." Haughty chin juts punctuated his rehearsed speech.

Ah, he was *that* C. Sloan, the American neurologist who dribbled trivial research into good but not first-rate journals. Dante settled himself in the chair opposite them and stretched his tired legs. "Alzheimer's is an amyloidopathy and a tauopathy, not a synucleopathy."

Sloan's head dropped and his jaw cracked. "You're in neuroscience?"

If Dante had been less enraged at the evil of the world or if he had eaten lunch, he might have been kinder, as befits a priest. "My research concerns molecular psychiatry. I have a paper in last month's *JAMA*," a better journal that Sloan published in. No need to mention Dante's recent papers in *Nature* and *Science*. Leave Sloan something to discover.

Sloan's fidgeting foot stopped twitching. "Wait, you're *D.M.* Petrocchi-Bianchi?"

Smoothly, from behind his steepled fingers, he said, "I prefer 'Father

Dante. It is nice to meet you, Mr. Sloan." He stood and opened the door for them to leave. "You must be in a hurry to return to your lab. Please send Dinah and Christina in."

"Christine," Mrs. Sloan said.

"Yes, excuse me." A headache was forming behind his left eye. Dante pinched the bridge of his nose. "Good night, Mr. Sloan."

SISTER MARY FRANCIS walked Dinah and Christine under the cathedral's vulturing saints to the library. The girls' ponytails twitched above their plaid jumpers. Earlier, Sister had tried to remove some books from the library, but Father Dante had raged that *no one* was to go in there. She complained to Father Samual, but Sam had shushed her and said that the new priest was from the Vatican and that he was God's man. Sam wouldn't even tell her what he meant or why he was suddenly nervous and pale.

And now she was about to throw two of her own little girls into the priest's lair.

At the door, she dropped to one knee. Their mother stood aside, struck mute. Sister said, "Just answer his questions. If you need anything, you call out, and I'll be right outside the door."

They nodded.

Father Dante opened the door. His curt chin jut suggested anger. She ushered the girls into the library. The wooden door closed but stopped before the door hit the jamb. Father Dante's handspan measured the distance the door remained open, about nine inches, and then withdrew.

CONROY ROCKED on his feet. His wife sat in a pew and regarded the lurid, crucified Christ suspended above the altar. The Protestants were smart to remove Christ from the cross and contemplate the abstract form of the torture device. Not that he understood them, either. He leaned on the pew where Beverly sat and asked her, "Why is he talking to the kids?"

"Something about the school."

"I don't like it." He didn't like that priest or his long black cassock or his long black hair. The guy looked like a hippie or a Renaissance relic. "You didn't tell me he was a scientist." He'd looked like a fool all day, first with Leila threatening him, now this.

Beverly shrugged and kept her eyes on Christ.

"I'll PubMed him, see if he's really who he says he is."

His wife didn't answer.

"So what's the matter with you? I thought you wanted counseling."

The overhead lights, dimmed to resemble candlelight, reflected off gold strands in her brown hair. She smoothed her beige skirt. "We'll talk later."

"There's something else?" There was always something fucking else. Maybe he could find Leila's hidden stash of scotch at the lab.

BEV ADJUSTED the piano bench and limbered up her fingers with a few scales. Minor keys suited her mood, dour, wintry music. The claxon fifth and descending minor scale were from the *Lieutenant Kije Suite*, Prokofiev, snow falling on spilt Russian blood.

Arriving choir members blew in, laughing in the January chill: happy, silly people who didn't snoop. Bev stretched her lower back, which had tightened while she'd crushed drives in the golf simulator at the pro shop that afternoon.

Father Dante strode out of the library toward the piano.

Bev gathered the sheet music she'd been using and the paper slipped sideways and fluttered. She snatched the sheaf and managed to catch half. The rest splashed on the floor.

Father Dante was beside her, sweeping the pages together.

"Could you choose the music for the Mass this week?"

"But I wouldn't know what to pick." She took the pages from his hands.

She might get the hymns wrong. She might ruin the Mass.

"Afterwards, you can tell me what they are." He sat beside her on the piano bench, which was far too small for two adults and her thigh rested against the black cassock over his legs. He handed her a list of names. "These people, are any of them in the choir?"

"Well, it depends." She pointed to the middle of the list. "*White* is probably Bill and Melanie. Melanie is a mezzo." She pointed at a frosted-blonde woman in the third row. "These people," she pointed to *Lawrence*, *James*, and *Douglas*, "only go to Mass and school events. *Dietrich* is Laura and Don. Laura is an alto. She's wearing the red blouse and khaki slacks."

Bev waved to Laura, sitting between Lydia and Mary.

LAURA WAVED BACK to Bev and whispered to Lydia and Mary. They'd been discussing that Father Nicolai was AWOL and that no one had seen him for two weeks. Father Sam had only muttered "transferred" with tight lips, and he was never tight-lipped about anything.

Laura said, "My, isn't our Bev cozy with the new priest?"

Mary, behind them, leaned in. "He's so young. What is he, thirty-five? What a waste."

Lydia said, "Yeah, what a waist, and his ass is nice, too."

Laura smiled. "Oh, Liddy, you're awful. How can you tell what's under that cassock?"

Lydia flipped her bottle-blonde hair behind her shoulder. "Anyone with a face that gorgeous is morally bound to have a nice ass too. Is it just me, or is there something especially sexy about a priest?"

"Intrinsically playing hard to get." Mary fluffed her naturally blonde hair, preening.

"Forbidden fruit," Laura countered.

Lydia said, "He can take you to Heaven because he knows the way."

"Liddy! You are *so* going to Hell." Laura examined a rough fingernail.

"If that's where all the fun people are," Lydia said. "And he's so cozy with our Bev."

Mary made a dismissive *hmmf* sound in her throat. "He should be up here flirting with us instead of wasting his time with our sweet little Bev."

The priest looked over then stood and climbed the risers toward them.

Lydia said, "Quick, Mary, wish to win the lottery."

Laura said, "Oh, crap," and her inner Catholic schoolgirl emerged and she flashed back to high school, when Father Joseph advanced to confiscate the note she'd been passing, a parodied song titled, "Father Joseph and the Amazing Lipstick-Colored Dream Condom."

Four lady friends watched Father Dante stride up the stairs.

One is oblivious and the most innocent, contrary to public opinion.

One has committed adultery with another's husband.

One will cause the priest to break his vow of chastity.

One is the mother of a raped child.

THE FULL CHOIR surrounded Father Dante and Bev. During the trial, they took sides.

Some blamed the wife because she was blind to what was happening in her own home. Some blamed the husband because his screwing around precipitated the whole thing. Some blamed the other woman, the only one who wasn't breaking sacred vows, as they always do. Some blamed the priest because God should not let murder happen.

Some sided with the priest, for surely he was the innocent one. Some supported the wronged wife for fear of being a victim like her. Some took the side of the husband, for they were not blameless themselves. A few sympathized with the other woman because they knew in their hearts that they were as much the very Devil as she.

BEV WAS LATE getting home because she circled the block four times. The January stars revolved around the cold suburban rooftops as she cruised.

She finally parked her car in the garage beside Conroy's Porsche—should a family man own such a smug, sexual car?—and walked into the hot house. The odor of the girls' no-tears shampoo drifted in the laundry room.

"Beverly?" Conroy hollered from somewhere in the house.

"Yes?" She set her purse on the washer, and her keychain jangled on the enameled metal.

"I missed dinner," he yelled.

She considered picking up her purse and circling the block until Conroy figured out that his plate was in the refrigerator where it always was whenever he was late, but she sloughed off her coat, hung it in the closet, and meandered toward the kitchen, where she removed his plate from the fridge and microwaved it.

The pork chop and corn soufflé rotated in the microwave. It would be easy to shake a little rat poison on it, but she didn't have any rat poison. She had some wasp spray. She sat with him in the dining room while he ate and said, "I hope counseling will be better tomorrow."

Conroy cut a slice away from the apple-glazed pork chop with a strong steak knife, then divvied that into pieces. "I didn't like him talking to our girls, alone, with the door closed."

Bev couldn't watch him tuck away that pork chop that she had spent an hour and a half perfecting. He didn't even chew. "He said it was about the school."

"Still inappropriate. He could have been doing anything in there with that door closed."

Conroy could have been doing anything to that whore in the hotel room that he had booked in the names *Conroy and Beverly Sloan*. Or that whore could have been doing anything to him. "Father Dante is a priest."

"The corporate culture of the Vatican warps all those priests into sexual caricatures of men. They're all perverts and pedophiles, like that one in Boston who sodomized those boys."

Yes, *sodomized*. Was that what Conroy did to his whore? Bev sighed.

"This Father Dante was transferred here suddenly." Conroy pointed at her with a square of pale pork atop his fork. "They say pedophiles get jobs in schools to have access to kids."

An image arose in Bev's mind: smashed meat and potatoes flying, the glass table top lifting and flipping onto Conroy, imprisoning him in a makeshift glass house. She said, "Stop."

"I don't want the girls alone with him. He might be a pedophile."

Pinpoint reflections shimmered in the table. "You shouldn't make such horrible accusations."

He held up his clean, blameless hands. "Hey, I didn't accuse anybody of anything."

Bev grabbed the tabletop with both hands. The glass was slippery as ice between her fingers. "You checked that woman into the hotel under my name. *Under my name.*"

Conroy stood, outraged. "You shouldn't be snooping around like that."

"You shouldn't be *screwing* around like that. Who is she?"

"Beverly—"

"*No*, she most certainly is not *Beverly*. Why would you do such a thing?"

"I'm sorry. I told you that it was over."

Bev's nose burned as tears boiled up. "You have to tell *her*. I want proof that you told *her* that it's over."

His blue eyes rolled. "Did that priest tell you to do this?"

"Stop it. Just *stop it*." He was heaping all of his own hateful sins onto Father Dante.

She prayed to Mary to intercede. *Pray for us sinners now and at the hour of our death.* That Conroy's whore had appropriated not only Bev's husband but pretended to her name and position and identity galled her, literally *galled* her, made Bev feel as if she had vomited out everything in her esophagus and stomach and duodenum, all the way down to her green gall bladder, and then vomited green gall and black bile.

No one had even checked the woman's identity. No one even cared.

Bev was so easily replaced that she was practically no one at all.

LEILA ARRIVED LATE at the lab the next morning. Even though she had driven home and showered, the hangover clung to her, snarling and raking her scalp.

Keyboard clattering rattled from Conroy's open office door. She sneaked past.

At her desk, her purse and backpack fell out of her hands. The purse bounced and fell to the floor. She let the stupid thing lie there. The way of the universe was gravity and entropy, and on that morning, the universe was winning.

Alcohol detox and caffeine jones warred in her head, pillaging and burning her brain cells. Aldehyde was the chemical. Ethanol metabolized to aldehydes, like formaldehyde. Even after brushing her teeth twice and gargling with acid-strip mouthwash, aldehydes excreting through her lungs scoured her dying tongue and irritated her digestive tract.

From his office, Conroy yelled, "Leila! Computer help!"

She steeled her head against her own voice and moaned, "Okay." She limped to his cluttered office and closed the door behind her. "I don't suppose you have any extra coffee."

"Here." He handed her a cup without looking up. Both his legs bounced at the knees.

"It's okay, Conroy. You don't have to give up your juice."

"S'all right, it's my fifth." He drumrolled his fingers on the desk.

After an experimental sip, her stomach relaxed, thanks be to all the caffeine gods in the Java Islands.

"Do you know this Petrocchi-Bianchi fellow?" Conroy pointed to the computer monitor.

Tiny-fonted PubMed citations filled the screen. The papers' titles were neuroscience, molecular to physiological. Each citation listed *D.M. Petrocchi-Bianchi, S.J., M.D., Ph.D.* as an author. She said, "That's a lot of alphabet soup after his name. I don't think I've met him."

Leila sat at the other computer. With distraction, her head pounded less, though as soon as she noticed this, the war drums crescendoed. She launched web software and searched for *Petrocchi-Bianchi, neurology,* and *Rome.* "Found his homepage."

Conroy leaned over. "You can read Italian?"

"No. Is he in there?" Leila pointed to a lab group picture. The caption under the photo read, *Dipartimento di Neuroscienze e Psichiatriche Molecolari, Universita degli Studi di Roma.*

Conroy pointed to a man in the back row. "That's him."

The guy was hot. He was wearing gothic black, and his thick, curly hair swept his broad shoulders. European, and Leila liked Europeans because they did the most passionate things in bed, but something was odd about his clothes. She leaned toward the monitor. His black shirt was cut by a Roman collar. "He's a fucking priest. Why the fuck are you asking me about a priest?"

"No reason."

She squinted, trying to will herself to read Italian or at least call up enough of her high school French and Californian Spanish to make an educated guess. "Goddamn priests. They're all sick bastards. The corporate culture of the Vatican subverts natural moral sense and warps their personalities into a hyper-chauvinist parody of masculinity."

"Yes, you've mentioned that."

Leila's opinions were sometimes too near her tongue. "That's what the *S.J.* after his name means: Society of Jesus. He's not *just* a priest; he's a

Jesuit. Christ, Conroy. What did you do to get the *Jesuits* after you?"

Conroy shifted in his chair. "Click on some of the links."

The links led to many papers in very good journals. "Damn," Conroy said. He closed the browser window on his own computer. A window holding a gel showed up.

A groan rose in Leila's throat. She needed to go home, drink fluids, and sleep it off, not stare at a glaring computer screen over Conroy's shoulder and point to icons that Conroy would laboriously drag the cursor over to and click. She said, "I'm not a hundred percent today."

Conroy looked surprised, and then he stared back at the screen. "We can do it tomorrow."

His monitor's engorged plasma screen showed a picture of a preternaturally schmutzless gel with five dark, smooth bands. She asked, "What is that?"

Conroy minimized the window. One of his eyebrows dipped and he frowned at her. "You look like hell. Go home."

When a neurologist who specializes in the end stages of organic brain diseases like Alzheimer's and mad cow–associated prion dementia says that you look like hell, you should go home and sleep it off. "Okay. I'll split cells and then leave."

"You can ask someone to split your cells."

Considering that she'd stepped over Joe when she'd left O'Malley's this morning, Leila doubted *he* was in yet. Danna went AWOL about three in the morning, when one of O'Malley's writer friends also disappeared. Yuri might ask why Leila had primary neurons in culture and what was grotesquely killing them. "No, thanks."

Conroy dropped his voice. "Are you all right? Do you need a scrip for antibiotics?"

"It's probably one of those twenty-four-hour bugs."

"Headache?"

"Enormous."

"You didn't pick it up in the lab?" His gray eyebrows clenched over his blue eyes. "Because God only knows what's growing in here half the time. Yuri's doing some secret experiment that he won't talk about. Lab accidents happen all the time, infections, contaminations, weird stuff."

"I'll bet I caught it somewhere else." She walked out.

In the tissue culture room, she pressed her face to the hood, and the glass cooled her forehead. On the other side of the glass shield, her hands efficiently pipetted media. Her poisoned body could do the work without any higher brain function at all. Miraculous, really.

She slid her flasks into the incubator. Mysterious dishes slathered with Conroy's handwriting tiled the shelf below hers.

Leila gloved and set one of Conroy's dishes on the microscope. Neuroblastoma cells half-covered the bottom of the dish. The bloated, dying cells looked virus-infected, but a chemical or cytokine or reagent virus or transfection might do the same thing.

Leila went home to sleep off her hangover.

Chapter Four

The Daily Hamiltonian:

CONTAMINATION AT NIH

By Kirin Oberoi

In an assumed accident at the National Institute of Health, a scientist, Dr. Joy Chan, was contaminated by carbon-14, a radioactive isotope commonly used in scientific research. The chemical was found on her lab chair last week. Though Dr. Chan is six months pregnant, the isotope is not expected to harm the fetus. "It is revenge," Dr. Chan said. "Americans don't like foreign nationals taking jobs." The NIH declined to comment.

DANTE INTERLACED the packing box's flaps and taped them shut. The books that remained on the shelves huddled, ashamed that they had sheltered the criminals rather than recoiled in horror and expelled them.

So many tapes and magazines and movies on CDs, some slickly commercial, others rickety and homemade, had been stuffed on those motley shelves. *Homemade*: these despicable tracts sullied that vanilla-cookie word. Dante's despair was bilious black. Angry acidity burned the mesochymal barriers between his gut and his heart, and the bile recirculated through his abdomen and thorax and threatened a coronary infarc, a heart attack. *Heart-sick*, Dante was heart-sick. Exorcisms and battling demon-strong men and women and expelling the Latin-spewing devils by holy water and crucifix had been easier.

Knocking pattered at the library door.

"Come in," he said and scooted the chairs to form a triangle.

The doorknob grated. The metal-studded door opened. The Sloans surveyed the library, its chairs, its shelves. Mrs. Sloan said, "Hello, Father."

Dante grasped the stuffed arms of the chair and sat. They sat.

Mr. Sloan jiggled his leg, eyed the bookcases and sighed dramatically. Mrs. Sloan, roused, looked over at him and then back down at her hands. She seemed ashamed that they had to be there, whereas he was annoyed. He studied them. A relationship is a sinuous, gauzy thing stretched between two people but not of either one.

Dante wove his fingers into a double fist at his chest and waited. He waited until the silence oppressed, until it hung from the ceiling and slouched in the corners, until it blanketed the room and no one wanted to peep out from under the covers lest the unspoken thing devour them.

"And who is the woman who left her underwear in your suitcase?"

Sloan leapt up. His fist twisted at his side as he turned to his wife. "You told him *that!*"

Mrs. Sloan shrank in her chair and clutched the arms as if acceleration drove her back.

God, that bastard had *hit* her. Dante rose to his feet. "Stop! Stop this."

Sloan's voice dropped and he snarled at her, "Who else have you *told?*"

She searched from Dante to Sloan as if one of them would save her from the other. Sloan took a step toward his wife. Dante jumped between them and glared up at Sloan. Dante was accustomed to being among the tallest men in the room, but Sloan was half a head taller.

Dante stepped toward Sloan, chest to chest. "Sit down. Now."

Sloan blinked and stepped back, and Dante advanced, herding him toward the chair.

Sloan stepped back again, the chair caught his leg, and he sat. He looked up at young and powerful and *towering* Dante. Men like this thought they could stick their dick in any hole they wanted and damn the consequences. Arrogance and selfishness like that begat pedophiles. A violent urge knotted Dante's throat. "What about your wife, and your children, and *what about the other woman?*"

Sloan shook his head and rolled his eyes, somewhere between dismissive and possessed.

Dante leaned down and braced himself on the arms of Sloan's chair, their faces inches apart. Onion-skinned wrinkles around Sloan's eyes stretched upward, and he jammed his white-haired head against the chair's upholstery.

Mrs. Sloan's fingers plucked Dante's black shirt sleeve. "He said he would stop."

Dante said quietly, with rancor, "Have you stopped?"

"Yes!" Sloan's eyes widened more, and the small folds in his eyes' skin turned to rigid lines. He dropped his head away and to the side, nearly leaning over the chair arm.

Rage clawed Dante, raking his heart and his temples, worse than the time a possessed priest had tried to escape, spitting blood, and Dante had hauled the old man back and flung him into the chair to continue with the exorcism.

Mrs. Sloan grasped his biceps and tugged. "That's enough."

This was not an exorcism. Wrath is a sin. Violence is a sin. Sloan was just a selfish old goat. Dante should calm himself. He pushed off the arms of Sloan's chair. "You will cease the affair. Until you have satisfied me that you have stopped, you will not receive communion."

Sloan, belligerent, chucked up his chin. "We'll join a different church."

Dante sat in his chair and stretched his legs out. "This is a small city, Mr. Sloan. If you were excommunicated, no church would admit you. Community ties are important to American universities."

Mrs. Sloan looked stricken. "You wouldn't excommunicate him."

Sloan rallied. "I give this parish a hell of a lot of money."

"I don't care," Dante said.

The Sloans, Mr. Sloan sitting and his wife standing beside his chair, looked at each other, their first sign of communication and common purpose.

No doubt a simple parish priest would have salved their wounds and encouraged them to rebuild, if only Sloan had shown the slightest bit of willingness to do that. Dante drew a deep breath and waved a hand to Mrs. Sloan's chair, indicating she should sit. "Now," he said, "Mr. Sloan, when did you begin this adultery?"

Unrepentant anger squinted Sloan's blue eyes. "Six months ago."

Mrs. Sloan said, "I don't want to know this."

"Then, Mrs. Sloan, would you wait outside?" Dante asked. He gestured toward the door and didn't dodge Sloan's stare. Lines of anger coalesced in the beige skin around Sloan's eyes.

Mrs. Sloan hesitated, but she left. The door clanked softly behind her.

The lines on Sloan's face strained upward and victorious smugness replaced his anger. He said, "Father, I wish to confess my sins."

"Confession is to beg God's forgiveness. You cannot use a sacrament for selfish ends."

Sloan didn't blink. "I want to be reconciled."

Dante leaned his elbows on the chair arms and pressed his fingertips together. "Can you say the prayer before confession with an open heart?"

Sloan grunted, "Okay."

Arrogance again. Arrogance that he could fool a psychiatrist who diagnosed lies and illness and the haunted and the evil and the damned and the possessed. If Sloan genuinely wanted to confess, and Dante wished he did and knew he didn't, Dante must grant him absolution and the conversation would be under the seal of confession. The sin would pass out of Sloan's soul like rotten chicken out of his gut.

But Sloan had to make a genuine confession. Loopholes didn't apply.

Dante smiled to unnerve Sloan. "Pray for your soul's salvation, and I will don the stole."

Sloan crossed himself perfunctorily and clasped his hands. He sped through, "Come Holy Spirit into my soul. Enlighten my mind that I may know the sins I ought to confess, and grant me your grace to confess them fully, humbly, and with a contrite heart."

"Stop," Dante said.

Sloan's mouth snapped shut. "What the hell?"

"Do not curse. Has the Holy Spirit enlightened your mind?"

Sloan flicked his hands apart, nearly an obscene gesture reminiscent of ablutions. "I know what to confess."

Dante watched Sloan's blank, blue eyes. "Are you contrite?"

Sloan's stare flinched away, but he caught himself and looked right back. "Yes."

Dante's cynicism won out. He leaned back in his chair. "This is not a true confession. This conversation is not covered by the seal of confession."

"A priest can't refuse to hear a confession." Sloan's anger dragged his rangy body to his feet, and he paced.

"Sit down, Mr. Sloan."

"It's *Doctor* Sloan. *Doctor.*"

Dante held his steepled fingers motionless though the rigidity strained his arms. "Sit."

Sloan paced in front of the two chairs. "You're supposed to help us. You're twisting everything I say. You're making it worse."

Stillness was key to retaining control. Dante's fingertips mashed flat against each other. His fingerpads and nailbeds reddened. Strain drained into his wrists. "You cannot repair injury with platitudes."

Sloan slashed the air with one hand. "You don't know anything about being married."

This objection, priests prepare for in the seminary. "One need not have cancer to be a good oncologist. You treat patients with neurodegenerative diseases. Do you have Alzheimer's?"

"Of course not."

"Marriage is a sacrament. As a priest, God and the sacraments are my domain." Dante added his own twist. "And I am a psychiatrist. I am not psychotic, but I treat the mentally ill."

Sloan's head bobbled, begrudging the analogy.

Dante continued, "And I have never been possessed, but I perform exorcisms."

Sloan stopped pacing. One sandy eyebrow dipped, incredulous. "You believe in possession and demons and all that superstitious crap?"

Believe? Mere belief could not endure a world rife with frailty and evil and sin and damnation: chairs that flew across the room, elderly priests breaking chains, young girls' faces transformed into hideous caricatures. "There are things I have seen that I do not understand."

"You're a medical doctor, a scientist." Sloan gaped at him.

Dante's stillness fought his agitation. "I am a priest."

Sloan waved one hand in the air as if clearing irrational incense fumes. "I'll believe in demons when you show me their molecular mechanism."

Dante sighed. "This is not the subject at hand. The subject is your marriage and adultery, Mr. Sloan."

"It's *Doctor.*"

At the tips of his steepled fingers, Dante's fingernails dug underneath each other. "You have forgotten your urge to confess the sins that so trouble your soul."

Being caught in his lies deflated Sloan's anger. He stared at the blue carpet as if the swirls of color might open under his feet. Dante glanced at the carpet, in case he had missed a flap in the carpeting concealing a subterranean dungeon.

Sloan pressed one hand to his weathered face.

Dante waited. He could wait for days if necessary.

"I don't know why Beverly wants counseling."

"You screwed another woman."

"I'll break it off." Sloan rubbed his face. "I don't know why that idiot woman hid her underwear in my luggage."

Dante adjusted his cassock over his thighs. "Because she wants you to leave your wife."

Sloan nodded. His silver hair swayed. "She's hinted, but I wouldn't."

Dante asked, "But why would you have an affair?"

Sloan chuckled. "Oh, right. You priests are celibate."

Derision would poison all the progress he'd made, so Dante ignored it. "Tell this woman that the affair is over. Do not see her again. If you do this, after counseling Saturday, I will hear your confession, and you can take communion on Sunday."

Sloan nodded. "And no one will know anything."

"Yes," said Dante, negotiating when he should have commanded Sloan. This must be a command. "If you lay a hand on your wife, if you so much as pinch her, this deal is off. I'll grant her an annulment, I'll excommunicate you, and I'll call the police."

Both Sloan's shaggy eyebrows rose. "What?"

Dante did not feel the need to observe more denial. He glanced at his watch. "I need to speak to your wife."

Sloan strode out of the library. He didn't say goodbye or even glance back. Insolent.

But, if Sloan did cease his affair, there might be hope.

At his desk, he stacked boxes and waited for Mrs. Sloan.

BEV KNELT BEFORE the Virgin Mary and prayed to her and God and Jesus and the Holy Spirit for peace. Unexpelled prayer constipated her. She strained with praying because, even though she had said the Rosary and was participating in counseling, she wasn't forgiven because she couldn't forgive. The situation was impossible: unforgiveness begat unforgiveness begat unforgiven sin. A spotlight raked the Blessed Virgin's left cheek and blue-robed shoulder. The Virgin's inert, white porcelain face gazed down on Bev.

The statues crowded into niches ringing the church walls personified stories about God's Love that she had heard as a child. Some saints were crazy or debauchers or drunks, but God loved them.

Even though Bev was a stupid doormat, God had loved her. Probably. But not any more.

Conroy's voice whispered, "Beverly!"

She turned, and dust grated under her prayer-bruised knees. Conroy wove from side to side like a gray cobra hypnotizing prey as he scanned the lines of pews looking for her.

She whispered, "Amen," and stood. "Over here, Conroy."

Conroy whipped his head sideways and saw her. His voice echoed in the shifting dark of the cathedral. He wasn't smiling, but he wasn't scowling, either. He was grave, serious, busy. "That priest wants to see you."

She slipped into Father Dante's library. He sat at his desk, sorting papers. "Father?"

His shoulders jerked and he turned. Father Dante sat in his desk chair and brought his prayer-folded hands to his lips. "There is one more thing we need to discuss. You would sit?"

She sat in her chair.

"Mrs. Sloan," he looked at her over his knuckles. "If you feel threatened, you should call me or the police."

Bev crossed her ankles and arms. "I don't know what you're talking about."

In his black cassock, brooding in this library fraught with shadows, Father Dante looked like a medieval Inquisitor. Anxiety rose in her lungs as if he was asking which of her neighbors weren't good Catholics. He said, "The Church offers you protection."

She tucked her arms and legs in tighter. "I'm fine."

Father Dante came over and sat in Conroy' chair next to hers. He took her hand—his hand was warm like a leather glove in a sunny car—and he slipped a card into her palm. Black ink curled across the back of the business card: phone numbers. He said, "The top number is the rectory. The lower one is my cellular phone."

Bev turned the card over. "I didn't know priests had business cards." The keys and tiara of St. Peter embellished the upper left corner, and Father Dante's name ran through the center. Italian words surrounded his name. Bev tucked it in her purse.

Father Dante nodded. "There is one more thing to talk about, but," he looked at his watch, "it may take some time. Will you be in the church tomorrow?"

"I'm substituting for the music teacher. I have a free period at two o'clock."

Father Dante nodded. "I'll be here. Tomorrow, then?"

Bev left the priest sitting at his desk, sorting papers.

In the church, Conroy was in the third pew, reading the hymnal. "Ready?" she asked.

"Yeah." He snapped the book shut and stood. Conroy said, "I'll drop you at home. I've got to get back to the lab."

Bev nodded. He probably had something very important waiting .

THE NEXT MORNING at nine, Leila slammed open the door to the mouse facility and found Conroy injecting a small syringe of liquid into a mouse's belly. Her breath puffed. She'd sprinted to the lab with her arms full of printouts. She said, "Tony translated the Italian webpage."

Conroy looked up from the mouse, startled. Behind the clear visor, his eyes, so oddly blue, were wide, and he glanced past her and then back to her face.

She said, "You will not believe this. The bottom links lead straight into the Vatican."

Conroy frowned. "Of course he has Vatican links. He's a priest."

He wasn't getting it. "He's not just a priest."

"So he says." Conroy resumed injecting the mouse then released it into its cage. He wrote a small note in his lab notebook and turned the page.

Maybe shaking him would wake his ass up. "First of all, it's not *Father*

Petrocchi-Bianchi. It's *Monsignor*."

Conroy cocked his head. "He said to call him 'Father.'"

"And everyone in his lab has moved on. He doesn't have a lab anymore."
Leila shoved papers into Conroy's latex-gloved hands.

CONROY LOOKED OVER Leila's sloppy stack of papers. Her slim,
tanned finger pointed to a link for *The Congregation for the Doctrine of
the Faith*. Leila's fingernail polish was the color of champagne. They sat in
wheeled lab chairs to examine the translation of the priest's web pages.

He reached for her thigh.

She pushed him and her chair rolled out of his reach. "Conroy," she
whispered. "The door's open. And God only knows what's on your gloves."

"No one could see." And it didn't matter if he was caught with her, too.
He rolled toward her and reached for her leg again.

"Conroy! Yuck! You smell like mice."

He stripped off his gloves. "Can I see you tonight?"

Leila's almond eyes, shaped by her Egyptian father's genes, slid sideways.
"I have labwork."

"Me, too." Both his hands clamped around her thigh above her knee.

Leila's eyebrows twitched. "More labwork? More than these mice?"

Conroy's neck stiffened as if the mere mention of mice induced
encephalitis. "Tonight?"

Leila peered into the cages. One black mouse staggered in its shoebox-
sized plastic cage, slammed its head into the clear plastic wall, and swayed,
stunned. She asked, "What in the hell is wrong with that poor thing?"

"Nothing." Nothing that she nor anyone should know about until he
was good and ready to tell the world. "Tonight?"

"All right."

Conroy's neck loosened enough to nod. His fingers climbed up the lean
meat of Leila's thigh. "I could give you a ride."

Leila shook her head and her hands rose in the air, warding off evil eyes. "Malcolm from Lugar lab drove up after you dropped me off Monday. His headlights almost hit your car, and that black midlife crisis–mobile of yours is too damned distinctive."

"Midlife crisis–mobile?"

"The Porsche. Come on, Conroy. Surely you lead a more examined life than that." Leila left him sitting in the mouse room, contemplating.

BEV CLUTCHED HER JACKET around her and hurried from the music room to the library. January mist drifted through the lines of plaid skirts and navy blue slacks and into the unbuttoned front of her coat. The cathedral nosed out of the winter fog ahead of her.

She knocked on the library door. The priest's muffled voice said, "Yes?"

She bustled in. Father Dante was slumped in his chair. His hands covered his face.

"Father, are you all right?"

She dumped her soggy sheet music on her blue chair and stood beside him. If Conroy or one of her girlfriends had been slumped over so, she would have put her arms around them, but a priest, how could she comfort a beleaguered priest? Priests moved in the company and grace of God, beyond her fumbling. She patted his shoulder with a tentative, arrhythmic tapping. Under his black shirt, his shoulders were rounded with muscle.

He rubbed his face. He stood and reached toward her arm but his hand stopped in midair and pointed to her arm. "Why you are wearing the long sleeves?"

"It's January." She tugged a sleeve over her wrist self-consciously.

His hand hovered inches away from her face. "And the collar, it is high on your neck."

"The music room is chilly."

Father Dante's hand dropped away, but he leaned closer, as when a man angles for a kiss but doesn't know whether the woman will acquiesce, and he whispered, "Did he hit you?"

"What? No. He didn't. He wouldn't." She sat on the other chair.

Father Dante watched and seemed satisfied. His hands came together on his chest and his fingers formed a sort of cage. "You see most of the children in this school?"

"I substitute often." She crossed her ankles, lady-like, as behooved her with a priest, especially a young priest who still looked like a man. "Sister Benedicta has health problems."

Father Dante leaned forward and rested his forearms on his knees. His fidgets reminded Bev of her daughters' machinations to delay admitting petty guilt. "Do you know of any children who were initially good students here, happy children, who became sullen and angry?"

Bev couldn't stop her wide eyes from blinking. She'd learned the symptoms of sexual abuse in her primary education courses in college. "That couldn't happen *here*."

Father Dante sighed.

"You mean like someone's uncle? One of the parents?"

"No." He pulled his hand through his black hair, raking it away from his eyes.

"That new janitor? The soccer coach?"

"No, Mrs. Sloan."

The rumormongers had stalwartly avoided that particular accusation about Father Nicolai's disappearance. Diocesan politics, the school's deplorable standardized testing scores, poor-box embezzlement, *whiskey priest*, sacrilegious snacking on consecrated host, Alzheimer's, selling the host to Satanists, those things had been mentioned, but molesting children was the sort of thing that happened in other places.

Bev folded her hands in her lap primly. "That's patently ridiculous. Father Nicolai was one of the *nicest* men I've ever known."

"I'm sure he was."

"All of us just walk right into the rectory, without knocking, without yoo-hooing. His sermons are about the transparent lives we lead, how God sees into out hearts and loves us. And about how we need to be compassionate, reach out to others, live with open hearts. He's so *compassionate.*"

Yes." He drew a hand through the black curls fringing his face. "Pedophiles are some of the *nicest* people I've ever known. They have a special rapport with children. They offer to babysit. Absolutely *charming.*"

Bev would be able to tell if someone was a pedophile. She could tell if a person was gay or straight. Father Dante had watched the women's sections of the choir, and he had opened his posture, hesitantly, toward Laura Dietrich. He was straight but restrained. She would *know.* "I don't believe it."

"Most," Father Dante glanced at the white-painted ceiling, "of these kinds of people," he sighed, "are especially *efficient* at concealing their crimes. They induce guilt in the children, or shroud the abuse as a game, or utilize their clerical authority. Two months ago, when the allegations reached Roma, a priest was sent here to watch and intervene."

Father Domingo had appeared two months ago, ostensibly to update the school's benighted curriculum that had caused the free-falling test scores, and both he and Father Nicolai had left last week. "Was he reassigned to some other parish?"

"No. Nicolai is in Italia, in a place where there are no children. I need to know if there are any other children who you think might display these behavior patterns. I am here to counsel them, to try to help them. That's why they sent a psychiatrist."

Oh, Lord. Father Dante had asked to see Laura. Laura had choked when Bev called her last night. "He hurt Luke, didn't he?"

Father Dante leaned back in his chair, and his eyes slid away from her.

"Luke Dietrich. You saw Laura after choir practice. She's been taking Luke to all kinds of doctors for his ADHD, but he hasn't gotten any better, and it came on *suddenly* last year."

Father Dante stared at the blue carpeting.

Bev's chest caved in at the thought of anyone hurting Luke. "Oh, God."

If that man had touched her daughters—she would, she would—and violence welled up. "My girls, did he hurt them?"

Father Dante said quietly, "When I talked to your daughters a few days ago, I did not see anything to concern me. I asked them about rumors in the school."

"What did they say?"

Father Dante paused, seemed to consider, and said, "The children had a system of not going to Father Nicolai's office alone but in pairs or groups, especially junior high boys, or they had Sister Mary Theresa wait outside, but it didn't always work."

Her daughters had been in danger, and they knew they were in danger, and they hadn't told her. They'd found a way to defend themselves from rape. "Was it just boys?"

"Nicolai was a primary pedophile. He was attracted to children. Their gender was not as important as their age, between ten and thirteen. It appears he abused both boys and girls," he said. "I trust you will not say anything about this."

Bev nodded.

"Because some families will want to keep this private."

Father Nicolai was her friend. Bev would have known. Bev's eyes were so dry they felt burned. "I just can't believe it."

BEV PICKED UP her email later that afternoon:

Dearest Beverly,

I have to work late tonight, so I won't be home for dinner. I've attached the proof.

Love,

Conroy

Fwd: an apology

> I can't see you anymore. > It was all a mistake. I love my wife. You know that. > I apologize if I hurt > you, if I let you believe that our relationship was anything other than what it was, or if you > believed so anyway.

Conroy

CONROY WAITED in his Porsche outside Leila's apartment building. The kung pao and mu shus were stinking up his car but he couldn't roll down the window because the rain would ruin the leather seats.

Something knocked on his window and he jumped. Outside, Leila was so rained-on that frigid water streamed from her long, black hair and dragged her clothes against her shoulders. She motioned him toward her apartment building. Her mincing shadow dodged through the foggy January rain. She unlocked the building's door and flung it back.

The paper bag greased his hands as he followed her. Her elevator closed its doors before he caught up. His elevator beat hers to the twelfth floor, so he ambled down the hall, rolling and unrolling the top of the crinkling bag. She strode past and unlocked the deadbolt on her door.

Inside, Conroy set the bag on her dining table. A freaky blue chandelier above the table looked like a church stained-glass window and threw spider shadows on the walls' blue and green moulding and ceiling medallions. The funky, faux plasterwork looked like the Palace of Versailles had relocated to New Hamilton.

Leila peeled off her soaked clothes and tossed them in the kitchen sink. Her black hair trailed water behind her. "Meth," she called. The old dog sauntered over, all black fur and muscle, claws scritching on the hardwood floor. It stood beside her and sniffed her breath, nuzzling. Leila said, "Good boy, go lie down," and he ambled away, doubtless to sleep again.

"How'd you get so wet?" Conroy asked.

"It's raining, and I walked home." she called from her tiny bathroom, past the rows of closets that held her silvery and black clothes. Once, while she was showering, he'd stroked the crotch of a pair of black pants with a red matador sash and she'd worn the pants the next day, unsuspecting. He'd been turned on all day, imagining his fingers in those pants.

She came out of the bathroom nude and fingerwalked through the clothes in her closet. Her body was lithe, even angular over her collarbones and pelvis. Her hair, usually sleek and black as a beaded curtain against his face, had tightened into slick spirals.

Conroy stood behind her and pressed his body on her chilly skin. The ice of her passed through his damp clothes. Shivery goose flesh peppered her arms and torso, and looking down from behind her, he saw that her nipples poked out hard. He thumbed one.

She wiggled her cold ass against him but otherwise didn't comment, just touched the shoulders of her clothes in the long closet, deciding.

Blood rushed in him, streaming into his dick and weighing it down until the mass rose inside his pants. Her skin was so cold. It would be like screwing an ice sculpture caught fire.

She shook a robe away from its hanger, stepped away, and flipped it around her. "Don't want those mu shus to get cold," she said.

"They'll keep." He spun her around and kissed her hard. It would be an easy thing to part that robe and her legs and crush her between his dick and the wall. She'd scream, maybe bite.

When he broke away for air, Leila said, "Yeah, the mu shus will keep." She grabbed his wrist, spun him, and the floor rushed up at him.

He caught himself on his hands and knees. Weight on his back forced him to the ground. His arm wrenched behind his back. She bit him lightly on the ear.

His shoulder hurt but didn't tear, as long as he didn't move. "Careful, I'm not young."

"You should be careful what you start. Sit up." Her voice was raspy in his ear. She didn't let go of his arm, still twisted behind him. Her weight left his back. Conroy sat back on his heels, kneeling. She said, "Unbutton your shirt."

He unbuttoned his shirt with his free hand. Leila might rip it off if he didn't, and explaining missing buttons might be difficult.

Leila's grip on his arm loosened and he tried to get away so he could twist her hands behind her, but she pressed his fist into his shoulder blades. His back bowed. She yanked his shirt down over his shoulders to his elbows so he couldn't move his arms and tied it into makeshift bonds. His dick was so stiff it ached.

Her hands slid in his waistband and he sucked in his belly to reduce the flab flap. She opened his pants. He said, "This isn't what I was thinking."

"You were thinking about it rough."

"Yeah," he admitted. She stepped back from him and Conroy stumbled forward. His hands were still knotted in his shirt. He couldn't catch himself. His arms pulled him backward, and he steadied. The shirt loosened, and one arm was free. He turned on his knees.

She pushed him backward. Still off balance from pitching forward and shuffling on his knees, he tipped, and she jumped on him.

He struggled but she was strong, so he fell back. One hand was still wrapped in his shirt, and she grabbed that one and his bare hand and forced them above his head. She held them there with one hand and pushed his underwear down. Elastic cupped his balls. The air polymerized into ice. She grappled in her robe pocket and found a foil envelope, tore the packet, and slapped the purple, corrugated condom on his dick.

She pressed herself onto him, around him, and he bucked as she fucked him. The hardwood floor bruised his vertebrae. Above him, she was a long, pale arc of flesh from his dick to his hands, holding him down, pressing at both ends, soaring between. When he'd grabbed her, he thought he could have her like that, but Leila turned it around on him again. She was a ball of twisted detonator cord, and he never knew which cut wire was going to blast her apart.

Idiot priest. Why did Conroy do this?

Because the whole rest of his life he craved this.

DANTE HAD FINISHED cleaning the bookshelves when a knock rattled his door. He squatted, never simple in an ankle-length cassock, and swept together obscene magazines and stuffed them in a box. "Yes?"

Mrs. Sloan came in. She clutched a scrap of paper in her hand. "You might start with these kids."

Dante took the list. Four of them he had already contacted. Three new names, though.

If Dante ever saw that bastard Nicolai, if Dante was ever within reach of his haggard, lizard throat—but he stopped. Wrath was one of the seven deadly sins. God's justice was more important than Dante's own outrage. He rubbed his eyes, which throbbed and ached all the time.

Mrs. Sloan was beside him, and her hand fluttered near his arm. "You've been cleaning the library," she said.

"It was filthy."

"The service should clean in here." She looked at the shelves and boxes.

His temple pounded. "Nicolai told them not to."

"Why would he—?"

"I have found things." He shouldn't tell her. "Books, pictures, videotapes, computer disks." Any information he told her might infiltrate the parish's common knowledge.

Nicolai had owned a digital video camera. Dante watched the video clips to identify the children, if you can call it "watching" to view a monitor with your head turned almost away, your hand clasped over your mouth the whole time, glancing back only when absolutely necessary to identify another child when a pause in the sound signaled a new clip.

In one, Nicolai stood and chanted the Eucharistic prayer while a dark-haired, black-eyed boy not older than twelve fellated him. The priest's chanting kept time with the rhythm of his balls hitting the boy's sharp chin. The sacrilegious suggestion that Nicolai was transubstantiating his dick into the body of God was nearly as sickening as the abuse. Afterward, the boy stood, but no expression rippled on his face. Not fear, not horror, not revulsion. The constant trauma had numbed the child. Dante said, "I cannot fathom. I cannot bear to think."

Horror widened her caramel eyes. She sat down in her chair as if her knees had given out. "There were things in the library, in the *church*?"

Dante was so weak that he had inflicted his pain and rage on this woman. He covered his face. His hands smelled like ink and dust. In another video, Nicolai and a different boy had masturbated each other, lying on the floor on a green sleeping bag. Afterward, the boy made another appointment with Nicolai for the next week, and Nicolai noted it on his desk calendar. Dante found the sleeping bag stuffed behind the desk, photographed it, notated it in his evidence log, stuffed it into a trash bag, and then scrubbed his hands hard with institutional, gritty soap. "Nicolai was very—" *evil, demented, psychopathic—*"subtle."

She demanded, "Why did you send him to Italy? The bishops said that there would be tribunals and that they wouldn't transfer child molesters around anymore."

Dante leaned back. He shouldn't have said anything, but it was a relief to tell her. He wanted to tell her everything, but he would not breach his confidentiality with the children, and he could not discuss the monasteries in the Italian Alps. It was too much of a relief to talk to her. He was isolated here in the benighted New World and separated from the Jesuit community and the Vatican and his fellow priests and even his sister and her family. He said, "There are no tribunals. I am here to find the truth, and to counsel the children."

She frowned. "But you're not a lawyer. You're a psychiatrist."

Dante had rationalized this on the plane while trying to sleep, and at night while trying to sleep. "In the 1800s, the coroner was a lawyer who looked for *legal* evidence of murder." It was also a relief to not discuss Nicolai and the abused children. "Now, forensic scientists examine dead bodies to determine if the person was murdered. In our tribunals, doctors look for mental illness, and priests look for evil. Perhaps a *magistrate* is a better comparison, an inquiring judge."

Her brows were still bowed down, troubled. "And they're transferred?"

"No. They remain in Italia. They repent and they commend their souls to God."

At this, she shook off her dismay. "Some sins are so grievous that they can't be forgiven." Her words were measured. "I think they're going to Hell, a real Hell, forever."

"Perhaps so." Dante pulled his black hair back from his eyes again. His head still ached.

Perhaps prompted, Mrs. Sloan smoothed her own hair back to where it was caught in a twist. "Father, how about a home-cooked meal tonight?" She was leaning forward, hands open, brows lifted, and a smile opened her lips.

"I—" *should scrub the library clean, should mail these boxes of offal to Roma, should call parents, should read about the pathology of child molesters, should view the rest of those horrifying computer CDs and figure out who that little girl is, should pray for my own soul that rages in the midst of such horror,—* "will be finished counseling at six, Mrs. Sloan."

Mrs. Sloan smiled. "Call me Bev. Supper at seven, then." She left.

Dante stood, brushed off his cassock, and glanced in his date book: Joseph Helbrun and his parents at four o'clock.

Dante had volunteered for this job. Hunting pedophiles was more important than his home, his work, friends, family, everything. Pedophiles hiding within the priesthood must be hunted down and stopped, by whatever means he could command.

Luckily, the Vatican owned Dante, a man who went to battle with demons and won.

JOSEPH SAT in a pew outside the library and kicked the pew in front of him. Stupid word: pew. Pee-ew.

Christine's mother Mrs. Sloan left the library. Father Dante was still in there. Christine's mother had probably been doing dirty things with Father Dante in there.

Father Dante opened the door and saw Joseph waiting, swinging his legs, tapping on a drum set of hymnals, being noisy, being bad. A tremor, something between hate and fear, wracked him at the sight of a man in a Roman collar looking out of the library, waiting for him.

Father Dante was wearing a black cassock, a dress like a woman, which hid his legs and his crotch and his bulge and his dick and his balls. Joseph started putting away the hymnals. Father Dante called over to him, "Is your mother here yet?"

Joseph looked around, even though he knew he was all alone. "No."

Father pointed past his own shoulder, back into the library. "I have just a few things to do. Could you look at your homework out here for a few minutes, until she is here?"

Joseph, still holding a heavy hymnal, nodded.

Father disappeared back inside the library.

It was a trick. The priest was trying to trick him into not being afraid, and then the priest would show him dirty movies and do dirty things.

And it would be all Joseph's fault. Father Nicolai had made Joseph swear on the Bible and on Father Nicolai's dick that he'd never tell anyone about how he made Father Nicolai sin. It was a terrible thing to make a priest sin. You went to Hell because you could never confess it.

LEILA'S BARE LEGS slithered under the silk of her robe, and she pinched a morsel of chicken with chopsticks. Conroy sat across the Biedermeier table from her, shirtless. Her body was comfortably ragged from fucking him, but her legs were still unsteady because Conroy had grabbed her and she'd fought him. No one grabbed Leila and fucked her.

The blue Tiffany glass chandelier above the table tossed glittering light shards on Conroy's skin like alms to the freckled poor. She asked, "What are those cells in the incubator? Primary neurons? Neuroblastoma?"

"Nothing." Conroy ate a mu shu with a fork and fluffed his thinning white hair with his other hand. "What's your experiment?"

"Viral apoptosis pathways in neurons." *How a virus kills brain cells.*

Conroy nodded. "Neurons don't apoptose. Which virus?"

"Retrovirus." And here was her little lie. "Mouse retrovirus."

He nodded. "Write the paper now. Make the mutant later."

One benefit of fucking the professor was these precious little moments. "Here's the thing, Conroy. If we wait until the mutant is finished, it'll be a much bigger paper, mechanistic, seminal."

Conroy shrugged and forked a kung pao chicken bit. "Two publications make your curriculum vitae longer. Give me a draft Monday."

He was wrapped up in his little world, the university, the department, the lab, and the next, small paper. Myopia. If he saw the whole paper, he must understand the whole story in rich colors like Darwin's paradigm-shifting book. Her paper shouldn't be a puzzle piece. It should be art. "You never answered about your mice," she said, "or your cells."

Conroy shrugged. "Just a confirmatory experiment."

Ye gods. Conroy endlessly performed confirmatory experiments, converse and inverse, backwards and forwards, examining results that were already published and then publishing them again. It was as if he had to ensure that the wheel was not only round but a flat cylinder with a center, a radius, a diameter, a circumference, and that pi still approximated at 3.1416, because if it wasn't, he might get to reinvent the goddamned wheel.

Conroy's plate had two bites left. Hers was empty. The last few streaks of sauce clung to the sides of the paper cartons. "Time to go."

Conroy looked up. "Going to the lab?"

"Gym," she said. "Then lab." *Then gay bar.*

DANTE HELD A LARGE, black umbrella above him and knocked on the Sloans' door with the cork end of a Chianti bottle. Winter-pruned rosebushes fringed the strong blue-painted wall. Inconceivable that Sloan would risk all this for a screw.

Dante knocked again, and Mrs. Sloan opened the door. Her smile contracted small wrinkles around her eyes, yet plumpness in her cheeks suggested youth.

Inconceivable.

They said hellos and he handed over the wine, chilled from the cold car trunk. The girls, Dinah and Christine, streaked toward him but stopped short of his legs. In Roma, his nieces and nephew scampered like a twelve-limbed ocean wave and splashed against his legs, spontaneously dividing into three giggling children. He missed that.

Dante shook their hands in turn, the older Christine first. "Pleased to see you again." He bent lower for Dinah, who wore a spiky ballerina's tutu. "And you."

"Good timing," Mrs. Sloan said. "Supper's ready."

The dining room glittered. The chandelier above the table looked like melting crystal, and the glass table reflected the scattered droplets of light up to the ceiling and out the windows that wrapped the room. Candles on the table tossed gold sparks though the glass.

Mrs. Sloan sat before he could offer to pull her chair, so he sat at the other end of the table, facing them all and those dark, reflecting windows that crackled with light.

"I hope you like lemon chicken," Mrs. Sloan said and she began passing plates.

Dante hesitated. He shouldn't be shy about blessing the meal. At his sister's house, he said the benediction in Latin because it amused Theresa. He said, "Shall we…?" and spread his hands apart, suggesting an arc within a circle.

Mrs. Sloan pulled her napkin from her lap and dropped it on the floor.

She picked it up and reached out to her children. "Girls? When Father Dante is here, we'll say grace before we eat supper. We don't need to tell Daddy."

The girls wavered, looking between their mother and Dante, until Christine reached for their outstretched hands. Dinah followed suit.

"Join me in the Lord's Prayer?" he asked.

Mrs. Sloan smiled. She was pretty, but she was not one of the sultry Roma beauties who tried Dante's soul. Dinner with the three ladies was pleasant. Absolutely pleasant.

Pleasant salved Dante's raw soul.

CONROY TYPED the grant proposal on his wide computer screen. The son of a bitch needed to be mailed soon so there would be time for encouraging rumors by February fifteenth, when the university committee decided who would be the new Dean of the Medical College. His barnacled heart quivered and pumped harder. *Dean Sloan. Dean Sloan.*

Finally, Yuri went home, and the lab was empty. One can't do experiments that should not be talked about when there are students and postdocs hanging around, looking at plates, asking *Whatcha doing?*

There are many reasons not to discuss experiments. Some experiments are wild shots in the dark and aren't worth discussing unless they pan out. Some experiments infringe on other labs' work, and you have to be politic. Sometimes, what you are doing is illegal or immoral or might cause a problem, like you might inadvertently create a deadly new superplague, or you might be working with virus strains or reagents internationally smuggled and furtively handed off at conferences, and you've got to be really careful when you discuss those.

Conroy wrote in his lab notebook: *8:30pm (22 hp pass), infected c 1000 PFU/mL RV-12.* Keeping careful notes is vital in science. If you screw something up, you can figure out what you did from your notes. An hour can make a difference in viral titer. When treating patients, careful notes can allow you to see a pattern you might not have considered and thus save a patient, or notes can save your ass during a lawsuit. Conroy kept meticulous, though coded, notes on everything.

Padded gloves protected his hands, and he opened the giant Thermos flask. Warm air seeped into the tank. The liquid nitrogen boiled, and the tank burbled like an ice volcano.

Labeled metal tabs ringed the mouth of the tank. Conroy selected one and pulled up an aluminum basket full of long aluminum canes. He pulled out one cane. Frozen vials, longer and thinner than thimbles, lined the cane. One vial, *RV-12*, he teased out with double-padded fingers. The tiny tube frosted over, obscuring the pink crystals inside and coating it in slippery ice.

The ice-covered vial shot from his encumbered fingers and tumbled through the air. He dropped the cane in his frenzy to catch the vial, and it splashed into the liquid nitrogen. A fine, freezing spray speckled his face. The tube brushed his cottoned fingertips, danced in the air, and fell into his palm, safe.

Jesus H. Fucking Christ. Conroy's hand clamped around the miniscule tube and shook. If the frozen, brittle vial had shattered on the floor, the virus would have burst into the air and aerosolized, and he might have inhaled it. This strain, isolated from the *Pipistrellus subflavus* bat, was particularly infectious. The virus would have burrowed into his tender lungs, leapt into his blood, infested his nerves, and swarmed up to his brain. His face flushed as if with fever.

He hadn't dropped it. He just needed to be careful. Very, very careful.

He set the vial on the counter and eased the basket down. The liquid nitrogen bubble-bubbled, toiled and troubled. He capped the tank and carried the vial to the tissue culture room.

In the hood, he set the vial down and stepped back. If liquid nitrogen had seeped past the silicone gasket into the vial, the vial would explode when thawed, splattering the hood with virus. Still, that was a better proposition than contaminated shrapnel flying through the lab. He shucked the padded gloves, slapped on latex ones and waited, interlacing his fingers behind his head to support his neck.

Outside the tissue culture room, the lab door crashed closed.

Conroy jumped and inspected his samples; they were all labeled with innocuous numbers. He draped a floppy latex glove over the vial of virus stock to hide it anyway.

Leila strode into the tissue culture room. She wore damp yoga pants and a sweatshirt. Her hair was slicked back in a ponytail. She opened the incubator, a warm contraption the size of a dorm refrigerator, and pulled out trays of cells. "What're you doing here, Dr. S.?"

"Tissue culture." He glanced at the glove-covered vial in his hood.

She slid a flask onto the microscope and stared through the oculars. The video camera displayed pink, spindly neurons like stretched fried eggs on the computer monitor. She said, "Oh, secret experiments again."

"No. Nothing important."

"Yeah. Right." She white-balanced the screen to remove the pink tint. The brain cells' splatted bodies and axon spikes sharpened on the screen.

His vial of virus stock had probably thawed and was, as they spoke, degrading in the caustic hibernation chemicals.

She focused the picture of the neurons, twiddling the knob on the side of the microscope. "So why are the Jesuits after you?"

"They aren't *after* me. I met Petrocchi-Bianchi and wanted to know if he was legit."

Leila tapped the space bar, and the image on the monitor froze. "I can't believe you got the Jesuits after you. The Jesuits are the radical fringe of the Catholic Church. Kind of cool."

"You don't think anything about the Church is cool." The heresies she promulgated, the scoffing and outright hostility she evinced, usually in bed, turned Conroy on.

"Well, the Jesuits aren't as sick as the rest of them. Some were killed in Latin America during the troubles. Others disappeared because they opposed Pinochet. They've nearly been excommunicated en masse a couple of times." She looked up, away from the cells, and a small smile curved her lips. "If I were a priest, I'd be a Jesuit."

"You can't be a priest. You don't believe in God." Conroy's virus stock was dying.

"Not to mention that I lack a necessary member...ship requirement, but it's philosophically impossible to prove a negative," Leila stared in the microscope, "so you can't say there is no God. Absence of evidence is not evidence of absence."

Good thing his wife didn't know that crap. She'd have his ass in Mass every day. "That waffling wouldn't be acceptable during the Liturgy."

Her jaw tightened and ligaments lined her neck. "I know the Liturgy, Conroy."

"Jesus, Leila. Are you Catholic?"

"Nope." She slapped the space bar, capturing a picture. She cranked the microscope, slapped the bar, cranked the scope, smashed the bar. She shoved her samples back in the incubator, "'Bye, Conroy," and strode out.

Conroy lifted the membranous glove off the vial of viral stock in the hood. The liquid was thoroughly thawed. He held it, and chill poked his palm through the latex glove.

Thank Whoever couldn't be proven not to exist, the virus hadn't gotten too warm. Virus stocks are notoriously delicate.

AFTER BEV AND DANTE FINISHED the Chianti, Bev's ears felt tickly and her balance was bobbly. She'd tried to let Father Dante drink most of the wine, but he had to drive home, so she'd helped. As a rule, she didn't drink in front of the girls, but the girls should see how responsible adults could imbibe a little.

She sent the girls upstairs for baths. "Father, shall we sit down?"

His unrelieved black clothes, Mediterranean skin, and black hair were an impossibly dark hole cut into the bright room. The incandescent light streaming from the harsh bulbs and rebounding from the white ceiling found him untouchable. "I shouldn't," he said. "There is work."

She walked him to the foyer and held out her hand. "Thank you for coming."

Father Dante took her hand and held it, not shaking. He smiled shyly, or wryly, just a curve of his lips. Expressions melted in her eyes when she was tipsy. "It was lovely. Thank you, Mrs. Sloan."

"Bev, call me Bev." She thought he was going to kiss her knuckles, so European, but he didn't lift her hand. Hand-kissing would have been too continental for this East Coast college town, for this Midwestern girl. "Everyone calls me Bev."

"Thank you, Bev." Father Dante walked into the porchlight, and the dark night gathered him in.

Her head spun as she closed the door and leaned on it, listening to his car drive away.

The alcohol buzz drifted in her mind and felt like the peace of God, but it wasn't. No Divine Grace could reach her until her penance was complete, until she forgave Conroy.

A tipsy plan formed itself.

She waltzed back to the dining room. The glass bottle tapped her teeth as she drank the last astringent swallow of the Chianti.

CONROY SAW the light in the master bedroom when he pulled into the garage at eleven. Beverly must be waiting for him, ready to start a fight.

Inside, the house was dark. A fir-green, empty wine bottle slanted in the recycling bin. He picked it up. *Chianti.*

Surely Beverly hadn't been drinking. She wouldn't drink in front of the girls, or alone. He let the bottle slip into the bin, and it clanked against the washed, unlabelled jars and bottles.

Upstairs, he checked on the girls in case Beverly hadn't gotten them to bed, but they were fine. Dinah's stuffed unicorn had fallen on the floor. He tucked it under the covers with her.

Conroy opened their bedroom door, expecting to find his wife full of the wrath of Hell or passed out drunk.

Inside, candles flickered on every glass-topped piece of furniture: dressers, nightstands, Beverly's vanity table. Red pillars, yellow votives, green tea lights, white tapers, emergency power-outage beeswax, and an orange three-wick pot flickered. Beverly lit the last one and clicked off the butane lighter. She was wearing a blue silk penoir set with lace froth at her bust and thighs. She always wore a robe of some kind until they turned out the lights. The scars still embarrassed her.

"Beverly?" he asked, as if he didn't know who she was, dumbass. "Have you been drinking?"

Her hands flipped and fluttered in the air for longer than if she'd been sober. "Father Dante brought a bottle of wine." She walked over to him. "What was I supposed to do?"

Beverly and ethanol were too miscible. Her personality was highly soluble in ethanol and chemically unstable. She had an edge to her when she was drunk. When they were younger, her sharp edge had attracted him, added volatility to their conversations and encounters. A thrill of uncertainty shivered in his flesh. "Was it just wine? Was it just one glass?" he asked.

"Maybe one and a half." She slid her arms around his neck. Wine soured her breath, a whiff of danger and promise. She was beautiful with pink cheeks and a hot glow to her body.

He laughed, picked her up in his arms, and tossed her on the bed.

She giggled, and her light brown hair bounced and shone in the candlelight.

THE NEXT MORNING, Bev gathered her robe around her and pressed the waffle iron closed. If she got to school early, she might have a moment to kneel at the altar, to see if her heart had mended.

Ah, last night, the wine had been so tasty, like chocolate, a glorified sugar buzz, a cell-level happy glow. She had the munchies for wine, just a little, just one glass.

Conroy wandered downstairs. The girls were finishing their waffles at the kitchen table, watching the empty swings outside meander in the chill breeze. Christine continued her diatribe about *Anne of Green Gables*, "And I have to read *a hundred pages* this weekend."

"I'm sure you'll be fine, honey." Bev set waffle-laden plates on the table.

Conroy ran his fingers through his hair so that it stood on end, obscuring the thin spot in back. "What was that priest doing over here last night?"

She poured coffee for herself and Conroy. "He came over for supper. He's alone in a strange country. He doesn't have any family here." She sat across from her husband.

"And the priest got you drunk?" Conroy asked.

"He brought one bottle of wine. I'm such a lightweight any more." Bev tucked into her waffle.

"It's strange," he said.

"It's not strange," she said.

Chapter Five

Friday morning, Leila's toe dragged on the hallway's industrial tile floor and she hopped over the stumble. Her coffee sloshed in its cup but didn't splash her. She didn't bother to look back to feign that a pebble had caused the stumble. Except for that damn experiment, she would have called in sick. Today was the type of day to be in a bar, drinking oneself unconscious.

Conroy was working at his computer, typing furiously, and she had almost sneaked past when he waved her into his office. "This gel turned into a big, red X again!" He flicked his middle finger at the monitor.

On the oversized screen, a square was slashed by a red, graphic X.

She drank coffee. A scalding line extended down her throat to her chest. Her cells waved villous receptors, trying to catch the cascading caffeine. She asked, "What did you do to it?"

"I didn't do anything," he protested. "I was writing, and I scrolled up to look at the gel, and the computer hung for a minute and, when it started scrolling again, all I got was this damned, red X! And now they're *all* like that! *Xs!*"

"All right, Dr. S. Let's see what you did. Get up."

His chair was still warm under her legs. Leila closed five other memory-sucking programs that he had running in the background. She scrolled the grant up, and the gel was back in its place. "There."

"How'd you do that?" Conroy leaned over her shoulder and squinted at the monitor.

"Magic." She walked toward the door. Her timepoint was already late. After that, she could get the hell out of the lab. He caught her forearm and she jerked away. "Don't grab me."

Conroy asked, "I'm not prying, but are you all right?"

"Fine."

"Do you want to talk about it?"

"Nope." She was too slow in reaching for the doorknob.

"Do you have a few minutes around six tonight?"

"Sure," Leila said. "Bring booze." A rough scrog might be just the way to begin the long, terrible weekend.

OUTSIDE CONROY'S OFFICE in the Sloan lab, Danna sat on a tall lab chair and swung her legs. On the paper-covered counter beside her, beakers, Erlenmeyer flasks, and graduated cylinders stood in glittery rows like fine crystal, waiting for the undergrad dishwasher to put them away. Danna said, "I think he's taking advantage of her."

Joe laughed. "Leila can take care of herself."

"He always has a computer problem." She scratched at the welt on her arm. It had been there for weeks but it hadn't grown or gotten infected, it was just kind of rashy, so she ignored it.

Virus crawled up the neurons in her arm, chewing toward her brain. Conroy had rescued them from that icy hell of liquid nitrogen. He must have a divine design, a purpose-driven life planned for them, something more than just those dishes and mice. They chewed and flitted and swung among the neurons, praying for grace.

Danna played with a pipetter, squirting distilled water in swirls on the white waffled paper covering the counter. "I think he's going to hold her back from graduating."

"He wouldn't." Joe pipetted microliters of blue-dyed DNA into a block of gelatinous agarose. The thought that naïve Leila needed their protection was enough to make him snort, but he didn't. He respected Leila's privacy, and she'd mentioned a pub crawl that evening. After one of Leila's pub crawls last year, he'd awakened with a leather snake-toy wrapped around his waist and wondered what Leila was up to, but then the leathery toy moved like an enormous penis and he'd had an alien abduction homosexual rape moment before he realized he was sleeping next to an elephant in the Bronx Zoo, and its trunk was snuggling him.

Danna shook her head and her frizzy pony tail swished. Dr. S. was monopolizing Leila, and he grimaced every time he looked at Leila as if demonic thoughts assailed him. Danna clasped her hands to her bony chest. "I'll pray for her."

Joe snorted. "You do that."

BEV KNOCKED on the library door. No answer. She pounded harder on the dark varnish. Nothing. She knocked again, a sappy shave-and-a-haircut-two-bits rhythm. Nothing. She opened the door.

No one was among the bookcases and chairs and desk and cardboard boxes littering the room. Two large boxes stood on the desk. Father Dante might be throwing away something useful. She walked over to them. The flaps were interlaced closed. One box was taped with fiber-embedded strapping tape.

Footsteps pounded behind her. A masculine shout, "*Alto!* Stop!"

Grabbed from behind and pushed, Bev stumbled and lost a shoe. She grabbed the chair.

Father Dante held her arm and nearly lifted her. "You should not look there. You are all right?"

Bev sucked in air. "Fine," she said.

"*Mi dispiace.* I'm sorry." He stepped back and rubbed his face.

"No, I'm fine." Bev toed around until she found her shoe and slipped it on.

Dante was still breathing hard. "You shouldn't look in those."

Bev sat on the chair arm. "Good grief, what's wrong?"

Father Dante laid his hands on the boxes, as if to assure himself that they were still closed, as if he could divine whether she had looked or not. "It's evidence."

Evidence. Evidence was for crimes. Bev's breath caught. "Oh."

"I'm sending it to Roma, for evidence. Nicolai made videos on the computer, of himself with the children. I had to watch, to identify the children. I want to *kill him.* I want to beat him to death. The things he did, oh God, *the things he did.*"

Before, she had understood the accusations, but now she *believed* them. "Oh, my God."

"Yes."

"*Father Nicolai.*" Her stomach cramped.

"He is a devil." Father Dante rubbed his hands together rapidly as if to warm them.

LEILA LAY ON HER BED on top of the scarlet, tasseled duvet, reading *Middlemarch.* Pale red light filtered through the chiffon curtains around the bed and stretched long stripes on the duvet and wall. In rhythm with her reading, she batted the glass-beaded fringe that edged the curtain. Meth snoozed on the floor. His spindly tail thumped intermittently.

Finally, a knock at the door. Leila kicked her nightstand drawer closed as she rolled off the bed. Her pistol clunked as the drawer shut.

At the door, Leila peered through the peephole and saw Conroy, holding booze. She unlatched the locks in a drumroll of rattling bolts.

The brown bag in Conroy's arms clanked. "I feel like I'm contributing to the delinquency of a minor." He set the bag on her table.

"That's not funny." Even if he had pedophile or adolescentophile—*ephebophile*—fantasies, she didn't encourage shit like that. No cheerleader outfits hung in her closet. She swallowed hard to push down the shaking sickness in her throat and casually inspected bottles in the bag: whiskey, beer, and vodka. "What, are you throwing a party?"

"I thought I'd have a beer. Maybe some vodka. What the hell?"

Leila recited, "Liquor before beer, in the clear. Beer before liquor, never sicker." Someone at O'Malley's party should have reminded her of that.

"Okay," Conroy said. "Got orange juice?"

Leila's fridge held towers of salad ingredients and two cartons of skinless chicken breasts. "Some pineapple-orange juice."

"Sounds like a screwdriver to me."

She poured one finger of the umber Macallen in a shotglass for herself and slammed it down—it burned so good, like a whiff of hellfire—and poured a jigger of vodka into Conroy's glass of orange juice. She stirred it with a blunt table knife.

Conroy frowned at her. "Why don't you use a spoon?"

Leila poured herself another shot. "People sniff spoons when they're looking for evidence of clandestine drinking."

"You live alone."

Conroy turned her television over to the all-golf channel. Leila handed him the pine-screwdriver.

She sniffed the burning creosote-scented scotch. "It's January twenty-ninth, and it's even a Friday. Shall we raise a glass to my dad?"

From the couch, Conroy raised his glass to the height of her eyes.

Leila raised her shotglass until it eclipsed Conroy's orange tumbler and his balding head and his blue, blue eyes. "May he not be burning in Hell."

Conroy's glass dipped, breaking the alcoholic juxtaposition. "Your father passed on?"

Leila pounded the shot, and it burned too, but less. "Yep." She went back to the kitchen to replenish. Her next shot went in a highball glass with bottled water. New Hamilton tap water had a pesticidal, nitrogenous finish.

Conroy said, "My father passed away, too, when I was ten."

"I was sixteen." Leila's arm fell in slow motion, and she guided it down to the counter. The honey-colored liquid swirled in her highball glass.

She'd bought good barware a couple of years ago. Her father would have liked it, good scotch in good crystal. Pouring a shot on his grave would have been a fitting tribute, but he had been cremated, and flinging a shot into the Floridian waves seemed like a waste of good scotch. And she was nowhere near Florida.

"Heart attack," Conroy said. "I don't even remember much about him."

"My dad was sick." She raised her amber-filled glass. "This was a big part of it."

"You should be careful about drinking. Alcoholism is genetic," he said.

"Bullshit." Her drink caught flickers from the blue glass chandelier above the kitchen table. "Phenylketoneuria is genetic. Huntington's chorea is genetic."

Conroy looked serious, older, wiser, older. "A predisposition."

"Tay-Sachs is genetic." The glass-enclosed chandelier warped and wefted through the lens of scotch and water. The cups of stained glass walked on the ceiling like an upside-down octopus in round boots. "Sickle cell is genetic."

Conroy was beside her, and he steered her toward the couch. "Your definition of 'genetic' narrows when you drink."

Pressure on her shoulder, and she sat. She held her drink with cupped hands. "Thalassemia and albinism."

Conroy set his drink on the coffee table. "I haven't thought about my father for years."

"I think about mine all the time." Every time she saw the red gauze above her bed, morning and evening. Every time her mother said he was burning in Hell. Every time she drank.

Conroy shook his head. "You should talk to somebody."

"Like who, a shrink?" *A priest?* Her stomach wrestled with the scotch. "Me?"

"You're leaving." In Leila's hands, the dilute scotch seemed to permeate the crystal. It spilled into her hands and ran through the veins in her arms.

"Jody's coming over at seven. We're going out."

Conroy sat beside her and leaned back. "I'm sorry about your dad."

"So am I." She gazed into her amber drink as if trying to penetrate the mythical veil, the one that charlatans and mediums and psychics talked about, that separated the living from the departed, or *crossed-over*, or some other such euphemistic bullshit for *dead*.

The flavors in the scotch separated in her mouth. Her dad described the flavors in booze as smoke and fruit and berry, but scotch tasted more varied to her than food flavors. They were almost colors, and she resisted calling the top note *honey*, because that suggested bee clover honey, but it was rich and sweet, maybe more like honeysuckle, or honey-yellow silk, or cold gold coins. One of the compounds that registered on the back of her tongue wasn't salty, but it had a mineral taste, cloudy white like gypsum.

Conroy took the drink out of her hands and set it on the coffee table. She didn't protest or reach for it. It was going to be a long night. There was plenty of time.

He said, "Tell me about your father."

Leila retrieved her scotch. The anniversary was not for morbid reminiscences. The anniversary was for drinking and her own memories in her own head. Her dad had hated whispers and rumors and cattiness.

"What did he do?" Conroy prompted.

"Lawyer. He moved to Florida when my mom divorced him."

"Did you see him much?"

"Summers." Three sunny months every year when she was freed from plaid and penguins and priests and to-do lists and the big, dry-erase schedule on the wall, scrawled with *Mass, Youth Group, tutoring w/ Fr. Sean, piano*. Those six years, she'd been a divided soul, a multiple personality.

"Read any good books lately? I'm reading *Middlemarch*."

Conroy sighed. "I wouldn't think you'd like George Eliot."

Leila blinked, a darkness dropping over her apartment and lifting like sped-up night. "Why not?"

He sipped his pine-screwdriver. "All the women do is get married, and who they marry is of such importance. It's practically a romance novel."

"But George Eliot told the story." Leila set down her drink and lay back on the couch, one arm above her head. She knew she was inviting being jumped on. "George Eliot was her own woman. She traveled. She lived with a man she wasn't married to, then married a buck twenty years younger than she was. Even Virginia Woolf thought Eliot was cool."

Conroy shrugged.

Fine. He didn't get it, the philistine. "In Victorian times, *marriage* meant *sex*. Eliot was talking about *sex*. Women don't want marriage. Women want sex. *Middlemarch* is porn."

"Of course women want to get married. It's all they talk about."

Interesting that he used the exclusionary *they*, as if no one present qualified. "Women don't want marriage. Men do."

He laughed more than just a snort. "That's not true."

"Women want sex. Women risk childbirth and death to have sex." She rolled to her feet and picked up her glass. "Eliot was a pre-Raphaelite," she muttered and walked into the kitchen.

"You didn't tell me about your father." Conroy sat on the couch, watching muted golf.

"My father has nothing to do with this," Leila said. "Do you know why you're here?"

Conroy looked from the television to her, wary. "In your apartment?"

"On earth and in my apartment," she said. "It's to pass on your genes."

Conroy set down his drink and stared at her, somewhere between terrified and pissed. "You aren't pregnant."

"Christ, Conroy. I'm not preggers. Get a hold of yourself." She sipped her scotch to emphasize *that* point. "It's all just to contribute genes to the next generation."

Conroy looked back to the television. "Reductionist, like your genetics. I thought you didn't like reductionism. Glorious big picture, and all that."

"You're trying to pass on your genes before you die and are burned up or decay and your atoms reenter the carbon cycle. Even my dad passed on his genes. But let me tell you something." Her voice fell, and somewhere her mind thought, *don't tell him this, he doesn't even understand Middlemarch.* "I'm opting out, like George Eliot."

"No you aren't." He didn't even look at her.

"I'm not having kids, any kids, ever."

He sipped his drink and didn't turn his stare away from the television. "You'll want kids when you're older. All women want to have kids." The asshole was dismissive, condescending.

Condescending.

Con can mean opposite. Con-descending, the opposite of falling, so *falling up.*

Con-roy, *roy* means *king*, so *Con-roy* means *the opposite of a king.*

"No, *men* want kids," she said. He treated her like a drunk teenager.

"It's selfish not to want kids." Some golfer did something to grass.

She said, "It's selfish to have kids, to believe that your DNA is so valuable that you should produce lots of kids to suck up resources and turn food into crap and keep passing on your DNA. It's selfish to make babies so that your own death is less terrifying."

"Baloney."

"Come on, Conroy. A woman who doesn't want children scares you. You think it's *unnatural.*"

"It is unnatural. Everyone wants kids. Women want to be mothers."

"No, Conroy. Women want *sex.* Women risk getting pregnant and giving birth which, except for the last couple of decades here but still in most of the world, is horribly painful and lethal a good percentage of the time, because they want *sex.* That's how much women want to *fuck.*"

"Bullshit," he scoffed.

He *scoffed* at her, the idiot. "It's why *men* were against birth control in the early nineteen hundreds and why the pro-lifer leaders now are all guys.

Two, four, six, ten. Why are all your leaders men? Men want children. Men want to get married so they can lock up the woman so they know the kids are theirs."

Conroy laughed. "There's an old saying, 'Men give marriage to get sex. Women give sex to get marriage.' That's the way it works."

Leila was betraying secrets to the enemy. He'd put sodium pentothal in her scotch and he *wasn't even listening* to her spill these secrets, the secrets that women kept hidden even from themselves so they couldn't betray them. "Listen to yourself. *Men* run the Catholic Church. The Church is against birth control and abortion and sex outside marriage and abortion."

Conroy shook his head. "I wonder which neurotransmitter you have too much of."

"Surely you don't believe there's a God that dictates that crap."

"Leila, you've had enough to drink."

She couldn't stop talking. This topic haunted her. "Consider gay men. Homosexual men are promiscuous and have anonymous sex in the back rooms of bars."

Conroy nodded. "Because they're men. Heterosexual men would have that much sex if women let them."

"You've got it backwards." She was almost yelling across her apartment at him, but she couldn't stop. He was an idiot and he thought *she* was wrong. "Gay men have a *woman's* sexual appetite. They like men, and they like *lots* of men as often as possible. They also like good shoes and pretty clothes and antiques."

"Leila, please stop drinking." He stood.

"But lesbians," she swirled the dilute scotch in her glass and thumped it on the kitchen counter, "who wear sensible shoes, have extended groups of lesbian friends, cut their hair short, and participate in team sports, *they* pair-bond for life and stop having sex within a few months. That's *men.*"

"Lesbians stop having sex?" Conroy took her glass away. "You're going to be drunk before you even go out."

He still didn't get it. "That's why hetero men fear gay men. Homos aren't the manliest of men, inhabiting an all-male society, unfettered by women. The gay underground is a matriarchy. Gay men admit it and call each other by female names, *girlfriend, Mary, bitch*."

He set her glass down on the bar, out of her reach.

She said, "It's why hetero men like lesbians. They can relate."

"Leila, let's sit down. You've had a lot to drink on an empty stomach."

"I'm fine." She couldn't make him understand because it scared him. He was terrified and mocking her and she should shut up. Leila's head swam. The digital clock on the stove said 6:45. "You've got to leave."

"I can't leave you like this." He sighed. "You're distraught."

"Just another word men use to make women seem weak." The room swayed so she held onto the kitchen counter.

"Okay, then you're drunk."

"Am not." She reached for her drink, and Conroy moved it farther down the bar. Asshole, just because he was taller, he could win at keep-away. "Jody is usually early. You should leave."

"Will you stop drinking?"

"Fuck, no."

"I'm worried you'll choke to death on your own vomit."

"Oh, attractive, Conroy."

"Okay, here," he said and he handed her back her glass, but it was filled with water. She drank it anyway. His vacant, recessive blue eyes crinkled at the corners with laughter. "Besides," he said, "you're forgetting something in your drunken, feminist theory."

"What," she said.

"Keep drinking the water. Men put little energy into making gametes and make millions of them. It's in our reproductive interest to spread our genes far and wide, hope a few take root."

At least he was listening, even if it was only to get his way, to keep her from drinking. "But—" she said.

"Not done," he said. "Women put so much energy into making one egg a month and then nine months gestation, and then eighteen years of child rearing, that it's in their best interest to marry a guy who'll help raise their offspring. Male competition and female choice, sexual selection. Darwin."

"Old theory," Leila said. "Victorian-era theory. Most men don't have the opportunity to spread their sperm far and wide, so they find one egg and guard it and the offspring that they *think* is theirs. Most men don't have sex with thousands of women."

"Rock stars do."

The alcohol buzzing softened as her liver chewed the ethanol in her blood. "Salmon exception," she said.

The doorbell bonged.

"Salmon, like omega-3 fatty acids," Conroy said.

"Salmon, the fish that spawn." Leila went over to her door and looked out the peephole. Jody was dressed in spangles and sparkling scales that confused the peephole's fisheye lens. She yelled, "Just a minute!"

Jody called, "If you're not dressed, that's fine with me."

"Getting my purse!" Leila went back to the kitchen and Conroy. "Nope. Missed the point again, Con-roy." She handed him his vodka pine-screwdriver, took his rough hand, and led him through her kitchen.

Enough ethanol laced her blood that Leila was too sharp, too clear, and she knew all the ways he was wrong. She led him to her hallway and said, "Male salmon come in two types: normal and rock star. When resources are scarce, they all turn into little male salmon that swim like hell upstream and have the energy to get there, and they find one female salmon, and they spawn exactly once and die." She tugged his hand and pulled him toward her closet. "When there are a lot of little male salmon around and competition for the females gets hairy, a few males grow bigger, shinier, redder, with big hooked jaws and can barely make it upstream. Testosterone poisoning. They're too big, too heavy, and the bears can see them. It's risky. They're rock stars, and if they make it, they get all the chicks."

"That doesn't happen."

"Look it up." She shoved him into the dark closet between her hanging clothes.

He held the closet door open. "Even if salmon do that, we're not fish."

Her head rocked forward and her eyebrows cocked. "Of course we are, Conroy. We're nothing but bald monkeys, and we're nothing but hairy fish. The whole point of life is to squirt your genes into the next generation."

He held her clothes apart and glared at her. "But you're not going to have kids. So you have no purpose, under your own theory."

"On the contrary, I can do whatever the hell I want to." She slid shut the closet door, and she mumbled against the wood, "I'm free. Not even evolution can trap me."

CONROY WAITED in the dark of Leila's closet. Light slid through the cracks between the closet door and the jamb, just enough so he could faintly see her clothes hanging around him. Her clothes smelled like floral laundry detergent.

One pair of blue jeans was hanging by his left side, and he traced the crotch of her jeans with his finger, slowly, then rubbed the bulky seam, imagining Leila's soft clit inside.

Outside the door, Leila whispered, "Lock up." Her footsteps clinked away. There were greetings of two female voices, some very European moist lip sounds, and the front door closed.

The apartment was quiet, and Conroy found a slippery black blouse of hers hanging beside him. He ran his hands inside the material, where her small breasts would be, pinched the fabric that would rub her nipples.

He could hardly wait until she wore that black, silky blouse.

SATURDAY AFTERNOON, Dante opened the door and let Conroy Sloan into his library. Bev waited outside.

Mr. Sloan crossed to his chair and lowered himself into it. Traces of sober consideration or light fatigue softened his usual twitchiness. Perhaps he was ready to confess.

Cordially, Dante asked Sloan, "Have you informed the woman?"

Sloan sighed and reached behind him. He tugged a bloated wallet from his hip pocket, sorted through its contents, and handed Dante a folded piece of paper.

The email:

Re: an apology

> Dear Peggy,

> I apologize for what I have to say to you, and for what I have to do. I'm sorry, but it is

> best if we end the affair. > You knew that our affair wasn't meant to be anything other than some fun.

> I apologize if I hurt you, if I led you to believe that our relationship was anything

> other than it was, or if you believed so anyway. > I'm sorry.

> Conroy

Dante asked, "You sent the woman an email?"

"Well, yes," Sloan said.

Typically callous and careless. Dante shook his head. The woman, Peggy, was reduced to a recipient, which was indicative of Conroy's view of her. Dante asked, "When did you send this?"

"Thursday," Sloan said.

"And she replied?"

"Friday morning."

"Where is her reply?"

Sloan blinked slowly, delaying. He said, "I deleted it."

How like him to tap the "delete" button so her objections were erased. "And it said?"

Sloan bobbed his leg. "That she understood and that we could still be friends. She was very nice, very understanding. She is very nice. Understanding. And nice."

That answer was obviously a fabrication. The physical twitches were indicative of unease. The rest of Sloan's answers were, most likely and rather troublingly, true. At the very least, Dante could not allow Sloan to confess while he continued to lie about the woman's reply. "Tell me what her email said."

The smug curve in Sloan's expression drew taut. "What do you mean?"

Sloan had never been called to account for his lies before. This must be a troubling week for him, the discovery of his affair, being called to account for his actions, and the ease with which Dante saw through lies. "Your explanation of what this woman, Peggy, said in her email is false."

"You don't know that!" Sloan's voice rose, indignant.

Dante's work afforded him many opportunities to see such tiresome displays. *You can't prove I did that! I am not possessed by a demon! The child is lying!* Dante said, "Her reply was different than what you told me. If your student brought you a micrograph of a cell, and the cytoskeleton and the nucleus were labeled with fluoroprobes, such that the cell looked like a glowing island in a black sea webbed with lime green topographical lines and capped with a scarlet pillbox hat, and he told you that the picture was of a virus, you wouldn't believe him. A virus looks like a virus, and a cell looks like a cell. Upon examination, truth looks like truth, and a lie looks like something else."

Sloan blinked, again stalling. Dante waited. Sloan's fingers curled around the arms of the chair. "She was angry," Sloan said. "She said I'd lied to her."

"What did you tell her?"

"I never said that I would leave my wife." The last part rang desperately of truth. "And besides," Sloan said and glanced up into the corner of the library, "the affair was actually a good experience for me. It tested my marriage, and now I know that I love Beverly and my family. It's brought me and Beverly much closer."

More lies, as much to himself as to Dante. Dante pinched his nose. A headache blossomed behind his eyes. "What about the other woman?"

"I broke it off," Sloan said.

"You used this woman." He pressed the heels of his hands against his forehead and he tried not to allow the diatribe to emerge *again*. Those words lurked in him, always ready to leap and devour. Dante had tried counseling pedophiles for a week before he decided to work with the victims. The men could barely talk about their crimes because they didn't understand that their victims were children, who had souls, who had dreams, who should have grown up whole. Pedophiles were all spiritually stunted and could not imagine what it was like to be repeatedly raped. Sometimes, Dante was tempted to turn the men over to the American justice system so they could learn that lesson like John Geoghan had. "You think only of how this woman affected *you*, but she is a soul, a soul whom you damaged. It could not draw you closer to God or help your marriage to use this woman and damage her. You are not closer to God. This has destroyed your marriage."

Sloan slouched in his chair, his eyes slitted, his lower lip curled in. "It's over with. What did you want me to do?"

The anger tore free. Dante's hands were tangled in each other, an enormous, wrathful fist. "Confess," he said, "confess with an open heart and know that you have offended God. You've broken your marriage vows, a sacrament. You've broken your wife's heart. She trusted God and she trusted you. You've hurt this other woman, Peggy, by lying to her. It was *rape*, having sex with her when she believed you loved her, when she believed she was worshipping you with her body, but you were just screwing her."

The next morning, Sunday morning, Dante confessed his wrath and his despair to Brother Samual before early Mass, and his heart felt like abraded, flayed muscle, as he pressed his palms on his knees, and whispered, "My brother Jesuits were recounting their affairs, enumerating the ways they had broken their vows and how this had benefited them as priests and brought them closer to God, and I shouted, 'What about the women? What did you do to them?' Wrath is my personal foible. Wrath stems from pride, an unjustified pride because I have not committed these particular sins since taking Holy Orders. But I am a sinner, too, in my pride and in my wrath."

Sloan, sitting in his chair across the library from Dante, drew one ragged breath.

Dante looked up from his hands, which cramped from clenching.

Sloan pressed his hands to his face so hard that his arms quivered.

Dante waited.

Sloan rubbed his eyes with his palms and stretched the skin from his eyelids to his temples. He said, "It never occurred to me."

Finally, *finally*, Sloan's focus shifted from himself to the people he had wronged. If Dante trod gently, he might coax Sloan along, save his marriage, and maybe his soul.

Sloan's spine bent, and his breath rasped and he rested his arms on his knees as if recovering from a belly punch. His pink scalp skimmed under the thinning, silver hair.

"If you want to confess your sins, I will hear your confession."

Sloan nodded without looking up.

"I'll be right back." Dante walked out of the library, past Mrs. Sloan praying in a pew in the cathedral, to the rectory to retrieve his stole.

Dante had been, perhaps, too confrontational, but what can one expect from an exorcist accustomed to casting out demons by the force of his will and God's grace in his voice?

BEV PUSHED THE DOOR to Father Dante's library open with her fingertips. Her husband slumped in the chair, his hand covering his mouth, staring at the floor. "Conroy?"

His eyes, when he looked up, were glassy. "I'm sorry," he said.

She hadn't realized that her chest had hurt for days, since she had found those horrible panties in Conroy's suitcase, but now it didn't anymore. She laid her arms around his shoulders and he leaned into her. Small shudders ran through him, not crying, just trembling, as if from the aftershocks of adrenaline.

Surely, since Conroy had repented, she could forgive him and love him again. Maybe that loosening in her heart was the beginning of grace. Maybe, if she went back to the altar and prayed now, hard, maybe the Virgin Mary would come to her and she wouldn't have to bother Father Dante with her inability to feel the kind stillness of God.

CONROY ROCKED in Beverly's arms. He'd been a selfish prick, fucking Peggy when she needed more, ripping apart his marriage and his wife, and gambling that no one would find out.

The priest returned with his purple stole around his neck, the ends hanging free. He said, "Mrs. Sloan, another moment?" She smiled at Conroy as she slipped through the door.

Conroy had been a cad, and he needed to toss away these stupid things he'd done. Confession was as good a place to start as any. If he did this, maybe the priest would help him with Beverly. Conroy stiffly lowered himself to his knees and whipped through the prayer before confession, asking the Holy Spirit, Virgin Mary, and the archangels, angels, and saints to aid in his confession.

Strange how there was no direct imploring of any masculine deity in that prayer, only the neuter Spirit, the female Virgin, and the multitudes. This irking concentration on the girly aspects of God was meant to feminize men, humble them, emasculate him so he could beg. Not to mention that he was kneeling in front of a guy in the blow-job position. Maybe gay priests thought about getting blown while penitents recited their sins, down on their knees.

The priest's black-robed arm moved above Conroy's head, tracing a cross in the air, and the priest blessed him. At least the priest's black robe was more than an arm's length away. The priest said, "May the Lord be in your heart and help you to confess your sins with true sorrow."

Conroy's knees hurt. "Bless me, Father, for I have sinned. It has been," Conroy stopped and counted, considered, and lied, "seven years since my last confession. These are my sins. I had sex with a woman who was not my wife."

"On how many occasions," the priest prompted.

This is where priests got their reputation for dirty minds, prying for details. "A lot."

"Fine. Are there any other sins you wish to confess?"

Conroy stared at the wooden boards under his knees. "Only mortal sins, right?"

"Correct."

"No."

The priest said, "Think harder."

Conroy glanced up. The Italian priest was staring above and past Conroy's head at the far end of the room. On the underside of his chin, black stubble poked through his swarthy skin. Conroy said, "I'm not sure what you mean."

"Bearing false witness, lying," the priest said quietly.

"Oh, the email. All right, I bore false witness."

The priest asked, "Why?"

The stupid priest sounded like Dinah when she was two years old. *Why? Why?* "Because Peggy was mad."

"What did you do to make her angry?"

"Broke up with her."

The priest sighed, more heavily this time. "She was angry because you lied to her."

"Oh, *lied*, that's right."

"And you lied to me about her reply."

"Yes."

"And you lied to your wife about being faithful."

When Conroy had gone to confession before, he'd just knelt down, said his piece, and it was over. It wasn't fair that this priest had inside information. "Right," he said.

"And thus you have borne false witness at least three times."

Conroy's kneecaps bore through the skin on his knees. "Right."

"And why did you lie?"

He *hated* this smug-ass priest. "Why don't you tell me?"

The priest's head bowed. "We should pray for the Holy Spirit to open your heart."

"Now?" His knees grated like stones grinding into a rubble of pebbles.

"So that you may know what your sins are and confess them."

"The lying was a sin. I've got that."

"But why did you lie, to her, to your wife, to me?"

"Because I didn't want to get caught."

The priest sighed as if the cross itself pressed the air out of him. "No, if you had gotten caught, it would have wounded your..."

"Beverly would've wounded me all right."

"No," the priest said. "There is a reason, within yourself, why you lied. An emotion, a feeling. It would have wounded your..." The priest waited.

Conroy had lied so he wouldn't get caught. Because he had got caught, he had come to counseling, and counseling was embarrassing, and everyone was going to find out about it and rib him about it. "Pride?" he asked.

"Yes!"

The priest was stupidly excited that Conroy had guessed correctly. God, his knees hurt, ached, stung, and throbbed as the skin ground away.

The priest asked, "Now, what is the root of your pride?"

This couldn't go on. Conroy's broken knees were pulverized. "I have no idea what you're talking about."

The priest sighed and asked, "Have you any other sins to confess?"

"Not right now." He needed to stand up. His knees could not stand the weight of his skeleton and gristle and flesh and blood.

"Then, for your penance—"

Penance, as if he was back in grade school and the penguins were cracking a ruler on his knuckles, or his knees, cracking a ruler over his kneecaps again and again.

"—you must apologize to your wife and to Peggy, for lying to them. You must not see this other woman. You must attend marriage counseling and try, with your whole heart, to mend your marriage that you jeopardized."

"All right."

"And the rosary, the entire rosary, before tomorrow morning."

That would take an hour, although more than once in grade school he'd sorted the beads while thinking about something else. "Yes, Father."

"Make a good Act of Contrition."

Conroy, mindful of his must-be-bleeding knees, recited the Act of Contrition fast and was glad he remembered the whole thing. In the Act of Contrition, he spoke to God rather than girly demi-deities, dreading the loss of Heaven and the pains of Hell, resolved to confess his sins, do his penance and avoid-the-near-occasion-of-sin-Amen. He staggered to his feet and rubbed his raw kneecaps under his pants.

The priest smiled, maybe a little smugly. "Shall we call your wife in?"

"Sure." Conroy's back creaked as he pulled himself down into the chair. He dreaded the pains of confession, that was damn sure. He massaged his patellae.

At least he'd never have to confess about Leila. He'd never lied to her about casual fucking.

Chapter Six

The Daily Hamiltonian:

SERMON SUMMARIES

By Kirin Oberoi

Our Lady of Perpetual Help Roman Catholic Church: Father Samual Sorenson will speak on "Our God-Haunted World." Monsignor Dante Petrocchi-Bianchi will assist. Masses are scheduled for 6:15am, 9:30am, 12:00pm, and 2:30pm.

SUNDAY MORNING, Dante and Father Samual celebrated the Mass together. Dante had attended Mass every day for over a decade, a part of his normal day as a novice, a scholastic, a regent, and a Jesuit priest. The Nicene Creed recited itself in his mouth. Parishioners sparsely attended the weekday Masses, and their few, desiccated voices buzzed in the forced-heat zephyrs that rebounded on the pale wooden floorboards between the stained-glass windows depicting the gory Stations of the Cross and the saints' statues lining the walls like a doll shop.

At the four Sunday Masses, however, Samual and Dante performed to packed houses. At the third, the air rustled as hundreds of lungs wafted it to and fro, each flavoring the air with coffee or tea or strong mint. The meat of their bodies absorbed the currents of the heating system. The metabolizing, tremulating, fidgeting bodies overpowered the grumbling of the church.

Dante hadn't celebrated a Mass for years. That morning, the vestments of the officiant—the white linen alb, the stole with the kissed cross at its center, and the embroidered silk chasuble—slipped over his head and lay on his body. The archaic garments and proscriptions on their wear were dictated as if for protective gear—a yellow moon suit with an air tank and face mask—to dig in contaminated, defiled, unholy ground.

All had been violated: the children physically, the parish spiritually.

But with God, all things were possible, even the redemption of His own Church.

Enrobing for the Mass seemed eerie, a concurrent flashback to the seminary and a déjà vu of future Masses, a glimpse of past lives and future reincarnations within the garments and rituals of priests since the Christ laid hands upon Peter, and Peter upon the next priests, and so on, until hands had been laid upon him, unworthy, wrathful, lustful Dante, who was now on the other side of the planet, two millennia hence.

Dante caught a last glimpse in the mirror to ensure that the alb wasn't tucked into the back of his pants. A proper priest topped by Dante's head filled the mirror.

Father Samual walked beside Dante down the aisle of the church through the congregation, a metaphor for being called out of the community. The entrance song welcomed them, and the priests knelt and kissed the altar. Father Samual extended his hands over the assembled Catholics and said, as had been said for centuries, "May the grace and peace of our Lord Jesus Christ, the love of God, and the fellowship of the Holy Spirit be with you all."

The cathedral rumbled with their response, "And also with you."

Father Samual, his voice old but strong, began the penitential rite. The oiled wood and stained glass reverberated with the volume of the voices and withstood their calls to God and Christ for mercy. Samual stood in front of them all, white-robed and gilt-embroidered. It is said, or at least some enraptured priests had commented to Dante, that Holy Orders stamps the human soul with God's seal, an ontological change. At his own Mass when Dante had taken Holy Orders, he tried to feel God's touch, but he was not sure if that seal would be a feathery molding of his soul or a branding that seared him. In the end, the Mass had seemed like any one of thousands of others, except that he had lain face down before the altar, and his nose was sore. His disappointment in the lack of a Divine touch had been palpable, and during his month-long Ignatian spiritual exercises he decided that his unfilled longing for God was the cellular-level change he'd anticipated. Within months, logic crumbled the tautology that feeling the absence of God was indeed experiencing the presence of God, and he'd descended to a utilitarian realization of Holy Orders, that he must have been indelibly stamped because he evidently was a priest.

Even if the investiture of priesthood did blast through a man's soul, time eroded all things, even souls. With time, the stamp that Holy Orders imprints on a man might smooth away like an over-thumbed Roman coin, though the alternative was that, like a scratch in the earth that catches the wind, a fiery mark might plow deeper, chasm, and wear away humanity.

Perhaps it depended on the man.

Father Samual had written a sweetly stupid homily about the joy of finding the Lord in all things, in dappled things and shining things. "Our Catholic world is a God-haunted world," the old priest said to the assembled, "and we find Him in all things and in our hearts." Samual spread his arms as though spreading a cape and raised his face to the gilt ceiling.

Dante's hand itched to find a staff and smite Father Samual on the back of his white head, where his shepherd's instinct slept, so that Samual's gelatinous gray matter rippled forward in a shock wave and splatted onto the inside of his pink-skinned face.

Perhaps Samual hadn't known that Nicolai was abusing the children.

Perhaps he didn't or couldn't believe the accusations.

Maybe he didn't give a damn.

The collection baskets were passed, and Dante watched the baskets and the pyx of hosts and chalices of communion wine brought forward by the deacons while the choir sang. Bev's somber choice of *Panis Angelicus* clashed with Nicolai's blithe homily but soothed Dante. Longing for peace should fill this unquiet church.

Nicolai had stood here at the perched altar, next to the altar boys, and looked down on the children, sprinkled in the pews with their parents. The Sloans, the doctor and the two girls, sat gravely on the left side of the church, a few rows back. Sloan absently massaged the scalp of the younger girl, Dinah, and she leaned on him. Her vermillion velvet dress was a cloud catching the setting sun against the landscape of Sloan's blue shirt and beige pants.

At the altar, Dante stood over the round communion crackers, which were wider than his splayed hand. As the choir sang the lilting lament, "Panis angelicus, fit panis hominum," *Heavenly bread, that becomes the bread of all mankind*, he breathed and whispered over the bread, "Blessed are you, Lord God of all creation. Through Your goodness we have this bread to offer, which earth has given and human hands have made. It will become for us the bread of life."

IN THE CHOIR LOFT, thirty feet of wafting air above the congregation, the choir sang the low, keening hymn. "Manducat Dominum, Pauper, pauper, servus et humilis." *This body of God will nourish, even the poorest, the most humble of servants.* Bev sat at the organ platform and directed with flourishes of her upstage hand.

LYDIA DIDN'T KNOW why Bev had picked such bummer songs.

Laura understood. Her breath hurt as if a blood clot blocked her windpipe. Bev had called Laura every day, several times a day, for months.

Mary sang the hymns. They were all the same to her.

Bev sweated in the choir loft, drumming the organ. The heat rose in the church from the furnaces and bodies below. Fans blurred the voices of the choir.

Up there, especially in the winter when the furnace heat rose past the congregation, it seemed a fallacy that Hell was below the ground and Heaven was above. Heaven should be a cool, quiet place, a basement or an old fortress enclosed by thick, earthen walls that retained the cool of the night. Hell was a precarious place where heat climbed and coagulated.

She pedaled and percussed the antique organ. Her wrists ached at the end of the four Sunday Masses from pounding music out of the huge, recalcitrant beast.

Between hymns, she watched Father Sam and Father Dante perform the Mass, and she looked down on her husband and girls from above. Sometimes, an inkling stole into her mind: that she was dead and watching them, not from God's choir but from hot and stifling Hell. Hell must have its own choir, a respite for lost souls who, even though they were denied the presence of God, could sing their longing. Lucifer was, after all, an archangel before he fell.

She'd taken communion at the six o'clock Mass with the rest of the choir. Her dry throat had accepted the wafer and she'd swallowed it past her misgivings. Since the host hadn't choked her, her penance must be complete and all must be right with the world and with Heaven.

CONROY WATCHED the deacons holding the long-poled collection baskets like fishnets skimming donations from the congregation, and he readied his bills. This offering was in addition to the tithe account with the church's treasury and the special donation for the new bell tower motor and the tuition he paid for two children's good, Catholic education.

Dinah leaned on him, and he slipped strands of her cobweb hair through his fingers. He'd meant to braid it this morning but had only had time to plait Christine's hair into a tight, neat coif.

Father Samual said the majority of the Mass. That other priest, Dante Petrocchi-Bianchi, mumbled over the host the super-secret words that the congregation isn't supposed to hear. Holding back parts of the Mass was juvenile, as if the patronizing Catholic Church couldn't trust the laity with the magic spells lest they escape and form their own church.

The Protestants had done just that, though.

Filthy lucre, the love of which was the root of all evil, rustled as the baskets neared. He turned to gauge their approach. The middle-aged deacon raking in the cash closed on Conroy's row.

Conroy gazed farther into the congregation, a reaction born of the flash of a familiar image striking his retina while he scanned, and that tremor in his optic nerve reached neurons that caused him to search the faces of men and women and children, the brown and gray clothes smearing into each other broken by the occasional blaze of a bright tie.

Leila sat three rows back on the other side.

Over her breasts and body, she wore the black blouse he'd fondled in her closet.

Conroy jerked back, and his damp body spasmed and chilled.

LEILA SAT PRIMLY beside an older woman, ankles and wrists crossed, and watched the priest-scientist hunch over the wafers and invoke the supernatural. Monsignor Dante Petrocchi-Bianchi looked like his web page photo, though he was a few years older. She could have clipped out his image and pasted him into a temple sacrificing a bull to Apollo or slashing apart a virgin for Quetzalcoatl.

The pulse in Leila's left wrist quickened. Last night's whiskey must have been contaminated, because fungus tendriled her tongue even though a friend, a resident, had hooked her up this morning with a pouch of Ringer's and a snort of oxygen to kill the hangover. Her chest and back were grungy with excreted alcoholic metabolites under her blouse.

Earlier, she'd spotted Conroy, but she had no intention of talking to him. Choosing the same Mass as he had was a bit of bad luck, though both flavors of luck were fallacies. There were four Masses today, so a twenty-five percent chance existed that she would choose the same one as he had. If one eliminated the early Mass at six-fifteen, which neither of them was likely to choose, the chance of juxtaposition increased to one in three.

Petrocchi-Bianchi held the crackers as if he believed that voodoo mumbo-jumbo.

But his publications bespoke a mind that was rational and methodical. It was impossible that the seal of Holy Orders and the mind that wrote those beautiful papers could exist in the same chunk of meat.

Leila's pulse traveled up her arm and knocked at her temple. Rotten aroma filled her mouth, and she gulped incense-scented air.

The problem was the supernatural. The priest and these people around her, like the elderly couple to her left who stole disapproving glances at her and nodded knowingly to each other, agreed on the mass delusion that the priest had the power to draw these people together and that eating a cracker was indulging in divine cannibalism. No scientist should countenance that. No man who had been castrated by the Church could write, as Dante Petrocchi-Bianchi had, that *possession, seemingly caused by supernatural diabolical forces, is a neurochemical phenomenon shaped by cultural expectations*, which means *the Church causes demons*, as if his papers had transubstantiated William Blake's poetry into science.

Leila recrossed her ankles and watched Monsignor Dr. Dante Petrocchi-Bianchi pray inaudibly over the pyx, raise his jewel-encrusted chalice above the green-dressed altar, and mutter incantations. A nervous itch worried at her mind, not that God would smite her with lightning, but that her damaged wiring and unstable elements might reach critical mass, right here, and detonate. Feeling the words of the Lord's Prayer in her mouth made her skin prickle with sweat.

DANTE STOOD at the top of the aisle holding a pyx of communion Hosts, intoning over and over again, "The body of Christ," as each parishioner came forward to receive the sacrament.

The next parishioner was an older woman, sixties perhaps, dressed in an autumnal, flowing dress. The garish rusts, cinnamons, and olives would have glowed to the Roman pickpockets, announcing that she was an American apple ripe for picking.

Dante held the wafer at eye level and said, "The body of Christ."

She held out her cupped palms and said, "Amen."

The apple woman turned away, chewing, and Sloan stood before Dante, his hands cupped. Bubbles of perspiration gathered around his white hair above his cold blue eyes. His eyes were wide, as if he expected Dante to deny him the sacrament. Sloan had fulfilled his end of the bargain. Perhaps he had been slack in the penance but at least he had confessed.

Yet, damp premonition gathered close to Dante's belly.

Dante presented the wafer with his fingertips. "The body of Christ."

Sloan said, "Amen," and Dante placed the wafer in his palm without touching him.

Sloan walked back to his seat, chewing.

Sloan passed a very young woman sitting in a pew, eyes downcast. She was pretty in a Mediterranean way, Greek perhaps, and she wore solemn, black. She'd readily responded during the Mass yet she hadn't joined the communion line.

She seemed lost. Dante understood *lost*.

THE COMMUNION LINE shuffled toward the old priest and the young one. Thirty vertical feet of air hovered above them, and the choir loft spilled music over wooden railings. The congregation did not ruminate upon the geometric permutations involving Dr. Sloan and Bev Sloan and Leila Faris and Father Dante as they waited to partake of wheat transubstantiated into the body of Christ, which their cells would molecularly rend and burn. Most of those calories would be spent. A few of the atoms from the Eucharist—carbon, hydrogen, oxygen, nitrogen or sulfur—integrated with their bodies.

A carbon atom from the wafer failed to repair the DNA in one of Nessa Akins's lung cells, and it became the cancer that killed her ten years later.

Carlos Valdez's gut proteolysed the wheat gliadin protein, and his neurons used the energy from those amino acids and from the five shots he'd had the previous evening to walk out of the church and to his car. It had been five years since, just after his eighteenth birthday, he'd threatened to beat the living shit out of Father Nicolai if he ever touched him or his sister again. Carlos still came to Mass at least once a month to pacify his father, a Hispanic Catholic of the old stripe, and he endured the ordeal stoically. At least this time, he hadn't had to watch that monster staring at him the whole time.

Josephine Thorgood's body used several kilocalories from the host to build the body of her son growing in her uterus, though you'd never know that a few molecules of the body of Christ had been incorporated into that mischievous, incorrigible child who was baptized Patrick Allen Thorgood. Father Dante was the only priest that Josephine would allow to touch her baby, even for those few moments, in his baptismal gown and under her watchful eye.

CONROY SHIED as he passed Leila sitting demurely in the pew. What the hell was she thinking, showing up at church, where Beverly and that priest would see her and *know?*

But they couldn't *know.* They couldn't read his mind or hers. If he jumped up after Mass and hustled the girls out, Leila wouldn't have a chance to confront him.

AFTER COMMUNION, after another hymn and a prayer, Leila grasped the cool wooden rail of the pew in front of her and readied herself to dash for the door. Bumping into Conroy and his kids on the way out would necessitate an explanation, and she didn't feel like it.

The white-haired priest said, "The Mass is ended. Go in peace," and the priests and deacons filed out as the quiet, simple music rose. Leila whirled around the end of the pew and fell in with the eager crowd that battled to beat the parking lot traffic jam.

The priests stood just outside the door in the chill sunshine. The old priest creepily held Leila's hand too long, nodded over her, and finally reached for the next person in line. Her damp palm left a crumpled place on her coat.

Monsignor Dr. Dante Petrocchi-Bianchi, S.J., M.D., Ph.D., black-haired and black-eyed like a pirate or a Mafia-made man, reached for her and said, "You did not take the communion."

Oh, God, he'd seen her, sitting alone in the pew, refusing communion. Shades of high school. "Leila Faris," she said. "Nice to meet you." He held her hand, and the bridge of their two arms drooped between them. She tugged but he wouldn't let her hand drop.

"You are Catholic?" He seemed concerned, too nice, fake.

The greeting line didn't seem the place for a theological argument about the untestable hypothesis of an omnipotent Deity. "Orthodox. Coptic."

"Egyptian rite?" he asked. His other hand settled over their linked hands, restraining her, trapping her. His fingers around her hand were too cool, as if he were dead or she were febrile. Or her hands might be boiling off last night's booze.

Her throat closed like she had inhaled a feather.

The priest said, "How interesting. Have you been to Egypt?"

"My dad moved here before I was born." Leila couldn't get away because the priest's cool hands and lab-strengthened fingers still wrapped her right hand like she was imprisoned in stone. For some asinine reason, she added,

"He passed away a couple years ago."

Beside her, the old priest idled the time by rocking back and forth, toes to heels.

Petrocchi-Bianchi said, "We should speak more. You could stop by the church?"

"This week is rough. Thank you, Father Petrocchi-Bianchi."

"Please-ah, Father Dante." They said goodbyes and his grip on her hand finally loosened.

She yanked her hand free and walked away without running. She clambered into her car and gripped the frozen steering wheel. Nausea coiled in her esophagus and she grabbed the door handle, but she'd survived without screaming or fleeing. The cold steering wheel patted her forehead like a mother's hand should.

She'd seen the enigmatic priest, all right, but she didn't count on him seeing her and grilling her about her father and her family in front of everyone while the hangover from her father's annual anniversary wake still gored her temples and jolted her stomach.

THE CHOIR DESCENDED the narrow stairs behind the jalousies and the altar. Laura glanced through the wooden lattice while the congregation zipped themselves into a line to leave the loft. She whispered to Lydia behind her, "Does Theresa Witulski look pregnant again?"

Lydia shook her head. "I hope not. You heard that she told Jolinda that they wanted at least two boys, so they were going to keep having kids until they got a second son."

"But they have *thirteen girls*," Laura said.

"God is punishing them for pig-headedness. Hasn't anybody told them that it's 'Thy will be done,' not 'my will?'"

Mary said from behind Lydia, "Frank should leave her alone. She's suffered enough."

Behind Mary, Bev smiled at Laura, who smiled back. Bev wasn't a gossip-hound like the rest of them. Laura appreciated that.

DANTE SHOOK HANDS with people in the bright, cold sunlight and smiled, glad that he had only one more Mass for the day.

The Coptic Orthodox woman, Leila Faris, something was odd there. Dante hadn't introduced himself, but she'd known his name. Of course, his name had been listed as a celebrant in the Order of the Mass in the program. That must be it.

Behind a few more people, Sloan pushed his girls out of the church. He caught Dante's eye, and Dante extended his hand.

Sloan looked around then straightened and his shoulders dropped. He smiled.

JESUS H. FUCKING CHRIST. Conroy wheeled the girls aside as if shielding them from a blast.

Leila was talking to that priest. Conroy never should have mentioned the priest in the lab. He had stepped into the no-man's-land that separated his family and casual fucking.

Leila shook off the priest's hands, trotted to her car, and hopped on one foot as she tumbled behind the wheel.

Leila probably hadn't said anything substantive to the priest. Conroy was off the enormous, barbed meathook that Beverly's putative divorce attorney would've rammed up his ass if the Leila situation ever came to light. He inhaled the metallic January air and said, "Hello, Father Dante."

"Hello, Dr. Sloan," said the priest. "Nice to see you. Hope you enjoyed the Mass. See you tomorrow."

"Monday?" Conroy asked. "Why?"

Father Dante said, "As usual, for our session."

"Yes," he said. If they thought he was going to more counseling after that last debacle, they were in a state of neural insufficiency, goddamn it. Conroy sauntered to his Porsche parked in the gravel overflow parking lot, trailing flitting daughters.

BEV ARRIVED HOME and stripped off her gloves, tossing them and her purse on top of the dryer. "Conroy?" she called.

"In here!" he yelled from the kitchen. Bev wandered over to the kitchen, where he was eating a sandwich.

Conroy said, "Something weird happened today. That priest said he'd see me tomorrow."

Conroy couldn't have forgotten. She whispered, "Counseling."

"No, I stopped doing that other," he glanced toward the doorway to the living room where the girls were watching cartoons, "*thing.*"

It looked like he was going to say *woman,* doing that other *woman.*

"I did everything that priest asked." He ate the last corner crust of his sandwich. "I broke it off. I confessed. I was heartily sorry that I had offended God."

Such rote verbiage sounded like he had faked it and deceived Father Dante and her. Oh, Virgin Mary, this was too hard. "We need more than one week of counseling."

He asked, "Aren't you happy?" and ate the end of a pickle.

The conversation would proceed: *If you're not happy, then we should get a divorce.* Instead she said, "If you were happy, you wouldn't have done that other *thing.*"

From the living room, television cartoons jingled and beeped. The set was on too loud, but if the girls ruined their hearing they wouldn't be able to hear their parents' fighting.

Conroy's mottled face was stiff. His thin lips barely moved. "It was a one-time thing."

"You said in counseling that the affair went on for six months."

He clarified, "It was only one affair."

That might be another lie, that there was *only one affair*. There might be more affairs. God, she hadn't thought of that. *More affairs*. Stupid anger welled up. "Was it only one?"

He dropped his dishes in the sink. Water splashed. "Yes. I broke it off."

Bev dug her fingernails into the wood of the kitchen table. Outside, cold wind blew a swing on the girls' swingset, like a ghost rode it. "How do I know?"

"I sent you the email. You saw it. We're quitting the counseling."

"No. That was the deal, Conroy. We go to counseling. Not for just a week. Not just until you give up your—" *whore, lay, bitch, cunt,* "—affair. Until I say we stop."

"Priests are always meddling. The whole Vatican is a sick, twisted, corporation that micromanages people's lives, everyone, the priests, the laity, everyone. I stopped the affair. You can't leave me now. How would that look?"

"Like you had an affair and I left you."

"It would look like I'd stopped and you *still* left me."

The solid edge of the kitchen table threatened to crumble under her fingers, leaving her holding sawdust. "You have a morals clause in your contract. The university would fire you." The cold tile counter pressed her hip and she gathered her breath inside to threaten him. His eyes were narrow, blue slits. She said, "The scandal would derail your career for years. And the chair is open now. It might not be open again for decades."

Bev started to push a strand of hair off her face.

Conroy gestured his disdain for her opinion.

Their hands rose at the same time, fast, and slapped in the air.

Conroy grabbed her. His big hand lassoed her wrist.

Her breath snagged.

The room spun around the point where his hand held her wrist.

Spinning howled around her head and her other arm wrapped around her head like a helmet. "No!"

Her wrist ripped from Conroy's grasp and she caught herself on the counter.

"I'm sorry," he said. "Are you all right? Tell me you're all right."

Air scratched at her closed throat and parted the clamped muscles. "Fine," she said.

"I thought you had been," he looked away, "drinking."

"How could you think that?" Bastard. Idiot.

"Last week, you drank with that priest."

"It's not like that." She hadn't broken her rules. There was no problem.

"I don't like that priest coming over here when I'm not home, and you shouldn't drink, especially in front of the girls."

"I haven't."

"I can't go to counseling every night. I have that grant to finish, and experiments."

Negotiate, she thought, *don't escalate.* "We could reduce the amount of counseling."

Conroy leaned on the edge of the kitchen table. "Once, every other week."

"You've got to be kidding." She rubbed her raw wrist.

"Once a week."

"Wednesdays and Saturdays," she offered.

Conroy stared at the ceiling Bev had sponged yellow to look like the plaster wall of a Tuscan farmhouse. "Just Saturdays. I don't know if I'll be home for supper at all next week."

"Fine."

Bev went upstairs to lie down. She took off her wedding rings and speared them on the ring-keeper next to her bed. They clittered down the post to the silver base.

Tomorrow was Monday, and after she went to the indoor driving range and smacked golf balls into the air like a repeating bazooka, she could keep their appointment with Father Dante. From her bed, she prayed to the Virgin to open Conroy's heart and for strength and peace and calm. Her crucifix chained around her neck itched, and she held the graven image between her palms and prayed harder. The head of the tiny Jesus pressed into her palm.

LEILA, DOUBLE-GLOVED and lab-coated, pipetted fuchsia fluid over the infected cells. The biological hood whooshed, and the air chilled her arms. Her white lab coat sleeves were wound tight around her wrists and sealed to her gloves with lime green masking tape.

The lab door from the hallway banged open. Leila pipetted steadily. If she blasted the sick cells clinging to the dish, it wouldn't matter if anyone discovered the experiment.

The tissue culture door slammed open and banged the refrigerator behind it. Conroy held the door open with one splayed hand. "Why the hell were you at my church?"

Media dripped onto the last gauzy monolayer of cells, and Leila capped the dish. She slid the long pipette into the tall bucket of bleach-spiked water. "Is anyone else here?"

"No one's here."

"You checked?"

Conroy stomped around the dark lab, slamming doors. Leila put her samples in the body-temperature, breath-moist incubator. She stripped off her gloves, inside out and inside each other, tossed her lab coat in the biohaz laundry bin, and washed her hands with antiseptic soap.

Conroy slammed open the tissue culture door again and rattled the refrigerator as she rinsed foam from her hands. "What the hell were you doing at my goddamned church?"

"I wanted to the see that scientist-priest." She dried her hands with a paper towel and dropped it in the biohazard box. The towel landed on discarded clear six-well trays, sallow latex gloves, and a haystack of inch-long, yellow plastic pipetter tips.

"That goddamned priest saw you. *My family saw you.*" He slapped the sheet metal hood.

Leila sat on one of the lab chairs and leaned back, glaring. "Shut up."

Conroy spun around and stared back. "What did you say to me?"

She held her eyes open wide and didn't allow her body to fidget. "I said, 'shut up.' You're being an ass. You didn't break down and confess everything to your wife, did you?"

"No." He slumped in the other chair. His head flopped in his hands. His elbows rested on his knees, curved around his vestigial stomach paunch.

"What did that damned priest ask you?" Conroy's vitriol was usually reserved for the anonymous peers who reviewed papers, but he seemed to be in quite a snit lately.

"He wanted to know why I didn't take communion."

He looked up and Leila was startled anew by his cobalt blue eyes. No, lighter than cobalt. His irises were the electric blaze of methylene blue cell stain. He asked, "What did you say?"

"Nothing. He wants me to talk to him. I'm not going to."

Conroy blinked slowly, unattractively. "Fine," he said. "Fine." He stood. "I've got to work on that grant." He left the tissue culture room with three strides of his too-long legs.

Leila exhaled and bent over in her chair. She was dizzy from holding her breath, hoping that he wouldn't demand to know what experiment required her presence in the lab on a Sunday night. He'd almost seen what was written on the tops of her dishes.

He would have freaked and thrown her ass out of the program.

She wiped out the hood with two percent bleach solution, which will kill anything from HIV to rabies virus to poliovirus to mad cow prions. You can't be too careful when you're working with pathogens.

Chapter Seven

Early Monday morning, Conroy was in his office pattering on his computer. Text filled the sprawling screen, yet the letters still fuzzed together. He would have to get reading glasses or a wall-sized monitor.

Leila slammed open his office door. The door bashed his bookshelves. "What in the hell is this?" Scarlet vegetative mush dripped from her fingers. She must have torn the head off one of the roses.

"We had an argument," he said.

Her jaw didn't move and words squirmed in her clenched teeth. "A florist's charge on your credit card and yet your wife didn't get flowers? Idiot. Don't do anything like that again."

She slammed the door and the window behind him rattled. The apoptosis poster on the back of his door was horizontally creased by the bookshelves.

MONDAY EVENING, Dante opened his library door and Bev Sloan walked in alone. Her clothes were monochrome, black skirt and gray sweater. Her smooth hair reflected auburn and dark gold as if her hair had wicked the color out of her clothes. "Where's Mr. Sloan?" he asked.

"He couldn't make it." She placed her handbag on the floor and sat in her chair. "He can't make it at all this week, or next."

Couples' counseling didn't work with only one participant, especially with the participant who had fewer problems. "Is there another time that is more convenient for him?"

"No." She folded her hands and stared at them.

"All right." He needed to type his notes for the last three counseling sessions, but Dante took his chair, crossed his ankles, and arranged his cassock over his legs. He would be up late, working, and then lying on his narrow bed in the rectory. Lines of thought were wearing creases in his mind: the children with the now ex-priest Nicolai in the library, Nicolai with his hand up one little girl's skirt while another little girl sat on a chair, reading a book, or Nicolai and Dante in a snow-bright monastic cell, with Dante holding a baseball bat or wearing heavy boots.

Obsession would kill him. Separating that part of himself was the only way to save himself from creeping rage. He settled back in the deep chair. "What troubles you?"

She didn't look at him. "Everything."

"Take your time." Dante could wait. Entire counseling strategies were based on waiting, either allowing the patient to come to you, or as a dominance game. In this case, Bev Sloan needed a minute to compose herself, and this wasn't a ploy for dominance.

She stared at the books on the walls of the library, but Dante didn't flinch. In the week since he'd arrived, Dante had cleaned the entire library, book by book, ruffling pages, until gray grit ground into the ridges of his fingers. Afterward, he'd blessed the room, sprinkling holy water in the corners, wielding a gleaming crucifix, and grinding out Latin in a voice hoarse from dust. He'd added a coda from the Rite of Exorcism:

Begone, now!

It is He who casts you out, from whose sight nothing is hidden.

It is He who repels you, to whose might all things are subject.

It is He who expels you, He who has prepared everlasting hellfire for you and your angels, from whose mouth shall come a sharp sword, who is coming to judge both the living and the dead and the world by fire.

Dante hadn't sensed an evil presence lurking in the corners, no black wraith flitting among the shadows on the walls and flowing into the darkness behind the bookcases. Yet, the specters of fear and hate wafting in the children's eyes, watering their eyes when they entered the library and stared at certain objects—the VCR and TV, a now-expunged stack of magazines, a certain slim candlestick—were like possession. Still, even speaking the words of the rite invigorated him. In his years as an exorcist, Dante had stared too long into Nietzsche's abyss, and the abyss had stared into him until he understood it better than the Light, and so fought it on an even footing.

Bev Sloan spoke. "Conroy can't come to counseling because he's busy in the lab."

Ah, the dominance game. Sloan had sent Bev as his proxy. Clever, and a cowardly tactic that dovetailed with his use of email to end an affair. "This week must have been very upsetting for you."

Tears filmed her eyes. "I'm fine." She stared past him at the bookcase beside his desk, beside the well-taped, Roma-addressed boxes. "My husband stopped the affair. Everything is back to normal. I'm fine." Her hands, folded on her lap, hardened into a statue of repose.

In this case, silence covered the truth. He prodded, "Your husband had sex with another woman."

Her hands clawed each other and settled into a cramped knot. "But it's over now."

"He wronged *you*. He broke *your* vows." A little thrill of the hunt quivered.

Tears flipped over her lower eyelids. "I *prayed* for a husband like Conroy, successful, a good father, a Catholic. I prayed and I got him and I'm *fine*."

Dante stayed still, almost non-existent. "What did you give up, for Conroy?"

"I don't want to talk about this. My husband had an affair. That's all." Her shoulders slouched, relaxed. She was moving out of the moment.

"Did you give up your family?"

"My parents passed away years ago." Her shoulders remained down, her face softened, and she blinked. Wrong question.

"Tell me about your marriage."

Bev fumbled with her hands. "Marriage is a sacrament. It's being loving and *faithful*, having children and being a family."

Odd emphasis. Conroy's affair may have been in revenge. "Did you have an affair?"

"Of course not." Still calmly, and thus he was wrong.

She said she prayed for a *Catholic* husband. This suggested a non-Catholic man existed. "Was the other man not a Catholic?"

She jumped to her feet and clutched her purse.

Dante was on his feet and between her and the door. "Was he not Catholic?"

She stood before him and stared at the carpet. Gold and brown hair swirled from the crown of her head and fell over the tops of her ears. "It was a long time ago."

Ah, that was it. There was a *he* and he wasn't Catholic.

"Did you love him?"

"It was before Conroy. I *married* Conroy."

The moment was gone. She had returned to Conroy. In a cognitive-behavioral sense, it was emotionally mature in that she did not dwell on the past and she sought to fix the marriage.

In the Freudian-analysis sense, however, she was repressing emotions and memories.

Dante held his hand out to Bev and gestured toward her chair. "Shall we sit?"

She looked up at him, defiant. "We don't have anything to talk about."

"Conroy's affair."

"I've forgiven him."

Dante doubted this. Children were better at facing their anger because they hadn't been brainwashed to be *nice*. He held her elbow and steered her to the chairs. "I'm worried about you."

She didn't answer. Her head bowed as if she were pulling against a heavy weight. They reached her chair and she sat. Her hair fell forward and curtained her face. She snatched a tissue from the box by her chair and pulled it inside the veil of her hair.

He bent his knees so that he was at the level of her face, though her eyes were hidden. He wanted to brush her dark gold hair away from her face. "I want you to keep coming to counseling, even if Mr. Sloan doesn't."

She sniffed. "What good would that do?"

Her left hand clutched the chair arm. He laid his hand over her tiny, pale hand, just as he had his first day in America when she'd been distraught. "We could discuss coping strategies. I'll expect you Wednesday. Are you eating enough?"

"I'm fine."

"Eat something when you get home."

She still didn't look up. She probably wouldn't eat.

"Do you still have my card with the phone numbers?"

She nodded, and her hair rippled like ruffled feathers.

"Call if you need to talk, anytime. I don't sleep much."

"Okay."

She slipped her hand out from under his, and the chair arm was warm where their hands had crossed. He said, "I'll see you Wednesday."

She left.

Everyone at this parish was hunted, stricken, damaged. Though Nicolai had been the predator, Samual had not protected the children, or their parents, or the women. Dante could have done a better job than this.

Dante brushed his temple, where a headache was beginning to worm in. What a thought, that Dante should have been a parish priest rather than a Vaticanista, and he smiled at the incongruity. The smile tightened the muscles in his temple, and the headache probed farther.

MARY, LAURA, LYDIA and the rest of the choir watched Father Dante watch Bev Sloan as he sat beside her on the cramped piano bench while she paged through the hymnal. The stained-glass windows above were dark. The winter sun had atrophied and fallen off the horizon.

Lydia asked, "Do you think he's going to nail our Bev?"

Laura whispered, "Stop it!" and the ferocity of it slapped Mary and Lydia, who leaned back. "Stop it!" Laura whispered. "Father Dante is a good man. He's a good *priest*. He wouldn't do anything like that." She turned away from both of them, disgusted. "And Bev is the sweetest woman. She'd *never* do anything like that, *never*."

Lydia raised her eyebrows at Mary, who raised her blonde, feathered brows in return.

Mary said, "Of course she wouldn't."

"Well, then" Lydia said, "Have you heard the one about Jesus walking through Heaven?"

"No," Mary said. Laura still wouldn't look at them.

Lydia said, "Jesus is walking through Heaven, and he sees a gambler running a dice game and prostitutes lounging around. Farther down the street, he sees a drunk lawyer screaming wrathfully at tobacco farmers. Finally, he can't take it, so he goes over to St. Peter and asks him why he's letting all these sinners and miscreants into Heaven."

Mary reached over and patted Laura on the shoulder, and Laura touched her hand without looking back. It hadn't been an accusation. There was something else. All right, something else.

Lydia rubbed Laura's other shoulder. "And St. Peter says to Jesus, 'I keep turning them away, but Your Mother lets them in the back door.'"

Laura chuckled a sad, low huh-huh-huh like a car engine straining to turn over after an icy night, and they sat, Lydia and Mary patting Laura, until Bev announced the next hymn.

WEDNESDAY MORNING, Conroy sat at his desk—the gels in his grant filled the wide computer screen—and watched Leila walk by his doorway through the white, sterile lab outside like a blue-clothed, black-haired bruise walking through the glaring day.

He watched the word-processing screen, and the black bands on the white gels blinked, shivered, and transformed into giant, red Xs. "Leila!"

Danna, his other female grad student, pretty in a scrawny and frowsy way, peered into his office. "She's taking off her coat."

Conroy's fist shook to dispel the athletic anger. He wanted to punch the huge screen and under his fist feel it break or bend or do whatever plasma screens did when someone pummeled them. "Grant, gels, screwed up." He caught his breath. "Turned into big, red Xs again." He stopped. "Danna, you wouldn't know what's wrong with it, would you?"

Danna turned sideways and yelled, "Lie-la! Dr. S. wants you!"

Lazy-ass grad students.

Leila walked in, holding a mug of coffee and scratching her sleek head. "What happened?"

"This, this grant." He held his hands toward the screen as if to prevent it from lunging at him. "It keeps turning this gel into a god-damned red X."

Leila flapped a hand at him to move him over so she could see the screen. She said, "You're overloading the memory again. There, I've spliced it into three documents. Work on 'braingrant3' and grab me the day before you mail it to format the page numbers."

"Okay." His beautiful gels were back.

"You've got to teach me how to run a gel that clean." Leila pointed one slim finger to the glowing screen.

"Western blot, monoclonal. Lots of blotter."

"Yeah. Right."

"And a fetal calf serum block." Damn, if she suspected the gel was faked, he couldn't show it to her anymore, even if the sonofabitch computer mutated his gels into red Xs again.

She probably didn't suspect him of fabricating the gel. Everyone knew he was hopeless with computers, and graphics software was especially obtuse, and there was no way that he could drag-draw ellipses, fill them, warp, blur, pixilate, and paste them onto a gray rectangle. Maybe he should add some smudges for non-specific binding, maybe a fingerprint.

"Leila," he whispered and cleared his throat. "Are you free tonight?"

The email received at noon, Wednesday:

Dearest Beverly,

I'm going to have to work through dinner again. If I get the grant, it'll mean that I have three R01s, which will better my position with the Medical College Dean search committee.

Yours, Conroy

The email sent at one o'clock, Wednesday:

Father Dante,

Since my husband is working late again tonight, why don't we have dinner about seven?

Bev

The reply:

Si. Grazie.

WEDNESDAY EVENING, Bev laid the good silverware and the contemporary china on the table. She rinsed wine glasses in case Father Dante brought wine again.

Her rules were strict. No buying alcohol. No keeping alcohol in the house. No drinking alone. No hard liquor. For social alcohol, none before six o'clock at night. No more than three drinks a week, and no more than two in an evening. Her girls would not have a drunk for a mother. They would not be embarrassed by their drunk mother showing up at school, stinking of whiskey. They would not have to hide from their drunk mother.

Because their mother was a better example, they would not endure delirium tremens before their own weddings.

The girls were upstairs, being quiet. The occasional cascade of girly giggles reassured her that they were not *too* quiet, like the time they had given their dolls crew cuts or tweezed out each other's eyebrows—*all* of their eyebrows.

The doorbell chimed its five-note cascade.

Bev answered the door a little out of breath. Father Dante was so Italian in the trim black silk shirt fitted with the Roman collar. "Supper is almost ready," she said. "Chicken and risotto."

Father Dante drew in his breath and smiled. "Risotto." He offered her a green bottle.

The girls vaulted down the stairs and stopped short of the priest. "Hello," said Christine, and Dinah said, "Hello, Father Dante."

They prayed without prompting this time. They'd practiced saying grace every night that Conroy missed supper, which was every night.

Not saying grace when a priest was in the house, good Lord, why didn't she just curse God, commit adultery, and kill someone, too?

"JESUS FUCKING CHRIST," Leila said, "what is wrong with you, Conroy?" They'd gone back to her place and now, standing in her bedroom, he wanted to *talk*. "I was drunk. Let it go."

Meth frowned at Conroy and began circling in preparation for a nap. His toenails clicked on the wood floor as his unbalanced circling wandered away from his blankets heaped by the side of Leila's crimson-draped bed.

"If you want to talk," Conroy said.

"Strip and get on the bed." She unlaced her boots, and the metatarsals and phalanges in her feet decompressed.

Meth, having meandered too far from his bed, ambled back to the blankets and initiated the circling routine again. Poor dog. He was getting so old.

"Do you only talk about important things when you're drunk?" Conroy unbuttoned his blue shirt and pulled it off.

"Nope. I only *decide* important things when I'm drunk." She yanked at her boot. The damned thing wouldn't come off, and she pulled so that her foot was almost eye-level. She was looking at her own stiletto heel. Leather frays hung off the saddle-stitched seam.

"Like what?" he asked.

If he didn't shut up, she was going to throw him out. In two hours, the Irish pub was going to be full of her rowdy, drunken friends who expected her to show up and would call her phones mercilessly if she didn't. "When I seduced you at the conference in San Diego last summer. When I committed to your lab. When I chose grad school instead of medical school."

Meth groaned as he lowered his tired dog body onto the blankets.

"Those decisions deserved careful consideration. They affect your whole life."

She wrenched off her other boot. "Shut up." She pulled off her socks, top and jeans but left on her push-up bra and panties. Lingerie is power.

Conroy had slipped under the covers, demurely. He looked like a spirochete, a skinny gray and white bloodworm, cozy in a crimson nest. She flipped away the comforter.

"Hey!"

She crawled on top of him and pushed him down into the bed, kissing him hard. The red gauze, twisted up in the wrought iron bed frame, fell around them, enclosing the bed in a claustrophobic bower, tinting the lamplight creeping in the window from the parking lot outside and pinkening Conroy's skin.

"It's cold," he said under her lips and groped for the comforter. His legs and arms dragged the sheets, trying to reach it.

She grabbed his left arm, wrenched it above his head and clipped the handcuffs hanging from her headboard around his wrist.

"Hey, what the hell?"

She handcuffed his other hand.

He grabbed the chains and dragged his skinny body across the red sheets. "Don't you want to talk?"

Maybe she should threaten him with the handgun she kept in her nightstand to get his attention, but she shoved that idea aside. You didn't aim a gun at anything you aren't planning to *destroy*. Leila had never pointed it at another human being. It was only for self-defense.

Leila sat, butt on heels, hands on hips. "What is wrong with you?"

His blue eyes were sappy as a sugar maple, weeping syrup. "I'm concerned about you."

"I don't know what the fuck you're talking about."

Conroy's lined face was earnest. "Your father," he said. "You miss him."

"It was an anniversary."

"You must have loved him."

"That's it." She stood up, pushed aside the red film of the bed's curtains, and tossed the keys from the nightstand on his naked, small belly above his garter snake dick. "Unlock yourself and get out."

"But you should talk about it. And I can't reach the keys."

Sonofabitch. "We don't talk. I am *not* your mistress. I'm *fucking* you."

"But we could talk." He emphasized his words with his open palms still locked to her bed above his head, as if he were handing her his idea.

"No, we couldn't. This is just casual fucking, Conroy. This is not a friendship. In the lab, you're my boss. Here, we fuck. And that's all." A little luck and he'd storm out, and she could stop worrying about how to break it off with him.

Conroy's lips compressed into an angry crease. "I just wanted to help."

"I don't need help." Leila leaned over him so that her face was inches above his. He could only cram his head into the pillow to back up. She widened her eyes. Anger is best dealt with wide-eyed. Narrowed eyes led to hysteria, a noun with roots in the word *uterus*, like hysterectomy, coined when men thought a woman's uterus could wander up her body and cause insanity, which stemmed from a fear of cuckoldry. Leila's uterus wandered wherever the hell she wanted it to. "Don't talk to me unless it's about my Ph.D. research."

Conroy blinked. "Fine."

"Do you want to stop doing this," her finger stirred the bedsheets, "and go back to being just labmates?"

"No, no." Conroy sighed. "You just seemed so sad last weekend."

"I shouldn't have gotten emotional on you." She was embarrassed and ashamed about it. Intimate knowledge was both a burden and power, and Leila feared Conroy having either. She unlocked his handcuffs. "Come on, Conroy. We both have other things we should be doing."

After she dressed and left Conroy sitting in her apartment, Leila sat behind the wheel of her car for ten minutes. Her gloved hands clamped the cold steering wheel, and she held it hard to control the terrified vibrations scrambling up her arms. Damn it, Conroy was getting too close. Eventually, she would destroy him, just like she destroyed all the other men in her life.

Her father was the first man in her life who'd died badly. Others, if they survived her, were ruined. Her only route to save them was to fuck them a few times and then throw them away. A few screeching notes played on their heartstrings were better than their damnation.

IN THE SLOANS' sparkling glass dining room, where the chandelier twinkled on the glass table and its reflection re-reflected on the window glass like a new galaxy just outside the window, Dante sipped the tart Pinot Grigio between bites of the excellent chicken and al dente risotto, and watched Bev Sloan and her preoccupation with the wine.

Bev helped herself to another scoop of risotto and drained the remainder of the wine from the bottle into her glass. She watched the pale wine dribble, and Dante saw sadness drag at her eyes when she contemplated the end of the bottle.

Christine and Dinah ate happily, squishing the risotto into sculpture, outdoing each other with towers and caves of rice. They didn't notice their mother becoming tipsy and obsessing about the wine. Her intoxication was not, then, something they dreaded. A child of an alcoholic counts drinks and judges drunkenness because there are repercussions.

Dinah's fork broke through the back wall of her cave, producing an arborio arch.

If Bev were so good as to invite him for supper again, perhaps he should bring flowers.

The girls ate their sculptures and asked to be excused. Bev granted permission and the girls folded their napkins and scampered off.

Bev swallowed the last of the wine in one gulp and licked her glossy lips. Her tipsy cheeks pinkened. She leaned on one elbow and rested her chin on her palm. Her head tilted to one side, perky, flirty, and odd in a woman and mother in her mid-thirties. "So, Father Dante, why did you become a priest?"

Dante sat back in his chair. He was a priest, her marriage counselor, a spiritual authority. He was not to be flirted with. He crossed his legs away from her. "That is a complex issue."

"Did you *hear* a call?" She blinked, twice, rapidly, *batting her eyelashes.* Her face was pretty, even when she resorted to girlishness. "I've always wanted to ask a priest that. It seems so mystical, so holy."

He looked down, watched his own rough hand toying with a fork. "It's rather private. It is like asking someone about their sex life."

"I didn't mean to pry." She sat back, and her hand fluttered before it dropped below the table. This seriousness and fluster, her usual demeanor, was more appropriate.

He said, "We discuss the Call *ad nauseam* in the seminary. The theologians simultaneously seek to discover if one has had a divine intercession and they strip all the mysticism away to make a priest who will toe the Catholic line, will adhere to doctrine, and leave superstition to the laity."

Bev lifted her eyebrows, less flirty. She looked prettier when she was less coquettish.

Dante leaned on his elbow toward her and uncrossed his legs. He responded to her not-flirting, reinforcing the mature behavior, and yet he ought not respond too much, as she could manipulate him with this if he allowed a pattern to establish.

Bev said, "I'm not sure what I imagined the seminary to be. Praying, I guess. Memorizing the Mass, special Masses, other rituals, but I don't know what else."

"Doctrine, homiletics, the history of the Church, dogma, theology, eschatology, Latin, Greek, Hebrew, Aramaic." Dante smiled and looked away from Bev, who hadn't looked away from him. "I finished my residency in psychiatry before I entered the seminary. The professors wanted black and white answers because Catholicism is biased toward good and evil. They wanted shining knights, defending the faith." He ducked his head, embarrassed. "I was a problem student."

Bev leaned over her elbows, not too flirty. "You argued."

"There is this old moral puzzle about the sacrament of reconciliation, and how a priest should divide his mind and act as if he does not know anything that is said to him under the seal of confession. It is this: If directly before Mass, a man confesses to you under the sacrament that he poisoned the chalice containing the sacramental wine, deadly poison, no antidote, an absolute death to touch your lips to it, what should you do?"

Bev raised her eyebrows, and her gaze sharpened. She didn't seem fuzzily intoxicated. "That's a horrible thought."

"The answer they want is that you should drink it, and you should allow others to drink it because you must act as if you do not know what is said in confession, because the seal of confession is sacred, and that our mere corporal lives are far inferior to the sacred nature of the soul and the hereafter. Martyrdom is also encouraged."

Bev wavered backward. "You would break the seal of confession?"

"I would not commit suicide, and I would not allow innocents to be murdered." He shrugged. "I will not be used as a tool of evil."

"But he confessed!"

"I answered that I would give the man the penance of confessing his crime and ensuring that no one drank the wine. If he did not do this, then I would know that he had not been truly contrite, that he was not dreading the loss of Heaven and the pains of Hell and he had not resolved to confess his sins, do his penance, and avoid the near occasion of sin. Thus, if he did not confess and save everyone from drinking the poison, he had not made a true confession and the sacrament of reconciliation was void, so I was under no obligation to allow the murders to proceed."

"So you'd break the seal of confession." She looked horrified, eyebrows down and upper lip contracted, as the old priest had.

"The hypothetical confessing man had not made a true confession, he was not forgiven for his sin, and therefore I was under no onus to act as if he had. Indeed, if I had not hypothetically acted, the sin of murder would have also stained his hypothetical soul." Again, the debate flared, not intellectual, but righteous. "A priest must not allow himself and the Church to be used as an instrument for evil. If the Devil exists, *since* the Devil exists, we must not allow the Church to fall into diabolical hands." It was a variation on Cardinal Newman's postulate—*If* God exists, *since* God exists—a desperate scrambling of belief.

Bev stared at her empty, cream-smeared plate. "It still seems wrong."

"They felt that I was quibbling with both the letter and spirit of the law. I was angry that the larger issue, that of the meaning of true confession, went unremarked upon."

She looked away and tucked her honey-brown hair behind one pearl-studded ear. "And they think the laity are superstitious." She shook her head.

"It is why they did not believe the reports of sexual abuse. They are generals discussing strategy of battle, lines of skirmish within semantics of doctrine. Most have not been in a parish for decades. They have been locked in the Roman Curia, debating the nuances of Aramaic words or the order of words as they were written in Latin, investing them, I think, with far more content than remains. They think all the priests are like they are: scholastic, ambitious, political. Since I have been here, working at a parish, which I have not done since my regency, I am astonished at how little the Curia knows about the people of the Church. They don't remember a normal life. Few of them have had normal lives, since many of them entered the Church when they were fifteen or so. They don't understand the world, or its pressures, or what children are like."

Bev shook her head and rested her temple on her hand.

Dante confided, "They thought 'streetwise youths' were tempting vulnerable, innocent, naïve priests."

Bev glared at him. Her alcohol fog had burned away.

The twinge twinkled in Dante's temple, a reminder of his sleepless nights. "The seminary was designed for right and wrong beliefs. It was easier to be admitted to a seminary if one believed in absolutes or if one was convinced of one's own partial divinity, meaning if one was emotionally immature or a narcissist. Especially, I have heard, in the States."

"No." She shook her head, straightening her silverware to square with the edge of the table, like the careful placement of the host on the altar.

The flicker in his temple grew insistent, became a sting. "American seminaries were notorious for demanding absolutes, encouraging shallow reasoning, admitting anyone who showed the slightest interest in the priesthood, even men who obviously, in their applications, were deeply repressing their sexuality and attracted to vulnerability. They turned away men who evinced interest in having a family because they thought, rightly, that these men would eventually leave the priesthood. Thus, they eliminated normal, heterosexual men and admitted those repressing their sexuality." The backs of his legs ached as he repressed pacing.

Dante tapped his fingers on the edge of the glass table. "They told the young men that the vow of chastity precluded sex with women. If they did horrible things to a child, that was sinful and they should repent, but it didn't break their vow of chastity." He shook his head. "They used to hand out paddles to young men in the seminary to tuck in their shirts, so they would not accidentally touch themselves and be tempted to sin. Insanity."

Bev grunted, an expulsion of disbelief.

"The horrible result was that the seminaries allowed the self-selection of many damaged, childlike men and then churned out classes enriched with pedophiles."

Bev stared, horrified, and yet Dante couldn't stop talking. "These emotionally stunted men were sent to dioceses where they were given the least prestigious duties: training altar boys and running youth groups. The young priests, impressionable, ignorant, saw the young men in the youth groups experimenting, searching, learning things they themselves should have learned as teenagers, and they identified too strongly with the young men, saw themselves as leaders of the pack, which indicates they were wolves. They established preferences, predilections, habits, and techniques."

The edge of the table creased Dante's palm. "In the Vatican, I saw the records, and I told them that these men would continue to commit crimes, that they considered children to be objects or contemporaries." Dante drummed the edge of the table with his fingers, fingerprinting the glass. "The cardinals believe reflection and hearty sorrow for their offences and penance will cure pedophiles. They think it is a sin, not a crime, not the pathology of an incurable disease. Some Vatican administrators and even some counselors believe that some victims harbor 'loving memories' of the monsters who raped them, though most psychiatrists now realize that those victims suffered from something like Stockholm Syndrome, where kidnapped victims are brainwashed to identify with their captors in order to survive. Transmuting traumatic flashbacks into 'loving memories' is a dysfunctional way to reconcile oneself with abuse. It assumes that the children consented, which they could not have, by the very fact that they were children."

Bev tugged a hank of her oak-brown hair, an unconscious diversion to direct her attention away from what she did not want to confront. She twisted the lock into a shining cord.

Dante said, "Most pedophiles do not even know what they are. They do not develop an aberrant theory of pseudo-theological sexuality, that demonic nymphets strut the earth, searching for their nympholept." He'd read and reread *Lolita* while studying pedophiles. "Pedophilia has as much to do with homosexuality as rape has to do with heterosexuality. Pedophilia and rape are violent crimes, not a manifestation of sexuality, even when accomplished by persuasion or intimidation rather than overt violence. Primary pedophiles want sex with children, and they do not discriminate between boys or girls. Age is more important than gender. Most pedophiles do not admit to themselves that they are attracted to *children*. It is only *this* child, this one *here*. This child is mature 'beyond her years.' I cannot tell you how often I have heard that. It harkens to Victorian child prostitutes, girls who were 'young in years but old in sin.' And there are thousands of pedophiles who are priests. *Six percent* is a conservative estimate. It is probably higher. At least *six percent* of priests have sexually abused children."

"It can't be," Bev said. "The priests I know are good men."

"It's one of the secrets. *Six percent.*" He rubbed his eyes, trying to ease his headache. "And now, *now* the seminaries are expelling or not admitting men who have delved into their own psyches and understand that they are attracted to adult men. They're throwing out the healthy heterosexuals and the healthy homosexuals. I cannot believe this will improve the situation."

"I can't believe it."

"Ninety-four percent of priests are innocent," he said. "Sixteen priests of seventeen have never harmed a child." He was reversing himself, flipping his statistics, emphasizing the innocent. He manipulated the numbers for his own reasons, when it suited him, because he was as hypocritical as the rest of the damned Vatican.

Damned was the operative word. If there was a Hell, *since* there was a Hell, he would see most of the Vatican there with the ragged omission sins gouging their souls.

"You haven't," she said, and it might have been a question.

"What?" He opened his eyes and electric blue dots poxed the dining room, smudged over the glass table, the chandelier, and Bev, whose caramel eyes held tears.

"You haven't hurt a child," she said.

"Of course not." His outrage at the accusation of pedophilia was blunted because, after those overwhelming statistics, it was a perfectly logical question from a mother with children in the house. "I do not fit the profile. I entered the seminary when I was twenty-seven after an undergraduate degree, medical school, a residency, a young life, and I have never worked with children before. In the fifties and sixties, some would-be priests entered 'minor seminary' when they were thirteen. It was a boarding school, and they were cut off from their families and girls and the normal world, even movies, even television."

Bev leaned closer. "Are you gay?"

He shrugged. "No. I am celibate." He smoothed his pants over his thighs. Shame scoured his face. Since he had taken Holy Orders, he had been celibate and chaste, anyway.

"Sorry." Bev picked up her dish and the children's plates. "Didn't mean to pry. I'm just going to tidy up. Girls!" she called, and the girls' faces poked around the corner. "Would you entertain Father Dante?"

They dashed in, each grabbing one of his hands, and tugged.

At his sister's in Roma, there was always one extra child dancing around, tugging at his pant leg or latching onto a pinky to propel him where Theresa had decreed.

The girls chattered about the board game they were playing, getting out of jail and retrograde motion.

CONROY TYPED WITH two cold fingers.

Beyond his closed door, a door slammed. The rectangular window glowed behind the fried-egg poster. Someone had arrived.

He had finished another paragraph when the doorknob turned. Conroy tapped the button for an apoptosis paper he was reviewing and it spread over the grant, hiding it.

Leila opened the door. She was wearing her lab coat buttoned all the way up to her sharp chin. Below the coat's hem, she wore black slacks and high-heeled boots. "Thought I'd say hi." She glanced at the screen. "Show me that gel again."

"Okay." He popped over to the grant, found the page, and sent it to the printer. The gel had to be good enough to fool a graduate student if it was going to slip by an NIH committee.

The laser printer ground out the pages. Leila looked at the gel and the text around it. She flipped one of the pages over as if she were missing something printed on the back. Her fingernails were the color of good claret. "What the heck is this?"

"New grant," Conroy said. "New direction. More of an anatomical focus than molecular."

"Come on, Conroy. We're spread too thin now. I'm doing viral apoptosis. Danna is studying Schwann cells. Yuri's doing immunology. Joe is working on the glial wild goose chase. Not to mention the summer of the Yucatan mini-pigs."

She didn't see anything odd about the gel. The recently added smudges must have blurred it toward realism. Conroy raised his hands. "No one's switching projects. This is a whole other grant that I'm applying for."

The paper wrinkled where she grasped it. She looked ready to throw the pages at his head. "You've got nine grants, including two R01's. We had to buy that sequencer last year to dump an extra hundred grand from an expiring grant. It looks like someone has a shopping addiction around here. How much more money do you need?"

"The lab's focus should be broader, more models, more applications."

She slapped her forehead. "More mice? More Yucatan mini-pigs?"

"Humans."

Her jaw dropped and jutted sideways. "We do *basic* research. We're not a pharmaceutical company. We can't file the paperwork for human trials. What's it called, an IND?"

"Part of this," Conroy tapped the screen, "is salary for a lawyer to do the paperwork."

Leila rolled the pages into a spanker and slapped her hand. "We aren't ready. In my first paper, you added the word 'suggests' to every sentence."

If anyone would understand his ambition and the path to glory, Leila would. "I presented my name to the Med School department chair search committee. It meets next Monday."

Leila dropped the pages and they scattered on the industrial tile floor. Her eyebrows raised so far that they dragged her eyelids up and white showed all the way around her dark, dark brown irises. "You want to start human trials because you want a god-damned promotion?"

He explained, "And because our data warrants it. In the conclusions of your first paper, we said that the next step was provisional clinical trials."

She leaned on the computer desk and covered her young, lean face with her hands. "We cannot rip out parts of people's brains and feed them poison to see if it slows down multiple sclerosis. Inhibiting fatty acid synthesis is contraindicated in people who want to stay alive."

"We wouldn't just scale up the mouse protocol, Leila." She wasn't seeing the grand scale. "Phase I trials are all do-no-harm. If I get this grant, they'll give me the department chair. If I were the head of the department, we'd have all kinds of resources, people, residents, funds, equipment. We could do the experiments to get to clinical trials."

Leila shook her head. "So if you get this grant, then you'll get this promotion, and then we could utilize the department's resources to do the stuff in the grant."

"Yes!" She did understand.

"So it's okay that you're lying on this grant, because you might be able to make it true."

"I'm not lying." She might have figured out the faked gel.

She stabbed the printing pages with her finger, pinning them to the printer tray, "You're relying on a self-fulfilling prophecy."

"If you want to engage in wordplay, I suppose you could call it that." Conroy examined his fingernails, which were rimmed with talcum from latex gloves.

"What is killing your mice, and what is growing in your cells? It doesn't even look like Yuri's research. The CPE is wrong."

He picked up the pages from the floor. The gel did look more realistic with smudges. He'd even managed a partial fingerprint, clipped and pasted from another gel. It might be his own. "You didn't touch those mice or cells, did you?"

She said, "I just hope it's not pathogenic. Your aseptic technique looks like a toddler in a bathtub." She slammed his office door behind her.

No one understood him. Not his wife, not his mistress, not even his casual fuck.

Leila should have understood. She should have appreciated the way the keys slipped into the lock, becoming the next key that would open the next door.

Leila should have appreciated the way he casually fucked the system.

BEV WASHED DISHES while Father Dante played board games with her children. The cast iron skillet thumped the rubber mat under the frothy hot water. She kept the white kitchen bi-fold doors open, watching the priest and her daughters.

Six percent, *at least* six percent.

If one out of every seventeen cars randomly exploded, the lawsuits would drive every car manufacturer out of business.

If six percent of dogs were rabid, people would shoot dogs on sight.

And yet, there were worse statistics.

Cigarette smoking kills two out of three smokers from cancer, heart disease, or stroke. If you drive ten miles to buy a lottery ticket, your chance of dying in a car accident is fourteen times greater than your chance of winning the lottery.

Statistics lie.

Women bear 1.8 children in their lifetimes.

One out of every two marriages ends in divorce.

When the good china was soaking, Bev noticed that it was five minutes past the girls' regular bedtime and called though the doorway, "Girls! Time to go upstairs!"

Protestations ensued: they weren't tired, they hadn't finished their game, and Father Dante wanted them to finish their game. Father Dante cleared his throat. "Indeed, it appears that I am about to be beaten badly. The game should end in a few moments."

"All right," Bev relented. They played quickly. Dante miscounted his moves twice, but Dinah didn't correct him because he landed on her property and had to pony up his railroad, so that she owned all four, then Dinah landed on an overbuilt street and had to turn it all over to Christine. The girls went upstairs without further ado.

Bev sat at the other end of the couch from Dante. Wine leadened her legs and heavy streams of mercury flowed around her calves. Dante's black shirt and Roman collar seemed predatory, like a vampire's cape.

Suspecting Dante was obscene.

Suspecting Nicolai might have saved Laura's son.

It was confusing to entrust your soul to, and suspect child rape of, the same person, the same collar, the same Holy Catholic Church. She asked, "The pedophiles, do you think they're real priests? Or do you think they faked hearing the Call and are just using the Church?"

Father Dante shrugged. "It seems to me that people use God or the Mystery to rationalize whatever they were going to do anyway. We rationalized the Crusades. The Islamists rationalize terrorism. That poor woman in Texas heard God tell her to drown her own children to save them from the Devil. People pray to God, but they hear their own desire or hate or insanity answer."

"But," Bev said, "maybe the Devil answered those prayers." An awful fear puffed smoke into her lungs. She grabbed his arm around his biceps, round, lean meat. He jerked, but she didn't let go. "How are we supposed to know if it's God or the Devil answering?"

He stared at her hand, at her fingers wrapped around his soft black shirt. "Mrs. Sloan."

"If we think God or the Virgin Mary is speaking to us, telling us to do something, how do we know that it isn't the Devil or our own desire or insanity? Really? How do we know?"

Father Dante examined her face, prodding her. He asked, "Why?"

"I felt something, once." Her own voice ached to scream, *How are we supposed to know?*

Dante lifted her hand from his bicep and held it between both of his own hot palms. "The Devil tempts us to sin, to do something that is ultimately evil." His hands were folded around her hand, like that first evening when she'd found that horrible lingerie, when she'd run screaming to confession. Dante's hands were tan, dusky, Mediterranean. Dante had been kind that night and now, holding her hand. Kindness was expected in a priest. It didn't mean anything, to have a young priest who looked like a da Vinci painting of the Archangel Michael, beautiful and ending the world with a flaming sword, holding her hand. It meant nothing.

He asked, "What happened?"

She inserted her other hand between his. "There was a man. He wanted me to marry him. I didn't know what to do. I prayed for guidance." And she'd received guidance, and it had changed everything. If she had been wrong, if she'd been tempted by the Devil instead of visited by the Holy Virgin, then her whole life was a lie and she shouldn't be here, and Conroy shouldn't be here, and her girls shouldn't be here, and she couldn't escape now because she had married Conroy and the girls had been born and she wouldn't leave them now. Not for *anything.* "And I didn't marry him."

"Ah," Dante said. "This was the not-Catholic. And you felt something?"

"No," she lied.

"What happened to him?"

She shrugged. "He went back to Israel."

One of Dante's eyebrows lifted. "He was Jewish?"

"Israeli, and a Jew." She chuckled, and her hand jiggled with reverberations, but his hands encompassing hers were steady. "Malachi hated that word, Jew-ish. He said it was equivocating, because no one is Russian-ish or Catholic-y. He was 'a Jew, through and through.'"

"And you weren't."

"He wanted me to convert, but I couldn't see myself as anything other than Catholic, and he couldn't see himself not being a Jew." Her eyes were unexpectedly bitter, sand dry. Dante was still holding her hand, and his warm, brown skin comforted her. "How do you tell if it's the small, still Voice of God or if you're hearing voices?"

Dante's fingers slid around hers, locking down. "Bev, you aren't crazy."

Her eyes burned, and the inside of her nose stung as if she was breathing in burning desert air. "How do you know I'm not crazy?"

"People who are schizophrenic hear voices and are aggrandized, believe that they *are* God or one of the chosen, or a prophet, or the Devil. But some people experience something else, and it humbles them. Their humility connects them to other people. They are sanctified by it."

His luminous eyes reflected the stacked lamp behind Bev, the ceiling flooded with light as if by floating fire, and the candles on the marble mantle doubled in the mirror.

Dante said, "The first type of people, the raving mad, are easy to discern, and they suffer so, from the delusions and from the treatment. The others are perfectly stable, but they may have touched the Divine."

"But you didn't hear a call," she said. Their hands tangled together. If Bev extracted one hand now, it would seem she was turning away from him. It seemed uncaring, especially after he had reassured her that she was not crazy, so she waited, her hands among his hot hands, and all of their jumbled skin lying on her chintz couch in the lamplight, while her children, upstairs, thumped across the ceiling.

"No voices for me," he said. "The Church needs me, especially now. It's also a self-serving, self-righteous, agoraphobic, hypocritical bureaucracy that strangles me, every day, in my every thought. Sometimes it makes me want to run."

"You aren't thinking about… not being a priest."

Dante shrugged. "I imagine it is how the whales evolved. The ancestors of whales were land animals once, long ago, with legs and feet, but they went back to the sea. Once you're far enough out to sea, you lose sight of the land. You can swim, so you swim, and the sea has its own charms." He smiled a bit, wryly. "I've been working on that for a while. And what would I do as a lay person?"

"You're a psychiatrist."

"I'm too accustomed to being a priest, safe, harmless. Can you imagine me dating? I would not wish a man such as myself upon a woman."

Bev turned her hand over so their hands were palm to palm. His hands were strong.

Running footsteps crossed the ceiling above them like poltergeists.

Dante looked over to the clock on the bookcase. While his eyes were away, Bev detangled her hands from his and they drew their embarrassed hands back to their own laps.

"I should go," he said. He stood. The front door was just off her living room, a few steps, and they walked onto the tile of the foyer. He took her hand and held it again, hanging between them like a twined pendulum, and he paused, breath drawn in.

Breath lodged in Bev's chest. She should back away. She shouldn't hold a priest's hand like this (a priest was owned by God and she was a married woman, joined at the soul, shriven by a sacrament) so close, too close, and a priest shouldn't look at her lips and her eyes, and his hands shouldn't be so warm around her palm and wrist, and she shouldn't turn her hand over, like that, so her fingers were caught and if he wanted he could pull her toward him with a quick flip of his hand, and catch her.

He hesitated, as if he might tug on her hand, and seconds stretched into breaths.

Dante dropped her hand and backed up. "Thank you for dinner." He opened the door.

"Any time," she said and regretted it. She was a silly middle-aged woman, a little tipsy and a little stupid, standing in the foyer with a priest like that, waiting, when there was nothing that she should be waiting for.

LEILA CLOSED her cell phone. "Damn. Danna's not coming. She has a headache again."

They sat in a booth near the back of the Irish pub, sipping stout and smoking. Joe sat beside her. His leg vibrated against hers. Malcolm, across the booth, drank Guinness.

The boys continued their bombast. "Sheep," Malcolm said. "Anthrax is a ruddy sheep disease."

Joe countered, "Rabies. Rabies in the mail would scare people."

"Lyssavirus, too bloody slow. People would have months or years to get vaccinated. No deaths a'tall. Dengue fever, now that'll *scare* people!"

Past Malcolm's wiry, black hair and through the mist of secondhand smoke, that priest from Conroy's church came down the stairs and peeled his black coat away from his open-necked black shirt.

Leila said, "Holy shit. Don't look." She gestured at the door with her glowing cigarette.

"What?"

"Wot?" The guys swiveled like bobblehead dolls.

The priest surveyed the crowd from the second step, elbowed through the mostly grad-age crowd, and seated himself at the bar.

"What about him?" Joe asked.

"He's a priest," Leila said.

Joe smirked. "Someone from your past?"

Malcolm said, "I don't see no collar."

Leila stared down at the table, letting her long hair curtain her face. Glimpses of the bar scene wove between her hanks of hair. The bar noise swelled and choked her. "Dr. S. knows him. He's from Rome, a Monsignor, and a neuroscientist." Her shaking fingers jiggled her cigarette, and the cherry fell off.

Joe prairie-dogged to peer over the people around the bar. "And he likes the good stuff."

Leila peeked around the edge of her hair. At the bar, Monty the bartender reached into the top shelf for a dusty green bottle.

Leila tossed her hair behind her shoulders and straightened. "None of our business, anyway."

"Kind of weird," Joe said. "A priest, drinking, in a bar."

Malcolm shrugged. "Wouldn't be odd for one of our Scots priests to be in a bar. Like a drop with the best of 'em. And he's a Roman priest, eh? Och," he said, "hardcore." He twisted in his seat and struggled to the edge of the booth. "I believe I need another beer."

"Christ, Malcolm," Leila said. "Don't bother the man."

"Hang on." Joe slid the remainder of his beer down his gullet. "I need one, too." He flapped his hand for Leila to vacate.

She said, "I'm going with, and if you get out of line, I swear, I'll take Dante's side."

"Oo-ew," Malcolm said. "Don-tay. On a first name basis, are we?"

Leila hated bar talk. If she had gone to her gay bar, she could have had a drink with the nice pre-op trannies in peace. The three of them threaded themselves through the crowd, up to the long bar crowded with people like ants on a stick of gum.

Malcolm edged up next to the priest and ordered a Guinness from Monty. Monty poured it slowly. He'd attended the company's model bar in Dublin to learn the proper method.

"So," Malcolm said to the priest. "What's a nice priest like you doing in a bar like this?"

Dante smiled but didn't look away from Monty, who watched Malcolm warily. Monty didn't like his high-end customers harassed.

"Come on, Malcolm," Leila said. "Monty'll bring us the beer."

Joe leaned over to Monty and ordered another Murphy's. Monty nodded and continued to lazily pour Malcolm's Guinness.

Dante noticed Leila and raised his eyebrows. "Do I know you?"

"You use that line on all the girls?" Malcolm asked.

The priest wilted, not that the guys noticed squat.

Joe and Malcolm laughed and Joe pulled out his wallet to pay Monty. "You want anything, Leila?"

"No, thanks," she said. The priest's eyes widened at her name. Damn.

"Yes," the priest said, "Leila, the Coptic Catholic who attended Mass."

"Leila, at Mass?" Malcolm leered at her. "Explains that lightning storm Sunday, eh?"

"Shut up, Malcolm."

Malcolm clapped Dante's shoulder. "What're you drinking there?"

"Macallen," Dante said and gazed into his glass.

"Well, any man who knows a good scotch knows that I'm one, too. Why don't ya join us there, eh, Father?"

Dante smiled. "Why not, indeed?"

Leila considered leaving, either for home and her dog or for the company of nonjudgmental drag queens, but Joe steered her back to the cigarette-burned wooden booth, and Malcolm and Dante sat across from them.

Introductions ensued. The priest shook her hand perfunctorily, no more contact than with the guys, and called himself "Dante, just Dante," no *Father*, no *Monsignor*. Maybe Leila could sic the priest on Malcolm so he would leave her alone.

Conroy would have a conniption if he knew Leila was drinking with his priest, of whom he evidently felt proprietary, but it was an opportunity to figure out how he was a priest and a shrink and a scientist, and it was an opportunity to prove to herself that she could survive this.

She plastered a calm smile over her trembling jaw.

MONTY FINISHED pouring the Guinness with a froth of head like whipped cream above the deep beer. Malcolm appreciated Monty's art. He slapped Joe's Murphy in a glass.

Leila liked lighter beers, though last Friday, when she'd been there with her other friends—some of them girls but all of them dressed like women—she'd been drinking scotch like a man. Monty had joined them at the other bar for dancing 'til dawn. He had been careful to dance with the girls, not with the he-shes. He held nothing against them, but he wasn't going to hold them against himself.

Nathanial, at the end of the bar sipping an expertly poured Guinness, had rechristened himself Natalie last weekend, just for fun, to fit in with Leila's funny boys. She'd drawn eyeliner on his lids in the women's bathroom, straddling his skirted lap, and told him how beautiful he was.

He'd popped a chubby, but she'd been polite and not mentioned it. That night, Nathanial, with his curly blond hair, huge blue eyes, and full lips, had been twice hit on by straight guys. Tonight, he had been hitting on chicks all night with no luck. If he was more attractive as a woman than as a man, what did that mean?

DANTE HAD NEEDED a drink after he'd left Bev standing in her house, face turned up, eyes dreamy. At the rectory, Father Sam maintained that there was no alcohol secreted anywhere. Sam had been vigilant about *alcohol*, because *alcohol* could be a problem with priests.

He had driven around the college town of New Hamilton, strangling the steering wheel and kicking the pedals, until he'd finally found the bar-lined main street. The sports bars were full of ebullient frat boys, not the atmosphere for liquor and remorse. The medical student hangout held the well-dressed crowd sipping martinis and smoking cigars. The Irish pub, a canopy above stairs leading down, a tattered pool table behind the jukebox playing rock, blond wood railings and an empty spot at the bar, seemed the place for whiskey and soliloquy.

Damn it, no priest held onto a woman like that, projected his own skin onto hers, felt her warmth and smelled her pheromones and perfume until his own mammalian body responded. Even if she was lonely, he could only harm her and, presumably, damn his own soul.

Part of his recent vulnerability was loneliness, he knew. At the Vatican, he and his friends gathered at each others' apartments or the Jesuit residence and played poker late into the night, or partook of culture, or drank and pressed books on each other. Dante's sister also took him in, like a good priest's sister. And he had platonic lady friends, Roman women, who were used to platonic priests.

Here, he was either judging or counseling everyone he knew.

But he shouldn't punish Bev for his temptations.

While this thought might have edged into rationalization in many priests' heads, Dante had inhabited the unfriendly territory of exacting celibacy and needy women for a long time.

So Dante drank and tried to hone his soul to a fine, sharp, rigid blade.

When a few regulars had challenged him, he'd held his peace. No use getting in a bar fight merely to release pent-up aggression.

But the Coptic Orthodox girl had been there, and she had picked him out of the crowd and told the men about him. The small collegiate town was enroped by gossip vines, and now he was ensconced at their table and had been introduced as "just Dante." He smiled at the requisite *Inferno* jokes and asked, "What else do you know about me, Leila?"

She blew cigarette smoke out the corner of her mouth into a part in the crowd and smiled. Dim lamplight silver-lined her as if she were a bronze cloud at sunset. Ah, before he had taken Holy Orders, when women smiled at him like that, his heart rate had doubled and his skin warmed and tightened with the hunt. His body responded to Leila's smile out of ingrained habit. His lips filled with blood. The gold-shaded lights in the bar brightened. Cool air brushed Dante's throat through his open collar and drained down his chest.

Dante said, "At Mass, you knew my name."

Leila said, "I searched for your name on the Internet. Found your lab."

"And how did you know to do that?"

She shrugged her thin shoulders, and her dark red blouse slithered and clung to her. Dante still liked to watch the silky movement of women's clothes on the litheness of their bodies and breasts. This type of woman, slender, beautiful, *una bella figura*, had haunted Roma for him like lockstepped legions of ghosts. They paced the stones of the streets, lingered on the fountains and smiled coyly at him because he was a harnessed, muzzled priest.

The bartender brought the beers and slid them across the table.

Leila said, "Dr. S. wanted information on you."

"And who is that?" Dante sipped his smooth, sweet scotch. He'd needed a strong drink since he'd arrived in America. The liquor lapped at his mind and soothed it, like being petted.

She said, "Conroy Sloan."

The scotch lumped in his throat, but Dante swallowed it. "Sloan?"

"Joe and I," she jerked her thumb at the beige man next to her, "are in Sloan Lab at the university. Malcolm is with Lugar Lab down the hall. We study some pretty similar things to your lab."

Joe raised his beer at Dante and asked Leila, "So who is this guy?"

Leila smiled at Joe, and they seemed chummy. She said, "He's modest, this 'just-ah-Dante,' but he is, and I'm not sure of the order of the titles, Monsignor Professor Doctor Dante Petrocchi-Bianchi, Society of Jesus, Congregation for the Doctrine of the Faith, the University of Rome, and the Vatican. His lab studies schizophrenia, molecules to anatomy, soup to nuts."

Dante, flayed professionally, felt his jaw click. He smiled at her. She was a landmine, this woman. If he trod wrongly, she would tell Sloan that his priest had been pub crawling, and gossip in this town ricocheted like a laser in a hall of mirrors. Yet, an information source about Sloan might be valuable. "You're thorough."

Leila shrugged. "So how can you be a priest and a scientist?"

Dante said, "There is an artificial divide between the rational and the spiritual, yet most people believe in God." He watched Leila's eyes flicker upward, an aborted roll of her eyes. Ah, an unbeliever. "But no one studies faith. It's too abstract."

Leila said, "I'll believe in God when you show me a molecular mechanism for it."

Sloan had used practically that exact phrase, demanding the molecular mechanism for possession. Dante kept his face passive. Like confession, counseling did not exist outside. "We believe the *Srk* kinase pathway is involved."

Leila laughed, and the men joined in. Dante stretched his legs under the burnt, graffitied table. He would exit as soon he finished this scotch. It was foolish of him to go to a bar in this small, gossipy town.

Leila leaned on the table. Her challenging eyes didn't flirt. "Really, how can you be a scientist, work in neuroscience, and still believe in God?"

Joe and Malcolm blocked the conversation by raising their inside shoulders, turning away from Dante and Leila and in toward each other.

Dante smiled back. In the seminary, holier-than-thou priests had disparaged science, rounding on him in stone-faced hallways and demanding to know where the Bible mentioned quarks or neurons or the hippocampus. His secular colleagues latched onto him in the tiled, sterile hospital halls and cited studies that equated religious practice with obsessive-compulsive behavior. "Why are a religious belief and science incompatible?"

Leila held her cigarette just beyond the edge of the table and shielded it with her jutted-out elbow. "Because religion used to be all-powerful in all areas: origin of man, creation of the earth, structure of the universe, and we had to worship Him or else He'd smite us." Her capitalization was audible and nearly spittle-flecked. "Science stole all that. The universe began with the Big Bang, and all the stars are red-shifted. The earth coalesced from a swirling disk of dust around a third-generation star. Humans evolved from apes, which evolved from other chordates, back to fish, back to cells, back to chemical reactions around thermal ocean vents. There is no *reason* for it. There is no one to *smite* us. So there is *nothing* to worship."

Dante smiled. "Reductionism. Interesting. But you can't prove that there is no God."

Leila's joking manner sublimed and re-crystallized as anger that stretched her black eyes and her lovely mouth. "In that you can't prove a negative statement, and absence of evidence is not evidence of absence. But, *Just-Dante*, it's still *absence*. We have found *absence*."

"If one apple falls up…"

"It will disprove the theory of gravity, but apples *don't fall up*."

Dante quoted, "'The Bible teaches us how to go to Heaven, but not how the Heavens go.'"

"Galileo," she said. "The Inquisition imprisoned him and forced him to recant the truth."

Dante flinched at the Inquisition reference.

"Guys, guys," Joe broke in. "How 'bout them Knicks?"

"Oy," Malcolm said. "The Knicks are overpaid, Neanderthal poof-kahs. The Suns, now *there's* a basketball team."

The ash from Leila's cigarette drooped, and she slid the ashtray out of the table's back corner to flick the cigarette. She smiled at Dante. "Basketball is skewed by the officiating."

"They can't call a foul if none is committed." The men turned back to them. Sports were safe. Dante asked Leila, "Do you have a cigarette?"

Her eyes smiled and she licked her lush lips, enchanted as he knew she would be. Indulging in alcohol and tobacco suggested he might have other vices. God, grant him strength.

She tapped out a cigarette and gave him her lighter. Her hand was smooth, and he brushed her skin when he took the Zippo. He flicked it open and lit the cigarette. Smoke rushed into his lungs, and those crying cells, starved for four long years, feasted on nicotine.

AT ELEVEN O'CLOCK, Conroy slipped into bed beside Beverly, who barely stirred at the jiggling. The grant was almost finished, and he needed to perform only one more experiment.

Beside Conroy in bed, Beverly flinched, sleeping soundly, dreaming.

Conroy smiled at Beverly dreaming. In the absence of stimuli—light, touch, sound—the brain could replay sensations and, while one can lucidly know one is dreaming, the dreaming neurons of the brain are the same ones that respond to the world, and thus a dream is a kind of reality, and thus reality is a kind of dream.

Francis Crick, of Watson and Crick, who discovered the essential double-helix nature of DNA, had said, "You're nothing but a pack of neurons."

Conroy settled his pack of neurons down to sleep, and their crackling quieted.

Chapter Eight

Thursday in the lab, Conroy pipetted while Leila, glove-deep in an experiment, muttered incantations into the whoosh of the radioactive hood. Joe blearily watched the PCR machine's red and green lights blink, indicating the successful completion of each of the hundred and twenty cycles. Heisenberg should have included *Taq* polymerase in his watched-pot theories.

Leila flitted through Conroy's field of view.

"Leila," he said and she screech-stopped, startled out of her concentration upon picomoles of wing of bat and micrograms of eye of newt. "Does Danna have an exam?"

"She had a headache last night." She shrugged, and her white lab coat lifted her arms. Twenty-two tiny vials in her hands, three between each of her blue-gloved fingers and two clutched by her thumbs, jiggled. She looked at sloshed teardrops in the tubes, "Damn," and bent over the breadbox-sized centrifuge.

"Joe, call Danna. Yuri," Conroy called, and Yuri paused, Groucho-Marxist eyebrows raised. Conroy said, "I'm ordering a new car. I'll sell you my old one for three thousand."

Yuri's eyebrows peaked happily. "Thank you, Dr. S."

Across the bench, Leila's mouth dropped open.

Maybe he should have sold the car to Leila, but that might look like favoritism, and he didn't want any whiff of that, especially when the selection committee's politics were flowing his way. Only another week and a half until Monday the fifteenth and their decision.

A frisson of happiness rippled his skin like wind-blown grass.

JOE AND YURI sat side by side in the tissue culture room, pipetting pink media onto Petri dishes of cells in twin hoods. Joe yelled over the hurricane-force hoods, "Did you hear the one about the professor, the postdoc, and the grad student who found a magic lamp on the beach?"

"Why would lamp be magic?" Yuri frowned.

"Like in Aladdin. The lamp had a genie, and the genie says they each get one wish."

"They should hold out for more wishes. Collective bargaining."

"So the grad student wishes to be in Las Vegas with a million dollars and a showgirl, and poof! He disappears. The postdoc wishes he was in the Bahamas with ten million dollars and three models, and poof! He disappears."

Yuri shook his head. "I should have argued Dr. S. down to two thousand dollars."

"And the genie asks the professor what he wants for his wish."

"Da?"

"And the professor says, 'I want those two back in the lab after lunch.'"

Yuri scoffed. "Dr. S. would only have given us half hour for lunch with models."

BEV LEFT CONROY'S SUPPER in the fridge when he wasn't home again. The girls had been in bed for an hour when his Porsche growled in the garage. She hid the vodka under the lettuce in the crisper and microwaved his barbequed chicken and au gratin potatoes.

Conroy walked quietly though the dark family room and stopped, startled, when he saw her in the kitchen. "I'm sorry," he said. "I thought I'd be home at seven, but you know the lab. Everything takes two hours longer than you think."

"Fine," she said. The microwave beeped. She felt the underside of the plate, and the warmth penetrated to the middle of the food.

"This grant will be done soon."

"That's good. I'm going up to bed." She went upstairs, carefully navigating the gray-carpeted staircase that rose and slid like the sea, and fell into her bed, which spun in both directions at once as if her body and her soul looped around and converged.

FRIDAY AFTERNOON, Leila met Conroy at her place for a quick fuck. "I've got to load that gel by eight," she locked the door's deadbolts, "if it's going to be finished tomorrow morning."

"Run it hotter." He sat on the couch in the living room and bent to untie his oxford shoes.

"I don't want to run it hotter. I want to run it at exactly the same voltage as my other two hundred gels. It messes up the molecular weight markers to run them at different voltages."

"They're standards." He dropped his shoe on the floor. "They should run the same."

"I don't know how you ran that perfect gel, Conroy." She stripped off her shirt. Cool air washed her back. She unzipped her jeans. "You do everything wrong."

"It's the washes, not the gel." He dropped the other shoe and it rattled, thump-uh.

She pried her shoes off and rolled her jeans down, the opposite of a condom.

Leila unhooked her bra. She dropped her underwear on the floor. "Are you still dressed?"

Conroy folded his socks on top of his shoes.

Leila grabbed his shirt, unbuttoned it and tossed it on the floor. He said, "It'll wrinkle." She unbuttoned his pants, pushed him back on her couch, and climbed aboard.

CONROY LEANED HIS HEAD BACK on Leila's couch, the toss into the sky from his orgasm still draining away. At least the casual fucking with Leila was still the same. He didn't have to pussyfoot around to appease her. It was all just hot sex. And some dirty talk. "Wow," Conroy said. "I don't care if I go to Hell for this."

Leila slumped on his shoulder. "You don't believe in Hell," she whispered. "Even priests don't believe in Hell. They make up rules and invent punishments to keep superstitious people in line."

She untangled. He lifted his thigh to free her ankle.

Ah, the cold and the freedom. Sadness at the end, and yet, still, the exhilaration of cheating, of winning, of fucking the entire society who sought to repress his instinct to fuck. When he fucked Leila, he fucked every woman in the world, and he gloried in that moment.

"Come on," she said, "I've got to go back to the lab."

As she opened her bedroom door, her old black dog, who'd never paid much attention to Conroy, sauntered out toward the kitchen.

Leila came back, denim-clad, pulling a clingy silver shirt over her bra-less chest. Her nipples impressed the shirt like machine-stamped rivets in silver metal.

She said, "Let yourself out, Conroy. I'm running late."

"Thought you were going back to the lab to run a gel."

"I've got plans for after." She pulled her gray coat out of the closet and patted her dog, who'd walked over to see her out.

Conroy stood and buttoned his pants over his messy groin. His underwear gummed onto his skin. "Who with?"

"Friends. Just lock the doorknob and pull the door closed."

He padded across the laminate wood to her. "Who with?"

"None of your business, Conroy." Her hand grasped the doorknob.

"Who?" He grabbed her wrist.

Her dog barked near his leg.

Leila twisted, an ampersand of black motion on the white wall, and

Conroy's arm twisted backwards. His wrist and elbow creaked, pulling to the tolerance of his joints. She held his wrist cranked into that position and asked, "What the hell do you think you're doing?"

The dog barked an angry streak of obscenities.

Conroy's attention rooted in his elbow. His ligaments strained against the pressure. A tremor increased the strain. He said, "I don't know."

"Don't ever grab me again. Next time, I'll break your arm."

A small tendon just inside his elbow pinged, almost tearing. "Okay."

"I could kill you, you know that? I could snap your neck or shoot you in the head."

"All right, all right."

Leila released his hand and stepped back, wary. The dog watched. Its yellow eyes shifted in its black, heavy head. She said, "Don't you ever, ever grab me again."

SATURDAY AFTERNOON, Bev arrived late for counseling. Conroy's black Porsche was parked away from the other salty cars, near the trees that sliced the sky like swords.

She trotted through the cold church. Afternoon sunlight struggled through the stained glass windows and left indiscriminate scarlet and turquoise smears on the oak floor.

At the library, she knocked and heard Dante say, "Yes?" Dante was sitting in his chair, reading, alone. His black cassock draped from his Roman collar over his body to the floor. She asked, "Isn't Conroy here?"

Dante shrugged and his black robe rippled.

Bev closed the door and leaned against it. She scraped her courage together like spilled salt on a countertop. "We need to talk about the other day."

Dante stretched his long legs and smiled at her. "It was nothing. We did nothing, and we were right to do nothing. I've had women friends.

Occasionally, you feel a little tug, a little tempt, but nothing happens."

"Yes, of course." Her heart jumped up. Oh, and she thanked the Virgin Mary, Dante didn't hate her, and he didn't even think she had sinned or tempted him or been evil or anything.

The Blessed Virgin was silent on the subject.

Behind her, the door knocked and fibrillated against her shoulder blades.

CONROY COULD HEAR THEM inside that library, his wife's alto and the priest's rough voice, but he couldn't distinguish words. He knocked on the door and there was a hesitation before the priest shouted, "Yes?" and the heavy door nudged away from the frame as if a secret had been lifted from it.

Conroy pushed the door open. "What's going on in here?"

His wife stood across the room from the priest, who insouciantly smoothed his robes as if they had been hiked up around his waist. Beverly looked inordinately happy. She was hiding something. Conroy repeated, "What's going on?"

Beverly smirked and sat in her chair. "Nothing."

The priest raised a groomed, Italian eyebrow.

Conroy sat in his chair, but the two of them, his wife and the priest, seemed to be sending each other subtle signals, flickers of eyebrow and eyelash, curves of mouth and fingers and hip.

"So this is how it's going to be," Conroy said. "The two of you, ambushing me."

"We didn't discuss you at all, Dr. Sloan." The priest steepled his fingers, a pose designed to be benign and thoughtful, but it looked like pondering harsh judgment.

Beverly said, "Conroy, we need counseling more than once a week."

Conroy shrugged. "I'm too busy."

Beverly said, "You weren't too busy to have an affair."

"I'm too busy at the lab right now."

The priest said, "We need you here, Dr. Sloan."

Trust this creampuff who had allowed himself to become God's prison bitch to not understand the battlefield of marriage, the subterfuges and feints. Trust him not to know that *talking* about a relationship is the woman's cavalry and field artillery. If, by some miracle of morale, if the battle tide turned and the man made some headway, her territory was mined with bouncing betties, old arguments that she somehow remembered and tossed up that shot off bamboo spikes, and the guy would be tweezing out eighteen-inch splinters of sneaky allusions for days afterward, and he'd still lose the fight.

DANTE RUBBED HIS ACHING EYES. "Dr. Sloan." He used the title to reduce antagonism. The skin on Dante's face itched and tightened as though he was driving while exhausted. He couldn't relinquish control of the conversation and reinforce Sloan's obstinate behavior. "Dr. Sloan, what do you want to be the result of this counseling?"

Sloan's forehead pleated.

Bev breathed quietly, leaning forward, and Dante watched her watch her husband.

Sloan drew a breath and said, "I want everything back the way it was."

Perhaps there was more to that answer than a mere wish not to have been caught screwing another woman or irritation at the effort to save his marriage. "Yes?"

"Routine," Sloan said. "I want everything to be calm and routine. No blow-ups. No worrying if I've done something that looks suspicious." He looked up at Dante, glaring. "She's holding a grudge."

As if it had been suspended in a spider web, Dante's heart fell, and the mass rattled his ribs and lay there. "It has been less than two weeks since you were caught having sex with another woman, and you want everything to be normal?" Air rushed into Dante like the anger of God. "You think that people are like puppets dangling before you, but we're not." Dante pointed to Bev, whose brown eyes were shocked wide. "She's not."

"Dante," Bev said. "Please stop."

"This is what is wrong!" Dante wanted *God* to hear this. *If* there was a God, *since* there was an absence of evidence that there was no God, He should know about the miscreants He'd created. "It is obsession with self. You don't believe in humanity. People are objects to you, Sloan," like children were objects to that damned, damned pedophile.

Sloan turned to Bev. "This isn't counseling. He's just a priest threatening damnation." He spun and flicked his finger at Dante. "You priests make up rules and then threaten everyone else with some stupid punishment that even you don't believe in. You have your own problems, asshole." He stalked out, leaving Dante ashamed at his temper and exhausted, alone with Bev.

Bev rubbed a tear off her cheek. "It took so much to get him to come to counseling."

"I thought he would see that he was hurting people. But he did not," Dante said. At confession the next morning, Dante drew a few prayers in penance for his outburst and another sad grimace from Samual.

Her eyes dropped tears. She rubbed them off her cheeks. "Now what?"

"It's up to you." He scratched his scalp and finger-combed his hair back. Dante wished he were back in his lab discussing brains and cells and proteins and not screwing up people's lives. "There are the children to consider."

"I don't know how this happened. A couple of weeks ago everything was fine."

Dante pushed himself up, walked past the neat bookshelves, sat in Conroy's still-warm chair and held Bev's cool fingers. "One thing leads to another. It is a succession, a chain reaction. I think that about Nicolai, too."

Bev scrubbed at her reddened cheeks with her other hand.

He petted her hand. Swollen veins sneaked under the surface of her skin like thick threads in raw ivory silk. "For pedophiles, first there is the pornography." Dante turned to Bev, who was leaning forward, staring down. "He told the Dominicans he was doing *research* on pedophile priests, that he wanted to testify before the American bishops."

"So Father Nicolai wasn't a pedophile!" Her hand covered her chest, her cleavage, her heart, which Dante broke anew.

"That's what they all *say*. They *all* say that it was research. Every last one of them tries to convince you that the boxes and crates and metric tons and terabytes of raped children are *research*. It's a cliché." Dante's hands fell in his lap, useless. "If he had been researching pedophiles, he would have known what a ragged old excuse that is."

Bev looked down, saddened again. Damn, he hated himself for bruising this sweet woman. The blue carpet in the library still smelled musty though he'd vacuumed it. His imagination picked up whiffs of spunk and turd. Beside his shoe, the carpeting was torn in a right angle, a handhold. He should rip it all up.

"Are you sure?" she asked.

"Yes." Dante couldn't even lift their linked hands, so he rubbed the back of her hand with his thumb. "It's incremental. First the pictures, then small transgressions which could be explained away as play or wrestling or an accident and, as they improve their lies and their manipulations, large transgressions."

"You make it sound so clinical."

"It's not. Each step is a betrayal and destroys people."

Bev rustled, shifting in her chair, and she turned her hand over so they held hands palm to palm. Her hair was loose. Usually, her dark gold hair was knotted or twisted somehow, but today it hung across her shoulders, and she looked so young, like the co-ed she had been when Conroy had met her. "So what should I do about Conroy?"

Dante was the Church, in his medieval mourning clothes and ringless fingers and blood rushing at the sight of the light on the gold in her hair, and he knew that she would take his slightest cue as the Word and that he was condemning her to living with an adulterer but he said, "The girls," and over their joined hands she watched him with solemn brown eyes.

"Well, then." Bev's fingers slid away and she stood, brushing wrinkles out of her skirt, "I need to think about it. Instead of counseling on Monday, do you want to come for supper?"

If he went to her house for supper, there would be the opportunity for another incremental movement toward each other, but Dante could handle women friends. Eventually they became sisterly and intensely platonic. He could guide women away from the romantic path because, before he took Holy Orders and had done his penance for betraying them all, he had steered crowds of them down that path to its final, dismaying, nebulous conclusion.

"Supper sounds nice," he said.

CONROY POUNDED ON LEILA'S DOOR, and she yanked it open and pulled him in. She held his biceps in her strong grip and whispered, "What are you doing here?"

"Nothing." Conroy grabbed her arms, crinkling her crisp, white shirt, and kissed her.

"It's never nothing." The covered buttons on her shirt slipped in his fingers, but he pushed each one through its buttonhole. She looked down, watching him.

He swept the shirt off her shoulders and reached for her fly. The rose perfume on her skin left a bitter residue on her belly, but he licked it as he worked at the yet-more buttons of her fly. The door lock clicked behind her, and then her young, bronze hands slid through his whitening hair.

He was not selfish. He licked lower.

BEV SAID, "One more thing," and fidgeted with her purse. She set it on the chair behind her because she had to do this even though she didn't want to. "Is Father Sam around?"

"He is at St. Jude's, celebrating Mass. Then he goes to St. Theresa's."

She swallowed even though her mouth was dry. "I need to confess."

"You've committed mortal sins since last week?" His head tipped, amused.

She'd grown up confessing to a priest. It was habit. It was comforting. She picked up her purse and stepped toward the heavy library door. "I could wait for Father Sam."

"Bev, I'm still a priest."

"All right."

He rummaged in his desk and pulled a slim, purple stole from the drawer like a recalcitrant purple snake from its den. Holding the cloth in his open palms, he closed his eyes, muttered, kissed the center, and looped it around his neck.

Confessing to Dante was going to make everything worse, but one must confess before taking communion. She held her breath, hoping for strength, but none came.

LEILA BURIED HER FINGERS in his hair and held on, gasping, then released Conroy. He sat sideways on the floor while she held the doorknob and panted. She asked, "What is going on?"

"Nothing." Conroy lurched to his feet and smoothed his hair. He slid his hands in his pockets and slouched. "Sometimes I'm unpredictable."

Unlikely. Something weird was going on with Conroy. He didn't go for cunnilingus. "Do you want a drink? I think there's still coffee."

"Got any of that vodka left?"

"Yeah." She tugged her jeans up over her hips and buttoned them on the way to the kitchen. Meth lay in his basket in the living room, asleep.

She poured one shot of vodka into the screwdriver and knife-stirred it. Conroy's odd behavior was unpredictable, and she didn't want him to be unpredictable and drunk.

He was sitting on the couch when she handed him the drink.

He sipped and seemed twitchy, like a dog with an itch. "Thanks."

He scratched his neck, put the glass down, and jiggled his knee.

Leila slid a silver coaster under his glass. That ornate wood coffee table had survived both world wars and both French revolutions before her father had imported it, and Conroy's drink wasn't important enough to sweat a ring onto it. She sat on the other end of the couch, posture open, the television remote behind her. Maybe he just needed a friend, which was not part of their deal but what the hell.

Conroy downed a third of the drink, ruffled the book by the Dalai Lama lying on the end table beside him, scratched a nubble on the couch cushion's upholstery, and picked up the screwdriver again. He was fidgeting in circles. He asked, "Why do women get married?"

Was he pimping her? "I'm not aware of any research on the matter."

"I'm not talking about research. You have it all figured out, that women are promiscuous like gay men. So why do women get married?"

Oh, that conversation, when she had been drunk, like two weeks ago. Mulling that dialogue around in his head for two weeks could explain why he was so weird. "Pressure from a predominantly patriarchal society."

"Don't give me that crap about the patriarchal repression."

"Women aren't repressed. Men think women are repressed."

"There's no difference."

"Sure there is. Subterfuge."

He picked a nub off her couch. "So why do women get married?"

She considered this miserable, post-middle-aged man. "So they can screw around."

He grimaced and flapped his head as if he'd been slapped. "Not if they're married." ·

He was going to birddog the subject until she expounded. Her theories had driven him insane. "Women do best reproductively if, first, they give birth to the children with the best genes and, second, if they have a spouse to help raise them. She gets the best genes from having sex with the best males, however you define 'best.' Frequent sex with the spouse suggests that the children are his, so he stays around. So marriage works best for women if the women are promiscuous but the men don't know it, and so women like sex, all sex, as much as they can get. Most men do best reproductively if they have sex with one fertile woman a lot and no other men have sex with her. So marriage works best for men if women are monogamous. So men tell women to be monogamous, and women pretend to be."

Conroy snorted and stared into his glass as if there were something other than opaque orange liquid in there. "But that's crazy."

"A study done a few years ago found that one out of every three children born within marriage was not related to the husband."

"One out of three? That's got to be wrong."

" 'There are lies; there are damned lies; and there are statistics.' "

Conroy shook his head. "You think it all boils down to sociobiology."

"Here's the thing, Conroy. It's like evolution. Evolution only talks about changes at the population level: gene frequencies and gene flow. Evolutionary theory doesn't apply to individuals: not individual people or ibexes or flies or viruses. The paradigm doesn't apply to me personally, except maybe that populations of people like me who opt out of societal norms tend to leave fewer children, so this trait is selected against, but it says nothing about *me*. That some women bear cuckold children says nothing about your children."

He blinked and gasped and sucked down the last of the screwdriver.

He hadn't thought of that. She wasn't helping shit and should shut up.

"Let me get you another drink." In the kitchen, she poured him straight orange juice and brought it back to him.

He said, "But that's wrong because men want sex. Men want all the sex they can get, any time they can get it." He sat back and crossed his legs, his usual posture at his desk when he was debating hypotheses. "According to you, men should be monogamous, so why am I here?"

"Well, sex feels good."

Conroy gulped his juice. "This is really weak."

"You can't taste vodka."

"There's got to be more to sex than just feeling good."

"The salmon exception."

"Yeah, the rock star salmon." Conroy sounded jealous of the fish.

"Rather than the efficient one. And, you know, it's adaptive to have sex whenever you can. People and monkeys who like sex leave more progeny who also like sex."

He drank half the glass and thumbed away a juice bead on the corner of his mouth. "But isn't that selfish?"

Leila settled on the sofa opposite him. "That depends on what you mean, Conroy. *Selfish* is a societal norm. It has nothing to do with biology. It's a construct."

"Constructed by society." Conroy nodded. "And the priests. So the Church represses people again." Conroy stared into his juice. "The Church has always repressed people, science, sex and men's natural instincts."

"God, Conroy, you sound like me. You better be careful. I'm nuts."

"So if the Church is repressing us, then it's wrong." He wandered out to the kitchen.

Leila followed him. Her dog rumbled, snoring. "Yeah, the Church is a sick corporate culture that produces twisted, deranged priests for the masses' consumption because the masses like to be repressed." In the kitchen, Conroy dumped several shots' worth of vodka into his juice. Leila said, "Hey, man, go easy on that."

Conroy stirred the drink with the knife. "If the Church is repressing us, then it doesn't matter." He drank a gulp.

She asked, "What happened, Conroy?"

"Nothing." He chugged the drink. Conroy set down his glass and picked up the goose-necked vodka bottle.

"Conroy, I don't think that's a good idea."

He swigged straight vodka.

Leila went over and rubbed up against him, located his car keys, and picked his pocket while he stared into space. She slid his keys behind a burgeoning arrowhead plant on her windowsill. Just because he was being a jerk and selling the Porsche to Yuri didn't mean she was going to let him drive with that much vodka in him. "Conroy, you can't get wasted here."

"Why not? There is no God. There's no reason not to."

"Nihilism is useless. Give me the bottle."

"I like to get drunk. There's no reason not to. The Church represses people, makes them feel *selfish* for doing what's natural." He grabbed her ass and slammed her pelvis against his. "And women. There's no reason not to grab as much pussy as I want."

"That's flattering." She wasn't afraid of him. If he got too rough, she could lock up his joints and force-march him out the door. The ultimate back-up was in her nightstand drawer, not that she anticipated any need for a gun with flimsy, skinny Conroy.

He said, "That's why you grab as much dick as you want. Because you've opted out." He held her jeans against his dick bulging his pants, and drank from the bottle again, a long drink, and bubbles flitted in the clear liquor.

"Yes, Conroy." His arms were stronger than she had guessed. She squirmed.

"You've got it all figured out, the casual fucking, the whole thing." He slammed the half-empty bottle down and lifted her by her ass onto the counter. His hands grabbed her bones and flesh, clenching roughly.

Rough could be fun. When she got rough, he cringed a little, as if someone were watching and judging. Drunk, he might fuck like a big, silverback gorilla.

He bit her neck and left a mark. Pain sparkled in her body.

BEV, BEREFT OF DIVINE STRENGTH, implored the Holy Spirit to enlighten her mind that she may know the sin she ought to confess, but it was obvious to her already.

Dante said, "In the name of the Father, and of the Son, and of the Holy Spirit, Amen."

And she had to say it. Maybe he wouldn't understand. "Father, I have committed adultery in my heart."

Dante blinked, and those long, lush, black lashes swept down to his cheekbones. "Two Hail Mary's and make a good act of contrition."

"Oh, my God, I am heartily sorry for my sins." She was sorry that her mind had strayed and was really sorry that she had confessed to Dante, who sat with closed eyes and no hint of a smile, like a Roman statue of Apollo at rest. "And avoid the near occasions of sin, Amen."

He gave her absolution without glancing at her and said, "Amen."

She gathered up her purse and coat. "Are you still coming for supper Monday?"

He removed the violet stole from his shoulders, kissed the embroidered cross in its center with his soft lips, and smiled at her. "I'll bring wine."

AFTER CONROY FUCKED LEILA on the counter, slamming his wrapped dick into her until she gasped, he lifted her and fucked her against the wall (a picture of an eggplant jumped off its nail and dropped to the floor) and finally on the linoleum floor.

Afterward, she laughed. "God, Conroy, what's gotten into you?"

"Nothing." And he felt the nothing, around and within him in that vacuum that gobbled up everything. The nothingness hungered, so he fed it more vodka.

"Conroy," she gently took the bottle away from him. "You have to go home. You can't stay out all night."

"Why not?" Her kitchen spun as if there were hidden gyros under the tiles as well as rubbers in the kitchen drawers. He braced himself against the refrigerator and stared at the magnets: an Eiffel Tower, several universities, a geometric tile, glittery things. They moved with his eyes like shining, cometary corneal scars. "Why the hell not? Nothing matters."

There was more liquor on the top of her fridge. Conroy stepped back and perused the selection: Macallen, Stoli, Woodchuck, Jack. He reached for the Jack.

"Hey, Conroy," Leila said. "Let's watch some porn."

He held the Jack Daniel's, stared into its deep mahogany silence. "You have porn?"

"Lesbian porn. *The Divine Secrets of the Ta-Ta Sisterhood.*"

He jiggled a starry magnet on her white fridge. "And I've been watching golf over here?"

The floor of her apartment lurched as if it was drunk, and he stumbled over to the couch.

Lesbians filled the television screen, pretty lesbians licking each other, and then they spun around him, flying and licking lightly furred, hovering cunts.

DANTE HELD THE RINGING PHONE to his ear and sat at the rectory desk, a small, shoddy affair of dark wood frayed on the edges with a chair so hard and easily tipped that it mortified the flesh. Dante was spoiled by the lush booty of history in the Vatican. Leila answered. He said, "Hello, Ms. Faris. This is Father Dante Petrocchi-Bianchi."

"Um," her voice was raspy. "This isn't a good time."

Dante straightened his black sleeves. "I'd like to invite you to Mass tomorrow."

"Thanks." Women's voices leaked through the phone line. She must have company.

"Perhaps we could talk after the noon Mass, about what we were discussing before Joe and Malcolm began talking about the sports. Philosophy. Theology."

"I'm really busy right now. Bye." The phone line went dead.

Dante hung up the phone and leaned back in the chair. The chair dipped back. Free-fall jerked him before the chair stabilized, and he stared at the ceiling of the rectory, his legs and arms extended, balancing so the chair wouldn't dump him. His gold crucifix bumped his cassock and his chest, then slithered aside and hung from his neck, pulling.

On the ceiling, one white-painted wooden board had no nails.

MOTION, LIKE SPINNING, only straight ahead. Cool air chilled Conroy's nose.

Leila was talking. "You hang in there, Conroy. Yuri will try to talk you down to two thousand if the car smells like puke."

Conroy turned his head to see who she was talking to but he had forgotten what she had said. Outside, light streaked and cars flew by as if they were broomsticks with women arching on them. He tried to talk, but the world spun and he spun the other way, fighting.

"Sit back!" His chest caved in, struck.

The world rushed by, streaks of cerulean and cinnamon, amber and chartreuse, and howls and scratches and twitters, and rage and remorse and screaming black. The dashboard undulated and spots glimmered on it, reflections in a hematite mirror of the insanity outside.

The images meant something.

As opposed to him, who signified nothing.

KNOCKING BATTERED the front door. Bev trotted to it and peeked out the window. Conroy's black Porsche was parked on the street. Red sunset reflected in its rear window.

She opened the door. A girl wearing jeans and a too-small white shirt under an open gray coat stood outside, staring down the block. The intermittent February breeze whipped her black hair and obscured her face. Chill air leaked into the house, carrying a faint odor of stale cigarettes.

"Mrs. Sloan, um," the girl said in a husky voice and looked back at the car. She clenched Conroy's keys in her small fist. "I'm Leila Faris. I'm in Conroy's lab."

That's where Bev knew this Leila from. The Sloans threw a Christmas party every year. Leila had been to the house two months ago for the party. "Are you driving Conroy's car?"

The girl tapped a cigarette pack, hesitated, and slid it back in her coat pocket. "I found him in his office. I think he's drunk."

In the car, a man's weedy form slumped in the front seat. "Oh, dear Lord." Bev ran out.

He was curled over in the front seat, his white head touching the dash like an accident victim trapped inside a crushed car. Bev yanked the door and touched the strong pulse in his neck. His chest rose coordinately with a raspy snort. He reeked like a bedsore-ridden corpse. His arm was sloppy in her grip. His torso shifted but he was stuck.

Leila, standing beside her, said, "Hold on, hold on," and leaned across his lap. "I put the seat belt on him."

"Did anyone see?" Bev leaned on the door in the cold air.

Leila ran to the driver's seat. "I don't think so. Weekend evening."

Surely a guardian angel had sent Leila to find Conroy and bring him home safely. Bev leaned down and looked through the car at Leila climbing over the driver's seat towards Conroy. "It was so nice, so nice of you to bring him home."

"It's nothing," Leila muttered. "Grab his arm, and I'll push from here."

Bev grabbed his arm and Conroy stretched like putty. He rocked forward from Leila's shove, and Bev lifted with her legs and dragged him halfway out.

He mumbled, "Damn," and dropped to his knees on the asphalt.

Leila ran around the car, lifted him from the other side, and roped his arm around her neck. Conroy's white-haired head flopped, fishlike, and he cursed again.

Conroy's body puppet-jiggled as Leila lifted from her side. She said, "Hey! Dr. S.! Walk!" and Conroy gathered his mantis-long legs under him. His weight, yoked on Bev's neck, lightened marginally but his lanky body sagged between them.

"Walk!" Leila ordered.

CHRISTINE PEEKED AROUND the edge of the bedroom door and watched her sick father curl up his colossal legs. Mom pulled up the covers but didn't kiss him.

The skinny girl touched Dad more gently than Mom did.

Christine sneaked downstairs to tell Dinah that they had to play quietly because Dad was sick. Christine kept Dinah quiet, even watching babyish cartoons over and over again.

BEV PUSHED CONROY'S SHOULDERS sideways and Leila, from the other side of the bed, pushed pillows behind him, like a foam wedge for propping infants. The girl found a trash can and set it on the ground near his head.

"If you want to be nice, you could pour some water down him," Leila said over the bed and Conroy's inert body. Leila pulled her cell phone from a belt clip, thumbed a button, and held it up to her ear. "Malcolm? You almost here?" She listened. "Yeah, he's fine. See you in a minute." She hung up. "I'll wait outside. I told him Dr. S. had the stomach flu. You should tell him that, if anyone asks on Monday, he ate some undercooked chicken or sushi or something."

This girl was an angel. Bev laid her hand over her pounding heart. Dragging Conroy upstairs had been an exertion. "I appreciate how discreet you were."

Conroy mumbled from the bed. His legs twitched but were tangled.

Bev lifted each of his legs and straightened it, unbraiding. "I called his office this afternoon, but he didn't answer."

Leila shrugged. "He's so drunk that you could have blown a foghorn next to him and he wouldn't have answered it."

THE NEXT MORNING, Conroy was a hangover-cursed, craggy, sea-pounded cliff. Barely, with the thinnest fingertip grip, buttered toast clung to the inside of his belly. A hammer pounded steel clips into his skull. Mountaineers swung from every hair, yanking. A cold storm salt-stung his eyes and nose. Slipped stones rattled in his blood. Stiff, dead tundra inhabited his tongue.

Beverly towered above him, an unpitying tsunami. "I'll take the girls to church," she said, "but the deal is that you attend Mass every Sunday, and just because you drank yourself stupid doesn't mean you get out of it." She set both the alarm clocks. "And take a shower. You stink."

She whirled like a water spout, a tornado drunk on sea water, and left him lying in bed, staring through his fingers as she walked away. A glass of water and a bottle of generic acetaminophen stood on the bedside table.

He had never been so unsympathetic after he'd scraped her off the floor and poured her into bed. He'd even prescribed a little helper when she'd needed to dry out before their wedding. Without that, she would have staggered down the aisle and slurped the communion wine to get her fix at their wedding Mass.

Then she would have stormed and raged like a snapping shark out of water.

DANTE HELD ALOFT the round communion wafer and prayed for the Holy Spirit to transform it, to rearrange the proteins from cracker's wheat gluten into divine flesh.

As a child in Roma, sitting between his mother and sisters at Mass, he'd conjured a heresy. He wasn't sure which entity of the Trinity but at least one of them, Dante figured, had to be a loaf of bread since the host was literally God. The uproar at home when he'd vouchsafed his epiphany—his mother begging forgiveness from the crucifix on the wall, his father's whipping—had locked such musings inside him.

He still liked the idea of the Holy Spirit as a bread loaf, an incarnation of the loaves and fishes distributed by Christ, so one could eat a toasted slice of God.

Dante broke the wafer above his chalice and mingled the bread and wine. The chalice was mostly silver, but the gold rim was his grandmothers' wedding rings, melted down. The gems that lined up three rows just below the rim were gifts from family. His mother had donated the diamond from her wedding ring, which is traditional in Southern Italy, where she was from. He turned the chalice so that his right thumb rested on that overly large diamond, to remember her as he sipped.

To Dante's left, Sloan sat with his daughters, holding his head.

On the other side of the aisle, Leila Faris sat with her eyes cast down.

THE CONGREGATION milled into the aisles for communion. The theatricality of the Mass inspired them to partake of the ritual as it has been and ever will be. Their souls walked the church, waiting to ingest the body and blood of God. They were immortal in those minutes, feeling the Almighty around them and soon, inside.

BEV TOOK COMMUNION for the last time in her life at the 6:15 Mass. She'd hurriedly swallowed the papery wafer to make way for Mary behind her. A floury bit stuck in her throat and she growled to clear it. The host shouldn't stick. It should slide down and assimilate seamlessly, melding her with God.

Now, at the 2:30 Mass, Bev glanced down from the choir loft.

Conroy's white head leaned on his arm as he waited for the communion lines to shorten. At least he'd fulfilled that bargain. She was willing to accept it as a sign of better things to come.

The choir muttered behind her, and she flipped the hymnal to the next pink sticky note.

In the choir loft, the furnace forced scalding air around her. If she had known that this was her last communion, she would have played more carefully. At the end of the *Ave Maria*, she hit a sad, Russian E minor instead of an E seventh, which would have rung more gloriously, but she held the chord, feeling it in her soul.

THE COMMUNION LINE shuffled toward Father Dante as he presented the fragile host and proclaimed it the Body of Christ. Eight women and two men lusted in their hearts for the body of Father Dante, but the music welled in their hearts and lifted them, burnishing them for better things, and then a chord clanged and saddened them, a note of their own deaths in the music. The line shuffled forward.

Richard the altar boy held the paten and stood straight in his miniature surplice. He kept waiting for Father Dante to notice him. So far, Father had called all the other boys in to talk. Richard wouldn't rat out Father Nicolai, though. If he did, Father Nicolai would excommunicate Richard and his father and his mother and his little sister Anne, and even if Richard was going to Hell, he could save them. He would save them, no matter what.

CONROY SHOULD JOIN the communion line. His desiccated tongue stuck to his arid molars, and prying it loose left membrane on his enamel. His vodka-seared mouth was so dry that his tongue might suck the trace of moisture in the gluey host and reduce it to dust. That might be heresy, too. Every goddamn thing was heresy.

The girls squirmed in the pew beside him, not quite misbehaving, edging towards infraction. They were whispering, trying to one-up each other in a petty contest.

The goal of the game was moral superiority. Christine had, she said, sat entirely still and not moved the entire first part of the Mass. Dinah was mortifying herself by breathing only when absolutely necessary, forgoing even oxygen.

They had both squirmed incorrigibly the whole time, so they were manufacturing virtues.

Perhaps this was how it started, little women deceiving themselves about their own honesty. Perhaps this was the training for how they would later gather superior genes and yet pen a submissive husband.

LEILA SHRANK in the ass-torturing pew and watched Conroy shuffle in the communion chain gang. She'd thought he would attend the noon one, damn it. His face had a hepatitis-virus pallor, and his walk was weak and slow, as if his blood wasn't carrying enough oxygen.

She'd have to leave quickly after the Mass and hope he hadn't seen her. He'd been pissed last week and, even though he had no right to any opinion about her Mass attendance or her talking to his priests, a shock might kill him in his hungover state.

Chapter Nine

After Mass, Dante waited outside for Leila Faris. The sun filled the February afternoon with brightness but a fog chill hung in the air. His breath gathered in front of him, obscuring his view, and he exhaled out the corner of his mouth to avoid frosting people.

Leila hurried out the door, squeezing past people waiting to greet the celebrants, and skipped down the stone steps.

"Leila!" Dante lifted his white, flowing alb to hurry after her. She turned and glanced back toward the church, then saw him stupidly loping after her in his ecclesiastical dress.

She waited for him to catch up, drawing a line in the parking lot gravel with the toe of her boot. Under her open gray coat, she wore a black skirt cut a whisper short of respectability and current fashion above her long calves and heeled shoes. She said, "I have to run."

Dante took her cold hand in his, ostensibly a handshake. "We could talk in my library."

"Can't right now." She glanced at the hand that was holding hers for too long, and her lower lip dropped. Wind bit through his white robes and pulled them as if his clothes whipped off his body and she could see everything, all the intentions he'd hidden from himself. His impression that she was lost and searching would damn him.

From the church, a frozen dust devil swooped toward them and resolved into a beige-clothed Conroy Sloan. Sloan grabbed Leila's upper left arm with a proprietary grip. "What the hell are you doing here *again*?"

Dante stepped toward Sloan to defend the girl but as he released Leila's hand, she grabbed her own captured arm, wrenched it away from Sloan, reversed the grip and twisted. Sloan gasped and staggered as her grip rotated his arm in his shoulder socket. His knees sagged.

Leila's eyes were black with anger. "I warned you about that shit."

Sloan crouched farther. He inhaled grunts, enraged, though Leila had wrenched his arm around so that his palm unnaturally faced the back of his own head.

One of them needed his help, but Dante wasn't sure which one. That Sloan was having an affair with her seemed obvious from his assertion of ownership and from the familiarity of their fight.

Leila tossed Sloan's hand away and stepped backward. She nodded at Dante. "Some other time, Monsignor." She strode through the parking lot to her car.

Dante rubbed his cold-stung eyes. "Would you care to explain that, Dr. Sloan?" Sloan was not going to false-confess his way out of this.

"She's angry because I broke it off." He rubbed his shoulder and staggered to his feet. "She's stalking me."

Dante doubted that Leila was the one who was stalking. Sloan was having an affair with her, instead of, or in addition to, the Peggy person. He should tell Bev about Leila.

But what did he know, really? Sloan had grabbed Leila's arm. Sloan said that she'd been stalking him since he broke it off with her. At supper with Bev, he would have to say something or be silent, but either option must be a considered one, not an accident.

Dante turned, braved the stiff wind, and walked back to the crowded church steps, leaving Sloan gasping for breath and holding his elbow.

CONROY SAT AT THE HOOD, careful not to press his forehead on the protective glass barrier and leave expanding-forehead oil marks, and pipetted sonicated mouse brain soup onto silver dollar–sized Petri dishes filmed with cells. His lab notebook lay open beside him, and he'd scribbled notes about sacrificing the mice and the state of their brains when he'd scooped them out and sonicated the matter in cell media. All the infected mice were dead now, and he could finish these few experiments, get his grant, and be crowned the new Dean of the Medical College.

After Mass, his hangover had receded like a storm tide, revealing debris scattered in his head and his neurons short-circuited by salt. An I.V. pouch of Ringer's and a few snorts of oxygen cleared that up, freeing him to contemplate Bev's response if that priest tattled.

That grant could use some more work before he went home. A lot of work. Hours.

Conroy brushed his silvery hair off his forehead with one latex-gloved hand. His fingers felt condomed. He idled, pipetting frothy pink inoculum through the glass pipette, mixing.

Outside, the lab door clanked.

Fear killed him all the way to rigor mortis and, scared stiff, he watched the door to the main lab. He heard light footsteps. He hoped it was Leila. Anyone but Leila was a disaster. But he wasn't ready for Leila, either.

Leila walked in. She glistened with snowflakes and sweat. "Christ," she said and turned.

His punching heart vibrated a frantic harmonic and one of its moorings creaked. His face stung, flushed and sweating. "Leila, wait!"

She stopped, turned, and leaned on the doorway. Her slim arms and legs wrapped her body like spiraling concertina wire. "What?"

His pipette dripped virus-laden inoculum into the dish. "I'm sorry."

Her black eyes narrowed, and she looked pissed. "You're an idiot."

"Okay." He finished inoculating that well, disposed of the pipette, and sat with his hands in his lap looking, he hoped, innocuous and contrite.

Her dark eyes were large with calm anger. She hadn't blinked yet, literally, no flicker of humanity or normal reflex. "Don't ever, ever grab me like you did, ever again."

"I won't," Conroy promised. There was the slightest tickle in his head, a déjà vu, that this power play was another form of her kink. His eyes felt dry for her lack of blinking.

"If you ever grab me again, I will fucking break your neck. I don't care if we're in the middle of Grand Central Station. I don't care if your wife is standing next to you."

"I understand."

This was all a corollary of her rules for casual fucking: Act as if nothing was going on, either in the commission or the omission of acts. "All right."

Leila sighed, looked away, and finally blinked. "What the hell is going on, Conroy?"

In the hood, he selected another fragile glass pipette from the sterile paper bag and began inoculating the rest of the cells. "It's a long story."

"You've been here late every night. You got shit-faced at my apartment yesterday. If I hadn't dragged you home, you would've stayed out all night. That's not normal." She flipped the switches of the other tissue culture hood, and the updraft whooshed and the neon light whined.

The chill air of the tissue culture room seeped through his damp shirt and stroked his back. "There's a lot going on right now."

Leila removed dishes from the incubator and slid them onto the stage of the microscope. She focused and said, "Secret experiments again?"

"Just confirming Yuri's results."

"Bullshit." She turned on the digital camera atop the microscope. The computer was behind her, and she stretched across the narrow room, wiggled the computer mouse to wake it, and tapped the space bar. The picture on the monitor froze. Neurons splayed their splatted cell bodies and long axon spikes. Sick, spindly neurons. Leila whipped the scope over the dish—the landscape blurred on the monitor screen like a roller coaster video—and she clicked pics.

"Malcolm tried to pimp me for information yesterday after I told him you had the stomach flu." (*click.*) "Butch from Liddy Lab had very specific questions from her boss about your NIH trips." (*click.*) "People are talking." (*click.*) "You need to be careful."

Leila could keep a secret. Conroy was surprised that, since their affair began seven months ago (*not an affair but casual fucking*), there hadn't been a tinge of scandal. One of the reasons he'd allowed himself to be seduced was that she wouldn't talk about any of her former men. Leila kept secrets like she kept her dogs, she said: until they were very, very old, and then they drifted away and she buried them someplace beautiful.

He leaned on the purring incubator. "My wife and I have been going to marital counseling."

Leila's head whipped around and she stared at him, angry. "Does she think you're screwing around?"

"Yes, but she thinks it's someone out of town, at NIH study group."

The angry tension in her face softened. "That's why Dr. Liddy was warning me. Do you have someone else?"

Leila approved! His stock rose and his dick got heavy with filling blood. Conroy looked down in mock chagrin and real dismay. "Well, yes." Conroy batted the air, trying to knock the foolishness away. "The woman left some underwear in my suitcase and Beverly found them."

Leila's jaw dropped. She sat in one of the rolling chairs and leaned forward, hands clasped in front of her, the posture of a person conducting an intervention. "Conroy, that woman is out to break up your marriage."

"No, it was just an accident." He waved his hand, cleaning the air as if wiping her words off a blackboard.

Her voice dropped lower, more serious. "You believed *that*."

Conroy pressed his palms against the incubator behind him.

"Let me guess," Leila said, "she wants you to spend more time with her. She does domestic things, like cooking, and she irons your shirt while you shower after sex."

Conroy studied his black loafers and the asbestos-inundated, faux-marble tiles.

Leila pressed her fingers to her temples. "And she wants you to stay over."

Conroy sighed. So he'd been seeing a sweet woman, someone unlike Leila with all her rules and her limits and her power plays. "Well, yes."

"Conroy!" Leila's voice was imperative, strident. "She's auditioning to be your wife."

"No, she's not like that."

"She's exactly like that. Women lie. They're all whores." Leila cradled her skull as if Conroy's hangover remnants had latched onto her. "I just hope she wasn't ovulating that week."

He looked up, startled. "Peggy wouldn't do that."

Leila crossed her legs and studied her boots. "She tried to sabotage your marriage."

"It's not like that. She's not like that."

Leila looked up sharply. "Conroy, tell me you've broken it off with her."

"She said the panties were an accident."

"You idiot. You *play* with *players*. Are you going to leave Beverly for this Peggy chick?"

"No." Conroy's heart shrank at that terrible thought.

"Then get rid of Peggy and go back to your wife." She crossed her arms and glared at him with calm, wide, black eyes. "We're through."

Damn it, first Peggy, then his wife, now this. "Oh, come on. That's not what I meant."

"Your life is too complicated. The Jesuits are after you, and that Jesuit saw you grab me. Your wife is suspicious and hurt. We're through."

"Don't threaten me." He turned and slammed his open hand into the flat, metal door of the incubator. He looked back, but Leila's expression was still angry and cold.

"It's not a threat, Conroy. It's the best thing. Go home to your wife. Get rid of the chick who's trying to break up your marriage." She shouldered him aside, put her cells back in the incubator, and slammed the door on her way out.

Damn it, damn it. Everything was slipping away. Everything was apoptosing and necrosing and decaying. He punched the steel incubator. It hurt and felt good so he reared back and threw his weight behind it and punched the gray steel hard. His knuckles crackled.

Leila was the only one who didn't want something from him. She was the only one he could trust. He shook his bruised fist.

Beverly and Peggy and all of them were suffocating him. He needed to escape. He needed somewhere to escape *to*.

All the anxiety that fibrillated in his chest, all the adrenaline that spurred him and sapped his reserves, it was all from staying too late in the lab and not sleeping enough and flinching in bed every time Beverly twitched because he was afraid that she had found some other silken whip of evidence to beat him with. He needed a place where he could sleep.

Just a little *pied-à-terre*, a hole to go to ground in, a trench for warfare, a priest-hole where that Jesuit wouldn't find him, where Conroy could think without anyone bitching at him.

MONDAY MORNING, Bev needed coffee. The coffee in the teachers' lounge was stale and reduced, but she drank it.

The door behind her opened. "Bev?" Father Dante asked.

"Yes?"

"You are all right?" he asked. In his Roman-collared black shirt and slacks, sometimes he looked like a Sicilian assassin instead of a priest. She imagined him producing a gun from behind his back and, with strong posture, gunning down Conroy's slut.

Bev pressed her fingers to her temple. Such thoughts, such thoughts. No wonder God and the Virgin Mary still shunned her. *Be with us now and at the hour of our death.* "I'm fine."

MONDAY AFTERNOON in the lab, Conroy dawdled and fretted and finally called Leila into his office. She had been out of the lab all morning, avoiding him. He hadn't looked at her face when he'd called to her from his doorway. Derision might lurk in her sable eyes or the set of her mouth.

Joe and Yuri busied themselves at the bench as Conroy retreated to his office and waited.

She followed him in and nudged the office door closed.

His newspaper was folded to the furnished apartment rentals.

When he looked up, he knew his eyes were too wide, his posture too anticipatory, trembling, as if someone holding his belt prevented him from falling over a precipice.

She smiled gently. "Friends, Conroy?"

He hissed out the breath that had ballooned inside him. "Yeah," he said. Conroy circled an ad that read *2 bdrm, 1.5 ba, furn, townhouse. Short-term, perfect for visiting faculty.*

Leila tapped his desk. "You were busy in the mouse room this weekend. The guys in the mouse facility have been nervous about your mice."

Conroy crossed his legs the other way and glanced at the closed office door. "There's a lot riding on this grant."

"You mean the department chair?"

"Not just that. There might be more. I want it all. I want the department chair, recognition, prizes, maybe the big one, maybe the Nobel Prize." Nobel, *the Nobel*, the big kahuna.

"Conroy, are you on drugs? Seriously, drugs?"

Conroy leaned in and conspired with Leila, whose eyes were shocked open. "I'm in my fifties," he said. "I've got a pretty big lab at a pretty good institution. If I get the chairmanship, I'll have more resources, more people, more contacts. I'm a dark horse, but I've got a shot. I've made good progress at the molecular level but I need the big one, the big, elegant experiment that shows, perfectly, something on the GUT level." GUT: Grand, Unifying Theory. "I need a GUT."

Leila's blink was exaggerated. "I can't believe you're the same person who ripped all the theory and conclusions out of my paper last year."

"God," Conroy clamped a hand over his heart that cartwheeled in his chest. The path to glory echoed: grant, department chair, resources, GUT, Nobel. "It makes my heart flutter."

"Nobel," she whispered, her tongue licking her lip.

Yes, yes. Those three little syllables that trip off the tongue, a touch on the teeth and two plosive presses of the lips with a zinging shiver at the end: No. Bel. Prize.

She smiled. "Are you turning into a rock star salmon?"

He quirked one eyebrow. "Maybe."

She laughed at him and left his office. Conroy watched her ass, an ass he liked to grab and lift while he screwed it.

He bet, he would wager money, he would risk his life, that he would fuck her again next week. He picked up the phone to call the rental agent.

YURI WALKED BY Dr. S.'s office and saw inside through a horizontal rip in the poster covering the arrow-slit window. Leila's dark head nodded.

He hoped Leila hadn't discovered anything brilliant. Dr. S. might give her the Porsche.

"You coming?" Joe paused, holding the door open.

"Sure," Yuri said. "Should we wait for Leila?"

"She visited Danna this morning. Took her a book. Danna said she wants junk food because patient food sucks worse than staff caff. I raided vendo land. Chips. Cookies."

Yuri surveyed the assembled cellophane. "That stuff will kill you."

BEV HAD NOT OVERCOOKED the gnocchi, thank goodness. Dinah had been suspicious of the dumplings until Bev vouchsafed that they were potato. Dinah was a big fan of anything potato.

Father Dante had brought a lovely zinfandel and, when the bottle ran dry halfway through dinner, Bev found a chardonnay in the fridge. The drier chardonnay complemented the robust gnocchi and broiled chicken even better than the light, sweet zin.

Dinah tugged at Father Dante's sleeve. "I have a joke," she said.

Christine rolled her eyes and sighed. "She doesn't tell it right."

"A little boy is bad in school," Dinah said. "And he disses his teachers and he fails his reading and his math."

Christine nodded and frowned.

"And so his mommy makes him two doors."

Christine said, "Tutors. Takes him to tutors."

Dinah shot her a dirty look. "But the little boy still fails his math. She teaches him math at home and he still doesn't do the math right. So his mommy sends him to Catholic school."

Christine nodded.

"And the little boy starts doing better. Especially in math." Dinah looked up at Christine.

Christine prompted, "So his mom asks him why he's doing better."

Dinah nodded. "And he says, 'I knew they were serious about math when I saw that they had nailed that guy to the cross.'"

"*Plus sign*," Christine said. "'I knew they were serious about math when I saw that they had nailed that guy to the plus sign.'"

Bev chuckled, caught herself, and looked at Father Dante. He laughed and she did, too.

After supper, the girls included Father Dante in their cutthroat board game long enough for Bev to tidy up. The French white casseroles were soaking when Bev noticed it was 8:30 and time for little girls to be in bed.

The girls climbed the stairs. Dinah literally dragged her feet on the carpeted steps, leaving scuffs. Christine hopped, a stealthy victory dance.

"My head," Dante sat up on the floor near her feet and pressed his palm to his temple. "I think I drank too much wine."

"Me, too." Bev smiled and laid her head on the back of the couch, enjoying the lightness. Elation spun behind her eyes. She recognized Conroy's absence. "Conroy isn't home." She stood, and the floor tilted but she held her balance. "I should call him."

The cordless phone was across the room, but she hesitated. She didn't know what to say to Conroy. She hadn't said anything to him since she'd bawled him out for being drunk Sunday morning and told him to get his butt to Mass and now she had to talk to him in front of Father Dante. Oh, good Lord. The floor tilted again, and she stepped to counter the shifting ash dunes.

Father Dante stood and held her elbow. An elbow is a friendly place for a man to hold, not the intimate touch of palms, not too near the swell of the breast.

She smiled at Father Dante and he let her go. She dialed Conroy's office.

CONROY FOUND his jingling office phone between stacks of papers under the split-open book *Immunobiology* and lifted the receiver on its third ring. To the phone, he said, "Sloan."

"Conroy? Everything all right?" Beverly asked.

"Yes, yes." She should have figured out by now that he just wouldn't be home for supper. "I'm sorry, Beverly. I should have emailed. Leila and I were editing her paper."

"Leila Faris? Oh, all right," Bev said.

"Yes, it's almost finished." Leila's svelte shadow sashayed by his open office door. "It'll be a few hours. Around eleven. I'm sorry, dearest."

DANTE, HORRIFIED that Bev had said *Leila Faris*, waited until Bev laid the phone in its cradle to ask, "He said something about Leila Faris?"

"Sure." Bev moved the phone farther back on the table. "Do you want a cocktail?"

His silk shirt clung to his back, which had sprouted sweat. "Sure."

Perhaps he could obtain enough information to interpret what it meant when Sloan grabbed Leila's arm and yet accused her of stalking him.

"What do you want?" She opened a cabinet and removed a couple of boxes of dried pasta to reveal a cubby stocked with liquor. "Screwdriver? Sloe gin fizz? Long Island iced tea? Neat?"

"Whatever you're having."

"Long Island iced tea." Bev tipped bottles, splashing several types of alcohol into each of the two glasses and a finishing jolt of Diet Coke, and handed one glass to Dante. The drink looked like tea. It tasted like tea to his wine-numbed tongue.

During medical school, after a spate of exams, he and some of his classmates had toasted each other with a similar drink ("We drink to cope!") and then there was a long white space and flashes of naked female flesh from various angles, like an ill-tuned satellite dish burping pornography, and he woke the next morning with two women twined around him and around each other, and he was ashamed not to feel mortifying disgust at his stupid, carnal self. They had cooked breakfast: omelet and fruit. Their names were a mystery.

Dante said, "I think we need to talk."

Bev blinked twice. "Okay." He followed her into the living room.

He raised his glass and sipped. If he drank much more, he would to have to call a cab to get back to the rectory, that whitewashed house where Father Samual sanctimoniously sat in the living room. Sam would glance at his watch when Dante tumbled in, belatedly snooping on his fellow priests, displaying for Dante's approval that vigilant Samual couldn't—*couldn't*—have deciphered devious Nicolai's intrigues.

Dante drank.

He should leave. He shouldn't pass on unsubstantiated conjectures that might shred Bev's home.

Sloan had admitted to an affair with Leila by saying that he'd broken it off with her. Now he was spending evenings with Leila, not avoiding the near occasion of sin.

Perhaps Sloan's admission was a lie, but in the church's parking lot, their fight looked like a lovers' spat. They were too familiar with each other's body. Dante would never have grabbed one of his grad students around the arm like that.

Dante had written down Leila's address when he'd looked up her phone number Saturday. The card was in his wallet. If he could find her, he could ask Leila if she'd had an affair with Sloan. Maybe they could talk about theology, too, or philosophy.

"I should go." He inched forward on the couch.

Bev stepped back. "You wanted to talk about something."

"I should go."

"All right," she said.

Dante would know better how to counsel Bev after he had talked to Leila. He stood and smoothed the creases from his pants.

Bev was too close to him, and he could smell her lemony perfume and see smile lines near her nose, minor, gentle mars that reminded Dante of the first few creases on the faces of monks who had meditated for decades upon compassion.

He had been doing so well staying away from her. His body wanted to step forward.

Bev had been wronged. Sloan had taken advantage of the softness of her skin and the sweetness of her spirit. Dante couldn't use her, too.

His hand reached forward, seemingly of its own accord. He didn't remember deciding to reach for the back of her neck, to cup her fragile skull.

Her head tilted, falling into his palm, golden and oak hair cobwebbing his hand.

She closed her eyes.

Dante opened his arms and stepped against her, a hug, an innocent hug. Anyone who thought differently had a dirty mind. It was practically research, it was so innocent.

The pressure of her arms around his waist was another step in an incremental, stuttering path, each individual pressure and touch seemingly innocuous. Her breasts warmed his chest, but her pelvis tipped away. He wondered if his own buried experience was gathering her body to him, if she was revenging herself on Sloan, if she was lonely, or if he was a fraud.

His chin rested atop her fresh, honey-brown hair. "I should go."

He untangled his arms from hers.

LEILA HAD NEVER FOUND a drunk Monsignor on her doorstep before. She stopped a few yards away from him in the corridor and asked, "Can I help you?"

Father Dante looked up at her, sideways. He looked younger, crouched and inebriated on the carpet, sipping Diet Coke. His voice lilted with drink, "Are you having the affair with Sloan?"

"No." Whether Conroy's priest wanted to grill or counsel her didn't matter. Before she'd met the priest, his publications suggested he might be interesting: surmisings about the origin of the notion of the Divine in the hippocampus and contrasting the symptoms of garden-variety schizophrenia with mental illness manifesting as possession by exotic species of demons. But Conroy's whole freak show was too much. Leila stirred her purse and found her keys.

"But, he grabbed you, and your reaction." The priest wagged his head.

He was trying to head-shrink her there in the hallway, where the walls were the color and heft of eggshell. Four doors down the hall, a grad student from chemistry was shacked up with a mycologist. The woman next door monitored Leila's comings and goings like she was Homeland Defense and Leila was a half-Egyptian, rootless wanderer. "My neighbors will talk. Let's discuss this inside."

He retracted his legs and steadied himself on his knees. "I just want to know."

She jiggled the key in the locks and pushed the door into the dark apartment. Having a drunk man in her apartment didn't worry her. She had a dog and a gun. She wasn't afraid of goddamned anyone.

"It's not your fault." The priest followed her inside. He reeked of ethanol metabolites: acetones, ketones, and aldehydes. "Sloan has a history of these things."

"It's none of your business." She flipped on lights and twisted switches under beaded lampshades.

The priest stared at her apartment, decked with thick silks, plaster moldings, delicate carved woods, and lush, muted hues. "Like Paris."

"Yeah." Leila set her purse on the Louis Quatorze entryway table. The priest was probably gay, considering the reverence with which he was eyeing the pink-gold plasterwork recovered from Parisian apartments, heavy moss-green drapes pooling on the floors, and rococo-framed paintings by minor artists. She shucked off her coat and tossed it on the coat tree. "My dad was into antiques."

The priest found a coaster, set his soda on the end table, and sat gingerly on her couch.

Meth slunk out of Leila's bedroom, glanced at the priest and found him uninteresting, and greeted Leila with a hand-snuffling.

She asked, "Can I call you a taxi?"

He sipped the soda. "I drove."

Leila slapped the counter of her kitchen pass-through and he jumped. "You're drunk." She walked over to him and held out her hand. "Give me your keys. I'll drive you home or call you a cab." Between the priest and

Conroy, she was the local drunk patrol, ensuring everybody got home.

He hesitated. She had come on too strong, especially considering he was not only an adult but Mediterranean with machismo appropriate for a descendant of Caesar, but surely he wouldn't balk. Surely an iota of maturity came with being a priest, and her own callowness amused her. Her hand was flat open between them, and she rippled her spread fingers, waiting.

"I would appreciate if you would call a taxi," he said.

Her hand fell back to her side. "I'll make sure you get in it." She called a cab company. They said a few minutes. She reported the schedule to him and he thanked her, pensively tracing the thick braid that rimmed the satin upholstery on the couch arm.

"I am embarrassed," he said. "I should not have driven like this."

"No one got hurt."

In spite of his prying into her personal life the way all goddamn priests think they have a right to do, Just-ah Dante was Byronic in coloring and tragic air and inebriation, and his body and his smooth posture cast a confidence, an ease around women that came from having nailed many. Priests shouldn't be like that. Sick chills crawled up her back.

"Just so you know," the priest said, "whatever you say, I will not tell. You could tell me under the confession seal, and I could tell to no one."

God, she hated busybody priests. "It doesn't matter. You'll say whatever you want, anyway."

He held his temple with one hand, quite the tortured Heathcliff.

"You priests make all the rules and get pissed off when people don't follow them, threaten them with made-up curses and punishments. You don't even believe in Hell, do you?"

The priest's eyes widened like speeded-up black roses blooming. "Yes, I believe in Hell."

He walked over to where she stood by the kitchen. His hand darted toward her face and retreated, and she jerked back. Her heart shook and her breath cowered in her chest. "Don't touch me." She stepped toward him, and the aggression in her step drove the priest backward. "Don't you fucking touch me."

Leila answered her ringing phone. "Your taxi is downstairs."

The priest stood and gathered his black coat around him. The white square of his Roman collar peeked out. "I would like to talk to you more."

Prying jerk. "Your cab is waiting."

He stepped into the hall and said, "Let me buy you dinner tomorrow, to talk."

"Goodbye, Monsignor." She closed the door. She watched from her window as the priest got into the cab.

Asshole. Thought because he was a priest that he could ask anything he wanted and pass judgment on her. Fuck him.

TUESDAY MORNING, Conroy sipped his coffee while his girls chattered and Beverly cooked. Only a few more mornings until he could wake up alone.

Bev asked, "Scrambled all right?"

"Yes, thank you." Maybe his cholesterol would go down if he didn't eat Beverly's eggs fried in butter. "I found another empty wine bottle in the recycler last night. Were you drinking?"

"No. Dante had one glass. I didn't have any."

"That priest was over here again?" His cup rattled on the table.

"For supper. Since you're never home."

This was turning into arguing and the girls were right there, but Dinah pushed two lumps of egg around her plate, racing them. Christine stared at her lap, oblivious. He asked, "If the priest only had one glass, why is the bottle empty?"

"I poured the rest down the drain."

"You did?"

"That's the rule. No leftover alcohol in the house."

"All right." Conroy drank the rest of his coffee and went to the lab.

DANTE'S HANGOVER tapped his temples but didn't ricochet inside his skull. He called a cab, ducked into the rectory's Volvo in Leila's parking lot, and drove over to Bev's.

He stood outside the strong door of Bev's house, toying with the brass knocker and trying to decide whether the affair between Leila and Conroy was ongoing or over. The cold February wind lapped his coat and ungloved fingers, and he stuffed his hands in his pockets.

He rang her doorbell, and moments lapsed. Relief played in his chest. He didn't have to do this, he could think more—but Bev answered the door.

"Oh!" Her brown hair was bound into a ponytail, and she wore slacks and a red tee shirt. "Come in out of the cold. Want coffee?"

His temple squeezed, the start of a dark caffeine jones. "Thank you."

Bev giggled. "I needed a little extra coffee this morning, too. How do you take your coffee? Light? Sweet? Irish?"

"With cream or milk," he said. In the kitchen, she poured two cups, and they sat at the kitchen nook with windows facing the tree-enclosed back yard. The trees were stark, frozen wood.

The coffee was weak and bitter. Hazelnut flavoring attempted to compensate but failed. Italian coffee was never so dilute, and Roma was never so cold. Weak coffee and cold air, the New World was a tepid place.

She studied him and laid her hand on the table between them.

He swirled his cup and stared into the beige opacity roiling in blue ceramic. "Bev, I'm sorry. I don't want to say, but I think Sloan was having more than one affair."

"Oh." She retracted her offered hand and stirred her coffee. Her spoon clinked, and scraped, and clinked. "How do you know?"

"I saw them together. I talked to the woman."

She set her spoon on her saucer and sipped. "It's not so shocking the second time."

The coffee cup cooled between his palms, imparting warmth into his chilled hands. He reached out and rested his now-warmed hand on her shoulder, near her neck. It was a priestly gesture, a measure of comfort after bad news.

Bev asked, "What should I do?"

Her shoulder was soft under his fingers: thin shirt, bra strap, softness, resilient muscle, and crisp bone. His words were asinine vibrations in the air. "I can't counsel you to divorce."

Bev sipped her coffee, and sinew and flesh shrugged under her shirt and his hand. "I'm a substitute teacher. I can't take care of my girls alone."

"There is alimony and child support," he said. Bev scooted her chair over so that they looked out the window side by side. He bent his arm so that his hand stayed on her shoulder closest to him and reached no further. He shifted, but retracting his hand was another injustice.

"The courts don't do that anymore. Women should be able to take care of themselves and their children and look foolish if they believed marriage vows. After divorce, the children always sink to the socioeconomic level of the ex-wife, which is always lower than the ex-husband's. Men are rewarded for divorce." She sighed. "The girls would have to go to public school. I know it isn't a tragedy, public school. OLPH feeds into Xavier Prep. Xavier sends ten or twenty girls to Ivy League schools every year, and the next fifty to top Catholic universities and the Sisters. None of the public high schools around here send more than the valedictorian to good schools. I know my girls can overcome challenges, but I thought I could give them a good education."

She laid her head on his shoulder. Her head wasn't heavy, but her weight squeezed the deltoid muscle. He was too aware of her weight and his body. He should back away, but he could stop this at any time and she was frail right now.

She said, "I haven't been alone for thirteen years."

Dante dragged his innocent arm around and held her shoulders. He was only comforting her. He wasn't a slave to his body. He would not break his vow of celibacy. He should be kind, supportive, and compassionate. This woman was in crisis.

She said, "I don't want to uproot the girls."

She turned her head on his shoulder. Dante stared at the red and yellow plastic swing set huddled in the winter grass husks. None of the colors in Leila's apartment had been so uncomplicated. Auburn and pinks burnished the old gold plaster in the living room. The mossy curtains were tinged with sunlight glints and navy blue, deep-water shadows, like being sunk in a pond.

He smoothed her schoolgirl hair. As a psychiatrist and a priest, he should maintain a professional distance from this woman's soft body. Heat drove through her tee shirt and melted his black clothes.

She said, "I don't know what to do."

He couldn't tell her to divorce. He wouldn't counsel her to stay.

Her arm wove around behind him. Outside, a straw-brittle vine clung to a tree skeleton. Her breath whispered on his neck, just above his Roman collar.

A discordant note rang in his mind and clenched his spine. His weak flesh that he had laid before the altar when he had taken Holy Orders, defied him, blooming and heating from that point where her breath touched his bare neck.

"Tell me what to do," she whispered, and her lips touched his neck, a spark jumping.

His voice leaked through his clenched larynx. "You have to decide."

He should leave. Thoughts skimmed: that Bev was storm-tossed in the choppy seas of her breaking marriage, that he had committed not to touch a woman's soft shoulders and hair like this, that his Holy Orders were the dividing line between a wasted era tipping women into his bed and a time when he looked higher and averted his eyes from his own flesh, that staying in her arms that were pulling him closer would cement for her that men were rutting beasts, that he was a beast, that she needed comfort and that pulling away would prove to her that she was undesirable, that he'd waited too long to pull away, that his soul was damned and that he'd never believed in the existence of the soul.

Her breath rasped on his neck and traveled down his veins to his heart, which slammed in his chest and splashed his blood in his arteries against his skin, and he turned to ask her to stop but her lips were on his, sweet with sugar and hazelnut and whiskey.

Her hands moved on his black shirt, and his shirt pulled on the scruff of his neck, and he should stop, he should stop, he should stop.

He stood, knocking over the kitchen chair, and she stood with him, still kissing.

Elemental habits were ingrained in his male body like striations in wood, deep through him, each the accumulation of years. The mortifications during his short time as a priest hadn't permeated his flesh or charred away the marks that years of women had left under his skin. The vestments, the alb, and the cassock had camouflaged the man who liked to taste women, touch them, and herd them into his bedroom.

He lifted her in his arms, that little bit of woman that he wanted to press himself into and pin to a bed, crash into her. Habit and lust ripped through his cloth-thin, priest-black plating.

MEANWHILE, CONROY finished the phone call with the dulcet-voiced apartment agent—he could have the townhouse Saturday and planned to move a few of his things on Monday evening, which was the fifteenth and the day of the department committee meeting—as Leila hurried into his office. She closed the door behind her and braced herself against it. "That priest showed up at my place last night."

Conroy jumped and his knees rapped the underside of his wooden desk drawer. "What?"

"Monsignor Dante Petrocchi-Bianchi, asking all sorts of stupid questions. He asked if I was sleeping with you. Are you sure your wife doesn't know about me?"

"She doesn't know." He should have kept Leila's rules. He shouldn't have screwed any of those other women. One of his eyelids twitched as if it couldn't decide whether to blink.

"Okay," Leila left his office, still preoccupied.

Conroy opened up a new window on his computer and typed, *Dearest Beverly*.

IN THE DEEP DARK of her curtained bedroom, Bev could barely breathe from Dante's weight, though he didn't move, and she closed her eyes as one last crest lifted her and her body clenched his dick. A sunlight sliver poked through the curtain gap and laid a knife of light on the sheets beside her hand.

Her body, ferocious bone and skin around her soul, had liberated her because she understood why her husband screwed around: it was just sex, instinct and friction, not her soul, not her heart. She'd barely touched Dante, her friend, her *priest*, and he'd leapt at her as if she were prey, and that's all that sex was, a movement of biology, a reflex. An orgasm, even a molten-spine, skull-blasting orgasm, wasn't a tremor of the soul.

Dante lifted above her. Air rushed in her lungs. His face still pressed against her shoulder. His breath was shallow, gasping.

"Dante?"

He pushed himself up and rolled away. He curled on the bed, his broad shoulders a night-shrouded mountain with a faint frost of sunlight that sneaked through the thick curtains. He clutched the sheet and gasped.

"Dante?" She rolled over and touched his shoulder. He was wrapped in muscle, but this had been obscured by his black clothes and the flowing cassock he wore. The dark of her bedroom was so black that it seemed they were both inside the priest's black clothes. She stroked his shoulder. He had the body of a young man, a beautiful, healthy, young man with chest and arm muscles of round, firm flesh, and he was uncircumcised. Ribbing on condoms must be to replace that cushiony, frictionous foreskin.

He remained turned away from her.

He must think she was too old. Her body had birthed two children, though she ate well and kept active, she was thirty-seven and in the last throes of fertility, not nubile, not virginal. And there were scars.

His hands covered his face. His breathing wasn't sobbing, more like the gasps after a punch to the solar plexus, the wind knocked out of him.

She shook his shoulder. "Dante!"

LEILA WALKED BACK into Conroy's office and slammed the door behind her, catching her fingertip. Paper stacks on his desk and the floor shuddered and verged on implosion. She shook blood down into her stinging finger.

Conroy looked up from his typing and raised one gray eyebrow.

She asked, "Who else knows about us?"

He frowned and squinted at his monitor. "I haven't told anyone."

"You haven't bragged to anyone? You haven't hinted that you were nailing a twinkie?"

"No." Conroy dipped one eyebrow and deleted something he was typing. He turned his calfskin-leather face to her. "Don't get paranoid."

"Yeah," Leila's face warmed. "Okay."

DANTE WAITED for the blinding flash of lightning, the deafening agony of a brain hemorrhage, or the paralyzing lurch of an earthquake swallowing the house. The cold sheet slithered on his skin.

When she'd touched him, when she'd kissed him, his body had shouted rebellion. He should have stopped his hands from tearing her clothes away. He should have stopped his mouth from tasting her skin and leaving a moist snail-trail of saliva leading to her breasts and her sex. He should have walked away instead of forcing his body into her, but it all seemed undeniably foretold or beyond his control, like possession.

The universe's silence rang in his ears, a piccolo's shrill and a television's dead channel static but, as he'd suspected, no retribution rained down on his ocean-sticky body.

Bev said, "Dante?" and her light hand fluttered on his shoulder.

His skin hungered again, already wanting her smooth body *again*.

His priesthood, which had led him to higher realms of the mind and scholarship, which he'd thought had saved him, was an empty, black hole he'd dropped himself into. His black clothes were a Swartzchild radius, the absence of escaping light, hiding the famished, warping singularity that was only a condensed body and the absence of a soul.

"Dante!"

His silence was upsetting her.

Habit suggested several alternative comments: *I'll call you tomorrow. I have a meeting early in the morning; shall I call you a taxi? When is your husband due home?*

Or, depending on his objectives: *Just this once. Your beauty makes me do terrible things. I was out of control. You seduced me. You make me a madman. You or I or we or all of us had too much to drink. You wanted me to do that. I couldn't stop myself.*

Dante said, "I am so sorry."

"No!" Her hand yanked him onto his back and she hovered above him in the dark. When he'd pushed her onto the bed, she'd bounced up and drawn heavy curtains and it was almost night-dark in the bedroom. Her loose hair hung around him, cloth-of-gold glinting in the sunshine glimmer that sneaked around one edge of the navy blue drape. "No," she said.

More guilt. "And now I should be the one comforting you."

She smiled at him, and she pulled the sheet up a little on her breasts in the deep gloom. "It was just this once. We lost control. We couldn't stop ourselves."

His breath caught in his chest, a cough, a coronary infarct, all corporal reactions. He couldn't summon outrage at her disregard for her marriage and his priesthood. He'd said those words so many, many times. His evil nature reflected in her and spun, winding him up.

His body had felt lust and leapt to its old habits, refined in the Roman Testaccio district night clubs. His virtue had been in his imagination. Holy Orders meant nothing. He was destroyed.

He rolled over on her and forced her down into the dark bed again, penetrating her mouth with his tongue. He'd show her that it wasn't just this one time, that this was sin, and that evil permeated him like smoke.

Her arms tightened around his neck, and her legs around his back.

CONROY WEDGED himself into his car and trudged the rush hour–congested highway through the suburbs to arrive home before six. The girls were watching cartoons while Beverly cooked something fishy for supper.

He leaned against the kitchen wall. Beverly turned and smiled at him, and hope blossomed in his chest. Maybe the priest hadn't ratted him out. "Um, hope I'm not too late."

"Nope. It's okay."

Supper was so pleasant he wondered if she had poisoned his food.

From the other end of the table, she smiled. "This weekend, maybe we could get a babysitter and go out." There was a little tilt in her eyes. "Sunday is Valentine's Day."

THE CRUCIFIX behind the altar glowered at Bev, hating her, and she smoothed her hair back, trying to press that image out of her head. That crucifix and its representation of her Savior couldn't glower. It did, however, need dusting. With that mundane detail, the cross and Christ solidified into wood again.

She should go home. There would be no torrid affair, humid and equatorial and Mediterranean, tree-shaded and reeking of shore leave.

Yet she had never passed the library's dungeonesque door without knocking and a quick word with Father Dante. She had to see him some time, even though this afternoon he'd gathered his clothes and sneaked away while she was showering. She knocked, confidently, forthrightly, with heavy and non-conspiratorial raps.

"*Sì?* Come in." Dante's voice scraped against her skin.

She cracked the door open and leaned in. Boxes partly packed with books built a half wall between the two counseling chairs. "Father?"

"Don't call me that." He was leaning over in his chair with his arms crossed over his stomach, as if sick.

"Are you all right?" She slipped sideways through the doorway and leaned on the door to close it behind her. "What are you doing?"

He held his head in his hands as if it might fall off. His shiny black shoes poked out from under his black cassock. He'd shrouded his young flesh in thick black layers. "I am so sorry."

"No, Dante."

"I broke my vows and betrayed you."

"No," she said. "No, we were swept away."

He gasped, as if punched. "There is no such thing."

The stupid words hovered in Bev's ears, meaningless chatter. "It didn't mean anything."

"It meant something to me."

A wall of boxes barricaded the room. "What are you packing?" She pulled a thick, doorstop book, *DSM-IVR*, out of a box.

"I am going back to Roma tomorrow."

She set the book on his desk. "You're abandoning those kids?"

"The Vatican will send someone else."

"Luke and the other boys need you. Laura said that he smiled this week, that she can touch him without him flinching like she'd slapped him."

"I have to go back to Roma." He sat hunched over, as if cancer consumed him from the center.

She didn't need to pray for enlightenment this time. Once again, the problem intrinsically lay with her. She'd seduced a priest. There was no good ending to this. The poor man, he was crouched in the chair as if the gray stones and mortar of the church walls were crushing him.

She had to give him up. She knew where to grab and yank.

She said, "Listen to me." Her soul flinched, but she grasped that thing that had lodged under her sternum and said, "We'll stop." The warm thing clung, and ripping it out took with it long strips of flesh and muscle and artery. Bits of light-reflecting shrapnel cut muscle as she yanked them away. "Conroy and I will quit counseling." The wound gaped in her side and the ragged edges rubbed when she breathed. "You can't leave."

Dante's fingers worked into the lanks of black hair at his temples. "I can't stay."

She wanted to hold him, stroke his silky hair. "It'll be okay. You'll see. We just won't see each other any more." She worked the doorknob behind her back and stepped out.

The church was silent. The choir had gone home. The gold wood overhead echoed her footsteps in the empty air. She wanted to fall before the altar and beg forgiveness from the Virgin Mary, but she didn't want Dante to find her there, and it seemed melodramatic, and she could reconcile herself with God later. This wasn't the only reason that she suffered His absence.

She snatched her coat from a pew and ran into the cold night and the spot-lit parking lot.

Chapter Ten: Dante

Dante's closed eyes burned as if phosphorus fumes inundated his dark rectory bedroom. His fingertips pressed his eyelids and cooled his eyeballs, but his mind flipped and tumbled, falling unparachuted.

The louvers over the silver-plated moon glowed, reflecting the rectory's whitewashed walls, milky furniture and bleached bed sheets. His body shadowed the white sheets and blotched the white-pickled wooden floor as he paced. He drank from a bottle of whiskey.

The room was too confining. He needed to walk.

His coat offered scant protection from February's mature winter wind. Soon, winter would grow feeble as spring sucked it away. Soon, he would return to Roma and sequester himself in the Vatican with the other celibates. The Roman sun could warm his scratched shoulders.

He unlocked the wooden doors of the church and slipped inside. The air echoed even though the wooden pews absorbed his footsteps as he hurried toward the altar at the heart of the cruciform church. He could sit. He could rest. Surely, if there was a God, *since* there was a God, he would find a measure of peace in the church.

He sat on the front pew and pressed his palms against his burning eyes. The sinuses behind his forehead were scalded, too. His symptoms might be psychosomatic or they might be due to insomnia, which had plagued him since his arrival on this infernal continent, peopled with pedophiles and adulterers.

He swiveled on the undulating front pew and lay down, setting the bottle on the floor beside the pew. Drinking himself unconscious in the front pew of the church to be found in the morning by a clucking Samual appealed to Dante's sense of irony.

Lying on a pew did not convey proper penitence. He pushed his insomniac, drunk body and kneeled on the wood floor, not on the padded kneeler, his arms folded on the rail. The rail was cool on his forehead, and he lay there, hurting.

He'd failed. He'd failed everyone. Dante had been tumescent with hubris and pride, believing he could rise above his body and inhabit his head. With the merest sough of Bev's breath on his flesh, he had dived like a hunting hawk into her body.

Her breath had sanded the skin on his neck, but her bites marked his skin.

The wood floor ground at his knees.

Let his weak flesh suffer.

Moonlight and lamplight seeped through the stained glass windows depicting the Holy Virgin Mary, striping the floor with shadows and random splinters of color. He tried to focus, tried to imagine a glowing cross floating a few feet before him in the dark church.

Glowing sunlight, insinuating itself around the curtains of the bedroom window, had trickled on Bev's body, brightening her breast.

All he wanted was an envisioned cross to pray to. God is with us even in our most forsaken moments, as that idiotic poem about sand and footprints struggled to say, but Dante couldn't conjure even a simple image of a cross. All that he had thought was holy in him had been nothing but his imagination and longing for a reason for life other than the mindless pursuit of sex.

The glowing gold that he tried to fashion into a crucifix was her skin. Darkness in the church was his body plunging into hers.

Pedophiles did not control their urges, either.

His body and its urges were no better than those beasts who tortured children.

He should have stopped. He was a Vatican magistrate. He should have walked away: he was judge and jury of sexual crimes, his Holy Orders committed him to the Church, and he'd hurt Bev again. She was a wounded deer in the woods and he'd wolfed her down.

What about the woman?

Hypocrisy stabbed him.

He focused his tired eyes on the wooden crucifix, the tortured and dying Christ, immobilized behind the altar.

His meat heart flailed.

He pressed on his knees and stood, glaring at the crucifix; he wanted to scream at it to speak to him or to fall to pieces, but insanity hovered in the act of speaking aloud in the empty church and in the wavering, gem-shining windows at the periphery of his vision.

He vaulted the prayer rail and strode past the altar to the Christ, crouched on the cross and ready to spring. Dante grabbed the only part of the Christ he could reach on the looming crucifix, the nailed wooden foot. Grit ground his palm.

If only the foot would warm, would drip blood on him, or would turn to light and fill him with grace—anything—but the Christ on the cross was a dead tree knifed into a human shape, encased in varnish, and in need of dusting.

Dante mumbled prayers, all the prayers he could think of, the Lord's Prayer and the Hail Mary and the Act of Contrition and portions of the Mass and bits of the Last Rites and the Exorcism, and he clung to that unyielding wooden foot. Splinters from the Christ's big toenail embedded themselves in his palm. He tried to believe that the Church itself was the miracle he needed, that life was proof enough, yet his cells metabolized without divine intervention, and he began talking to himself in the dark church.

"If there is a God, *since* there is a God," and his grip on the wood loosened and he glanced away, protesting, lying.

He had imagined it all, the Call, an invigoration when he prostrated himself at Holy Orders, his priesthood. He'd run away from his body, but his skin under the rough wool coat and cotton pajamas had rebelled.

There was no priesthood, not for him. His life in his mind was an illusion, every bit as fallacious as a dream or a psychotic hallucination.

He had nothing but biology and an empty church.

Chapter Eleven

Around ten o'clock Wednesday morning in the green-tiled hallway, Conroy tapped Leila's arm.

She carried a potted dieffenbachia on her hip like a toddler. She said, "I'm on my way to visit Danna. They said it's viral."

Conroy shrugged. "Did they say which virus?"

"No, just 'viral.'"

He snorted and glanced down the green-tiled hallway, preoccupied. "Then they have no idea what's wrong with her."

Leila shifted the plant. "Could you take a look at her?"

Conroy said, "I've visited Danna four times. I took her some papers to read."

"I mean look at her chart. The attending doesn't seem interested."

Conroy's attention flickered across the crowd of green-smocked surgeons and blue-clad staff, like color-coded workers from a dystopian film. A pharmacy student, garbed in raspberry scrubs, wandered as bright as a berry in a salad. "One does not poach another physician's patient."

"Just stop by and take a gander at her chart," Leila said and struggled with the Mexican clay pot that sprouted foliage. "Consider it a *favor.*"

Her glaring innuendo promised sex. "Okay."

"It couldn't be something that she picked up in the lab, could it?"

He scoffed, "No. We don't work with anything that needs more than a P2 lab."

"You're sure? Your mice were acting weird. Really sick. They were moribund. If your secret experiments could infect a mouse, they could infect other mammals, like humans, right?"

He scoffed harder to cover up that he was worried. "God, no. What could she get, vaccinia? Or pig herpes? She probably got something at one of those terrible bars you take her to."

THAT AFTERNOON, Dante rang Bev's doorbell. The chime tintinnabulated through the house.

Bev answered the door and she bobbled, startled. He pushed his way into her house, slammed the door behind him, and vised her between the wall and his body, the crushing type of kiss detailed in the Kama Sutra.

She pushed against his chest. "Don't."

He kissed her harder to make her shut up, even though women's protestations excited him. His famished body thundered so that he could hardly hear her.

"Dante," she said, under his lips, her mouth open, her tongue curled.

"It's just this once," he said, and he knew how to lie and what she wanted to hear. Holy Orders, that sham demarcation in his life between the carnal and the intellectual, couldn't stop him now. "You're so *bella*, beautiful. You make me a madman. I can't stop myself." He dragged her shirt off her shoulder. Her fingers ran into his hair, grasping. He licked the pale espresso cup of skin between her clavicle and her neck.

"I can't do this," she said, and her larynx thrummed his lips. She dragged her shirt back up and over her shoulder. "I can't give you up every night and have you come back every morning."

With this, he knew how to spin her around and catch her. He said, "I can't stay away from you."

"Dante, I can't."

He lifted one of her hands away from her eyes, turned it over, pinned it to the wall above her head and, that old Valentino trick, kissed the blue ribbons of veins on her thin-skinned wrist. "I can't stay away from you."

"Then no more pretending to leave."

"Sí."

He would have her here, against the wall. He lifted her other arm and held her wrists, pinned above her, and chewed down her arm to her breasts under her open shirt.

WEDNESDAY AFTERNOON, Sister Benedicta called Bev's house looking for a substitute teacher for that afternoon. Bev, wrapped by Dante's hot flesh from behind in the blackened bedroom, had said that she, too, was indisposed but imagined she could be on her feet to sub tomorrow.

THURSDAY AFTERNOON, Conroy was typing the letter to Beverly when Leila walked in. Her shirt was unbuttoned so far that he could see a curve of breast. She shut the door. Leila popped open another button on her shirt, and her black bra spanned convex curves, and he glimpsed nipple. "Did you take a look at Danna's chart?"

"Hmmm? No. Sorry. Haven't had time."

"Conroy, I promise," her voice was husky and his ears and dick pricked up, "that if you take a look at her chart," Leila leaned on his desk with her fingertips nudging aside the paper sprawl, and her breasts fell forward and kissed, "I will blow you under this desk," she tapped the hollow wood, "while everyone is in the lab."

"I'll drop by this afternoon."

CONROY FLIPPED THROUGH Danna's chart while Leila smoothed Danna's damp, frowzy hair back from her feverish forehead and spoon-fed her clear broth. Heavy drapes masked the room from the afternoon sun. He squinted at her chart in the gloom, held the paperwork aloft and aslant to catch sterile fluorescent light leaking from the hallway, and wrote careful observations in the margin with a thick, black pen.

Danna had no problems swallowing the broth. That was good. The subject of his little side experiments would produce throat spasms if it jumped into humans, so whatever Danna's problem was, it wasn't his fault. He didn't need to explain his moribund mice to anyone.

The preliminary diagnoses included febrile encephalitis, non-bacterial or viral, or encephalomyelitis. Her bloodwork showed counts typical of viral infection. Could be anything. Could be a herpesvirus from a cold sore that had headed into her central nervous system. Or an adenovirus. Or a retrovirus. Or an endogenous retrovirus stimulated to excise itself to infectivity by an innocuous, infectious retrovirus. Or a trick of autoimmunity. Or a poison.

Conroy lifted an edge of a curtain to see the hasty, illegible handwriting scrawled in the lab column by one of the overworked, inattentive residents. Negative gonococcus screen.

"Conroy?" Leila said. "Migraine. Put down the curtain."

Danna's trembling hand covered her eyes.

Conroy smoothed the curtain into place. "Have you been working with anything unusual in the lab?" he asked Danna.

"I found a bottle of ricin in one of the freezers," she said.

Leila's outraged jaw hung. "You have *ricin?* The chemical weapon from castor beans?"

Conroy mentally sorted through the freezers. "In the minus eighty? Third shelf?"

"Yeah." Danna nodded and rubbed her neck with one floppy hand.

Conroy shrugged. "We used it for tissue culture back in the Stone Age, before organelle-specific fluoroprobes. It's very dilute. You didn't drink it, did you?"

Danna snuffled, laughing. "Not even a little."

"Besides, ricin causes bleeding, hemorrhages. Anything else?"

Danna said, "No. I was worried about touching the ricin bottle."

"I'm sure that's not a problem." He waggled Danna's limp foot, and Danna watched without much interest. "I'll be back to check on you later. Leila? In the hall?"

"I'll be right back, honey." Leila followed Conroy into the searingly bright hallway. "Yeah?"

He tucked his pen into his pocket and whispered, "Has she called her parents?"

"No. She doesn't want them to worry." Leila glanced at the closed door beside them as if Danna could overhear that confidence betrayed.

"I'll call them." Conroy shook his head. Breaking bad news was one of his weak points. "This doesn't look good."

Her slim jaw worked, gritted, and she swallowed. "Come on. She was fine a week ago."

"She went to the Paris conference with us two years ago, didn't she?"

"Yeah."

Conroy plucked his pen out of his pocket and clicked the blue ballpoint open and closed, twice. "They were having their first cases of BSE and new variant Creutzfeldt-Jakob disease then."

"She has *mad cow disease?*"

"Long, asymptomatic incubation. Rapid onset of symptoms. No hydrophobia. Photophobia. Encroaching paralysis. Is she a vegetarian?"

"She says that if God hadn't wanted us to eat animals, He wouldn't have made them out of meat."

"She ate beef in France?" he asked.

"Worried about anemia without it. But nvCJD doesn't have an immunological reaction. She has a fever and WBC elevation."

"Atypical presentation." Conroy sighed. He'd hoped to hear that he'd misremembered, that she hadn't been to that conference, that she was a militant vegan. "Damn."

AT EVERY MOMENT in Bev's creaking bed, Dante thought he should stop, but she had lain on him in the dark, and her skin was so smooth.

If God wanted him to abstain, why had He made Bev so beautiful and so soft? The Church's misogyny and celibacy seemed to be an affront to God's creation of women, His perfection of the human model, Man 2.0.

The room smelled oceanic, like a sun-roasted Mediterranean beach.

LEILA SHUT CONROY'S OFFICE DOOR and locked it. The paper stacks on his desk trembled.

Conroy was talking on the phone and waved her quiet. "Yes," he said into the phone, "I'll see you Sunday. I wish it were under better circumstances." He hung up and picked up his notebook.

"Danna's parents?" Leila asked.

Conroy nodded. "If it is nvCJD, Danna might have contracted it on that university trip, and once I ran that by the legal department, they had a conniption fit. The university is flying her parents in and putting them up, just in case it is nvCJD, so they might not sue." Conroy's hand draped over the hung-up phone receiver. "I'm glad you convinced me that she needed looking at."

Leila cleared her throat. "I came to pay up."

Conroy's forehead creased, confused, and then he waved off her approach. "Let's talk about it next week."

He flipped to a fresh page in his notebook and wrote *DANNA KERRY* in block letters.

Leila said, "This is all awfully nice of you. What's next week?"

"The Dean committee is meeting on Monday."

BEV ROLLED OVER. A flake of sunlight jumped from the curtained dormer window and touched Dante's amber skin. She said, "I'm not asking anything specific about Luke, just how you knew about Nicolai if the kids didn't tell."

Dante slid onto his back, away from the window, and the sunlight shard glinted on silver strands embedded in his black hair. He dragged his fingers through his hair, tugging it away from his eyes. "We couldn't trust what the children said, either because they might make false accusations or because they might not make true ones. Once we eliminated their accusations, only heresy remained, and that the Church understands."

Bev's arm chilled, and she slipped it under her pillow. "I don't know how you can just up and decide something is heresy."

"There is an organization here in America that seeks to help pedophiles, to say that the rape of children is normal and good, to decriminalize it, even promote it. They have a website."

"Everybody has a website these days."

"We, the Congregation for the Doctrine of the Faith, declared the organization to be committing heresy. Priests who belonged to it or advocated for it were guilty of heresy." Dante sat up on one elbow. "A few months ago, the Congregation that I work for reabsorbed the I.E.A., the Institute for External Affairs, to which Father Domingo belongs."

"Father Domingo, the guy who revamped the school's curriculum."

"Yes. They're the Vatican's C.I.A., 'God's left hand,' so to speak. They hacked the pedophile organization's computers, membership rolls. Everything on a computer leaves a trail. Of course, many men who were members were not priests, and many pedophile priests were not members, so we cross-referenced, studied contacts, acquaintances, correspondences and coincidences, chat rooms, address books, mailing lists, purchase orders. Father Nicolai was acquainted with unscrupulous men. We sent Father Domingo, and he found evidence."

Bev decided not to mention her sacrilegious theory—the grace of the

Holy Spirit working through Dante's muscular yet limber body to show her the meaninglessness of sex—to the Monsignor.

CONROY FINISHED TYPING his letter to Beverly at eleven o'clock Friday night and printed it with whirring gasps and one last, grating rattle. He called the university's tech support to come and fix the printer Monday morning, during the time when the Dean committee met. He hoped to be busy then, called out of the office. Excitement whirred in his cells. Sympathetic neurons fired and he was ready to fight for the neurology chair and his future and the Nobel Prize.

Later Monday, he could move a few things into his apartment and take Leila there, where no one would find them or squawk at them or harangue them or damn them or counsel them.

Monday, it would all come together for him *Monday*.

SATURDAY AFTERNOON, slamming cold air filled the converted warehouse, the Wallball Hall, where Christine's soccer game was being played. Conroy refereed the game as a lineman, whistling short bursts and flashing yellow cards, and Bev sat in the bleachers above, smiling, and served hot cocoa when the girls substituted off the field.

Jolinda and Pat didn't know what to make of them. "They stopped going to counseling," Jolinda said.

"They must be doing better." Pat's girl, Giorgi, the goalie, hovered near the edge of the goal but the halfback got the ball before the other team had a shot, and the game swung down the field. Pat hoped the Sloans were doing better, because Madge in the finance department had said that Conroy had booked a ticket back to Washington, D.C., next weekend, and she'd just bet that Conroy was going to order "room service" again.

"Isn't that Father Dante?" Jolinda pointed to a man wearing a black coat clanking up the metal stairs toward the spectators over on the other side of the field.

"And he's sitting by Bev."

Bev Sloan pointed to the field, her hand following Christine, and the priest nodded. Father Dante sat on the metal bench, leaned back, stretched out his long legs.

Pat grabbed her arm. "Did you see Conroy's face?"

Jolinda looked. Conroy Sloan, down on the field, his face bulging with anger, ignored the other team passing the ball offside to score a goal past Giorgi.

The referee whistled the offside call and yelled at Conroy. The whistle echoed in the fuzzy-insulated, metal beams above.

A few weeks later, Jolinda and Pat shook their heads, dismayed. It was obvious, looking back, that wrath, and hate, and insanity, and murder were in the air.

CONROY STARED AT that goddamn priest who insolently sat next to Conroy's smiling wife and watched Conroy's eldest daughter charge down the field after the buckminsterfullerene ball. Conroy's younger daughter, her loyalties easily swayed, ran to the priest and hugged him.

Beverly and that priest inclined their heads toward each other, and collusion lingered in the shadows their heads cast on each other's shoulders from the overhead fluorescent lights.

That priest had been at Conroy's house lately, staying for supper, bringing wine. The priest had tracked down Leila.

Goddamn, meddling priest. The priest was a pair of scissors between Conroy and his family and his other women, slyly cutting Conroy out.

Beverly covered her mouth, laughing, and the priest glanced up at the cold, metal roof that reverberated with shouting and kicking and thumping.

He understood it, now. Beverly wanted a divorce and she'd enlisted the eunuch priest to snoop so she'd have evidence. Those two were in it together. They had ganged up against him. They were colluding, string-jerking svengalis, cunning spymasters, betrayers and Inquisitors and executioners. And the priest was perverting Conroy's daughters' minds against him, probably preaching about what Conroy *should* be doing.

Beverly was cutting Conroy out of their life, replacing him with the Church as personified in *that sneaky, goddamn priest*. Beverly had a cultish streak. When he had first begun dating her, she'd talked too much about the Virgin Mary, like they were roommates. He'd worried that she was having hallucinations. Now, he saw her method. She used the priest, she manipulated the children, and she was disposing of Conroy. They were all ganged up against him. He stood against them and their machinations alone.

He needed somewhere to think, alone, about this.

His townhouse was ready today, though he'd planned not to move in until Monday.

Conroy left the field, climbed the stairs, and walked over to his wife and that priest, sitting on the bleachers in the sweaty air of the Wallball Hall. "I forgot something in the lab," he said mildly. "I need to go to the lab right now."

"Ah," the asshole priest squinted up at Conroy, his too-young skin creased around his black eyes. "I can drive the girls home."

Conroy left and ran through the cold, cold air to Beverly's car. He would drop the Volvo at home and pick up his Porsche. He needed his Porsche. His new one was going to be delivered next week, and he'd promised to sell the old one to Yuri.

Chapter Twelve

Dante stayed for supper after he drove Bev and the girls home from the soccer game. Bev sliced vegetables for pasta primavera while the girls taught Dante the intricacies of video games. His character died within minutes, so he watched the girls traipse ruins and kill people.

He joined Bev in the simmering kitchen and held her around her strong shoulders, most likely so different from slight Roman women.

Bev smiled and stirred the fuming pot. "After supper, Laura and Luke are taking the girls to that new kids' film."

His body pined for her touch and the slip of her skin. Dante whispered, "and Sloan?"

"He always works late." She glanced toward the family room, frowning. "It's funny. He must have picked up some of his books before he went to the lab. One shelf in his office is bare."

LEILA'S CELL PHONE chime-chirped and she stumbled in her dark apartment, blind-searching under scarves and knit hats on her entryway table before she found the screaming baby of a contraption. "Hello!"

Conroy's voice, buzzy as if speaking through an empty soda can, said, "I'm here."

"Where?" She crammed the cell phone between her shoulder and ear, shrugged her white shirt over her shoulder, and buttoned.

"My new apartment."

The sandbag stupidity of *my new apartment* smacked Leila. "*What?*"

Static. "Down by the university, off Woolf Road." Whirling screech. "Can you come?"

"Those white townhouses?" Her own voice echoed out of phase, *houses?*

"Yes. Number fifty-one."

Leila clicked on the Tiffany lamp. Jody looked over Leila's shoulder, and her blonde eyebrows dipped. She pulled her dark blue sweatshirt over her moonlight skin that glared in the floral-toned lamplight. Leila asked Conroy, "Did you leave your wife?"

Jody's mouth opened like she was grunting a disgusted *uh!*

Conroy's voice squeezed through the cell phone's signal. "I left her a note."

The idiot. The *idiot.* "Conroy, don't do anything stupid. I'll be right there."

BEV WAVED to the girls clambering into Laura's earthshaking SUV. Dante stood behind the open door, his shirt open, and she toyed with his bare chest with her out-of-sight hand. Wine insinuated among her nerves, sparking sensation in her fingertips and drifting in her head.

Warmth slid up her bare arm, and she shut the door. Dante massaged her forearm and bicep. "You exercise?"

"Some. I golf." She unwove her arm from between his fingers, grabbed his hand, and led him up the stairs to the darkened bedroom. He shoved her and she bounced on the quilt-covered bed. The pillow crackled. One of the girls had probably planted a crayoned picture.

"Hold on a minute," she said, but Dante was already on top of her in the dark, his mouth growling on her neck, his hands pulling at her blouse and pants.

Under the pillow, her hand found three pages stapled together.

Dante's leg forced her knees apart, and he mouthed her collarbone. "What is it?"

"I don't know." She flicked on the lamp and looked.

Typed: *Dearest Beverly,*

Something from Conroy. Unease flitted, as if he was somehow present through his note. She dropped it, and it fluttered beside the bed.

Dante asked, "What is it?"

"Nothing." Her belly heated as his warm body insulated her. She reached for the light.

Dante crawled across her and lay crosswise, his hard stomach pressing her, looking over the edge of the blue-draped bed.

"Wait." He sat up and handed the paper to her. His expression softened, turning remote and priestly. "You should read this."

....

Selections from Conroy's note:

> Dearest Beverly,
>
> It's not you and it's not the girls, but I need some time alone to think. My life has taken some turns lately that I hadn't foreseen, none of us could have. I've rented an apartment, just to have some time alone. I won't be home tonight, or for a few nights.
>
> 51 Vita Place.

Three pages of meaningless drivel about obligations and commitment and meaning well and Beverly had become *unsympathetic* and something about the priest making him feel *cornered* and *claustrophobic* and *under surveillance.*

> And: Don't be surprised, but there will be some papers delivered tomorrow. Legal things, for both of our protection, legal separation. I know you'll understand.
>
> Love Always,
>
> Conroy

Bev's heart knotted, and her fist shivered, shaking the dry paper. A pulse thumped her temples like being cuffed on both ears, and sound rushed, falling away then slamming back into her head. She swung her legs around, grabbed the bedside phone, and dialed Conroy's cell phone.

The phone clicked. Conroy's distant voice muttered, "Yes? Beverly?"

The weight of air crushed her chest when she tried to breathe. "What is this?"

"You've found the note."

"Why?" Her voice echoed in that crappy cell phone of his, *Why.* "*Dearest Beverly*, and you're leaving me? *Love Always*, and you want a divorce?"

"Beverly, we need some time to think." His speech was metered in tone and tempo like he was reciting the damned note by rote.

"Come home."

"Beverly, we should take some time to think."

"Fine. I'll come there."

Conroy's voice squalled "Beverly, no!" through the air like a screaming, flying bug as she hung up the phone.

She said, "I can't believe this." She pressed her palms to her eyes and blue dots marched in regiments across the dark field of her vision.

Dante, his voice huge and dark after the squeak of Conroy's cell phone, said, "He has made a mistake."

"You bet he has." She buttoned the blouse over her chest.

His voice strengthened, and he sounded more like a domineering doctor. "You shouldn't go."

"I just want to talk to him." She stepped into her shoes.

"Don't go over there tonight."

Bev stood, buttoned her shirt and, despite Dante's fingers plucking at her clothes, she walked downstairs, coatless, into the February-cold garage and started her chilly, sensible car, next to the empty space where Conroy parked his stupid Porsche. A black oil blot the shape of an elephant with an extended trunk and stringy tail stained the cement. That damned old car was always half-broken. It drank money and leaked dirty oil.

He had to see that he couldn't leave them. She revved the car's engine.

DANTE FOLLOWED HER to the garage. Cold air sucked into his shirt and clung to his chest. His collar flapped beside his cheek. He leaned on her car window. "Bev! Wait!"

Bev thumbed the tab on her door handle, and all the car doors thump-locked in unison. Her staring eyes were tearless and unblinking, shocky.

"Bev!" He ran around the car to the passenger side, flipped the handle uselessly, and pressed his hand against the car window as if he could keep her there. "You've been drinking. You shouldn't drive."

She flipped levers on the dashboard. Her hair floated around her face from blowing air.

"Don't go," he shouted through the glass and the locked door and above the car engine and fumes. "Don't go!"

The garage door rattled and clanked like a drawbridge, flooding the garage with freezing air. She grabbed the back of the seat and wrenched herself around to look behind the car as she reversed.

The car rolled away into the icy night. He stepped aside, blown back, and she drove away.

The garage door clattered down, leaving Dante in the harsh neon light. She'd left him for that bastard.

In the note, Sloan had typed his address. Dante sprinted up the stairs. The carpet thudded under his feet and he found the papers beside the bed, scrambled through them trying to find the number, and wadded the whole mass into his pocket.

LEILA STARTED YELLING when Conroy opened the door hung with the wrought-iron 51. "You idiot! What the hell are you doing?"

Conroy's thin body jerked. "Come in, come in."

She flung her gray coat on the rose-flowered couch. The colonial-cliché townhouse was a decorating parody. A bowl of red wax apples catnapped on the cherrywood veneer coffee table. The shining gold guts of a black-lacquered grandfather clock peristalsed. Blobs of chintz imitated furniture. The kitchen was probably stocked with television-sold knives and peeling non-stick skillets. Her father would have set fire to it and danced around the flames.

Leila asked, "Did you leave your wife?"

Conroy's blue eyes were too wide. "I needed a place of my own." He spread his arms as if he expected her to hug him, as if she had ever *hugged* him. "I needed a place to think about us."

"You don't *think* about *fucking*. There's nothing to think *about*."

Conroy sat on a chair and covered his eyes which one vein-riddled hand. "Beverly and that priest ganged up on me. He's helping her find evidence for a divorce."

Leila's rigid, indignant knees kept her standing. "Priests don't help people get divorced, and so what? We aren't fucking anymore, and you broke up with wifey-wannabe, didn't you?"

"Peggy's gone."

"Conroy, if you had sat tight, they wouldn't have had anything. But now, this," she whipped her arms around to encompass the generic townhouse. A brass and brittle glass lantern-like fixture glimmered above her head. "You've screwed it all up now. You've given her the perfect excuse. At best, you've got a love shack. At worst, you've abandoned her in the legal sense. She's got you by the *heuvos* now."

"No," Conroy said. "They ganged up on me. That's the important part."

"No, the fact that *you left* is the important part. When she caught you fucking around, she forgave you. After she found Peggy's panties, she didn't throw you out." Leila settled into the creaky couch. The cushions rustled as if there were plastic under the chintz, a sensible precaution in a rental. "Women don't leave when men screw around. Women leave if men fall in love with another woman. Did she ask if you loved the other woman?"

Conroy nodded.

"And when Beverly found Peggy's panties, you assured her that the screwing was nothing and that you didn't love that Peggy chick or anyone but her, *right?*"

"But she still would have dragged me to counseling."

"Conroy, you've *fucked* this up. You need to *go* home, *right* now, pray to God that she hasn't found that note—a note, *a note!* You coward."

"She found it." He rubbed his hands over each other, like washing.

"And you *tell* her that you *love* her and that you'll never, *ever* do this again, and that *none* of your screwing around ever meant a *damned* thing, because *it didn't mean anything.*"

Conroy looked away from the pastel, smeared art print, and his eyes acquired a melancholy, lugubrious, sentimental sheen, somewhere between a basset hound and a needle-startled mouse, and Leila started swearing at herself, calling herself a whore and a hungry cunt.

He said, "But it did mean something to me."

"Stop it. Stop it *now.*" She punched her hand.

"You're the only one who hasn't turned against me. No one else cares about me."

"Shut up."

His hands fell to his sides, palms forward, a studied gesture of baring one's soul. Leila should punch that idiocy right out of his head.

"I want us to be together," he said.

"Shut up. This was nothing but casual fucking, Conroy, nothing more."

"We could have children."

"You're fucked in the head. I don't want kids."

"Everyone wants children. They're fun."

"Children are not *fun.* The world is a vale of tears that destroys people. Children are people you create to suffer for your own amusement. Creating new people to watch them suffer smacks of sadism. If you want fun, get a Ferrari. A Ferrari is cheaper."

"Listen, you can have it all. The career, science, me." His eyes were wistful, religious.

"I don't want it all." Even though she'd told him that it was all casual fucking, explicitly, at the beginning, in the interest of full disclose, he'd still fucked it up. "Think, Conroy. Even if we did shack up in this insipid condo, how would shagging one of your grad students look to the department chair committee? You wouldn't get the chair, and you wouldn't get the resources, your grants will be stripped, and you'll never make it out of this pretty good university. You'll have wasted it all for fucking."

He blinked, as if released from a thrall that he'd cast on himself.

She said, "If you ever, ever talk like this again, I'll switch labs. You won't have my research. Everyone will wonder why I switched, even if I never say a word."

He sat on his chintz chair and looked confused, glancing away and around, as if he didn't understand how he'd arrived at the cheesy little townhouse. "But, I love you."

"Go back to your wife before you fuck everything up." Leila scooped up her coat.

"I love you." He grabbed her arm, and she dropped the coat, pulled her wrist out of his grip, and punched him in the face. His flesh around his left eye compressed between her knuckles and his skull. He fell down heavily on the floor and held his eye.

"I warned you," she said. "I warned you never to grab me again."

He covered his face with both hands. "Why would you have an affair with me?"

Leila gathered her coat off the floor and said, "We were nothing but a casual fuck. I thought you understood that it was *just fucking around*. I always end up in bed with men, every time. From the way you drooled on Valerie Lindh at every conference and the two of you strutted around arm in arm blabbering in French, I figured you were fucking her already."

He nodded.

"Then why did *you* do it, if it wasn't just fucking? You're the one who's married."

"It was just screwing around, but when you said you wanted to break it off, I couldn't stand it." He prodded the flesh around his left eye. "I want more. I want you."

Shrieking filled her throat at this net he was throwing at her, trying to drag her down into the rip tide of everyone else's life, but she widened her eyes and, though her breathing rattled in her chest, she said, "Stay away from me."

She walked out into the February night that had turned ice-floe frigid, leaving him alone in that asinine townhouse.

CONROY STOOD AT THE FRONT WINDOW and watched Leila stalk between the dead bushes and cold-charred grass toward her car. He touched the skin around his eye. A ring on her hand had abraded his temple, and the skin was sore over the orbital.

Blindsided. She'd blindsided him. She hadn't seen that he was free, unencumbered, and ready to face the world.

Outside on the sidewalk, Leila stretched her fingers into her gloves.

A harridan's clawing hand grabbed Leila's arm.

Conroy watched from a slit between two vertical blind slats.

The window turned the sordid scene into a silent movie. Beverly's face dilated and released a howl that popped back Leila's head, but Leila shook Beverly's hand off her arm. Leila drew herself up like climbing into her own slender, dusky skin, glared down at Beverly, and mouthed something that infiltrated Beverly and twisted down her body to her feet. Beverly, coatless, hunched against those words and the cold, turned away, and ran to Conroy's door.

Leila started forward, saw Conroy peeking through the slats, and retreated. Headlights from the parking lot beyond transiently illuminated her like a lighthouse beacon searching storm waves.

The doorbell chimed. The door thundered.

No use making her stand out in the cold and angering her further.

He turned the cold knob.

AS SOON AS the doorknob clicked, Bev shoved the door open.

In less than three weeks, the whole sham had fallen apart. Her whole marriage, her whole life, every choice she'd ever made, all sucked away.

She shoved that cheap door in his bony face. The door thumped Conroy, and he stumbled and reached behind him, flinging one arm to the ceiling.

He should stumble, damn him. He should fall. He should fall and keep falling like she was falling and there was no one to catch her, though she prayed *Hail Mary full of grace, pray for us sinners now and at the hour of our death* under her breath into the silent ether.

Conroy slammed his open hand against the wall. "What the hell?"

Bev grabbed the doorjamb to steady her shaking legs. "*Why?*"

Conroy squirmed like poison wormed in him. "You and that priest thought you could catch me. You two were working together."

"That Leila is your mistress, isn't she?" Nerves alongside Bev's eyes spiked into her temples, and she rubbed the left one, trying to rub away the stabbing. "You're screwing her."

"What if I was?" Conroy slammed his palm against the wall. "Would you tell the priest? Would he go to Leila's apartment *again* and interrogate her *again?*"

Bev's horrified eyes hurt, leaked heat. The stone of her heart pendulumed in her chest, battering her ribs.

The lantern-shaped light fixture above Bev threw glassy light on the two-story ceiling of the living room. If she had a golf club, she would piñata-whack that brassy light fixture. If that coffeemaker on the green counter in the kitchen were full, she would scald the chalky walls. *Jesus, Mary, and Joseph,* the violence swayed her, roiled in her arms like the Atlantic.

Our Father, who art in Heaven, she tried to pray but her thoughts seemed to go nowhere, like talking into a dead phone. The flesh of her back felt striped, and she tried to reach around to feel if blood were soaking through her white shirt, dripping abstract crimson slashes. She shut the door behind her and walked through the gray and white rental.

The condo came equipped with the fake apples on the coffee table and shiny impressionist prints on the walls, an artificial milieu, a play house.

The coffeetable was stacked with entertainment magazines, diverting digests, popular ephemera. She picked up one of the slick, fake apples. A velvet leaf dangled from the plastic stem. She wanted to throw it at the staircase wall with a sideways whip of her right arm that would have smacked a golf ball in a duck hook, wanting a splatter of red molten wax, but it would probably pop and roll down the stairs intact. She wanted *splatter*. She tossed the apple and swiped it from the air, overhand. "Was it something I said? Is it because I'm not a scientist? Is it because I believe in God?"

"You forced me out. You and that priest."

She turned and found Conroy halfway to the kitchen. "Don't you blame it on Dante." She followed him as he walked away from her. Later, she thought that *following* him was the mistake she'd made: following him back East, to the apartment, and into the kitchen. "Don't blame it on the Church. You weren't supposed to leave. We're married. We promised."

The kitchen was equipped with a clean coffeemaker, a chrome toaster, a blinking-noon microwave, and a block heavy with knives.

IN THE KITCHEN, Conroy unbagged the supplies he'd bought for Leila: vodka, scotch, Riesling, orange juice, soda, all of it useless now. He opened a soda. Hissing, sugary mist irritated his nose. "Go home, Beverly. We'll discuss this later."

"When? After the *legal things* are delivered?" She grabbed the bottle of scotch.

"Beverly!" He reached for the squat bottle as it receded past him, but her arm was a snatching ghost. He stashed the other bottles on top of the refrigerator. "What are you doing?"

"Having a drink. You've had quite a few lately, haven't you? At the office? With Leila?" She twisted off the top of the bottle and slugged, her smooth throat working to contain the scotch.

God, horror, the way she used to be when she was an undergrad, all shrieking and fists pounding on tables and running. "Beverly! You shouldn't drink hard liquor."

She touched the corner of her mouth where a drop of scotch beaded. "Why not? Because I'm the little wife?" She tilted the bottle back and gulped two shots' worth. She choked but swallowed it down. "I need a drink."

"Give me the bottle. I'll drive you home."

She rested the bottle on the cheap laminate counter and stared into the coffeemaker as if trying to evoke spirits. "Looks like you have everything you need. Alcohol," she waved at the fridge top and opened the door to peer inside, "milk, bread, granola bars." She stalked around the kitchen opening cabinets as Conroy leaned on the counter, out of her way, waiting. "Pots and pans," she pointed to each. "Silverware," she inventoried. "Knives."

AS DANTE PARKED at 51 Vita Place, his headlights swept a thin girl in a gray coat slouching in the stairwell to dodge the needling wind. She lit a cigarette. The tip glowed red near her black hair. He stopped the car, climbed out, slammed the door.

"Did Bev see you?" he called as he strode at her.

Leila frowned. "Goddamn priest. What do you care?"

"Did she see you here?" She was so small, crouched against the wall, and his height and black clothes and Roman collar intimidated even the strongest men, but he needed to know if Bev had found Conroy's mistress at his new apartment.

Leila nodded and turned her face away, swinging her black hair. She lifted the trembling cigarette to the other side of that slick, black partition. Dove-gray smoke streamed into the air.

He wanted to knock the infernal cigarette from her hand and stomp on it or smoke it himself. A smoke or a drink might dull him. He was a sharp ax, chopping through people's lives. "Where are they?"

With her cigarette pinched between her thumb and finger, she gestured to a green door past the stairs past them and to the left. Ash fell off and splatted on the frozen cement. "They're yelling."

Dante leaned his cheekbone against the icy wall, and his jaw ached as he eavesdropped.

BEV LET THE cheap three-tined forks and hollow-handled knives fall out of her fingers, clanging. "You gave your mistress one hell of a Valentine's Day present, didn't you?"

"What?" He snagged the whiskey bottle and cradled it.

"Valentine's Day. Tomorrow is Valentine's Day." Bev opened the freezer door, stepped into the emanating chill to fingertip the vodka bottle off the top of the fridge, and caught it midair.

"Beverly, don't. You worked so hard."

She twisted the bottle open and the tasteless, odorless liquor stung her throat, like a chemical weapon. She hopped up and sat on the green countertop. It creaked. The whole counter might crumble. He might not get his security deposit back. She leaned against the coffeemaker and the block of knives—the row of knife handles poked her back across her lowest ribs and spine—and pointed at him with the neck of the bottle. "I'll contest the divorce."

"Please, Beverly, stop drinking."

"I'll get a lawyer and contest it. You have to be there for your daughters."

"Beverly, don't drink any more."

"Don't tell me what to do." She reached behind her with the hand not locked around the vodka bottle and grabbed the protruding steak knife that was poking her back.

"Beverly." Conroy set the scotch on the counter behind him and held out his open, empty hand. The riverbeds on his palm all seemed to run off into a delta where his thumb connected. Some of those lines that crossed Conroy's pink palm must be love lines. Many, many love lines intersected and crossed and cut each other off.

Her own palm encoded one love line, a fortune teller had told her when she was in college, a short one. Father John, her confessor in Chicago, who had a six percent chance of being a child molester, had told her that fortune tellers were agents of the Devil. Bev regarded Conroy's love line—rich pink palm and gulped another swig of tasteless flame.

"Beverly, you shouldn't drink that."

She set the vodka bottle behind her so that Conroy, the thief, couldn't reach it and stared at her palm. If she just knew which faint trace on her palm was the love line, she could carve an offshoot, a crease, just so she could hope that when Conroy left she wouldn't be alone forever.

"Beverly?"

The witch had read her right hand, so Bev tossed the knife to her left hand and stared at her right. On her ring finger, the underside of her right-hand ring was worn and sandpaper-scratched. The two major creases across her palm missed each other like airplanes veering off a near-crash. She pressed the tip of the steak knife to the feathered end of the lower contrail and sliced into her skin, just the top layer of the skin because it didn't hurt, or she couldn't feel it, and a pea of blood rolled down the groove in her palm to her wrist.

CONROY WANTED TO snatch the knife away from her because she looked like she might do herself harm in another one of those cry-for-help suicide attempts but, with the point poised so daintily on her palm, grabbing it might cut her. Little tendons and muscles crisscross palms and wire the fingers, and Beverly was a pianist. "Beverly, give me the knife."

"No." Overhead light rained on her wavy brown hair, which fell in folds around her elfin face. A tear leaked down one cheek, and she brushed it away with the back of her hand, the hand that held the knife. The knife was near her throat but pointing out and away from her.

Conroy jumped, grabbed her knife-wielding hand, and slammed it into the cabinets above her head. The steak knife, pointing out, swiveled in her fist like a snake head.

He thumped her hand against the cabinets again, but she didn't drop the knife. Her other hand slapped and smacked his head and shoulders. A scramble, kicking, and he pushed her knees aside, away from his balls.

Her latte-colored eyes widened and she struggled. Her arm rippled from where his hand clamped around her wrist down to her shoulder. Her other hand flailed. Trembling attacked her body. "Don't hurt me, please don't hurt me."

He strangled her wrist in his fingers and against the wood cabinet above their heads, trying to open her fist and make her drop the knife. "Give me the knife."

"No!" Tears tinged with mascara soot striped her skin.

"It wasn't supposed to be like this," he said. His own eyes heated, and shameful tears impended. "If that priest hadn't butted in, it wouldn't have been like this."

"I needed him." Her voice was harsh in her throat, as if the words shredded her larynx fighting their way out.

"But I wasn't going to leave until that priest screwed everything up."

"*Don't blame him.* You did this. You *left.* You *left* me and Christine and Dinah. *Let me go.*"

Beverly sucked in a sob, and she keened a wavering note. The vibration rattled up her knife-arm and into his hand pressing it against the cabinet. Her keening grief rose in the kitchen and hovered. She hadn't been as distraught and enraged as this when she'd found Peggy's underwear. Whatever she and the priest were conspiring, it wasn't divorce. If it had been, she wouldn't have been grief-stricken at his leaving. She would have been vindicated.

It was just as Leila said, that Beverly wanted him to stay.

He could have Beverly back, if he worked things right.

Indeed, if he worked things very right, he could demand concessions for his return.

He readjusted his grip on Beverly's wrist, and her hand clutching the steak knife swiveled as if the knife was seeking something to bite, but his hand was below the slashing orbit. "You and that priest ganged up on me and I had to leave, but I didn't want to. I don't want a divorce."

Beverly sucked in air with a moist slurp. Her arm clutching the knife that he wedged against the cabinet stilled. "What?"

"It was the priest, and you two ganging up on me. I thought you wanted a divorce."

"I never wanted a divorce." She looked back at him. Clay gumbo makeup smeared from her eyelashes to her temples as if wind-whipped.

He had to tread delicately. He had to work her around to his advantage. First, that priest had to be out of the picture. "I didn't want to leave. It was that priest."

She blinked rapid-fire, more vibration than movement.

"He meddles. I don't want him around."

Beverly rubbed her temple as if from a migraine, and her earthy eye makeup feathered up. Saline tears popped out of her eyelashes and ran down her nose and cheekbones. "Okay."

He tightened his grip on her hand, pressed against the cabinet doors, above their heads. He had worked so hard to twist away from his marriage.

All the men who moved and shook science ended up with beautiful, young wives of dense mass and high gravitation who gathered vortexes of admiration at parties and drew yet more powerful men into the man's circle. A spectacular wife was every bit as important as a prestigious grant or a prominent publication record. He needed someone *attractive*. Beverly was losing mass and gravitational pull. The skin on Beverly's wrist that he held against the cabinets seemed loose, compared to Leila's flesh when he'd grabbed her young arm.

But Leila had dumped him, and being alone was worse than a less-than-premium wife. Alone provoked pity; respect and awe did not jibe with pity.

Her hand holding the knife above them was limp, loosening, and he relaxed his grip to compensate, in case she dropped the knife.

If he was to go back, he had to be the one in control. Elation dizzied him, the alpha male, the big fish, and dragged him to the top of the metaphorical pyramid, the Pharaoh and the Mayan priest and the Illuminatus.

He said, "And if I come back, I want an open marriage. No more fights and sulking. If I come home at night, then I'm home, and if I don't, it's none of your business."

LEILA ROLLED AGAINST the chilled wall and glanced up at the priest. "It's too quiet."

The priest shook his head, and his hair swished in his eyes. "Maybe they're talking."

At least he had that funky Italian accent rather than an Irish one. An Irish accent is stereotypical of hypocritical, evil priests.

They skulked closer, two shuffling spies skirting the circles of hallway light that stuck to the breezeway wall and concrete floor. When Leila touched the brick wall with her head, harsh voices infiltrated the bricks, talking.

Talking meant they had a chance. When Leila was a child, her parents had had horrible screaming fights, but even the shouting was better than the last fight, when her mom and dad had sat across from each other in the living room, unspeaking, frozen. Leila had crept out of her bedroom that night and listened from the hallway. For hours, one of them inhaled, held it, and then leaked out a wordless breath. And then the other did the same thing.

BEV TOUCHED HER TEMPLE. The pain felt like a bullet slowly working in. *An open marriage.* He was crazy. *Virgin Mary, Mother of God, help me,* she prayed to the silence.

"After all," he said and he looked up near the ceiling, past her head, past his hand imprisoning her left hand and the knife, "It's not your fault. Women want marriage."

"Stop it," Bev said. Poison laced his words and shut down her body. She was numb.

"Men want sex. It's only natural." He shrugged, and his shoulder bobbed his hand that pinned hers to the kitchen cabinets.

"It's not *natural.*" Bev wanted to cover her ears but Conroy still jammed her hand against the cabinets above their heads and stretched her shoulder and chest.

"Of course it's natural. Men spread their seed. That's why they make many sperm. And, when a man becomes powerful enough, famous enough, he has the chance to do that."

"Stop." All this was stupid. It was against God's plan. It was the slobbering of beasts. It reduced Man, created in the likeness of God, to sperm. Conroy strangled her hurting left arm, and the knife was hot in her cold hand.

Here was the clickover: her perspective shifted, and her aims changed from *maintaining the family* to *dealing with the divorce.* Her face changed, from the naked, raw soul of an intimate family relationship to a defensive posture that she might take with a stranger.

Her foreign face was stiff. "No. I want a divorce."

His face contorted on one side, an asymmetry of unbelieving, contradicting. "Come on, Beverly. We have to be honest, here."

Dinah and Christine could not be subjected to such degradation. They shouldn't be indoctrinated that infidelity and selfishness were acceptable. Conroy, her older, wiser, doctor husband, who had kneeled with her before the altar—how she had loved him!—wasn't worth it. She struggled again but his fist still bolted her sore hand to the cabinet. Her wrist crushed inside, sharp bones snagging vessels and tendons in sharp pains. She said, "I want a divorce."

"What about the girls?"

"I'll get custody. You were screwing around." Numbness crawled down her left arm. "You told Dante you were."

"That was under the seal of confession or doctor-patient privilege, and Leila will deny it, too. You can't prove it."

Proof? The bastard wanted proof? He'd harangued her with science all these years, belittling God and religion and her faith. Those who live by science should die by science. "I kept those pink panties from your suitcase. The DNA on them will prove you were screwing around."

"You can't mean this." His entire face drew up at a point in the middle, forehead, eyebrows, upper lip, as if a fishhook snagged his hairline.

"I mean it."

The incredulity in his face collapsed and he *laughed*. The *bastard* laughed. "Oh, come on, Beverly. We'll have an open marriage. It doesn't matter if I screw Leila or Peggy or Valerie or anyone else."

She mattered. Marriage mattered. Dinah and Christine mattered. *Peggy? Valerie?*

She had to leave. She had to go to the Church and to Dante because Conroy's words were killing her. Adrenylated or God-granted strength rumbled in her body and geysered up her pinned left arm. With her other hand, Bev grabbed his wrist from her arm and yanked, and his hand lifted off her arm and flung back through space.

She'd been straining against his weight and stringy strength, and her hand he had crushed against the cabinet, holding the silver steak knife, fell and arced, a whipping golf swing. She turned the knife and pushed out and pushed Conroy and his *stupid* ideas away from her and poked Conroy's chest, on the right side of his bleached white shirt.

The knife slid between his third shirt button and his pocket that contained two ballpoint pens, one blue, one red, all the way up to its simulated maple wood handle.

Chapter Thirteen

Conroy watched the knife fall and intersect warmly with his chest. The knife was hot, not scalding or searing but gently burning, like sunburn.

His heart, which had thumped routinely, pulsed like a sun consuming itself and grabbed the knife, fought, and slashed itself on the serrated edge.

He flopped to the linoleum floor. Beverly's astonished face followed him down. Her hands flapped in front of him and her knee knocked his thigh. She scooted her knees under her and ran. Her footsteps floated. The door banged open, hitting the wall. His legs swam on the floor and, finding no traction, flailed bonelessly. "Beverly!"

She stood in the kitchen doorway, clutching her keys. "Conroy?"

He tried to roll over and crawl to the phone, but his arm jostled the knife in his torn chest and he fell back. He gasped, and his lungs' breathing ripped his heart against the serrations of the knife's edge, forged to slice meat. "Help."

Beverly grabbed the kitchen phone. Banging, clanging. "It's dead. There's something wrong with the phone." She dashed about. A clatter, a ruffle in time with his tripping heart, the rattle and jangle of her purse spilling on the counter, three beeps, and she said, "Hello? Hello!"

His heart swung on tough cardiac muscles lifted onto the knife by his lungs. He tried not to breathe, and it was easier than he'd thought.

Beverly's voice whispered into the phone, "I think it's his heart," and "Fifty-one."

Beverly's hands were on his chest. The knife vibrated all the way to his flipping, ripping heart. He grabbed her hands. She shouldn't pull it out. It should be removed in an operating room. Ripping it out would drag the serrations through his chest and cause more damage.

"Conroy." Her whisper raced at him and zoomed away, like he was falling asleep.

Gravity descended and settled over Conroy, pressing on his chest. Indigestion bloated and squeezed him, and his organs shifted.

Stop, stop, stop. Make it stop. Undo it all. Please God. Please, Jesus, Mary, and Joseph.

Every time Bev blinked, the instant of darkness relieved her that it was all a dream and every time her eyelids parted Conroy still splayed on the linoleum, squirming.

Please, Mary Mother of God, if you can hear me, make it stop.

Be with us now and in the hour of our death.

DANTE LIFTED HIS HEAD away from the cold bricks. "Can you hear anything?"

"It's too quiet." Leila glanced around, back and forth, skittish. "I don't like it. Let's go."

Dante's cellular phone rumbled in his pocket, and his chilled skin retracted from the vibrating. The screen read *Sloan, C.* He flipped it open. "Hello?"

Bev's terrified whisper: "Dante? Something terrible." Her voice crackled with crying. "Can you come to 51 Vita Place? Near University Hospital."

"I'm here." He ran to the door and thumped it with his fist. "I'm here."

A thud on the other side of the door, fumbling, and the door opened. "Oh, Dante. He's hurt, he's hurt," she whispered and rocked toward him. Bev looked past him and her whisper focused to a hiss. "What's *she* doing here?"

Leila nudged Dante aside and ran through the apartment.

Dante followed Leila inside and tucked Bev under his arm. Bev leaned on him.

"Where's Conroy?" Dante asked.

"In there." Bev said and hid her face against Dante's coat. "He's hurt."

Dante snatched the cellular phone out of her hand and scrolled back through the numbers called to make sure that she had called an ambulance. The number below his was 9-1-1.

Leila ran past them. She hit the door to the kitchen and it slammed behind her and she screamed a hoarse, wordless burst.

Dante untangled Bev's arms from his waist and ran.

IN THE KITCHEN, Leila grabbed Conroy's pulseless throat and tried to listen to his gasping chest, but the knife bumped her forehead.

She'd stabbed him. His bitch wife had *stabbed* him.

Conroy's breath gasped, shuddered, and pressed out. He needed more air. No one could live on so little air. He was suffocating. Leila wrenched his head back, pinched his nose, and blew into his gaping mouth. She did that three times, and she should pound his chest but she couldn't find a way to do that without wrenching the knife deeper so she kept blowing in his mouth.

The priest whirled into the kitchen and stared at her perching over Conroy, sucking air, crunching over, and spewing it into Conroy's mouth. The kitchen faded. Breathe, fold over, blow. She turned and hacked a deep smoker's cough and gasped, "Help me!"

The Monsignor fell to his knees beside her and inspected the knife. "Stop for moment."

Leila sat back and panted, and the world expanded again in her vision.

The priest searched under Conroy's jawline and listened at his chest. Conroy sucked in a rattling breath under the priest's dark head. The priest said, "He's breathing."

"But it's not enough," Leila said. "He needs more air. He's suffocating."

"I can feel the pulse."

"But he can't breathe!"

Conroy rattled another breath.

The priest said, "He is breathing."

"He's not breathing enough! Do you want him to die? Don't you care he's dying?" Leila sucked in a great draught of air and blew it into Conroy's mouth. His neon blue irises glinted under the gray lashes of his slit-open eyes.

The priest laid his hand on her shoulder as if to pull her away and she swung her fist through the air, punching him in the jaw, knuckle-bone to mandible. "Get away from him! He needs more air!" She gulped in air and blew into Conroy's mouth again.

A siren whined outside and wound down. Beverly Sloan yelled for them to hurry.

Chapter Fourteen: Conroy

Conroy drifted off the floor, floating. His body shuttled blood away from his extremities to keep his brain alive, so his limbs lost sensation and, with no input from the floor under them or the pressure of gravity, his brain interpreted that as floating.

That was a bad sign.

Nausea, motion sickness, a roller coaster had caught hold of him, and he closed his eyes. Motion sickness is due to the clash of competing sensations; here, the lack of feedback from his skin felt like floating but the steady visual input from his eyes maintained that he was lying on the floor, so he closed his eyes. He floated, and his stomach settled.

Wind blew over him, another sense stimulus from his brain unable to interpret a lack of sensation from the body. Light reddened his eyelids, and bright corneal scars pocked his visual field: floaters, often mistaken for ghosts.

A weak voice, screaming through the hurricane wind, said that the paramedics were coming, and that was a nice thought.

The typhoon-force wind brightened, and sunlight blasted him, as if he had floated so far up that the solar wind streaming with photons and subatomic particles and cosmic radiation and neutrinos had caught him, and now he was falling into the sun, spread-eagle, like a parachutist slowing his descent by air friction.

The light couldn't be that bright. He was in the kitchen, it was night, and the fluorescent fixture overhead emitted flickery photons from electricity-excited neon or argon noble gas.

Ah, his other senses must be shutting down, and his brain was filling in the details.

The body's view of the world is like living in a darkened room and looking through a window at the bright sunshine-reflected landscape outside. The light reflects on the oak tree and the swingset and Beverly's face, and the reflected light particles transmit through the clear cornea of the eye, enter the vitreous humor, and excite cones and rods in the eyes' retinas. The photosensitive cells transmit electrical excitations corresponding to the light's color-imbued wavelengths to the optic nerve that innervates the retina, and the optic nerve carries the electrochemical potentials along its axons to dendrites that release neurotransmitters, and these stimulate action potentials of other neurons, and eventually the pattern of neuron firings builds a mental image of sunlight and the yard and Beverly pushing the girls on the swingset.

And now, the rods and cones in his eyes must be shutting down, ceasing to receive light and signals from the outside world, like the sun outside the window going out.

Standing inside a lit room and staring at a dark window, reflections inside the room look like they are outside. Because all the images Conroy had ever seen were merely excitations and patterns and runs and clumps within his pack of neurons, there was no difference to him between the time when his neurons were stimulated by light-excited rods and cones in his eyes and now, with his neurons sparking inside his head, and Conroy's father walked out of the sun and shook his hand. His smooth palm was warm and somehow huge.

Conroy had no externally derived evidence to refute his father's existence. His father, auburn-haired and green-eyed and gold-tanned skin, the colors and musky scent of early autumn, was preserved, formaldehyde- and mummy-wise, in his late thirties.

Conroy studied the brilliant, whirling nimbus and said to his father, "I'm a doctor."

His father, his red-gold hair glowing around his head in the slanting gold sunlight, a reflection on the glass of Conroy's frontal lobe, smiled.

Conroy's brain filled in the sensory void with an image of his father, as the brain uses color or continuous detail to fill in the empty spot in the visual field where the optic nerve infiltrates the retina, but it was pleasant to see his father again, even if it was only for a moment, and even if it was only an illusion in this calm space they floated in.

Conroy said, "You have two granddaughters, Christine and Dinah."

His father nodded, still smiling blankly.

"I'm doing some interesting experiments, using recombinant rabies virus to trace the neuronal pathways of infection in the brain. Well, mice brains."

His father nodded again.

Wild, shimmering light bulleted silently past them, like standing unperturbed between the tracks of two opposing, rushing trains. Painless light like laser ablation began to eat through the midsection of his father and himself.

"Damn, huh Dad?" Conroy asked and watched his legs decompose.

His father nodded, sadly this time.

"Well, good-bye, then."

Neurotransmitters shuttled between his crackling neurons while Conroy stood beside his smiling, eroding father, occasionally venturing a comment about his life and his research, and then fewer of the protein-loaded bubbles floated in the interneural areas of his brain, and then the light and his father and Conroy dimmed and sputtered, and apoptosis began its work on his neurons in the dark.

Chapter Fifteen

Carl and Menz, the paramedics, bagged the knife-pinned man lying in the kitchen and pumped air into him with a hand-held balloon while the priest and the two women stood around them in a silent triangle. Brown-lined, scarlet blood stained the guy's shirt around the knife handle. Carl turned and spoke into his shoulder-mounted microphone. "We've got a white male, fifties, with an apparent knife wound to the chest." Carl squeezed the bag, and the guy's chest lifted. Air did not rush around the knife as his lungs inflated. "Not a sucking chest wound."

Menz recognized the patient and nudged Carl. "It's Dr. Sloan. Neurology."

Carl said into his shoulder mike, "Page Dr. Kumar for surgery."

Menz found no pulse at Sloan's throat and listened to his silent chest. He frowned at Carl, indicating his unwillingness to pull the knife or press his chest around it. "Let's transport him."

Carl nodded.

They lifted him onto the gurney, wheeled him past the priest and the women, and settled him in the ambulance. After a lurch and a jostle, the ambulance screamed into the cold night.

In the ambulance, leaning against a tight right turn, Carl checked Dr. Sloan, who was unconscious and barely breathing, and asked Menz, "Which of them do you think did it?"

Menz shrugged. "They all had blood on them. Twenty on the girl, if you'll give me three-to-one odds, and if she's not his wife."

Carl shook his head. "I could give you three-to-one on the priest, but two-to-one is the best I can do for the girl."

BEV WATCHED the paramedics wheel Conroy out of the kitchen and rubbed the trickle of blood off her arm with a paper towel. The drying blood left a crust in the crease of her hand. Bev said to Dante, "He hasn't had Last Rites."

Dante's hand was tangled in his black hair. "It was just a small knife."

Leila sank to the floor and held her head in her hands.

Bev said, "He's Catholic. He has to have Last Rites."

Leila said, "He had that death rattle." She covered her face, and her hair drooped forward. With the smooth mask of her fingers behind the black fall of her hair and black clothes, she looked faceless.

Dante shook his head. "His breathing was irregular, but that can be due to cardiac tamponade, pressure from blood pooling inside his chest."

The countertop beside Bev rose, towered over her, and she sat on the floor. Dante had jumped the space between them, the white floor marred by a comet-shaped smear of darkening blood. "Bev?"

"We need to go to the hospital," Bev said.

Leila was still a blank-faced, black-ragged lump on the floor.

Dante lifted her by her right arm and she gathered her feet under her. His hand whipped and pushed up her sleeve on her left arm. "My God, Bev. What has happened?"

"I don't know." A livid red bruise swelled under her skin around her left wrist and up to her elbow. Her arm began to throb, dully, then more sharply, and then pain ripped into her arm. Cold grabbed her like frost had sublimed on her skin.

Spinning, and Bev flew through the air. Dante's chest was beside her, and the apartment rushed by and cold air shocked her. He said, "We will be at the hospital soon."

A car engine roared, and Bev flopped and tried to hold her arm against her, and it hurt more and more, grinding pain, spiking pain, and then Dante hoisted her in his arms again and sprinted into manic lights.

His yell for help was a distant wind rush when the pain cracked her swelling, distended arm and the white lights on the ceiling sprouted black, consuming holes that drank the light out of the room. She lay back and her legs rose without her volition. Cradling surrounded her, as if the Virgin Mary's arms wrapped her, and the Virgin Mary's black robes swept around her and blotted out the light.

DANTE STOOD OVER Conroy amidst the monitors. Lines flowed across, but the alarms were silent. Conroy's chest was an open barrel of bloody organs, his broken ribs splayed. His dripping lungs swelled and collapsed with the whooshing ventilator. His pale skin was bluish on his torso and sun damage peppered his limbs but not his feet, which were like closed white tulips.

"I can't wear the gloves," Dante said.

The blood-splashed surgery team stood back, masked and gloved and goggled. "It's procedure to glove until we disconnect him." The surgeon wouldn't look at Dante, tacit understanding or unease in the presence of unscientific religious ritual.

"It isn't our procedure." Dante stripped off the latex gloves, inside out and inside one another, and tossed them in the biohaz waste bin.

The nurse wearing mint green scrubs, his flowered mask trailing behind him by its strings, sprinted in, holding a tiny vial. "Found it in the chapel."

Dante took the glass vial and turned it over. A computer-printed label read *Oil for Extreme Unction – Catholic – blessed by Bishop Thomas O'Henry.* "Thank you, Luis." He twisted open the vial of oil and tipped it. The olive oil moistened his thumb and a green-tinged bead ran into the crevices of his wrist, near the green surgical gown that covered his clothes.

Extreme Unction confers grace sacramentally; that is, all Conroy's sins would be forgiven as if he had confessed and been reconciled. By fiat, he was destined for Heaven: the selling of indulgences all over again.

If Conroy had sinned since his confession, his sins would slide off with the application of the oil. Greasing him with olive oil wouldn't prevent damnation, if God willed. Surely.

Such blasphemy, such sin, to think of the last Catholic rite as no more than a dash of olive oil to prepare the faithful for a hellfire sauté.

Dante recited, "Through this Holy Unction and His own most tender mercy, may the Lord pardon thee whatever sins or faults thou hast committed," Dante painted Conroy's freckled forehead with an oily cross below his moonlight hair, "by sight," wiped olive oil over Conroy's closed eyelids, taped down for surgery with papery strips, "by smell," touched the enlarged pores on Conroy's nose, "by taste," moistened Conroy's pale, thin lips around the white, plastic ventilator tube that ran down his throat, and bloody trickle speckled the hydrophobic oil, "by touch," he dribbled warm olive oil on his own hands and slipped unguent lines down Conroy's cool palms, leaning over Conroy's open chest stuffed with raw meat chunks to reach his other hand, "by walking," and anointed the thin, calloused soles of his bare feet that protruded from under the green surgical drape, "or by carnal delectation," lifted the surgical drape and smeared the remaining oil on Conroy's rusty, disinfectant-smeared naked lower belly and catheterized, shriveled penis.

Buzz, a quivering among the surgical staff. "What was that?" They bobbled like shoving, green penguins. "That's not how I've seen it done."

Dante raised his blood- and oil-streaked bare hands and prayed over Conroy's open chest, scarlet organs, sawed ribs, and papyrus skin. Machines pumped his lungs, though his stilled heart did not push the blood through his dying body and tattered soul. "Amen."

"All right," Dante said. "Call it."

The staff surrounded Conroy's stringy, blown-open body.

Luis said, "Time of death, one-o-seven A.M., February fourteenth."

THE AUTOMATIC GLASS DOORS rushed out of her way and Leila walked into the ER. In the sherbet-hued chairs, the black-draped priest hunched, his miserable head caught in his hands.

She wasn't here to console anyone. On the phone, the nurse had said Sloan was conscious and responding at admission and would be out of surgery soon. Her heart had leapt up.

Two fluttery male nurses wearing baby blue scrubs manned the nurses' desk, running back and forth, shouting anxious numbers at each other, *eighty over thirty, two liters, three units, twenty bucks for Taste of China.*

Leila approached the priest. "Are you all right, Monsignor?"

He swiveled and blinked in the fluorescent glare. "Leila."

Contrary to her stiff spine, an apology bubbled up. "I won't cause a scene."

He rubbed his left temple with his thumb. "Please sit."

"I'm just going up to see Conroy when he's out of surgery. Do you know if he's out?"

"Oh, God, Leila. Please sit down." The rasp in his voice was a warning.

Her hands fluttered in the air. Turquoise fluorescent light reflected on their shocking paleness. "I'm just here to see Conroy."

The priest's tan fingers interwove with her pale hand and tugged. Her body followed her hand down, and her denying knees folded. The metal seat chilled her legs. "I'm sorry, I'm very sorry," he whispered, "but he didn't make it."

Ridiculous. "They said he's in surgery."

"They are wrong. Bev is in surgery."

"It was just a tiny, little knife," Leila said, and her shrill voice rang in the ER despite the bright, new acoustic ceiling tile, replaced after last summer's leaky pipe epidemic. Father Dante held her one hand but her other hand floated and signed complex emotions that someone else must be feeling. "It was only a steak knife."

Dante fished her grasping hand and held it low between them.

"It was this big." Her spidery fingers formed a void an inch, two and a half centimeters, twenty-five millimeters apart, and in unreal parallax it looked like she was pinching his sanctified head between her fingertips. "*This big.* He couldn't have died from *that.*"

"The surgeon said that the injury was to his left ventricle."

The heart's muscular left ventricle collected oxygenated blood and pumped it into the entire body. A slash to the left ventricle would gush blood and push it nowhere, like clapping in water. Her own heart sloshed.

"I'm sorry," he said. Both his hands wrapped around her pale, cold hands but she couldn't feel them. He said, "I'm so sorry."

DANTE READ A BIBLE he'd found in a drawer while he sat beside Bev's hospital bed, waiting for her to wake from the anesthesia.

Bev had been out of surgery for—he consulted his wristwatch that read four o'clock—an hour, yet she hadn't regained consciousness.

Bev coughed. The cylindrical steel cage on her arm bristled with steel pins and hovered midair in a sling, like a multi-antennae satellite flying in space, radioing messages. Bev's eyes cracked open, each an edge of bloodshot sclera interrupted by brown iris, rimmed by lashes and faint, radiating lines. Her free, uninjured hand pushed a hair wisp off her forehead.

Dante flipped the Bible over and laid it on his lap. He leaned toward her. "Bev?"

She whispered, "Conroy?"

The lump in Dante's throat sharpened, but this wasn't the time to tell her Conroy had passed away. Another sharpness, a thin glass sliver, cut deeper near his sternum.

Her eyes crimped shut.

PANCHA LOOKED UP from the romance novel she was hiding at the nurses' desk and glanced at Beverly Sloan's door. Father Dante, who spoke Spanish so nicely, had said he'd alert her when Mrs. Sloan woke because Pancha needed to take Mrs. Sloan's vitals when the sedative wore off. Maybe he'd fallen asleep. Four o'clock in the morning was a tired time. Madre Dios knew that Pancha had read three times the passage describing Izabella's frothy, flowing, voluminous, lavender gown that scantily clad her heaving bosoms.

LEILA WAITED in the doorway until Beverly Sloan went back to sleep.

The priest was leaning forward almost off his chair, positioned to fall on his knees beside the hospital bed. His black eyes were open and raw. He touched the white sheet near Beverly Sloan's leg. It wouldn't have surprised her if he'd scooped Beverly Sloan into his arms, or howled to God, or wept, but he sat back and his throat under his Roman collar clenched as he opened the Bible. His eyes swept the page, a roving bulge under his eyelids.

Leila breezed into the room as if she'd been walking down the hall.

The priest looked up, professional and cool.

She flipped her hand at the hallway. "The cops want to talk to you. They're eating chips in the vendoland down the hall."

"She shouldn't be alone when she wakes. Tell her I'll be back soon." He said it offhandedly, casually, as if a moment ago he hadn't been heart-wrenchingly reaching for her.

"I've got to go see a friend of mine. She's two floors up."

"I'll be back in a moment."

He left Leila alone with the sleeping Beverly Sloan, who twitched and bobbed her head, almost waking, until Leila wanted to run out of the room screaming.

THE YELLOW-PAINTED ROOM was not Bev's bedroom. It was a hospital, the university hospital. Yellow walls. Yellow meant orthopedics.

Both her hands were bandaged. Her right hand was wrapped with gauze across the palm, and her fingers stuck out. Her left arm was pinned in the air by bright silver stakes. She trailed the fingers of her gauzed right hand with sadly chipped fingernail polish down her left arm from her shoulder to the pins. Just above the pins, her skin changed from normal skin, sensitive as a tongue, to dull neoprene, like a Novocained cheek or a foot trapped in ice.

A thin beige blanket covered her legs, and she jostled her thighs and calves against each other under the starchy sheet. Sandpaper abraded the skin on each of her legs.

She must have done something odd to injure only her left arm. She might have been in a car accident with her arm hanging out the window. The girls might have been in the car. *The girls,* and Bev struggled because she had to go see them right away right this minute now.

"Mrs. Sloan." Hands pushed her back onto the bed. "I'll call a nurse. Don't get up."

Bev followed the pale hands and arms pushing her against the bed up to Leila.

Bev choked. The hospital room was a prison and this girl was keeping Bev from her little girls. Leila tapped the nurse call button. "Father Petrocchi-Bianchi will be right back."

Her leg jerked, trying to fling out of bed. Puked-up spider webs wrapped Bev's tongue. "My girls," she said. "Christine and Dinah."

"They weren't there. They're okay." So-young Leila Faris gazed out the door, didn't meet Bev's eyes.

"You're not just saying that? They're really okay?"

"They weren't at his apartment. Please lie back—your arm, the pins."

Relief settled in Bev's chest. "What happened? Why is this thing," she pointed at the shining metal contraption, "on my arm?"

Leila lifted her hands off Bev's shoulders but she hovered. "I don't know. You hurt your arm and needed some surgery. Father Petrocchi-Bianchi will be back in a minute."

Bev leaned back on the pillow. "And Conroy?"

The resigned floppiness in Leila's neck dissipated, and she drew herself up like a straightening giraffe. "He's fine."

DANTE TOUCHED the cold door with his reluctant fingertips as he walked in. Everywhere, hospitals were cold, as if trying to avoid the spoilage of so much meat. Leila stared at the floor. Bev was half-propped up on her right arm, the sling still levitating her left arm in midair, staring at Leila.

"Bev?" Dante's voice croaked, rasped around her name, and he swallowed to clear his throat.

Both women looked up at him, startled, two pairs of brown eyes, one face shrouded by hair shining like a raven's wing waterfall by night, one topped by untidy tousled oak-colored waves.

Leila said, "See, he's back," and walked away. She checked up next to Dante and grabbed his wrist, and his skin lapped at Leila's fragile hand. He wanted to jerk away. Her skin abraded his arm, which felt as sensitive as if he was burned. His unleashed body wanted to maul another woman like the rabid beast it was.

Leila said, "She's asking about her kids."

From the bed, Bev watched Leila and her hand clamped around Dante's arm. He said, "They're with Laura. I haven't checked on them, but Laura has them."

Bev curled as if her heart tried to suck her whole body into itself. "Thank you, God." She sighed and asked, her voice a tenuous straight line, "Did something happen to Conroy?"

God and all the saints in heaven, how could she not remember?

Leila's hand loosened and her footsteps clapped away, leaving Dante and Bev alone in the chlorine-permeated hospital.

"Dante?" Bev's trained voice projected despite a quiver. "*Father* Dante?"

Perhaps it was shock at her husband's death or guilty repression of a homicidal memory or the physical shock of traumatic injury and subsequent administration of sedatives and previous administration of alcohol or the mercy of God or a lie, but she said that she didn't remember.

"Bev." He didn't know whether to be her priest, her friend or her lover.

She leaned forward in the bed, but her arm was still trapped in the suspended pin cage.

He dragged the chair close to the bedside, and the metal legs screeched like a crow.

She watched him warily from the side of her eyes, barely breathing.

"I'm so sorry, Bev, but I have bad news." Her gauze-bandaged right hand rested on the bedcovers, and he held her clammy fingers in both his palms. Cotton padded her hand. She was strung between his grip and the tractioned pin cage. "Conroy passed away last night, suddenly."

She blinked a few times. "Did you give him Last Rites?"

A memory or a repetition? "Yes."

She straightened in the bed—her arm pendulumed—and shook her head like a cat flinging earwax. Her fingers slipped out of his hand. "Was it a heart attack? His father died of a heart attack."

The police had warned Dante not to talk to Bev about that night, but damn the police, he could talk to her about anything in the world because priest-penitent communication was privileged. He was still a priest. Even though he broke his vows and hers, he was still a priest.

"Wait, Bev." Dante searched his pocket for his purple stole, carried from habit. He muttered the prayer for strength and wisdom, kissed the cross at its center, and laid it around his neck.

"Why are you doing that?" Her gauzed fingers drew a line in the air, indicating the stole.

"Because now we are under the seal of confession."

"I don't have anything to confess."

"Still, it's better this way."

"All right." She shook her confused head. A tear dripped, and she rolled her shoulder to wipe it off. "Was it the fighting that caused the heart attack?"

"I don't think so." Lying with the confession stole around his neck was merely an additional stain on the sullied rite of reconciliation and an additional crack in his parched, creviced soul, if he had a soul.

BEV UNTANGLED her fingers from her hair and settled her bandaged hand on her chest. Her heart percussed at an adagio tempo. It was inconceivable that, somewhere, Conroy's heart did not also abide by the time of a waltz, lub-dub-pause, lub-dub-pause. Somewhere below her, Conroy was lying still amongst the other still, chilled people, and her mind flinched back and her heart somehow, inexplicably, pulsed and shot blood through her body.

A phantom limb is an amputated limb that the brain insists is still there and so creates sensation for it. What was the opposite of a phantom limb, a limb physically there but that the mind can't reach? A zombie limb, perhaps. Her heart worked hard to push blood into her zombie arm.

A lanky form walked past the doorway, and Bev glanced up expecting to see Conroy's khaki pants visible below the hem of his long white coat, fidgeting with the pens in his left shirt pocket, but the man had citrus-orange hair and a three-quarter-length resident's white coat.

WES AND HARLEM stood outside Beverly Sloan's room. Wes whispered. "She looks groggy. If we arrest her now, a judge will throw out anything she says because she was on drugs."

"Yeah, but we're here now," Harlem said.

"We don't have a warrant."

"No, but if two people are in a room and one of them gets a knife in the chest, we arrest the other one."

"Yeah, but this isn't two gang members."

Harlem frowned at him.

Wes lowered his voice. "A judge should take a look at what the witnesses said before we go around Wyatt-Earping everyone in sight." Wes gestured to Beverly Sloan. "Her doctors haven't released her yet. Her arm is tied to the ceiling. She's got two kids and a priest standing over her. She isn't a flight risk."

IN THE LAB on the third floor of MedLabs, Leila sat at Conroy's desk and held his brown lab notebook to her chest. She had unlocked his office with the key they hid in the minus-twenty freezer.

Leila had stayed with Danna during the wee morning hours while Danna wove in and out of consciousness. The nurses said that she freaked out if she woke up and no one was there. They were trying the one experimental therapy that had shown a little promise during the English epidemic of nvCJD, but it wasn't helping. Danna's illness was driving Leila crazy.

Maybe Conroy had written something in his lab notebook about Danna, that her illness might be something else, that he might have thought of another treatment. Anything. Dear God, please, anything besides an untreatable, fatal, horrible prion.

Leila opened Conroy's notebook and stared at his amorphous handwriting.

The office fuzzed in and out of her perception, but returning home for a good night's sleep was too callous to contemplate, considering that Conroy was dead and Danna was going to die of mad goddamn cow prions. The clock wedged into Conroy's teeming bookshelves crunched as the wrought iron arrow locked into place at quarter past six, and the second hand chewed crispy time as it roved.

Yesterday, Conroy had been here, thumbing these lab notebooks and stacking ever-higher, teetering paper skyscrapers for her to godzilla around to get to his chair in order to talk to him. His body had imprinted his faux leather chair with the sink of his skinny butt, the curve of his back, the smooth grunge from his hands on the arms. His DNA was embedded in the chair vinyl. There was enough DNA from the chair and shed skin cells in the shelf dust to clone him.

A thin sliver of cheap steel shouldn't be able to undo the inconceivable number of chemical reactions that had built and maintained his body over decades. Each reaction started with atoms, was catalyzed by an enzyme, and produced a protein or other molecule within a cell within a tissue within an organ within a system within his body.

Physics doesn't understand time. Time as a vector has no ordained direction. The equations work just as well backward as forward, so they don't describe reality. Leila was constantly pinned between the past and the future with no *now*, no point of reference, just her foreboding slowly becoming memory, sliding, draining from her head down into the belly of her soul.

A slip of steel into a pocket in an organ, and Conroy's arrow of time had ceased, as if the knife had deflated his soul.

Such idle speculations were not like her. Conroy's body had lost its fight with entropy. That was all. It meant nothing else.

Leila flipped open Conroy's lab notebook to his last entry, yesterday. He'd written lab notes in that horrible prescription scrawl on the alternating pages of white and yellow graph paper. It was a wonder that the pharmacists hadn't killed him. He'd done tissue culture, passed cells and virus, and mouse work.

No notes about Danna. Damn it, where were his notes? Conroy wrote everything down. If he had bought heroin, he would have written a note in his lab notebook: its cost, color and consistency, and effects. He should have written down what he thought about Danna and what tests he'd ordered.

An experiment was titled: *Rhabdovirus neurovirulence factor 1: glycoprotein targeting and amygdale involvement.*

Rhabdovirus? No one in the lab was working with a rhabdovirus. They didn't even have any rhabdovirus stocks. God only knew which rhabdovirus he was talking about, the way a generic herpesvirus could be the virus for chickenpox or genital cold sores or mononucleosis, or a retrovirus could be chicken cancer or horse anemia or HIV.

Basic Virology: Rhabdoviridae is a dangerous virus family that includes haematopoietic necrosis virus (the kills-your-stem-cells virus), hemorrhagic septicemia virus (the bleeding and putrifying virus), vesicular stomatitis virus (VSV, a common gene vector for experiments), and rabies.

Maybe Conroy had a VSV vector. Leila flipped through the reference pages, but there was no link to a viral vector, just a strain from the ATCC, the American Tissue Culture Collection, a cell and virus bank.

Their lab didn't even have any rhabdo stocks. She turned on his desktop computer and waited for the huge screen to fizz and crackle to life. Her chest ached. She launched the web browser, pulled up the PubMed search engine, and typed in *rhabdovirus* and *neurovirulent.*

All the papers cited were about rabies viruses.

The monitor vented desert wind.

Emerging Pattern of Rabies Deaths and Increased Viral Infectivity.

Human Rabies – Iowa, 2004.

Differential Stability and Fusion Activity of Rabies Lyssavirus Glycoprotein Trimers.

All the papers were about *rabies.* The only neurovirulent rhabdovirus was *rabies.*

Motherfucker.

Leila smashed the keys with her typing and brought up the ATCC catalog page. She typed the reference number that Conroy had written in his journal into the search field.

Lyssavirus, the entry read, *rabies virus, isolated from Pipistrellus subflavus (bat), replicates in most strains of Mus musculus and mouse-derived tissue culture. P4 containment required. Restricted access. Submit restricted access order form and supporting documents.*

A hot saliva drip gathered at the corner of Leila's mouth and she snapped her jaw shut.

That motherfucker Conroy had live *rabies virus* in the lab, their lab that was only rated a P2, and the live rabies virus was floating around and growing in cells.

Conroy's strange-acting mice were *rabid,* and they had been kept in open cages.

And, oh God, oh God, Danna was sick with *viral encephalitis.*

A flush burned Leila's face like the exhale of a steam autoclave and her heart rate jogged double time. She felt feverish, and that panicked her: feverish meant symptomatic and that meant too late for vaccination. She was dying. Death crawled up her arms and legs toward her head.

Leila grabbed the lab telephone directory hanging on the wall next to Conroy's phone and a tape dispenser loaded with yellow biohazard tape and strung the locked lab door with tacky yellow ribbons crawling with red ophidian symbols before sprinting for the emergency room.

DANTE LEFT BEV sleeping and rubbed his stubble-overgrown jaw as he headed through the emergency room. The ER was harshly lit but quiet. Mint-clothed nurses drank coffee. The chairs area was empty but for a man sleeping on the floor. His straw cowboy hat covered his face, and his arms and boots were crossed.

A swinging door slapped open hard behind him, and Dante turned.

Leila sprinted past him to the nurses' desk, skidded on the tile and half-flopped over the desk. Pens flipped. Papers swished. She said, "I need help."

Dante had just left Bev's bed, but if something had happened to Bev, a blood clot or shock, someone not knowing Sloan's circumstances might have called Bev's emergency contacts. Leila might have answered Sloan's lab phone.

Dante ran.

"There's a problem," Leila said, and Dante grabbed the nurses' desk to stop himself beside her. "I've been exposed. Other people, too." She shook a list of phone numbers. "And the lab. And there's *mice*. I need a consult from I.D., *right now*."

I.D., *Infectious diseases?* Dante waited.

"I'll page the resident," Luis said.

"Get the I.D. attending, not the resident. And the police. And Danna's attending, Marlin Pettid, neurology. Why the hell didn't Conroy *tell* him?"

It didn't seem to have anything to do with Bev. Dante asked, "Leila, can I help?"

She jumped sideways away from him. "Jesus. Why the hell are you here?" She stopped herself and stared at her spread-open hands. "Jumpiness, irritability, my God. I'm sorry. Oh, my God."

She was exhausted and panicking, almost manic. He asked again, "Can I help?"

Leila's slanted black eyes widened. "Yes. Nurse! Nurse!" She grabbed a handful of Dante's black shirtsleeve.

Luis covered the phone and said, "I'm paging the attending I.D. physician."

"And the police."

Luis dialed three numbers. "What do I tell the police?"

"Hazmat team," Leila said. "Biohazard. Get the bioterrorism unit."

Her slim, ungloved hand clutched Dante's black shirt. Her hand seemed suddenly malicious, contaminated with something that required a bioterrorism team and an infectious disease consult. Leila grabbed the nurses' desk, contaminating it, too.

The nurse gasped. "Airborne?"

"*Pipistrellus* is a bat. Bat strains can be aerosolized. Yeah, maybe airborne. At least one infectious patient, Danna Kerry, up in neurology, maybe more. I have a phone list. We have to call them all, get them here. Do you have Conroy Sloan here?"

"Dr. Sloan's remains were taken down an hour ago."

"Disinfect everything. Decon everyone. The EMTs, ambulance, surgical staff, the O.R."

Dante had scrubbed his oily, bloody hands after he'd performed Extreme Unction for Conroy, but he was contaminated if there was a pathogen. Blood had seeped onto his shirt sleeve.

Luis set down the phone. "Hazmat team's on its way. What agent?"

"Rabies," Leila said and a tear leaked out her panicking eye. Dante reached over and grabbed her cold hands. Her straining fingers twisted under his and held on. "Rabies virus. I need to start vaccinations *now*. Everyone in the lab does. This is *Dr.* Petrocchi-Bianchi, a physician." She jiggled Dante's hands. "He can tell you. It's infectious. It's dangerous."

Ah, so she needed him for his medical knowledge. All right.

"I thought you were a priest," Luis the nurse said. "You gave Dr. Sloan Last Rites, and said Mass."

"I am both. We need infectious disease consult." He wrapped one arm around Leila's narrow shoulders and said, "And an exam room."

"Exam two is open." Luis ran to the door.

Dante walked Leila to the E.R. corridors and whispered, "Did you lock the lab door?"

Leila nodded. "And taped it with biohaz tape, but it's been contaminated for months."

"You did what was right. You're all right."

"I can't feel my feet. It's neuropathy. Paralysis starts at the feet. It's already started."

"You're panicking. They'll start vaccinations. You're going to be fine."

"Why was he working with *rabies?* What kind of idiot would grow live *rabies virus?*" She dropped her head against his shoulder and sobbed. "He's killed us. He's killed us all."

He eased her away and she sat on the exam table. Her slim face pleated into sobs. She reached for his shirt so he stepped into her drowning arms. Her torso was only skin stretched over her thin rib cage, more waif-like than a fashionable *la figura bella*.

She said, "Even when Danna got sick, he didn't tell anyone. They might have been able to try something, but he didn't tell them. He's killed us all." Her voice muffled on his shirt.

He smoothed her soft black hair.

Leila clung to his hand even while a gloved, gowned and face-shielded Luis drew blood, nervously watching her maroon blood fill a tube. Luis said, "We need saliva samples, but they're going to start vaccinating you. At least they don't do it in the stomach any more."

Dante would have held onto her even if he hadn't already contaminated himself in the operating room performing Sloan's Extreme Unction. This felt right, holding someone because they were mortally afraid, even if they were infectious. Priests had always attended the lepers.

HOURS LATER, after dialing the cell phone's tiny keys with her thumbs, Leila listened to the rattle of Father Petrocchi-Bianchi's phone ringing. When the priest's answering service cut in, *'Allo, this is Father Dante Petrocchi-Bianchi*, she hit *end* and redialed, and it rang more. This time, a click, a beep, scrambling like a coyote clawing its way out of a hole, and the priest's hoary voice, "*Si?*"

"Monsignor Petrocchi-Bianchi? Dante? This is Leila Faris," she whispered. She glanced down the hospital corridor. "I'm sorry to call you."

"Ah, it's all right," he said. A scuffle. "What time it is?"

"It's 6:30 Sunday night."

"*Merda.*" His voice croaked.

"I'm sorry, but the hospital minister isn't here, and," Leila pressed the side of her face flat against the chalky plaster wall and shielded herself with her arm from the eavesdropping nurses' desk and the wandering residents and med students, "and some folks are about to get some really bad news about their daughter, a friend of mine," Leila's scratchy throat closed and she blasted a cough to clear it, "and her dad is a minister, and I'm really sorry, but could you come here?" Leila's damned vocal cords slapped. "I don't know who else to call."

Stupid hot lines dripped down Leila's cheeks.

DANTE LOOKED THROUGH the half-open door to the darkened hospital room. Inside, a shaft of hallway light picked out Leila, dressed in baggy green surgical scrubs, sitting near the foot of the girl's bed while the girl's parents wavered on either side. They didn't touch the girl in the bed. Her head twitched when one of them came close to her, but the rest of her body didn't move.

He cleared his throat. Leila looked up, a trace of silvery light from the hallway lights limning her face. She left the bed and whispered to him, "Let's go down here," and fluttered her hand down the door-lined corridor. Each door sported a chart. Each chart summarized someone's life expectancy and organized their remaining time into dosages and intervals.

She led him to the residents' crash pad, a small room with a bunk bed, a table, a couch, and a kitchenette. "I'm sorry." In her eyes, lacework of fine blood vessels covered the whites of her sclerae around her black irises. Her lank hair was damp. "Conroy should have been here. I tried calling some of the other professors but I couldn't reach anybody. They have to tell her parents."

He gestured to her green scrubs and high-heeled black boots. "Have you been home?"

"No. A friend of mine is a resident. I should page the attending." Her exhausted eyes quavered and she listed to the side. Leila flipped out her cell phone, thumbed numbers faster than a video game, and flipped it closed. "He'll be here in a minute."

"Sit down, Leila. Just for a minute."

Her eyes blinked, slowly, almost falling asleep standing up. Her hand drifted up and pressed her temple. "He went for coffee at Staff Caff." She looked out the door. "He'll be back."

The lack of sleep was punishing her frail body. "You haven't slept at all, have you?"

She smiled, a minimal weary lip curve. "I'm fine."

"Is Danna conscious?"

"The paralysis is creeping up her body. The doctor said it will paralyze her diaphragm and she'll suffocate. It seems like she should be unconscious but she's not. She's aware. She responds. She answers questions." Leila shook her head. "She's not paranoid or demented, like you would expect from an organic disease like Alzheimer's or fronto-temporal dementia or AIDS-related dementia. Her brain is fine, except that she's dying of rabies."

Leila looked out the door. "Marlin's back." Her polished black boots clacked on the hallway tile, and Dante followed her to the girl's bedside in the darkened room. Leila whispered introductions: Danna Kerry who flinched even at the whispers, her parents the Reverend and Mrs. Jebediah Kerry, and Marlin Pettid, Danna's attending physician who wasn't a marlin but a jellyfish with glutinous, translucent skin and a boneless, floating manner. Leila reeled off Dante's degrees and honorifics and surnames, which lasted too long and was mortifyingly accurate.

Dr. Pettid said, "There's a conference room down the hall." He waved a hand toward the door.

They reached a small, clinically blue conference room with a round table. Marlin Pettid sat between the Reverend and Dante, and Leila sat between Dante and Mrs. Kerry. Mrs. Kerry patted Leila's hand. "It's so nice of you to be here," she said.

Leila stared at the dark wood veneer table. "Dr. Sloan should have been here," Leila said, "but he passed away early this morning."

Mrs. Kerry said, "He didn't sound sick."

"It was sudden," Leila said.

As Marlin Pettid efficiently explained the cause of Danna's viral encephalitis, his jellyfishiness starched. By the time he explained the unavoidable, fatal outcome of advanced rabies virus infection and her probable proximate expiration, his face was raw potato white and his clinical vernacular obfuscated connotation. "She was symptomatic at presentation, so vaccination would not have been efficacious. Presenting symptoms were atypical," he explained, "unlike a canid-origin infection. An inaccurate differential diagnosis of prionic new variant Creutzfeld-Jacob Disease further complicated accurate diagnosis, before the viral encephalitis was established as due to a neurotropic lyssavirus, rabies virus. Palliative care is recommended."

The Reverend Jebediah Kerry stared across at Dante, unblinking. His gray eyes became shiny. Hearing such news about his nieces or nephew would have driven Dante eye-gouging insane.

Mrs. Kerry still gripped Leila's hand, and Leila's fingertips were bright red where the woman squeezed them. Mrs. Kerry grabbed Leila's other hand. "Danna has *rabies?*"

Dante glanced at Leila, but she didn't look back at him. His thigh was sore where they had injected the first of the vaccinations that morning.

LEILA HUDDLED UNDER the priest's black coat in the passenger seat of his car as he drove her home. The cologne that his coat had rubbed off his neck smelled like musk and spice. Her crumpled, autoclaved, steam-damaged clothes and coat filled a bag at her feet. Road grumbled under the tires. She tried not to flinch every time the car slowed down and said, "I wouldn't have pictured you as a Volvo man."

"It's the rectory's car." Headlight glare swept over his face. Every third beam picked out the white square on his Roman collar.

When he clipped that white plastic strip into the snaps in his collar every day, was he reminded of his decision to take Holy Orders, or had the ecumenical collar become clothes to him?

When she donned her lab coat every day, it didn't remind her of her commitment to rational interpretation, the empirical method, and Koch's Postulates. The lab coat protected her skin and clothes from dyes, acids, alkalis, isotopes, and viruses. What did that white collar protect him from?

When he slipped the white lab coat over the Roman-collared black shirt, the juxtaposition of the rational and the supernatural must do something in his mind. The convergence of the lab coat and Roman collar must be like a reactive metal engaging an exothermic reaction, magnesium metal sparking blue fire in the air, or lavender metallic sodium skittering and smoking on water.

"I could've driven myself home," she said. "I'm fine."

"You haven't slept. You're exhausted." His sonorous voice was amused. He sounded like God making the joke to Moses about His name, *I am what I am. Tell them I-am sent you.*

Maybe that was just in the Charleton Heston movie. Movies always screwed up books.

Headlights brightened his collar and Roman centurion face. He might be less a centurion than a patrician, reclining in a Tyrian purple–edged toga, watching tigers maul Christians. Dante might be more an antique Roman than a Dane, like Horatio. Leila was babbling in her own head, but it distracted her, which was calming.

Dante pulled the car into Leila's parking lot and stopped. She slipped out of the car as soon as it was at rest and waved to the doorman, who smiled and nodded before shaking open his newspaper. She said, "Thanks for the ride, Monsignor Petrocchi-Bianchi."

She heard him say, "Just-ah Dante," as the car door clanked closed behind her.

MONDAY MORNING, Bev was due to be discharged from the hospital. The doctors had removed the cage of pins around her arm and plastered a cast over the remaining, protruding spikes. The two policemen loitered near the nurses' desk, one of them flirting with the nurse. Dante sat next to the bed, peering out the round window.

Bev asked, "Why are the police here?"

Dante frowned. "I don't know. They're the same ones who asked questions."

The nurse came in with the discharge papers and Bev signed the unread forms. The nurse kept glancing out the door, distracted. Bev smiled at her, but the nurse didn't see or didn't care.

"That's it," the nurse said and riffled the pages, checking. She inhaled deeply and her voice projected as if speaking to the back row of a theater. "You're all checked out."

Bev glanced at Dante, who'd also looked up, startled.

Two frowning policemen stepped into Bev's room. "Beverly Maria Sloan?" one asked. The other stared at his feet.

She nodded.

"You are under arrest for the murder of Conroy Robert Sloan." They stood on either side of her. The spokesman handcuffed her right hand and continued reciting Miranda rights.

Denials and shock and dismay clogged Bev's throat. "It was his heart," she coughed out. "He had a heart attack."

Dante said, "What are you doing?" He reached toward the handcuffing officer, and the cop flipped his arm over and slammed Dante against the wall next to the window, his forearm jammed under Dante's chin.

The black cop's mustached upper lip twitched, and he said, "Do not interfere with this arrest or I'll arrest you for interfering in a lawful arrest. Do you want that?" His voice escalated. "Huh? Is that what you want? Do you want me to arrest you?"

The other cop clanged his flopping handcuffs on her numb pin-studded cast. "Harlem, he's a priest, for Christ's sake. Sorry, Father." He slapped the handcuffs at the cast again, and they bounced off. Vibration speared Bev's wrist. "These won't fit."

The cop backed off Dante, who rubbed his throat and glared.

"I can't get her into the handcuffs."

The officer stared at Bev's pin cage. "Latch them around her upper arm and we'll chain them together in back."

"You don't have to," Bev said. "I won't do anything."

"I'm sorry, ma'am," the Hispanic officer said. "It's for your protection as much as ours."

Chapter Sixteen

The Daily Hamiltonian:

Neuro Doc Passes Away

By Kirin Oberoi

Tuesday, February 16 – Prominent neurologist Dr. Conroy Robert Sloan, 53, was pronounced dead at UNHHC early Sunday morning, February 14, due to cardiac arrest. He was transported by ambulance from 51 Vita Place. The hospital was not forthcoming with details about Dr. Sloan's sudden death. The police were called to the townhouse and the hospital, though no reports are available. Police forensic technicians are at the townhouse but will not comment.

AT THE LAB that morning, Leila typed a carefully worded email to Valerie Lindh, breaking the news of Conroy's death and mentioning his off-book rabies experiments. Leila delicately refreshed Dr. Lindh's memory that the rabies virus was abundantly present in saliva and if Dr. Lindh had had any contact with Dr. Sloan's saliva—say drinking from the same glass—she should be tested and begin vaccinations immediately.

Dr. Lindh replied a half hour later, thanking Leila and telling her that she had a doctor's appointment within the hour.

BEV TRIED TO STAND straight beside the lawyer at her arraignment, but the lock-up's pharmacist had filled her prescription with something potent. Her lawyer, the judge and the bailiff slurred their words like they'd been drinking Jack and soda, and their voices rose and fell and rose and fell.

Her eyes burned. Her arm, immobilized by pins and plaster, itched.

Her lawyer, recommended by Father Samual, was a silver-streaked blonde, a transplanted Californian. His teeth shone. His skin was cast bronze. His notes were neat and his delivery crisp. His hands wove in the air like a pair of mated swans, preening and dipping over her head.

The lawyer elbowed her and she said, "Not guilty," just like he'd coached her.

AFTERWARD, as the lawyer hurried Bev to the bail bondsmen, Lydia and Mary met each other's confused eyes. Mary asked, "Did she seem okay?"

"I've heard about lawyers handing out Valium," Lydia said.

"Maybe she got Percocet or Oxycontin for her arm."

Lydia shrugged. "Maybe she'll share."

"Liddy, you're going to Hell." Mary's voice was dejected, and she said it out of habit.

"If that's where the party is," Lydia said and stood on her tired legs. The insomnia was taking its toll. Her husband had begged her to sleep, but Lydia had been too busy interpreting the insurance forms that Laura had dropped off, trying to get Bev some money to live on for the next couple of months until she was acquitted. And, dear God and Jesus and Holy Virgin, Bev must be acquitted. Lydia had been vetting the Sloans' finances, trying to figure out how much Bev needed versus how much she had, and forty thousand dollars was missing from the Sloans' joint accounts.

Mary stood beside Lydia and stretched. Mary had lain awake in bed because resting was almost as good as sleeping. She'd arranged Conroy's funeral at the church, four days hence, though she'd been creeped out the whole time. She'd also convinced the suave California lawyer to take Bev's case, though he said he normally didn't take hopeless causes.

Heath Sheldon already hated this case. The forensic evidence, what little there was this soon, was damning. Her fingerprints were on the knife in the vic's chest, yet the fingers from her crushed arm had printed the knife. That might work in favor of a battered spouse defense, but that defense hadn't played well lately due to the feminist backlash demanding that women extricate themselves from abusive relationships, and Beverly Sloan had no suspicious hospital admissions. The existence of her 9-1-1 call supported that she hadn't tried to conceal a crime, but what she had said during the call, like not mentioning the knife, was a torpedo barreling at any affirmative defense. Her lack of memory was implausible.

Damn it. Heath didn't have a toehold here. He was slipping.

Near the back of the courtroom, Kirin Oberoi scribbled quick notes in English and Punjabi on a yellow legal pad. Though the attorneys had spoken in dispassionate vernacular, she'd heard titillating stuff. This case could make her career. A murder this lurid could end up on LawTV. Probing articles questioning the institution of marriage and the Church and that growling pretty-boy priest could lead to prizes, maybe the Pulitzer, and a book deal. She thumbed the wobbly keys on her cell phone as she ran outside into the brittle February sun.

THAT AFTERNOON, Leila pipetted twenty-five microliters, two dozen snowflakes worth, of lightly salted water onto a speck of DNA in a bullet tube, a plastic vessel the size of a .32 bullet, and twiddled the tiny tube. With Conroy gone, she didn't have to hide her side project, which wasn't even dangerous. Nothing like rabid mice, anyway.

Past the other counters and shelves, the lab door snicked open.

She ejected the yellow conical tip off the end of the pipetter into a jar filled with pipetter tips and looked across the lab, through shelves laden with clear bottles of salt buffers and bright kit boxes. The black specter of Monsignor Dante Petrocchi-Bianchi magnified in the buffer bottles like funhouse mirrors as he strode in and looked around. Leila's knees buckled. She sat on the floor behind the lab bench, still twiddling the tube.

Joe wandered over. "Father Dante, are you lost?"

The priest said, "Hi, Joe. I'm looking for Leila Faris. She works here?" From where Leila sat, the priest's dark voice brimmed with undertones, viral in its malevolence. Her pulse cantered, and cheekbones felt windburned. She appreciated that he'd helped with Danna's parents, but she didn't want to see him right now. She needed more time to deal with everything, Conroy' death, Danna's illness, having been alone with the priest in his car, everything.

"Yeah," Joe said. A pause. "She was just here. Leila?"

Leila sneaked her hand up over the bench and pressed the DNA tube into an insulated bucket of ice. Moist cold slipped through her gloves to her fingertips.

Joe said, "She probably went for coffee. You could wait for her."

Crap. She slowly twisted the knob of the cupboard door below the whooshing radioactive fume hood and removed a liter bottle from the cabinet that smelled like overripe peaches. A cup or so of acetone swished in the bottom of the brown bottle. "Joe!" she yelled. "Do we have any more reagent-grade acetone?"

"Oh, hey!" Joe turned. "Hey! You have a visitor."

"Oh? Had my head in the fume hood. We're out of acetone, Joe. Could you do me a favor? I'm in the middle of a kinase assay."

Joe frowned. "I thought you were cloning."

Leila continued, "And I desperately need acetone to precipitate the protein. Biochem Stores closes in a half hour and I can't leave this," she gestured toward the ice bucket. "Could you get me some acetone? I'll bring donuts tomorrow."

"Jelly donuts?" Joe poked around in his desk drawer for the University Stores credit card.

"Raspberry."

"Deal." He chucked his chin at the priest and walked out of the lab.

Leila spun around and faced the priest. "What can I do for you?"

His eyes were bloodstained near the black irises. Bruising purpled the skin under his eyes. He said, "I need to know what you told the police."

She rolled her eyes. "In America, we call this 'witness tampering.'"

"I just want to know what you told them, not change your mind." He looked down, and his eyelids covered his black eyes.

"She killed him." Words left her mouth before her brain vetted them.

He dropped his fists on her lab bench. "We don't know that."

"He didn't stab himself."

He pleaded, "We don't know that."

"You priests always cover for the criminal. What did you do to help Conroy? He's dead." This had turned ugly. She hadn't meant it to. She was still too raw, mentally, and tired. "I didn't mean that. I'm sorry."

The priest's hands rose and shielded his eyes. "I don't know how-ah I am ensnared in this." He rested his elbows on the lab bench and his head against his hands. "I was trying to help." She could reach over to him but it was probably a trick and he was talking again, fast. "I am a scientist, an academic, not a crusader running around the world trying to solve all its problems. I'm a Vaticanista, not a real priest." He looked so miserable, a scientist out of his element, yet that Roman collar creeped her out.

Leila opened a tube, and pipetted miniscule quantities of reagents.

The priest looked at the black box labeled *Clonetech*. "That is cloning, not kinase assay."

"Yeah." This was ridiculous. If she told him what he wanted to know, he might go away. "Look, I just told them that we were outside, she called your cell phone, we went in, and Conroy was on the floor."

The priest stared into her ice bucket. "Vpu? Gp120? Are you working with HIV?"

"A few proteins in transfection."

"How many secret experiments are going on in this lab?"

Leila shrugged. "How many were going on in your lab?"

"None."

Leila laughed. "None that you knew of." She felt stupid asking, but she did. "Would you mind taking your collar off?"

"All right." He reached inside his shirt collar and unsnapped the sides, the first step when he stripped off his clothes, and a nervous, steel wire wrapped her ribs and squeezed. The white strip fell into his hand and he slid it in a pocket. "That is better?"

The stamp of God lingered around him like heat shimmering off asphalt, but it was better without the stupid white square. Leila nodded.

"Actually," she said and tapped the bullet tubes down into the ice, "since you're here, I'd like your opinion on something."

He shook his head and his hair flowed as if he were drowning. "I am all out of opinions."

"A scientific opinion."

He straightened. "Perhaps, then."

"You've worked with fMRI scans, right? There're some scans among Conroy's results. I have no idea what he was doing."

He shrugged. "It has been a while." He smiled with one side of his mouth.

She slid onto a tall stool and handed Conroy's notebooks to him. Dante settled beside her. She thumbed through manila folders to find the scans, comic book–colored images of brains magnified to a foot across. "Here."

Dante's mouth opened, horror-struck. "What is wrong with these people?"

Leila should give the man some context. "They're mice."

"Oh," he sat back and grinned. "Thank God. Their cerebrums and cerebellums are all wrong." He shook his head and his hair brushed around his face. "All right, *mice*."

Leila flipped to a new page on her writing tablet and uncapped a pen.

Dante finished detailing the implications of the fMRI scans.

"How about this one?" She handed him a blossoming rotund cerebrum, imploded.

"This is human," he said.

"Yeah, what do you make of it?"

"It is terrible," he said. "It is awful." The scan swirled with malignant color, a plugged volcano ripping itself apart. "He is dying."

She nodded. "Yeah, she is."

Dante asked Leila, "Then all these mice were sick?"

"Rabid," Leila said.

Dante pointed to Danna's brain. "The same phenomenon is occurring here, with these structures heavily engaged in pathology."

Leila nodded. "That's it. Thanks for the help."

"Are they important, the scans?"

Leila shrugged. "Phenomenological. No mechanisms. No grand unifying theories."

Dante stood to leave. "Sloan's funeral is Friday."

"Yeah. Everyone else is going. I'm not."

"You were his graduate student. It will look odd if you do not go."

Leila added a drip of ligase to each cloning reaction, crammed the tubes in foam cushions, and floated the tubes in a body-temperature water bath. "Katherine Hepburn didn't attend Spencer Tracy's funeral. I don't want to cause a scene."

"I'll make sure everything is calm."

"Yeah, well, we'll see. Look, if you need something," and she couldn't believe she was doing it but she wrote her number on a quarto-sized paper scrap, "call me on my cell."

"It's all right. I have it." He took the scrap from her outstretched fingers anyway.

LATER THAT AFTERNOON, Bev waited by the front door for Dante. Her muscles slithered like wriggling worms all the way to her nervous toes. "Could we stop by the church before we pick up the girls?"

Dante nodded. His eyes wandered over her and settled on her sweatshirt, the arm slit to accommodate the ridiculous pins and cast.

In the car, Bev rested. Dante drove in silence.

In the church, Dante genuflected with the blessed water by the door. Bev dipped her fingers toward the water and stopped, and she mimed touching the water and pressed her dry fingers to her brow, sternum, and shoulders. Together, they teetered up the aisle toward the altar. Dante held her elbow and helped her kneel, then retreated to the front pew.

Bev needed help. Telling her children that their father was dead would be too hard if she didn't have some measure of divine grace. Just a taste, just a glimmer. The golden wood beams and pews echoed her breath in the transparent air. A wave of dust motes crested in a slanting beam of afternoon sunlight. She muttered the Lord's Prayer and still felt only loneliness.

She turned back. Dante's head rested on his hands, bowed over the prayer rail. "Dante?"

He stepped over to her, held her good elbow, and started hauling her to her feet.

"No, just a minute. Could you pray with me?"

Dante blinked. Bloody light stained the black stubble that crept up his jawline. He rubbed his forehead as if warding off a headache. "All right." He lowered himself to his knees and glanced up at the graven image of the Christ.

Bev extended her unpinned hand and he held it. His cold, tan fingers touched the swollen fingertips protruding from the bandage. "Our Father," began Bev, and Dante recited aloud with her, his canorous baritone an octave below her alto. Near the end, "Forgive us our trespasses," her voice cracked as if she were a pubescent boy in the middle of the word *trespasses*.

She grabbed her throat. The Lord wouldn't even let her *ask* for forgiveness.

"Bev?" Dante asked. "Are you all right?"

"I can't," she said, and her throat closed up again.

"I have a bottle of water in the library." Dante stood and lifted her elbow. He held her arm until they got to the library door.

"I can't. I can't say it." The church was empty to her.

"You are dehydrated." He unlocked the library door and helped her inside. From his desk drawer, Dante took a bottle of water and twisted the top open. The bottle hissed. "Drink this."

She sipped from the bottle. The lukewarm water seeped into her leathery tongue and gums. The water absorbed so fast that there wasn't any of that first sip left to swallow. She sipped again, and some of that water ran to her throat, which closed, choking her. "I can't swallow."

Dante's mouth opened slightly. "Have you seen the doctor?"

"What, for my arm?" She sipped again and choked less.

"No, to start your vaccinations."

"I'm current on my tetanus shot."

He reached out, took her good right hand, and said, "We have to go back to the hospital."

DANTE DROVE BEV to the emergency room carefully, calmly, because if they had an accident it would delay them and they could not be delayed.

The ER resident swabbed Bev's tonsils for lab tests and started the rabies inoculations. Dante badgered the terse resident until he called the neurology attending physician for a consult.

Dr. Feiffer, a chubby blonde woman, ran through the neurological exam. She assured them that she'd recently read up on rabies, considering the situation, and that Mrs. Sloan had no symptoms at all and was most likely not infected, but she'd had the first of the vaccinations anyway. The throat spasms were probably not related and indeed, Bev sipped water while the attending examined her, tilted her head up, twisted her head to the side, until Dante was pretty sure he would have choked.

"The agent of infectivity," Dr. Feiffer lectured, "is more similar to the bat strain of rabies virus, which doesn't cause hydrophobia, and no throat spasms had been in evidence in any of the presenting patients."

"Patients?" Dante asked, "plural?"

The neurologist had snapped her teeth shut and walked away, holding her white coat tightly around her.

CHRISTINE AND DINAH sat belted in the back seat of Father Dante's car and each looked out their respective windows at the houses being sucked behind them, old Mrs. Trout's house, young Mr. and Mrs. Trout's house, and the Witulskis' (one boy, thirteen girls, and pregnant again). Dinah had been upset when she saw the pins sticking in Mom's arm, but Christine had been relieved. Christine was old enough to remember September 11, 2001. Her teacher had had the television blaring in the classroom all day, announcers crying, people screaming and pleading for their families to come home. New York was only an hour away, and she'd seen the smoke column. Before she saw the smoke, there had been an inkling in her mind that it was like Orson Welles's *The War of the Worlds* that they'd listened to the year before, but the smoke had stayed in the sky for days, like the Pillar of Fire on Mount Sinai. Ever since then, she'd watched the skies, afraid that she'd see a pillar of smoke over her house.

WEDNESDAY MORNING, Leila sat in Conroy's chair where his skinny ass had rested and read his lab notebook. Funny scents drifted like poltergeists: soapy antiperspirant, fruity phenol that he used to extract DNA the old-fashioned way because he didn't trust kits, foot odor whiff from his running shoes in the bookcase behind her, and the pine needle powder that repressed it.

His lab notebook was atrocious. The proper way to keep a lab notebook is to write down what you are going to do (the protocol, or recipe), what you did (actual weights of reagents, sample numbers, microscope settings), what happened (results and observations, like *the cells all died*) and what that means (conclusions, like *that protocol didn't work*, or *the protein killed the cells*, or *the virus kills people*). Conroy, however, obviously knew that his rabies experiments were illegal and couched his language in the most convoluted, abbreviated, bizarre statements. Nostradamus hadn't obfuscated like this.

On a legal pad, Leila listed experiments, trying to figure out why the hell Conroy was using rabies virus. She flipped through his notebooks and found key words scratched into titles of experiments: Lyssavirus, rhabdovirus, neurotropic encephalitis virus.

He was paranoid, but he had been wrong about who was out to get him. He might have been a genius, but she was beginning to suspect that he had only been a paranoid idiot.

DANTE WAS WRITING counseling notes in the library—*John Williams refuses to be candid concerning salient details but is forthcoming with tangential matters. N tasked him with vacuuming the library and asked the boy to perform chores without his shirt and later only in underpants.* A shy knock rattled the door. "Come in," he said and flipped the file folder closed.

Bev, wearing black pants and a black sweater with the arm cut off for the cast, wove around the heavy door like thick smoke and pressed the door closed behind her. "Father, I need to talk," she said.

Father? He gestured to the chair where she sat for counseling and seated himself as he had that first day when she was distraught, when she had clung to his hand and he should have recognized her brittle fragility.

She settled herself in the chair and laid her black pocketbook on the carpet by her slim, black shoes. "I need to discuss God."

"God?" Dante shifted back onto his complaining left leg. Too much flapped around his head right now, and theology was yet another fluttering thing, slapping at him.

Bev said, "When I pray, when I'm in the church, I can't feel God."

Depression is common after the death of a spouse, especially an unexpected death, and Bev seemed to be following the stages of mourning. In the hospital, she'd used the present tense about Conroy, denial. There was no sign that she had reached bargaining yet, though some skipped stages and the order was hypothetical, but perhaps that was what she meant by the inability to feel God. God wasn't properly negotiating with her. Dante's sore jaw clicked. "So God is not doing what you ask Him to do."

"That's not what I mean," she said and shook her head. Her brown silk hair fell in tumbles on her shoulder. "I just can't feel anything, like the church is empty, like I can't even breathe the air."

Panic attacks, perhaps. "Do you feel anxious?"

"No." She scratched the chair arm.

He shouldn't be guessing anyway. Leading a patient was detrimental. "Then what?"

"I used to be able to feel God's presence. I can't anymore." She toyed with the fraying plaster edge of her cast. "I was afraid to mention it."

Ah, a motivation for secreting a feeling was something a psychiatrist could work with. "And why did you feel you needed to hide this feeling?"

She tapped the table between the chairs. All those gestures, the patting, the tapping, focused her eyes away from him, which either meant that she didn't want to look at Dante due to embarrassment or sadness, or that she might be averting her gaze because she was lying.

Bev scraped her fingernail on the edge of her chair. "Because if God has turned away from me, that means I committed a mortal sin, and that might mean," she swallowed hard, "that I did something to Conroy." She scratched her elbow above the white cast. "If I can't remember a sin, if I can't remember committing it, deciding to commit it, actually doing it, is it on my soul?"

"This scenario didn't come up in the seminary."

"I suppose it would be easier if I'd merely poisoned his communion wine." Bev tucked under the frayed edges of her sweater. "I've always felt a Presence before," she said, and her alto voice emphasized the capital. "Whenever I've needed reconciliation, there's been a hole in my stomach like a bleeding ulcer, like when you were in the confessional. The hatred was eating me. I knew it was sin. But now I don't feel anything."

"You are feeling grief for your husband's death," he said, and ache wedged in his ribs.

"Of course," she said.

Dante clutched the arms of his chair as if wind buffeted his head. "Do you miss him?"

"All the time. Last night, in bed, I couldn't sleep. I moved down to the couch." She nodded as she said this, a sign that she believed what she said.

The hurricane gale stuck him to the chair. The impulse to drop to his knees pounded his shoulders lower. Indignation that she hadn't picked *him*, that she loved that cheating Sloan bastard so much that she ran to him and, in her rage, killed *him*, yanked Dante and the world squalled around him. "He was cheating on you, with Peggy and Leila."

"Who's Peggy?" Bev turned, looking at him.

It was still all Sloan for her. Dante crossed the room and sat in the chair beside her. "And he drove you to have an affair, with me, with *me*, and he abandoned you and Christine and Dinah." He was drowning and his body rolled like a ship taking on water with every breath. "He *crushed* your arm. He destroyed your home. How could you miss him? How could you *grieve* for him?"

She whispered, "He was my husband."

"I tried to help you." Even though his own corporal form, his flesh, had propelled him, there had been something angelic in it when he'd been driven into her arms. There must be a reason. The world and their lives and his vows were not *meaningless*. The affair, breaking his vows, even Sloan's death, surely all this had been prescribed. "I could not stop you from going. You would not stop." She looked shocked, horrified at what he was saying, but he couldn't quit talking. "You wanted *him*."

"He was my husband."

Wind-driven rage rammed him. *"You wanted him back."*

She nodded.

He wanted to drag her to face him but the plaster cast on her arm was heavy and he didn't want to hurt her. Her eyes, caramel like toffee, flickered as she tried to see all of his too-angry face. He whispered, "You wanted to go there and fight with him."

"I wanted to hold my marriage together."

"Do you feel remorse?" The need to shake her, slam her, screw her against a wall quaked in his biceps and forearms. He was flailing at her because he was drowning.

She said, "I don't remember what happened."

"So you feel no remorse," he badgered. This was wrong. He was wrong.

She cringed. "I'm not sure what happened."

Everything slamming in his head crashed down. "Then you cannot confess." Twin, opposing instincts—to beg her to love him and to run away from yet another woman who had used him—battered his skull, and his hair brushed his face. "Then you went there of your own free will, then you wanted to go there and fight with him and that was your sin, and you cannot confess."

"But I can't feel God. There's something wrong."

"That makes no difference. It might be depression. It might be grief. If it is sin, and you cannot feel remorse for the sin, then you cannot confess it. It would not be a true confession. It would not be under the seal of confession and you would not be forgiven." He stood and the chair fell over behind him. "You should go."

THAT NIGHT, Leila and Joe thumped down the hollow stairs, shaking snowflakes out of their hair, to the Dublin Underground. A black-draped form crouched at the bar. "Ah, shit," Leila swore under her breath. She grabbed Joe's arm and turned back to the stairs.

"Hey!" Joe said and waved. "Father Dante!" Joe tugged Leila's arm forward. "What, don't you want a beer?"

Joe bellied up to the bar and slapped the priest on the shoulder. "Hey, Father."

The priest nodded and stirred his drink with a swizzle stick.

"How are you doing?" Joe asked and shook Father Dante's shoulder.

Leila sidled to the bar, keeping Joe between her and the priest, and looked around Joe.

Father Dante was exceedingly drunk. His blood-veined eyes wavered. "Allo." He twitched a fragment of a smile. He recognized Leila and leaned on the bar, asking, "Do you have a cigarette, eh?"

Joe said, "I didn't think he had that much of an accent."

Leila felt for the crinkled pack in her purse and tapped one out. "You okay there, Padre?"

"Me? *Si. Bene.*" His hand wavered in the air as he plucked the cigarette from the pack. "*Ha un fiammifero?*"

"Is he so drunk he's forgotten English?" Joe asked.

"I'd be looking for a light about now." Leila held the flaming lighter close to the end of the cigarette, and the priest puffed. She turned and waggled her fingers at Monty and he wandered over, still flipping the television channels with the remote. "How long has he been here?"

Monty frowned and flicked the television to a basketball game. "Three hours. Slowed him down the last hour. Been making him drink water."

"You're a kind soul, Monty," she said.

Monty bobbed his head and frowned. "Calls down the wrath of the Almighty when a priest gets sick in the bar. Not that I know what I'm going to do with him. It's only eleven."

Leila sighed. "I'll take care of him."

Joe cocked an eyebrow at Leila. "What is it with you and this guy?"

"Nothing."

Joe whispered near her shoulder, "He was in the lab this afternoon. You knew all about him when he was here before, and he knew you from *church*. Since when do you go to church?"

"It's nothing, Joe. Drop it."

Joe's expression resembled the time he had hunted down a cracked methyl ether bottle in the back of a cabinet by sheer bloodhound persistence. "Now you're looking out for him. Are you related to him? Long lost cousin?"

"He's Italian." She leaned over to his ear and a memory of mouthing Joe's bare shoulder rose in her mind. She whispered, "I'm half *Egyptian*, not Italian."

Monsignor Dante's collar lay open on his chest, a shade more bronze than Leila's half-breed skin, and his forlorn white collar flopped when he shrugged, mumbling to his demons.

Leila pointed at the dark brown liquid in Dante's glass. "What's he drinking?"

"Diet Coke." Monty clicked the television.

Joe patted the Monsignor on the back. "How you doing there, Father?"

"Fine. Just fine." He inhaled on the cigarette and smiled. "I gave-ah these up when I took Holy Orders, idiotic idea about dedicating my body. Idiot, eh?" He sucked another long drag off the cigarette, and his plume of smoke boiled out of him across the bar and through the air like a deep-ocean volcanic vent. "I miss-ah the smoke."

Joe whispered to Leila, "Do you think we can have a beer before we roust him out?"

Leila looked at her feet and leaned near Joe's shoulder. Joe smelled like phenol and cologne. "He might sober up if we wait."

Joe nodded. "Hey, Father, you want to join us in a booth?"

The priest nodded at the bartender. "I was just saying to this good man, Monty, here, that I think I've had enough. I don't remember why I came here, so it must be time to go home."

Monty raised an eyebrow and clicked the television.

Joe held the priest's elbow and lifted it up. The priest's body followed his rising elbow. "Come on, Father. Monty, another one for our friend here."

Joe led the priest to a booth near the back, and Leila followed, bringing their drinks like a serving wench, raising the drinks with both hands above laughing groups and avoiding the pool table and Attila, who rammed the yellow one-ball and sent it cruising over the rip in the pool table's felt, plummeting into a corner pocket while his Mongol Horde yee-hawed.

When she got to the booth, holding two pints of beer and one soda, Joe sat on one bench and the sloppy priest sat on the opposite one. The drinks obscured cometary burns and carved initials in the polished oak. Leila scooted in beside Joe and smiled. Fine, if she had to be here, if she had to talk to Jesuit Just-ah Dante, this was a good time to drag those silly secrets out of him. "So you've forgotten why you're here, Father?"

"No," the priest whispered, "but I couldn't say."

"Oh. All right," Leila said. The conversation would wend its way back there later. "So why did you close your lab again?"

"Ah, you want me to talk about the Vatican," the priest said and tapped his cigarette with exaggerated caution into the ashtray. Ash crud tumbled off the end. He raised his bleary eyes to heaven, or at least to the cigarette smog that clung with gecko feet to the wood plank ceiling. "I don't know why the Vatican and the Curia and priests fascinate people."

Joe shrugged and sipped his beer. "It's a secret society with that whole mystical bent, like the Freemasons."

Dante nodded. "*Si*, I noticed your handshake."

Leila turned to Joe, with whom she'd worked for three years, with whom she'd had a sweet little affair, and who didn't have a shred of Masonic paraphernalia in his apartment. "Oh?"

Joe's frowning eyes dropped to his beer.

The priest asked, "What level?"

"Thirty-seventh. Not something I advertise, by the way."

"Then you should change-ah your handshake." The priest tugged at his collar. "Not that I am accorded anything so subtle as a handshake. I'm-ah branded with Holy Orders for all to see, an ontological change. It burns my soul."

Shuddering recognition scraped her spine. "Damn that James Joyce. Screwed it up for everybody," Leila said and watched Dante to see if he'd meant the allusion.

"Yes," Dante nodded. "He commandeered a sacrament and-ah made it a metaphor, decimated its relevance until it was inferior to the epiphany of the stork-girl on one leg, and yet imbued it with inaccurate physical reaction, like D.H. Lawrence confiscating women's sexuality."

The priest was verbose when falling-down wasted. "And how would you know that?"

Dante smiled and sipped his soda. "I shouldn't-ah drink," he said. "I wax eloquent."

"Not at all," Leila said and leaned on the table. She dredged up her best line: "Go on. I'm just fascinated."

"You see," Dante said to Joe with that modest pride of a man who's knowingly being led by a bull nose-ring. "It's-ah the priest thing. It's-ah like I'm harmless, or a eunuch, or caged." He leaned toward her, holding his soda. His ethanolic breath intoxicated her. "Look at this girl, her lovely eyes looking at me like I couldn't reach across the table for her." His empty hand flickered through the air at Leila like a lightning flash.

Leila snapped back and her spine and skull banged the wooden booth. His hand had hovered close to her cheek. He could have grabbed her.

Joe toyed with the head on his beer. "Yeah, Masons don't get that."

"It is not that good, when you're a priest."

Joe sucked foam off his finger and said, "Must be the celibate thing."

"It is more than that," Dante said. He regarded his soda. "Leila, you are experienced in being a woman," and how she was supposed to take that, she didn't know. "Why do women, ordinary women, sweet kind mothers of children and good wives, throw themselves at priests?"

And that must be why the Monsignor was drinking tonight. Somewhere, either a woman had screwed herself a priest tonight and he was numbing the guilt, or else she hadn't scruffed him and he was imbibing chemotherapy for blue balls. "Anybody in particular we're talking about?"

The priest's expression fell to wariness. "Just the women in general. Why priests? Why the *sex*?"

"Maybe it's carnal lust which, as we all know, in women is insatiable." He might be too drunk to recognize the allusion to the *Malleus Maleficarum*, the *Hammer of the Witches*, a medieval Catholic document that dictated witchcraft stemmed from carnal lust.

He toyed with his glass, pressing rings of condensation onto the waxed oak table. "It's witchcraft, then, why women chase the priests. Do you know much about the Inquisition?"

"Not much." And he'd recognized the quote. Frightening.

Leila cupped her hands around the cool beer. The Dublin was too warm for February, when most people wore sweaters and had hung them on the ends of the booths, rows of oversized knitwear for an alcoholic Santa to fill with beer.

The priest's drunken gaze sharpened. A few of his neurons had managed to fire through the whiskey sludge, or he hadn't had as much as he'd suggested, or his liver was the size of a side of beef. "Tell us why women flock to priests."

"I'm sure I don't know," she said, "*Father*."

"It is just-ah Dante." He was Just-ah Dante when he was incognito, when he was aping normal men, when the arrogant holy Monsignor was walking among the patronized masses, thinking all the chicks dug him. No wonder priests landed in so much sexual trouble, walking around thinking all the women (or little boys) were moist for them. The priest said again, "Tell us why the women are so wild for the priests, eh?"

"*I don't know.*" The beer hadn't muddled her, yet she didn't shut up. "*I don't know* why a woman would want a man who traded his sexuality to a supernatural, imaginary Agency for unearned power." The priest sat back, and his wary black eyes appraised her. "*I don't know* why men would make a Faustian bargain for a Pyrrhic victory, leaving half of life—women, logic, pleasure, family, destiny, free will—in abeyance to gain nothing." Words long shoved down belched in her throat. "*Nothing* but the stunted life of emotionally immature men congregated for nonsensical reasons, making up arbitrary rules and mythological systems for everyone else to abide by, when they don't even believe their own shit."

Attila the pool player glanced at the scene she was making over his black-leathered shoulder.

Leila, half-standing, her thighs pressed against petrified gum under the table, lowered herself into the booth and studied the trailing effervescences in her thick, brown beer. She finished lamely, "And the monochromatic wardrobe is boring."

Just-ah Dante's Italian visage retracted around his sorrowing eyes. His smooth, tan hands surrounded the soda on the wood table.

Joe touched her shoulder. "You all right?"

She sucked in bar air, creamy with secondhand smoke. "Fine." Joe held her shoulder, and the warmth of his hand permeated the fibers of her sweater to her hot skin. Adrenaline soured in her blood because she had neither fought nor fled. She bopped her cigarette pack against her palm, plucked a cigarette, and busied herself lighting it. Undiluted smoke lapped her lungs.

The priest sipped the last of his soda around the ice chunks. "I should call a cab," he said and slipped around the edge of the table. He touched the oak table with his fingertips for balance.

Leila couldn't look at him. Carving scarred the blonde wooden table, years of drunk bar-goers happily chiseling their initials and names and profanities and hearts and, in a few cases, chipping them out again. Knife marks, half-filled with wax and grunge, mangled a heart bearing the initials H.P. + H.G.

Joe patted Leila's shoulder to get by. "Come, Padre. I'll call you a cab."

"Wait," Leila said.

Joe stopped patting her shoulder. Dante held his glass.

"I'm sorry. Don't go," she said. Spiked lines gouged the initials V.W. + V.S.W. in the wood. "I was out of line."

"It is all right, Leila," the priest said. "I have had enough of the soda tonight."

"Sit down." She rotated her glass. "Joe hasn't finished his beer. Nobody needs to leave."

The priest settled into the booth like a flock of ravens landing. He asked gently, "Are you sure you are all right?"

"Sure," she said. Attila and the Horde, disappointed that they weren't going to see anyone's eyes scratched out, turned back to their pool table.

The priest said, "I didn't mean to pry."

"It's fine." She sucked on the cigarette. The initials inlaid in the table read: T.J., T.C.B., F.C. The letters' edges were sanded smooth. They'd been there for years, decades, maybe when her father was alive, before she was born, and now after Conroy. Time was a blindfolded bitch.

The priest flicked his fingers at a passing waitress and asked for a pitcher of Guinness.

Joe frowned. "You sure you should drink more, Father?"

Dante shrugged. "It's just American beer."

Leila nodded. "Yeah. 'Liquor before beer, in the clear.'"

The priest smiled. "'Beer before liquor, never sicker.'"

Leila exhaled smoke. The nicotine was beginning to calm her. "Don't you Italians have your own saying, in Italian?"

He shrugged. "What did you want to know about the Vatican?" He scooted the ashtray with the remains of his cigarette toward her.

"I don't know." Leila tapped off her cigarette ash with a thumb-flick. Nicotine circulated in her chest and numbed a gash there. The half-smoked cigarette weighed a metric ton in her fingers and bent grooves into her skin. Dove-gray smoke streamed from the coal at the end of her cigarette, found turbulence, and raged in the air.

DANTE TOUCHED HIS FOREHEAD, an abbreviated genuflect. The alcohol coating on his mind was wearing thin, and a patch was necessary for threadbare spots. He was acting like a student again, searching out friends in a bar, lonely without trysts.

Leila stared at her beer and the table. She glanced at him before looking away, and the capillaries in her eyes were dilated to a pink haze. Some psychiatrist, he scoffed at himself. She'd been jumpy from the first time she'd met him. She'd been twitchy at Mass. He'd assumed that she was hiding her relationship with Conroy or what she'd told the police. When he'd reached across the table for her, she'd recoiled like he had slapped her. Fear shimmered in her, or horror, something more than political opinions.

Perhaps his first opinion, outside the church after that first Mass, when he'd seen fragility and damage commensurate with an abuse survivor, perhaps that assessment had been correct.

Jesus, Mary, and Joseph, he wanted to be wrong.

First, he had to gain her trust. That was always first. He could give her the information she'd asked for, as far as he could.

The waitress brought the pitcher of dark Guinness. Dante poured and said, "The Vatican has within it several Congregations, or divisions, like the State Department."

Joe removed his hand from Leila's shoulder to drink his beer. "You don't think of a church as needing that kind of thing."

"The Vatican is a semi-elected, theocratic, oligarchic dictatorship and an independent state." His beer tasted of yeast. "I'm a consultor for the Congregation for the Doctrine of the Faith."

"Thought you were a Jesuit," she said around the filter of her cigarette.

Dante half-smiled and laid his palms around his glass of beer. "Divided loyalties."

"And a scientist."

"Further divided."

"Bloody schizophrenic, aren't you?" She flicked her glass with her large, green-stoned ring, and a tolling *ping* sounded.

He sipped the beer and his alcohol buzz swarmed. "It is difficult, sometimes, to keep track of who I am with and where I am."

Leila lifted an eyebrow and resumed studying her beer.

"It sounds hypocritical," Dante said. "It feels hypocritical to monitor everything you say because people's world-views are so easily challenged."

Leila exhaled cool, blue smoke. "You didn't challenge my world-view."

Another blunder. "I meant other people. My English, it's-ah not so good."

Leila's shoulders twitched, a suppressed chuckle.

He continued, "I meant within the Vatican and the University. Even in Roma, people are sensitive. It feels like a war zone. Both sides assume I'm a spy."

"Oh?"

He smiled at her casual conversational punctuation. "Each Congregation guards its own territory. When the IEA returned to the CDF, the Secretariat of State had-ah, how do you call it, puppies."

Leila smiled and toyed with the foam on her beer. He'd amused her again. Her champagne-colored lipstick was fading, and a half-ring of it marked her beer glass above the foam line. "So this Congregation of yours," she said.

She was listening. Alcohol relaxed the neural connections from his brain to his tongue. "According to Article 48 of the Apostolic Constitution on the Roman Curia, the 'Pastor Bonus,' which was promulgated by John

Paul II in 1988," Dante recited, "'The duty proper to the Congregation for the Doctrine of the Faith is to promote and safeguard the doctrine of the faith and morals throughout the Catholic world: for this reason everything which in any way touches such matters falls within its competence.' And after His Holiness ascended to sit with God, the current Pope was elected, and he is one of us. The CDF controls the Vatican now. John Paul II started to reform the morals of his priests, and His Holiness will finish that work with an iron staff."

"So you're the morals police. How Orwellian." Leila wiped her foamy finger on a cocktail napkin. "I thought only Islamic theocracies had morals police."

"But, again," he waggled an unsteady finger, "we are a theocratic dictatorship. There are also four sections within the Congregation: the doctrinal office, the disciplinary office, the matrimonial office and that for priests. Morals, faith, and priests."

She inhaled from her cigarette. "So what do you do for this thing?"

Dante shrugged. "I used to read books to determine if they contained heresy. I met with priests who were accused of heresy to distinguish the mentally ill from those committing apostasy. Occasionally, I stripped a priest of his Holy Orders and excommunicated him if he was expounding heresy. Mostly, I did research and studied neuroscience."

Leila shifted in her seat. "You determine what is heresy. You excommunicate heretics." She said offhandedly, a throwaway remark, "Sounds like the Inquisition."

She'd guessed it, and it wasn't a secret per se, so Dante nodded. "There were several name changes over the years, but yes." He sipped his beer and watched her disbelieving eyes. "The CDF is the Roman Inquisition."

"The Inquisition doesn't exist anymore," she said and turned to Joe.

Joe shrugged and sipped his beer.

Leila swiveled back to face Dante. "Oh, come on."

Later, he blamed the alcohol for his indiscretion, but he wanted to tell her. He wanted her trust. The whiskey and beer lined up his thoughts and conveyed them to his mouth. "In 1542, Pope Paul III formed the Sacred Congregation of the Universal Inquisition, which was renamed the Congregation of the Holy Office in 1908 by Pope St. Pius X. It became the Congregation for the Doctrine of the Faith in 1965 under Pope Paul VI. John Paul II clarified our mission in 1988 with that Pastor Bonus. The current Pope gave us more authority and power and resources."

She looked at her beer and laughed. "So you're in the Inquisition."

"Yes." His lips didn't close. She met his stare, and he didn't smile.

"*The Inquisition?*" She held her beer near her delicate chin but didn't drink.

"In our own defense, the Roman Inquisition had only tenuous ties to the Spanish Inquisition, though we did have words with Galileo."

She set her beer down on the table and leaned in, unsmiling. "Are you a spy?"

"That is the IEA, the Institute for External Affairs. I am with heresy and priests."

"What is *the Inquisition* doing in New Hamilton? Looking for witches to burn?"

"It has been snowing. The wood is too wet."

"This is unbelievable." She shook her head and slapped the wood table. Dante shrugged again.

"I don't get you." Leila looked mad. "I don't get you at all. You're a scientist and a Jesuit, and that I can *almost* see. Jesuits are less irrational than most priests."

"Thanks," he said.

"But getting mixed up with the *Inquisition.*"

"Please keep your voice down."

"How in the hell did that happen?" She tapped her beer mug on the table like a gavel, and the beer clapped inside the mug but didn't slosh over the rim.

Beer sloshed in Dante's skull. "It started just after the seminary. I was working on exorcism."

She coughed in her beer. "And now it all makes sense."

He ignored that. "A Franciscan priest in India wrote a book correlating liberation theology with the Marian movement and the Eucharist and some polytheistic, Hindu-like notions. The book was heresy. It contradicted dogma on many levels." He rubbed his forehead and suspected a slight fever. "But there was a question whether he was insane or possessed."

Leila rolled her lovely, dark eyes. Ah, if he were a single man in Roma again, and he dispelled that thought.

"And we went to Calcutta, to his church, and interviewed him."

"We?" Joe had turned and was listening to the monologue with more interest.

"Monsignor Gaetan Silvano of the CDF, an expert on heresy, and I, a psychiatrist studying mental illness and possession. I could not reconcile the Indian priest's actions with mental illness, even paranoid schizophrenia, even multiple personality disorder." The beer was as black as the bile that had bled from the old priest's eyes. "He was eighty-three. He broke ropes that bound him. He broke chains. It was my first exorcism."

"Have I fallen into fairyland?" Leila asked. "Exorcism?"

Leila glanced at Joe, who shrugged. "I'm a Mason. I see weird stuff all the time. I got an award for the most improved ritual a couple years ago."

"It's like there's a whole magical world hidden around here. Exorcisms. Freemasons." She turned back. One limber eyebrow cocked down. "Have you done many exorcisms?"

"Not as many as some. Monsignor Silvano and I worked as consultors for the Congregation, to determine whether a heresy was due to illness or possession."

"So there's a mass outbreak of demon possession in New Hamilton?" Leila turned to Joe. "Isn't there a television show where a blonde chick slays demons?"

Joe said, "Was."

Dante shook his head. "It is not possession. I can't say more because it violates patient confidentiality, but I am here as a psychiatrist. When the Congregation took over the current project, they recruited every priest and ex-priest with counseling credentials. I couldn't say no."

"Sounds sinister." Leila sipped her beer.

Here was his chance. "It is not supernatural, but it is a terrible problem." Dante looked at her over his glass. "I think you know the problem that I mean."

Leila settled her mug on the table and stared directly back at him, too steadily, rehearsed. "I have no idea what you're talking about."

In his peripheral vision, Dante saw Joe's head swiveling from Dante to Leila and back again, but Leila didn't look away so neither did he. Dante maintained a calm, neutral expression softened by compassion. No smile. That would be knowing or gleeful. Just a softening of frown muscles, a widening of the brow, an invitation to speak.

Her expression was studied neutral, but the outer corners of her eyes expanded, and adrenaline dilated her pupils. Her eyes spread open. Fear swarmed inside.

Joe said, "What?" and broke the charm.

Leila looked over at Joe. "Nothing."

Dante nodded, wishing vehemently that he'd been wrong about Leila, but he didn't think he was. She tolerated his presence admirably well, for a child who'd been abused by a priest. Maybe she had recovered from it. He would like to know how she had done that. Knowing how might help in his counseling. He needed all the help he could get.

Chapter Seventeen

Friday morning, at Conroy's funeral, Bev shied at the font of holy water where she was supposed to bless herself before entering the church. The water in the smooth rosa marble font enticed her, as if she could plunge into and it would engulf all of her, sucking her sordid body into itself and extracting the horrors, and she might emerge rebaptized, but she couldn't. That little dish, rippling from footsteps entering the church behind her, couldn't hold her terrible soul. Nothing could. A Baptist full-immersion baptismal tank would redden like a plague of Egypt had descended on it. Her soul would kill all the fish in a river and poison the riparian land.

Her fingers brushed the air above the water and traced a dry cross over her face and torso.

AFTER THE PROCESSIONAL, Dante stood before the gathered mourners and in front of Conroy's white pall-draped casket. Bev sat in the front pew with three friends nested around her, a patting, stroking cluster of support.

Dante's notes lay on the lectern. Hopefully, St. Augustine and St. Thomas Aquinas had been correct when they expounded that a sacrament performed by a priest who was in a state of mortal sin was as valid as if Christ Himself officiated at a sacrament, and the *alter Christus* ministering the sacrament meant nothing. He placed his hope in his own insignificance. *Those whom Judas baptized, Christ baptized. So too, then, those whom a drunkard baptized, those whom a murderer baptized, those whom an adulterer baptized, if the Baptism was of Christ, Christ baptized.*

Dante raised his arms and said, "In the name of the Father, and of the

Son, and of the Holy Spirit." He genuflected in that exaggerated manner that Samual used to prompt the holiday Catholics. "May the grace and peace of our Lord Jesus Christ, the love of God and the fellowship of the Holy Spirit be with you all."

All responded as proscribed and written on the cheat sheet to the Mass furtively distributed to the Protestants, "And also with you."

Bev and her bevy occupied the first two pews, Sloan's professional acquaintances sat behind her, and their friends scattered over the rest of the church. Conroy's lab was seated in a block near the back, with Leila hemmed in by Joe and Malcolm and Danna's parents sitting behind them, respectful and curious to observe the pompous, splendorous idolatry of Roman Catholicism.

Leila peeked over Joe's arm at the notes, though after her recent Mass attendances she remembered the responses. Dante's voice soared past the altar rail and echoed in the expanse above the pews, maybe four stories of air space under the wood-beamed ceiling, and the priest said something about gathering together and started blessing the holy water.

Mary, Lydia, and Laura's hands slid off Bev's shoulders as the Mass began. Bev had said her goodbyes earlier, though the preserved effigy of Conroy lying in the magnificent box had only partially resembled him.

For an instant within a moment, Bev thought that Conroy was late for Mass again and she listened for his footfalls sneaking in and his reedy body whispering as he genuflected at the end of the pew, his grin sheepish, and yet he was already there, in that magnificent box.

Lydia steadied Bev's swaying arm and watched Father Dante walk the aisle. Yesterday when they had driven over to the florist's, Mary had mentioned to Lydia that Bev looked stoned that morning and that she worried about the pills.

Dante flicked vestigial drops of baptismal water on the congregation while he walked down the aisle toward the back of the church. Leila and her men sat back there.

Droplets of holy water smacked Joe and the others where they were sitting in the penultimate pew. Joe whispered, "Are you going to take communion?"

Leila said, "Me? I'd crumble into dust or something." She turned away from Joe, crossed her ankles under her long, black skirt, and watched Dante resume his place at the altar.

Dante said, "My brothers and sisters, to prepare ourselves to celebrate the sacred mysteries, let us call to mind our sins."

The church fell into silence and Bev bowed her head. Conroy needed to hear those words, but Bev sat in the hard pew. God wasn't listening to her. The church, despite all the people, seemed empty air, but she prayed for a mistake to have been made, for Conroy to push up the lid and fight the white cloth draping his face and shoulders, but nothing moved except her breath.

Father Dante recited, and everyone joined in, "I confess to almighty God, and to you, my brothers and sisters, that I have sinned through my own fault, in my thoughts and in my words, in what I have done, and in what I have failed to do; and I ask blessed Mary, ever virgin, all the angels and saints, and you, my brothers and sisters, to pray for me to the Lord, our God."

Dante said, alone, "May almighty God have mercy on us, forgive us our sins, and bring us to everlasting life."

The church rumbled, "Amen."

The swaying, shifting people in the pews seemed to have sprung up in the church rows as orderly as gardened rows of basil. Dante intoned, "Kyrie eleison."

Leila's breath caught in her uppermost rib and she couldn't speak when everyone responded, "Kyrie eleison." Her face flushed. That priest shouldn't be using the Greek incantation. Roman Catholics used the English translation, *Lord, have mercy.* The priest at her father's Mass had used the Greek because the nearest Orthodox church was Greek, when she'd stood in the front row with his friends, without her mother, in the baking, smothering, Floridian church.

Dante said, "Christe eleison."

Leila clutched her purse and bowed her head. Her lips moved, but she couldn't say "Christe eléison" with everyone else. This was ridiculous. She had to hang on because she had to survive hours more of the Mass. Her skin oozed cold sweat.

Dante said, "Kyrie eleison." and the congregation thundered it back."

Dante led the recitation of the Gloria since they had no music, and the congregation blended with his voice. At the end, he said, "Let us pray," and consulted his notes, which said that his prayer was to start *Lord, we stand together in this community,* but he couldn't read his scant, fatuous notes in the presence of these people who were here because they believed, because he stood before them in a state of mortal sin, daring to lead them in prayer. He said, "Lord, we are all sinners, all of us, but Your mercy astounds even the most callous among us."

Pain spiked Bev's palm, and she dragged a handkerchief from her purse with her good hand. Her eyes were unaccountably dry, but she needed something to clutch. Her fingernails dredged into the fleshy meat of her scratched hand and curved around the cast and dug into the gauze and plaster, driving her fingernails back into her nail beds, the inverse of pulling them out. She should scratch at the coffin until Conroy stopped pretending, until God heard her and gave Conroy back. Conroy had brought this all on himself. He'd allowed himself to get mixed up with Leila and that *Peggy* woman, whose name had shocked Bev, even though she'd known there was someone else, somewhere. That this *Peggy* had such a prosaic name seemed yet more insulting.

Her left eye burned and tossed a tear down her cheek. She dabbed it with the handkerchief. If God gave her another chance, Bev wouldn't confront Conroy with those pink panties. She could live with his affairs. She could offer the suffering to Christ as her cross to bear.

God, she needed one more chance.

Dante said to the people on the other side of the wide altar rail, "A reading from the Holy Gospel according to Mark." Shoes scraped the wood floor of the church as everyone bobbed up.

Dante leaned on his pulpit and listened to the deacon read about the crowd that had mocked Christ and dragged him, literally, to crucifixion. He glanced up at the deep wood carving of the crucifix that threw a shadow of a low mountain range intersected with a Cheops-sized pyramid on the floor of the apse behind the altar. The stained glass windows tossed sparks of vibrant light that clung to the wood.

John the deacon read Christ's words, *"Eloi, Eloi, lema sabachthani?"*

Dante hadn't read the Aramaic since the seminary. Even Christ had cried to God about abandonment when he was on the cross, in pain, alone. Even Christ was lonely in his very soul. Perhaps the abandonment and isolation are the natural state of man.

Bev curled inward and adjusted her pinned arm in its sling. She would have been a member of that crowd, mocking the Christ. She never recognized a good thing when she had it.

Leila toyed with the edges of the pamphlet. She would have been reading the Torah while the crowd dragged Christ to Golgatha, having long since chopped her hair and impersonated a boy to gain entrance to rabbinical studies. The veil in the temple would have rent itself in the midst of her studies as Christ died, and she'd have debated the meaning with her fellow scholars. The tearing of the veil would have been mysterious unless they'd known that the man who called himself the Christ had died. Context was everything. Results had to augment each other for the context to be understood.

John closed the Bible and whispered to the book, "May the words of the Gospel wipe away our sins," and looked at Dante, the cue. Dante recited, "The Gospel of the Lord," though his hands shook as he tapped his note cards. The congregation responded and Dante cleared his throat for the homily while people swished, sitting down.

"Lord, we come before you today to give to you our brother in Christ, Conroy Robert Alexander Sloan." Within the Mass, the homily should be short. Eulogies were scheduled for the funeral home afterward. Dante was here not to praise Sloan but to bury him. His note cards were pathetically brief. Last night, he'd wandered, distracted and drunk, through the empty rectory and church, knowing he'd cuckolded Sloan, hadn't kept him from harm, and had stood aside while a knife dove into his heart.

Dante stood at the podium and said, "Dr. Sloan was an important man in this community and a sinner in the deepest sense of the word." Some grumbling, some fidgeting of bodies out there amongst the pews that Dante looked across. "As we are all sinners in the deepest, darkest aspects of that word."

Redemption eluded him, but the Church's dogma was a safe bet.

"Sin pervades us, haunts us, turns us against ourselves and each other, and Conroy Sloan was no exception. Those who knew him, knew that he suffered as we all suffer and as the Christ suffered. In the Gospel, the Son of God cried out, 'Eloi, Eloi, lema sabachthani?' which translates as, 'God, God, why have you forsaken me?'"

Dante said, "Yet this is a fallacy. God did not forsake Jesus that day in Golgotha when He suffered. The Lord God could not have forsaken Him. The Father is a part of the Son, an indivisible quantity. Their essences cannot be put asunder. They were both crucified. They both suffered. But neither was forsaken. Neither was alone.

"And this, finally, is what Jesus, the Christ, wanted us to know: our fundamental spirit cannot be divided from Christ and from the Lord, our God, Eloi. Though we sin, though we feel alone and forsaken, we are indivisibly a part of God and part of our community. God cannot forsake us. Though we feel pain, though we sin, though we are sinners all, we are also the blessed of God, and God is with us. Even when we feel most alone, we are never alone, though we suffer, though we ache, God is with us, and

He shares our loneliness and our pain."

Dante bowed his head and recited the Nicene Creed with the congregation. "We believe in one God, the Father, the Almighty, maker of heaven and earth, of all that is seen and unseen. We believe in one Lord, Jesus Christ, the only Son of God, eternally begotten of the Father, God from God, Light from Light, true God from true God, begotten, not made, one in Being with the Father." He recited the rest, considering the unseen, the begotten, and Light.

"He was born of the Virgin Mary, and became man," Bev said. God and the Holy Spirit had been a part of Bev, a slice of her soul, but Dante was wrong. That part had been torn away, and she was forsaken. The Virgin Mary was her only hope for intercession.

"He suffered, died, and was buried." Leila crushed her fingers together. It was all superstition and fiction. People believed it to make themselves feel better because they were going to die just like Conroy, who was in that horrible box under the white cloth. She should have helped him when that knife slid into him, when the blade touched and sliced and internalized.

"On the third day he rose again in fulfillment of the Scriptures; he ascended into heaven and is seated at the right hand of the Father. He will come again in glory to judge the living and the dead, and his kingdom will have no end." Peggy read the Creed from the pamphlet but she had no fear of a Catholic judgment. Peggy was a Lutheran.

"We believe in the Holy Spirit, the Lord, the giver of life, who proceeds from the Father and the Son. With the Father and the Son, He is worshipped and glorified. He has spoken through the Prophets."

The air wavered between Dante and the congregation, out there past the altar rail, reciting. Heat isotherms rode over their heads, and mirage shimmered between Dante and the church. Dehydration parched him. He touched the altar for balance. The stone altar cooled his fingertips. He wanted to lay his febrile forehead on the cool stone.

There was more to life than what he measured in the lab. There was more than his previous bacchanalian code. There had to be more that that, but he was alone, and he ached.

"We believe in one holy, catholic, and apostolic Church."

Yes, yes, Dante agreed, *but what else, what else?*

"We look for the resurrection of the dead, and the life of the world to come. Amen."

Reverend Jebediah Kerry whispered to his wife, "These Catholics might have something, here. I like this creed they have. Did you see them all recite it, the whole thing, memorized?"

Mrs. Kerry nodded, but she was thinking about Danna, who was barely conscious.

"I think we should have something like this," he said.

"Jebediah, not right now," she said gently. He always touted new ideas for their church.

"It's the whole thing, the whole faith, all wrapped up, and they say it every week, or every Mass. I'm going to write us something like this." He smoothed the pamphlet on the scratchy fabric of his pant leg.

She sighed. "People won't like it. Too formal. No Spirit moves you when you're reciting something you've memorized."

Dante stumbled through the offering of sacrifices on the altar, remembering the words an instant before he said them. "Blessed are you, Lord, God of all creation. Through your goodness we have this bread to offer, which earth has given and human hands have made. It will become for us the bread of life."

The tenor sang another psalm *a capella* over his incantations.

Leila murmured to Joe, "Have you ever been to a Mass before?"

Joe shook his head and wondered if this rite was indeed Christianity. It seemed so foreign, ritualistic. Maybe that was why Satanists appropriated Catholic symbolism and rituals, because the Catholics *had* symbolism and rituals, like the priest at the altar, waving his hands in a thaumaturgic approximation over platters of bread and chalices of wine. A Protestant

Satanist would just read from the Satanic Bible and people would stand up and witness about how Satan jus' transformed their lives, and during the prayer, different members of the Satanic congregation would stand and jus' let Jesus out of their hearts. No wine, no alcohol at all, of course, in a Protestant Satanist church. No singing or dancing or playing cards, for that matter.

At the altar, Dante raised his hands and said, "Jesus taught us to call God Our Father, and so we have the courage to say, Our Father, who art in Heaven, hallowed be thy name," and the congregation joined him for the Lord's Prayer.

Dante consecrated the host, and once again the bread lay on the altar, transformed and yet not discernibly so. Then he called the people to offer each other a sign of peace.

Bev held onto her friends while they hugged her, holding her. She turned back to the rows behind her and shook offered hands.

A petite, plump woman sitting two rows back, a dingy redhead with the coloring of an overwashed floral blouse, leaned through the gap between Mary and Dr. Lugar to shake Bev's hand and say, "Peace be with you."

"And with you," Bev said. The faded auburnette, her khaki eyes, her plump cheeks, seemed familiar. She held onto Bev's hand. Bev asked, "Did you know Conroy?"

"I'm Peggy Strum, the department secretary. We spent a lot of time together," the woman said, and her graying eyes flickered, searching Bev's face. The little bitch smiled with her pastel lips pressed together, primly, knowingly.

Bev yanked her hand from that woman's clutches and pivoted to face the altar. Another of Conroy's sluts had shown up. Damn her. Damn *him*.

John the deacon chanted, "Lamb of God, you take away the sins of the world, grant us peace," and watched Dante. Dante broke a communion wafer, mingled it with the wine in his chalice, and recited prayers over the pyx and the cup. "By your body and blood, free me from all my sins, and from every evil." The flat cracker in his fingers was soggy with red wine and almost disintegrated. A drop of watery wine trailed down Dante's thumb and beaded in the creases.

Bev's knees trembled, and she sat while her friends shuffled past her to the center aisle. Mary's eyebrow lifted when Bev stood back to let her by. Bev couldn't breathe and she couldn't look at that gorgeous, magnificent box bearing Conroy's body.

At least two of Conroy's whores sat behind her. They should be more careful. Bev might have a knife. According to the police, she was capable of killing anyone.

Damn that Conroy, lying in that box, shriven.

God shouldn't forgive Conroy. She sure as hell didn't.

Dante stood next to the deacon, held the wafer aloft and above an elderly woman, and said, "The body of Christ." The woman responded, "Amen." She opened her mouth and extended her tongue. Several of her teeth were gray with silver amalgam. He touched the wafer to her tongue, and she retracted it into her mouth, lizard-like.

Bev's friend Lydia was next in line, and she held her hands cupped in front of her, so Dante laid the cracker in her hands and she walked away.

He looked over at the long pew, and Bev was sitting alone, hunched over, pressing her forehead to the railing. He shouldn't stop communion to go to her, but he held the plate of wafers on one hand and walked toward where she crouched.

Leila watched from the back of the church the short communion lines receiving wafers from Dante and the deacon. Each person came forward, received the little bread crumbs, and walked away, hands clasped in front of their chest. Saps. Suckers. It was like the communion wafer stopped them from thinking, made them stupid, killed brain cells.

Leila remembered that the dry communion wafer adhered to her tongue as soon as it touched. It had seemed mystical when she was a girl, the way the wafer burrowed into her mouth.

Now, it seemed viral, the way a virus clasps a molecule on the outside of a cell, climbs the receptor hand over hand like a gym rope, and slinks into the cell. If the host was a virus, the wafer would travel though her alimentary canal until it reached the vagus nerve and, prion-like, propagate like a string of firecrackers through her peripheral nervous system to her spinal cord and up to her brain, gumming everything in its path with insoluble gunk plaques, streaming through her cerebrum like ribboning bullet trails, sending all neurons into irrevocable apoptosis, programmed cell death.

That made the communion wafer a neural apoptosis ligand. Leila snorted *ha* at the biochemical heresy.

That knife had entered Conroy's chest the same way: it touched his skin and, biochemically propelled, the serrations chewed their way inside to his left ventricle and killed him. That made the knife an apoptosis ligand, initiating a caspase cascade causing the programmed death of all Conroy's cells. Maybe the knife was an apoptosis superligand.

The knife and the communion wafer were both ligands initiating biochemical events. The knife ripped apart Conroy's heart. The cracker caused apoptosis in brain cells.

Heresy.

Leila shifted her legs on the hard pew and watched Dante set a wafer in a woman's hands. The Inquisitor handing out communion wafers might burn her at the stake for such heresy.

If she took communion, and the wafer adhered to her tongue and internalized, she might spontaneously combust for her heresy, then the wafer would be an apoptosis superligand like the knife, but it wasn't, of course. The wafer was much more like a viral factor, insidiously inducing apoptosis over time, with exposure.

Maybe that had been her father's problem: all that communion he took had a neuron-specific apoptosis factor, and that's why the AIDS-related dementia ravaged his brain and he hallucinated God and angels until he forgot how to breathe and drowned in his own flooded lungs.

Conroy's rabies virus, however, infected brain cells without killing them, until the very end. It didn't produce neural apoptosis ligands, so the virus was killing Danna but not her consciousness.

Together, her own clandestine HIV experiments and Conroy's secret rabies experiments coalesced into a terrible beauty. Neurons must have their own apoptotic cascade that was different from other cells' death throes. HIV had a neuron-specific apoptosis factor that it secreted from its roost in the microglia and killed brain cells, and her father had died demented and raving. That was why she couldn't find classical apoptotic activations in the HIV-infected neurons even though the neurons were definitely apoptotic, because neurons had their own, unique pathway.

Rabies must encode a neuron-sparing factor, or it short-circuited the neuron-specific apoptotic cascade, so Danna was going to die perfectly lucid as the virus burned away her nervous system.

Leila and Conroy had run the same experiment from two different ends of the question. HIV killed neurons without infecting them. Rabies infected neurons without killing them.

If Leila looked at Danna's fMRI, she could see Danna thinking but not dreaming about God. And, if she called Florida and got her father's fMRIs, she could see his demented dreams of God.

It was awful, and wonderful.

Oh, Conroy. They had it. They had evidence for a grand, unifying theory about consciousness and the neural locus of God in the brain.

They'd proved that the brain dreams of God, and they had proved that God is all in your head.

They just didn't know what they'd done because they hadn't talked to each other, because they were both running secret, dangerous, illegal experiments.

God, she missed him.

Leila should have stayed inside his apartment. She shouldn't have left stupid Conroy alone with that crazed woman. He'd probably said something stupid. He was such an ass. He couldn't even stop skinny little Leila from wrenching his arm around behind him. He'd stood no chance against a furious wife with a knife.

Oh, Conroy, you mad, tragic scientist. The church blurred and swam as if a flood had burst through it. Leila tried to stop the damned tears dripping out of her stupid eyes.

At the front of the church, Bev rested her cast on the communion rail and bent over. That bastard. That bastard who lay in that box. That bastard had left her and her girls far more irrevocably than if he'd merely moved into a love shack with his honey. He'd left. He'd left them. Her eyes flicked raging tears down her cheeks. Her arm throbbed.

Warm flesh pressed Bev's good hand. She looked up from the railing.

Dante asked, "Why do you not take communion?" His whisper echoed in the church.

"Oh, Dante," she whispered. "I can't."

His black eyes looked narrowed because he stood and his head was above her, like when he had been on top of her. She couldn't receive Holy Communion from his hand. The sacrilege frightened her. She couldn't add *that* to the sin that cut her off from God. She shook her head and dropped her forehead back to the rail to shut him out. His black shoes under the white robe hesitated for a moment, then walked away.

In the coffin, Conroy's body, cold but still supple from the preserving chemicals, reclined. The embalmer had used a Formalin variation, a low-odor formulation, but the scent that lingered around his body was reminiscent of that which he brought home with him from the lab, aldehydes and ketones and metabolic breakdown products.

His body also smelled of his aftershave cologne, which Bev had tucked into the pocket of the suit and which the embalmer had discovered and splashed on his preserved skin. He'd had the cologne blended in Paris when he'd trysted there with Valerie Lindh. Dr. Lindh was one of his lovers not in attendance at his funeral, but Bev, Leila, Peggy, and Mary were present.

He would have liked that they were there, had any of his pickled neurons fired to produce an emotion, or registered the docking of aldehyde and ketone molecules at his olfactory bulb, or responded to the light reflecting from the white silk to his corneas from where the lid ill-fit the dark box.

BEV TOOK TWO MORE green pills in the car going to the funeral home, and she didn't remember a thing about any of the eulogies, thanks be to all the saints, and neither Leila nor that horrible Peggy woman had come to the funeral home, so she didn't think they'd come to the reception at her house, so she wouldn't have to toss either of them out of her house onto her skinny little ass or fat bloated ass, respectively.

Mary and Lydia sneaked out early from the funeral home to set up the reception. Sister Mary Theresa would bring Christine and Dinah over afterward. The eulogies droned on. Dante, sitting beside her, held her hand like he had that first terrible day, tenderly, as a priest. His gentle hands covered her exhausted fingers.

People began to arrive, Dr. Lugar and his wife, professional friends.

The phone rang. Bev answered it in the kitchen. "Hello?"

A man's unctuous voice, "Hello? Is Conroy Sloan there?"

Bev's cheeks burned. "May I ask who is calling?"

"Katana Porsche dealership. I was just making sure you were home."

"Why is that?" she asked, but the man had already hung up. She added a bit more whiskey to her coffee and went back to the living room.

"I think I'm going to sell the house," Bev said to Mary, Lydia, Laura and Dante. Laura's son Luke, after following Christine and Dinah's examples and furtively hugging Dante's leg, had retired to the backyard with the girls to swing. "It's too big," Bev said, "and it echoes. Conroy's life insurance isn't going to last forever, and some needs to be saved for the girls' college."

Lydia said, "Honey, let me finish figuring out where you guys are financially. I've still got files and whole accounts to go through. There may be more there than you think. You might even have time to pick up a master's degree."

"I don't know," Bev sipped the coffee. Her throat closed on the acerbic whiskey. "I didn't have a Plan B. I should have. Conroy's father had a heart attack before he was fifty."

Lydia and Laura glanced at each other, no doubt musing about the viability of a Plan B if Bev was in jail for the rest of her life. She sipped the coffee and waited for it to interact with the little green pills so those thoughts would float away.

Dante, looking out the front window, asked, "Do you know that man?"

Bev glanced past Dante through the treeless front yard. A man in a black suit slid sideways out of a black Porsche, closed the door and polished the handle, and walked up to the door. The doorbell buzzed in the foyer.

Bev frowned at the ladies, who frowned back, and she answered the door. "Yes?" she asked him.

The man held out a set of chunky black keys and said in that oily voice, "Sorry about the delay, but I think you'll agree that your new Porsche 911 Carrera 4S is worth the wait."

"I didn't buy a Porsche," Bev said. She stepped back and prepared to close the door.

"Sign here," he said and held out a clipboard with a pen attached.

She swallowed the hot saliva materializing in her mouth. "There's been a mistake."

The guy leaned back to look at the house numbers. "Is this *Doctor Conroy R. Sloan's* house?"

The air around her thinned, as if the house teetered on a mountain top above the clouds. If she fell out the doorway, she would keep falling and bounce off rocks protruding from the cliff. She said, "He passed away."

The man backed up a step and appraised the black dress she was wearing. "I'm sorry."

"It's all right." She pressed on the door.

The door half-closed before the guy pushed it back and breezed off, "So you don't want the car?"

"No," she said and punched the door open wide. "We don't want the car." He backed up. "We don't want Conroy's stupid, ridiculous car." She stepped outside, following him down the sidewalk. "How could he buy a *new Porsche*, when he has two daughters to send to college? What sort of an idiot would spend a hundred thousand dollars on a car when we don't have a tenth of that saved for the girls' college?"

"Hey, lady, I'm just delivering it." He backed up and held the clipboard in front of him, as if she might stab him in the chest. "And it was only eighty-four grand."

The other women ran outside. Mary grabbed Bev's arm.

Lydia said, "Let me see that," and grabbed the paperwork out of the man's hand and slapped it open, perusing. "He put down ten thousand, so there's still thirty missing."

"Why would he do it?" Bev turned to Mary and demanded. "Why would he have affairs, so many affairs, Leila and now this horrible Peggy woman, and buy a new Porsche and move out and leave his children?"

Mary gathered Bev against her soft chest but didn't say anything. Mary's perfume was sultry, tropical. Bev yanked away from her to go after the Porsche guy again.

The guy snatched the paperwork from Lydia and sprinted to the car.

"Let me see that!" Bev yelled. "I want to know what that bastard did!"

The guy climbed into the car and zoomed away in a black smear across the cold afternoon. It was a Porsche. It could zoom.

"Bastard!" Bev yelled after the howling Porsche and against the frigid air blowing by her head and blowing icy trails from the corners of her eyes into her hairline. Mary and Lydia wrapped their arms around her and walked her inside the house.

"Bastard," Bev sobbed.

DANTE SIPPED TEA in Bev's living room while everyone else filtered away. The cleaning crew showed up, cleaned up, and got out. Finally, he and she were the only two left, sitting across the living room from each other, sipping lukewarm tea from the only two unwashed cups.

They sat, not saying much, drinking tea, listening to opera, until dusk. Bev looked so tired but didn't cry more than that one tear, and she slid farther into drunken stupor. He supposed she needed it, yet, when he tucked the girls in at nine and settled Bev in her bed at ten, building up a pillow battlement for her arm, he removed her other arm from his neck, gently drawing her fingers from his hair, saying that he was needed elsewhere, even though the soft skin on her hand roused him when he kissed her palm then covered her breasts with the blue blanket.

He took a cab downtown. He was embarking on the road to his drinking problem again, and he knew the terrain well enough to realize that he shouldn't drive at night any more. He drank slowly and steadily until after midnight, amongst the other folks in the Dublin, waiting for Leila to show up. After seeing her professor-lover prayed over by an Inquisitor, Leila would need a drink, too.

At one o'clock, he gave up.

Fine. She had to go back to her apartment. He realized that this assumption, that she had to go home, was not necessarily accurate. Moderately buzzed, he bought a paperback at the bookstore next door and called a cab to take him to her apartment, where he leaned on the doorjamb and waited for her.

At two-thirty, he began to doubt. He read the little book, a mass market edition of a minor prize winner from two years before, and the alcohol slowly metabolized out of his veins, leaving his blood volume inadequate and his head dizzy.

At five minutes until three, his deadline, the elevator doors creaked open and Leila stumbled out. Her golden dress rode high on her slim thighs. Priests should not notice thighs.

She stopped when she saw him. "Jesus, Dante. What the hell are you doing here again?"

The pathos of it was shocking, him waiting at a girl's apartment in the wee morning hours. "I need to talk to you."

"This is ridiculous. It's three in the morning. Don't you ever need to talk during the day?" She found her clanking keys in her purse and shouldered past him. "Go home, Monsignor. Are you too wasted to drive? Do I need to call you a cab again?"

"I can call my own taxi. I need to talk to you. I must understand why."

She pushed the door open. "It doesn't matter *why*. There are more important things than rehashing the past, like taking responsibility for your own life." She stepped inside and turned, her hand behind the door to close it in his face.

He didn't want to be aggressive but she was closing the door and he would have to go back to the empty rectory with nothing but questions again. He pressed his fingertips against the door with his hand arched, the least threatening posture that kept the door open.

She rolled her eyes. "This is turning into stalking."

"I just need to talk to you. I promise, I will not repeat what you say. I need to understand." From an internal coat pocket, he extracted his thin purple confession stole. The embroidered gold cross shone on top. "I can wear this. Anything you say will be under the seal of confession. Lawyers could not ask me to reveal it."

"I'm not afraid of lawyers. I didn't kill anybody." She gazed at him steadily.

"Roma would not allow me to discuss it with anyone, no matter what."

"I don't care about your religious magic. I'm tired and I'm drunk, and I'm going to bed."

"Please. I don't understand why you had the affair with him."

The door had less inward pressure on it—she must have dropped her hand from the back side, and he pressed the door open a few inches.

"Fine." Leila stepped back, leaving the door open.

He decided this was tacit acquiescence if not an invitation. He followed her in and closed the door behind himself. Was he halfway back to his old habits, half-drunk in the living room of a woman's apartment, or had the priesthood tempered him? His drunken sex with Bev rode up in his mind and he cringed. The road he'd traveled in the priesthood had been steeply uphill but not long.

Leila returned from the kitchen with a bottle of scotch, a bottle of water, and two highball glasses. "Go ahead," she said. "Put on the stole."

"Do you wish to confess?" One loop of the fabric flipped out of his hand and swung in the air by his leg.

"No, but you said you'd wear it, pervert." She set the glasses and tall, full bottle on a gilt tray on the coffee table. The mirror on the bottom of the tray doubled the dark bottle, and the green glass torpedo stretched down though the wood table. "Put it on."

"You do not even like the collar." He kissed the cross in it and tossed the stole around his neck. The free ends hung down his chest.

"Yeah, but I'm very drunk, and I've had a very weird day, Monsignor."

"Do not call me that. Just-ah Dante."

"Just-ah Dante, the incognito Inquisitor."

"Don't say that."

Leila kneeled beside the coffee table. With her long, slim legs tucked under her, she looked childlike. She unclipped her hair, and the long, black silk of it spilled down her back, again so young, almost a child-woman, and the pedophilic connotations revolted him. He should shrink his own head to ensure that innocence was not becoming too appealing to him. She tipped the scotch bottle and poured one expert ounce into each highball glass. "Water?"

"Yes, *per favore.*"

She poured three ounces of water over the scotch in his glass, a nice ratio, and set the bottle on the tray. "Cheers," she said and tossed her shot back, no grimace on her smooth features, and poured herself another. For all his musing, Leila was no ingénue.

He stared at the azure chandelier above her dining room table. The cups around the light bulbs looked like miniature stained-glass windows depicting tulips. Cardinal Varchetto had one just like it in his office in the Vatican, but he had not allowed restorers to rewire it, lest they damage it. "Holy Mary, Mother of God, is that what I think it is?"

"Depends on what you think."

"Is it a Tiffany, circa nineteen forties, perhaps?"

"Thirties." She added water to her glass this time. "No one's ever recognized it."

"I've never seen one lighted up. *Bella.*" He sipped his drink. "Where did a graduate student get a Tiffany chandelier?"

"Inherited it."

"That's right. Your father." He looked up, startled. "And-ah, the Louis Quatorze table in the entry way? And the rest?" He pointed to the French antiques around them, inventorying. "Genuine?"

"Yeah."

"And the plasterwork?"

"Turn of the century Parisian."

"Which century?"

"Nineteenth," she admitted.

"The Vatican would love them. Cardinals would stab each other to get them. They'd tear each other's red robes and trip each other down stairs and send the IEA to steal them."

His line of sight drifted up to the chandelier, which cast blue-tinged, watery light over the apartment.

She said, "I had a revelation today during Conroy's funeral."

"Ah?" Dante picked up his diluted scotch and leaned forward.

"Conroy was working with GFP-labeled rabies virus to trace neural connections from the gut up the vagus nerve, extremities, optic nerve, to the brain. That data's pretty good. I'm planning a couple of papers out of Conroy's and my data."

"LPUs?" he asked.

Leila smiled. "They're not Least Publishable Units. I think some of them are big enough for *Nature* or *Science*. I owe you one for interpreting the fMRIs, and for helping with Danna's parents."

"I did nothing." He sipped the smooth, layered scotch.

"Her dad liked you." Leila chuckled and shook her head. "He thought you made up the Nicene Creed." Leila sipped. "How can you believe it? After everything, how can you believe those fairy tales?" Leila gulped her drink. "I can't believe I'm saying this to a priest."

"Why should you not discuss religion with a priest?" He wasn't sure whether that was the Socratic questioning of a psychiatrist or the ecumenical debate of a priest. It didn't matter.

"I'm usually not so mean when I drink. I'm more of the I-love-you-guys type." Leila held her glass up to the light and studied the diluted scotch. "You've taken Holy Orders. Why would I want to convince you of anything else?"

He could return later to her seeming reticence to challenge people's prior commitments. "What makes you think you could convince me?"

Leila squinted at her scotch. "Self-evident truths. If there were a God, then he's an evil son of a bitch. Wars. Famines. Genocide."

"That's your problem with God, that bad things happen in the world?" Dante laughed. "But that's the argument of a child. There are many answers for that."

"They all suck," Leila said.

"The world is a vale of soul-making, a chance to do God's work."

"They're all cop-outs, Dante, even Keats, even C.S. Lewis. We should discuss this when I'm not wasted." She stood on her long, unsteady, naked legs and braced her feet in her stiletto-heeled pumps. Her calves were gorgeous. His hands could span her thighs, perhaps her waist.

Ah, the scotch was going to his head. Perhaps, all questioning aside, all counseling aside, it was a mistake to be in the apartment of a drunk young woman in the darkest part of the night, when he was aware of his own proclivities. He said, "I should go."

"So soon? You've only had one drink." She sipped her drink and teetered. "The night's still young. We don't have to debate theology."

"You weren't at the Dublin bar tonight."

"I went out with friends, a girlfriend, Jody, dancing." She swayed a little, and her lithe body must have swayed in the music, dancing in a crowded, tangled club like Persepolis in the Roman Testacchio district, music drumming their skin. His cheekbones heated.

He dragged the confession stole off his neck from one end—friction burned the nape of his neck—and he wrapped the stole around his hand like a boxer taping his fist. He stood and buttoned his coat around him. "I should go."

She looked up at him, sideways. "I'm not so skittish around you. God, I used to want to claw my way up the walls to get away from you, but I'm getting used to it. You shrinks call that *desensitization*, don't you?"

He nodded. "Thank you for the drink," he said, and walked out, closing the door behind him. He waited until he heard the lock click into place.

He could live with the questions for another night rather than risk her presence. She was the type of woman with whom he'd been helpless in Roma: beautiful, intelligent, and drunk.

SLAIN DOC FINED FOR HAVING AFFAIR

By Kirin Oberoi

Before his death two weeks ago, Dr. Conroy Sloan was fined a total of thirty thousand dollars under a morals clause in his contract with the University of New Hamilton College of Medicine for continuing an indiscreet affair with an unnamed woman within the College of Medicine. As specified in his contract under a standard morals clause, Dr. Sloan was warned to discontinue the affair and, when the conditions of the agreement with the College of Medicine Board of Directors were not met on a timely basis, fined ten thousand dollars six months ago and a further twenty thousand dollars three months ago. The unnamed woman works for the University of New Hamilton College of Medicine but was not fined or disciplined. Under the University of New Hamilton College of Medicine's Sexual Harassment Policy, only the person in a senior position is held responsible because it is assumed that the other person was under duress.

TWO WEEKS LATER, Leila sat in a booth at the Dublin, drinking beer to quell the caffeine jitters, when the door above her opened and spring sunlight swarmed into the dark bar.

Two undergrads were playing pool in the back. The balls snicking off each other sounded like a switchblade released near her ear.

Footsteps clomped down the stairs, and Father Dante—open Roman collar, black shirt, wrapped in his black coat—trundled down the stairs, watching his feet. At the middle of the stairs, he steadied himself by grabbing the railing and surveyed the room until he saw Leila, sitting sideways in the booth. His head bounced in recognition. He walked over to her. "*Buona sera*," he said. "May I join you?"

She shrugged and he seated himself opposite her. Leila swallowed a gulp of her light, sweet brew.

Dante ordered a pint. "How are your papers coming along?"

"Almost ready. You're second author. Danna is third. 'A Novel Neuron Apoptosis Pathway Is Activated During HIV Infection and Inhibited During Neurovirulent Lyssavirus Infection.'"

Monty the bartender brought a well-poured beer to Dante.

Dante's question was quiet. "You had live HIV in your lab?"

"I labeled it biohaz, used the glove box and sealed flasks, put it in sealed incubators, and bleached everything. My aseptic technique is impeccable. Only-child, paranoid control freak."

Dante sipped his beer. "Why HIV? Why not something safe?"

She used the moist bottom of her glass to imprint a Mandela ring pattern on the bar.

Dante said, "I'm sorry to pry. How about them Knicks?"

Some secrets, Leila hid. This wasn't one. "My dad," Leila sipped her beer, "died of AIDS. A decade ago, or so. Back when AZT was the only stuff."

"I'm sorry." Dante sipped his beer, and his hand flickered toward her, then retracted.

"He used to take me to gay bars with him when I was a kid, when I visited him in Florida." Those wild, parrot-colored summers.

"Those are no place for children." His tone was conversational, not condemning.

"I was with a crowd of boy-moms every night, adored, dressed in trendy clothes, went to theater and arts performances, danced all night with men who had absolutely no bad intentions. I was a hell of a lot safer with my dad than I was in California. I ran away every August before he had to send me home. When I was fourteen, I got as far as North Carolina before the Queer Patrol found me. Dad tried to get custody but," she flipped her fingers in the air, miming the impossibility of catching smoke, "a gay man in court, against the mother, who had a 'stable home' and a bat flock of priests testifying that she was a staunch pillar of the Church. Poor guy didn't stand a chance."

Dante rested his elbow on the table. Without the white collar, his shirt looked almost like a flat Nehru collar.

"The virus attacked his brain more than most people's. Back then, most people died of pneumonia," Leila said. "My mom didn't want me to see him at the end, but one of his friends, Ducko, sent me a plane ticket. The way the virus ate his brain, it was like Alzheimer's or prion disease."

"Did your father know who you were?" Dante's eyebrows hovered above his eyes, sad, not derisive. He swirled his beer.

"It didn't matter. I knew who he was." Leila brisked up her manner. Moroseness reserved for one day a year. "Anyway, the first paper is the molecular one, the neural apoptosis pathway. HIV causes apoptosis, nice, planned, orderly death, and not some random, rampaging dying. I'm planning the second paper's figures, which I'll write just as soon as I finish submitting this one."

Dante nodded and sipped the last of his drink. "And what's that one?"

"I wondered if you want to be on it. I don't think you will."

Dante quirked an eyebrow. "A scientist turn down an authorship? Even though I think that fMRI interpretation doesn't warrant a spot on even one paper, let alone two."

"I'm sending it to *Nature*. I bet it'll make the evening news." Seismic tremors quivered through her muscles. She wanted to tell him, but he might scoff, and he shouldn't scoff. He should be afraid that she was right.

He smirked. "Come now, what apoptosis pathway could generate a sound bite on what you Americans call news?"

"It's not molecular. It's neurological. People who are dying of HIV have near-death experiences. They see angels and light and their loved ones and all that crap. I got scans from some people who were dying of HIV. My dad was a religious nut at the end. People who die of rabies don't see anything. I mean, they never, ever do."

"HIV doesn't infect neurons." The green lampshade beside Dante's head cast a sick pallor on his skin.

Leila said, "HIV infects microglia, and those cells secrete an apoptotic factor. The lyssavirus infects the neurons yet they don't die. And there's a structure in the brain that HIV infects. The apoptosis pathway must be different in there, or else it's killing around the structure and thus allowing that part of the brain to go haywire, removing the repression. The blood circulation in there goes crazy right before death. It's even in the visual cortex. The lyssavirus infects everything around that place in the brain but nothing happens to that structure. It's dark. It just lies there.

"I've found the neural locus of the brain's flight up to Heaven," Leila said. "I've got it all, the bright light, the angels, the soul, and how the brain works to make it seem real." She sipped her beer. "I'm putting the Catholic Church out of business."

"The Catholic Church has existed for two millennia," Dante said. "Mere proof that the soul is an illusion or an artifact of neurology won't bankrupt the Church. We've survived worse press than that. Besides, our business is faith, not facts. But yes, if you want, if you would be so generous, you may add my name to the paper. Perhaps the addition of *S.J.* to the header would, indeed, alert the media."

"Maybe it will." Leila sipped her beer. "So what're you doing in a bar in the afternoon?"

Dante shrugged. "I was on my way back to the rectory."

"Seemed like you were looking for someone."

Dante's head inclined to one side, between a shrug and an admission.

She said, "Malcolm thinks you're stalking me. He says you show up here, have a drink, and watch the door the whole time."

Again, his dark head inclined. Priests shouldn't have movie-star good looks, verging on ethereal angelic beauty. Priests were too dangerous to look like that.

What was that line from *Macbeth?* Something about how angels look. Her neurons probed other neurons, finding connections. "Have you been waiting down here for me?"

Dante sipped his beer slowly, a delaying tactic. For a psychiatrist, his tics were transparent. "Sometimes." He sipped again and wiped the foam off his upper lip with his thumb. "I like to talk to you." He looked up, and his black eyes were too vulnerable.

Flattery was an obvious ploy. She'd expected a smart-ass answer or something priestishly waffling. "Me? I'm cocky, I'm arrogant, and I'm a pain in the ass. Did I actually tell you that God is an evil son of a bitch?"

He smiled and ducked his dark head to sip the beer again. "You were intoxicated."

She looked off at the bar and smiled at Monty, chopping limes that aerosolized citrus oil, their fizzy scent detectable over stale smoke and rancid beer. "I can't believe I let you in my apartment when I was so tipsy."

"Nothing happened, if that is what you mean." He sounded as if he were explaining it to a child. His studied, careful expression left no lines in his face, and he looked younger.

"I didn't black out. I wasn't that wasted."

"Nothing would have happened. I am a priest." He glared at his beer. "I am no danger."

He was so bitter about that. How many times had he mentioned it? Every time she'd seen him. "And how do you feel about being *not dangerous*?"

He looked up and his mouth half-curved in a weary smile. "Are you analyzing me?"

Psychiatry is easy. Just ask questions. "Do you need psychoanalysis?"

He squinted a little. "Why do you ask if I need psychoanalysis?"

"Why aren't you answering the question?"

"What do you want to know?"

Leila leaned on her folded arms. Nice of him to give her carte blanche like that. "Were you quite the Lothario before you decided to be a priest?" *Lothario*, that was Rowe, not Shakespeare. What was that Shakespeare quote about angels? Angels, something about angels and what they look like, their brows.

He stopped smiling and looked down at his beer again. "I'm sorry?"

"Lothario," she tapped a cigarette out of her pack and examined Dante's chastened eyes, "Don Juan, Casanova," found her slim lighter in the side pocket of the laptop's case, "a playboy, a debaucher," held the papery cigarette between her lips and said, "a letch, a libertine," she ignited the lighter, inhaled sweet smoke, and blew a stream of it over the unoccupied booth on her right while Dante worked on a tentative smile, "a philanderer, a womanizer, a swinger, a player," she offered him the pack of cigarettes but he waved it off, "stud, dog, tomcat, wolf."

He stared, waiting for more, then chuckled. "*Un donnaiolo*, in Italian."

"They're so much better than the female equivalents."

He inclined his head, acknowledging this, and flicked his glass of mahogany brew with one finger. More bubbles joined the head at the top. "Why would you ask that of a priest?"

"Because you keep saying that you're harmless, tamed, or *caged*. Loaded words. They imply that you think your nature needs caging, that it's murderous or dangerous, that you're a criminal who needs a jail or a wild animal that needs a zoo, like a wolf."

Dante stared at his beer, unblinking, and his lower eyelids stretched open just a bit more. He reached out with his left hand, and his bare ring finger quivered before he grasped the glass.

"Of course," Leila leaned back in the booth, "this could all be bar talk, ethanol and caffeine. Idle language, full of sound and fury, signifying nothing." More *Macbeth*. Her neurons must be finding ethereal bubbles of neurotransmitter sparks.

Dante grimaced a smile that didn't touch his eyes. "You would have made a good psychiatrist."

She hadn't meant to pry, but if he was going to hint all the time, that was going to happen eventually. "How about them Knicks? Them Madrid Real? Them Manchester United?"

"No, you're *right. Caged.* It is a—how you say—a *tell*, like in poker."

She hesitated, wondering if she was trying to be too smart, but surely he knew all this, and if he didn't, he was fooling himself. "There are other things, like the condescending way you look at other guys, like you could tell them stories, but you refrain."

"No," he said, frowned, and shook his head.

"And the way you behave around women. A couple of weeks ago, when Joe and I were here and you were shit-faced at the bar," Dante winced at her choice of words, "you reached at me across the booth, but you didn't reach over to touch my cheek. Your hand was too low and cupping upward. You were reaching for the back of my neck to drag me over to you. You've done that a thousand times."

"I wasn't going to do it."

"Come on." Her fingers touched her anxious chest. She knew his moves as well as he did. She'd dated men like him. She liked men like him. Hell, she *was* men like him. "Consider who you're talking to, here."

He looked up at her out of the corner of his eyes.

"And you have this stillness about you, a restrained energy, kind of Robert Redford, around *Gatsby* or *The Natural*." Remembrance of those films, of sunlight haloing on Redford's bright blonde hair, touched her, and the words *Angels are bright* resolved in her head. "It's crouching, like you're ready to spring, like you're always sizing a woman up, deciding whether or not you want to have her."

"Surely not." He sounded dismissive.

She rapped the cigarette on the ashtray. "You even do it in the communion line."

"No." He sat back.

"Didn't you ever wonder why eighty percent of your line is women?"

"Because women go to church. Skewed population sample, self-selecting."

"Good try, but no dice." She smoked. "They want you to feed them."

A faint smile curled the edges of his mouth. "Now I know you are teasing me." He bit his thumbnail, smiling over his hand at her.

Do you bite your thumb at me? No, that was *Romeo and Juliet.* What was that *Macbeth* line? *Angels are bright still, though the brightest fell.* Yes, closer. "So you were a player."

"I'm a priest, now." He sipped his beer.

"How long ago did you take Holy Orders?"

"Five years." His shoulders relaxed. Perhaps confession was good for his soul. "I was almost thirty."

"So *why*, if you were a player and a doctor and a scientist, *why* did you become a priest?"

Dante held both his hands around his half-full glass. "I was studying madness and saints."

She shook her head. "That isn't enough of a reason. Especially since you'd already been to college and medical school."

"Are you saying I was too old?" He smiled, and his black eyes twinkled, flirting. He didn't even know he was doing it.

She was so right about him. She blew smoke down and away from the table. "I'm saying you should have known better."

He nodded, a sage oscillation from his strong neck that swished his black hair around his cheekbones. "In medical school, I challenged the professors. If the statistics are true and so many people believe some religion, why do we discount it, especially in psychiatry? If we're trying to heal the mind, why don't we ask about their soul?"

"And so you went to the seminary?"

"I was in Roma. If you're asking about God, there is one place to go for answers. I asked my seminary professors the same things you are asking me. I challenged them. Why is God an evil son of a bitch?"

At least she hadn't offended him with that drunken comment. "And?"

"Eventually, to answer those questions, I had to explore farther."

"So you fell into it."

"I studied at the seminary, but I never intended to take Holy Orders.

They accepted me, knowing that I was a scholar, not an aspiring priest."

"So you were still a swinger?"

"At first." On the lip of his glass, a drip of foam threatened to ride over the edge and fall, and he wiped it off.

Angels are bright still, though the brightest fell. The brightest fallen angel was Lucifer, light-bringer. Bright angels become beautiful devils. "So some woman broke your heart?"

"No one broke my heart."

Whatever. "I still don't see why you decided to be a priest."

"One of the old priests who taught at the seminary had heard of my— what do you call it?— tomcatting around."

Casual fucking is what Leila called it.

"Some of the other seminarians discussed my indiscretions, commented that I dragged my sorry carcass into morning Mass wearing clothes from the day before, smelling like perfume and hangover."

"Walk of shame." *She* was flirting. She straightened, crossed her arms over her breasts, and smoked her cigarette.

He scratched his ear. "I was atrocious. I try to pity my former self. I flouted every rule. They were lucky to have a doctor working for them, a psychiatrist no less, and I knew that nothing I could do would make them kick me out. No one could say that I was unsuitable for the priesthood. I would have agreed. The old priest asked me to meet him in his office."

The idea of a priest beckoning toward an office knotted her chest.

Dante rotated the empty beer glass slowly between his palms. He tested the air with one finger, and Monty glanced over at them, brows raised. Dante called, "The usual, thank you." He continued, "The old priest called me into his office, regarded me seriously and solemnly, and asked me why I screwed the women."

Leila snorted a chuckle. Stupid old priest.

Monty delivered a small glass of light amber liquid to Dante.

Dante said, "I laughed, too, but he smiled. He was a kind, thin, pink man with white hair, and smoked a thin cigarette while he waited for me to finish laughing, and he asked again."

Dante cupped his hands around the watered scotch. "I said, because they were *women*." Dante socked down more liquor. He seemed casual but that draught of scotch was the air-gulp of drowning. His shoulders coiled inward as if he were cold, though his tone was light.

Leila leaned on the table, listening. Her own response to that question would have been similar: derision and tautology, and maybe the panic that clinched his shoulders.

Dante's face was a slim, soft smile, empathetic, practiced. "And he asked again why I had sex with the women, what in me was so empty that I pursued women, women in plural, needing a different woman every night, staying out all night getting drunk and screwing women when it was ruining my theological studies and my practice of medicine. He asked me what was driving me so hard that I couldn't sleep alone or sober or in my own bed. He asked what I was looking for. I laughed at him." Dante's face remained serene with that slight, superficial smile. "He asked what I wanted that these women couldn't give me, that I needed so much that I was destroying myself."

Leila's hands were clamped over her own hollow chest, and she pushed her hands down onto the table. "What did you tell him?"

Dante splashed back the last of his dilute scotch and tamped the highball glass down on the table. "I didn't tell him anything. It was as if I was flailing in deep water. He'd stripped me until I wasn't anyone any more. I spent a week in my apartment, dead drunk."

Leila's hands pressed over her boxing heart.

"I knew there was something, and that women were not it." He rotated the empty scotch glass between his thumb and index finger.

"And the priesthood was," she prompted.

"I took Orders."

"And you found your answer."

Dante slid sideways and stood up. "I should go," he said. "You look like you have some reading to do." He dropped a twenty dollar bill on the table and set the glass on it. He hitched his coat collar up over the nape of his neck and walked up the gloomy stairs. He stumbled, nearly fell, but righted himself and walked up.

Angels are bright still, though the brightest fell. Though all things foul must wear the brows of grace, Yet grace must still look so.

Shakespeare meant that angels and fallen angels, devils and demons, are bright and beautiful because they are both, at their core, angelic. A third of the Heavenly Host fell with Lucifer.

This bright, beautiful priest was either angel or demon, for Leila.

Chapter Eighteen

The Daily Hamiltonian:

WIFE TO STAND TRIAL FOR KILLING DOC

By Kirin Oberoi

At the preliminary hearing yesterday, prosecution attorneys sketched their case against Mrs. Beverly Maria Sloan, accused of murdering her husband Dr. Conroy Sloan, on February 14 in his recently rented townhouse near the UNHHC. Prosecutors presented forensic evidence showing that Mrs. Sloan's fingerprints were on the murder weapon, a steak knife, and that Mrs. Sloan's clothes bore traces of Dr. Sloan's blood. The defense offered no evidence or rebuttal. The judge determined the evidence was sufficient to warrant a trial. The trial date has not been determined.

AT MASS, Dante stood at the front of the communion line and listened to the light hymn while Bev played one-handed chords. He presented wafers to the long line of women and watched their eyes. Most muttered "Amen," as he presented them with "The body of Christ," but some of them did seem to look into his eyes a little too long, and their eyelashes fluttered over brown or black or green or blue irises as he laid the wafer in their hands or on their tongue.

John the deacon assisted Father Dante with the sacrament of Holy Communion. Bev Sloan's music drifted down on John and them all from the loft, sweetly, angelically, even with one arm broken to pieces. "The body of Christ." "Amen." A woman like Bev Sloan couldn't kill her husband. Maybe Beverly's fingerprints were on the knife because she'd tried to pull it out of Conroy's chest. There were a thousand possible explanations.

Herman Burkett received Holy Communion from John the deacon in his cupped hands and ate the wafer. He liked Beverly Sloan's choice of light, fluffy hymns lately. They were easier to sing along to. He wondered who was going to take over the choir when she went to prison because, as everyone knew, she murdered that cheating bastard of a husband and, if she got away with it, every wife would murder every cheating bastard and then where would we be?

Up in the choir loft, Bev picked out a majestic E-major with her right hand and bobbed her head to conduct the choir. Ever since the hearing, everyone had stared at her, and she worked hard at holding her cringing head up. Dignity was all she had left.

Gomez Hererra sang the deep bass line of the hymn and watched Bev Sloan. Her head snapped back, and they all stopped singing, right on cue. It was amazing she'd figured out how to play the pipe organ and conduct at the same time using only one arm. He appreciated amazing. He appreciated Bev Sloan, who was a stalwart, staunch Catholic when lesser people would have begged off. He appreciated Bev's strong soul and her suffering, like now, when she thought no one was looking, and she bowed her head and her face creased with grief and pain.

THREE WEEKS after Conroy's funeral, Leila stood by the bed as Danna suffocated. The paralysis had seeped inward and paralyzed her diaphragm, and a ventilator prolonged her deeply medicated life. Eventually, when the virus had swum up her peripheral nervous system and adequately eaten her brain, her parents acquiesced to the ventilator's removal and signed a DNR. Her father proselytized that she was seeing Jesus as she died.

Leila didn't tell him that rabies victims don't have near-death experiences, that there are no welcoming relatives or bright, friendly lights because lyssavirus short-circuits that particular set of synapses.

For Danna, the screen faded to black.

TUESDAY NIGHT, Bev rehearsed the choir. Dante sat in a pew several rows behind her. Mary, Laura, and Lydia sat on the risers while the tenors sang their part.

Lydia motioned at the church pews in general and whispered, "I think he's just tired. Look at how much he's slumped over." She hoped he didn't ruin his looks with overwork.

Laura said, "I'll bet he is tired. He celebrates Mass every day, goes to the other churches to give their Masses, and other stuff, too." Luke, her baby, her angel, had begun drawing again, just two weeks ago. His pictures were dark, angry, and she'd taken some of them to Father Dante, worried. The priest's eyes had lit up, and he'd asked Luke careful questions about them. Luke talked animatedly about the weeping crucifixes and smoking ruins. The priest told her later that he had been worried because Luke had no way of expressing himself, and this was *bene, bene*. Sure enough, as Luke crayoned more pictures, his appetite improved, he played outside more, and he hadn't had a stomach ache worthy of skipping school for a week.

Mary said, "I don't know." His face seemed puffy to her. "I think something's wrong. Look at how he lays his forehead on his hands, like he's praying, like he's so sad."

Bev left the piano and joined them during the break.

Lydia bent her head toward Bev and whispered, "What do you call that flabby bit of skin around a penis?"

Air dove into Bev's lungs. *Caught.* She was caught. Lydia knew Bev had been sleeping with Dante, and that was why she was asking about *foreskin*. She even knew the *particulars*. She had to warn Dante. She was a widow, but he was still a priest. "What?"

Lydia whispered, "A man."

"What?" Confusion buzzed in her head.

"That flabby bit of skin around a penis. *A man.*"

"Oh, I get it. *A man*, of course. That's funny. A man." Bev pressed a hand over her sternum, where her heart fought to free itself.

ONE SPRING NIGHT, Bev let herself into Conroy's laboratory with his key from his home desk drawer. Christine and Dinah were at the movies with Laura and Luke, so she had the evening to herself. Her version of her and Conroy's lives was missing something. She needed to understand.

Conroy's office door was closed, and a thin line of fluorescence lay on the floor under it. Light irradiated the white paper over the arrow slot window. Surely his office light hadn't been burning for the last month and a half. She unlocked his office and pushed Conroy's door open.

Black-haired, dark-eyed Leila, sitting in Conroy's chair amongst Conroy's stacks and piles of white papers and slick journals and thick books, looked up, startled, but her wide eyes narrowed, glittering. Leila asked, "What are you doing here?"

"I didn't know anyone would be here." Her good arm cradled her cast. Bev was intruding on Conroy's little tramp sitting in his office. Her guts twisted, but no violent fantasy entered her mind. That thought train was too dangerous, and Bev didn't ever, ever think about violence any more. "What are you doing in my husband's office?"

"Figuring out if your husband was trying to kill us with anything else."

"Oh." Tension still racked her, but this trashy lingerie of a girl had raised the alarm that ensured Christine and Dinah and Bev's own safety, and she had been cordial at Christmas parties, and she'd dumped Conroy at home when he'd been drunk, though Bev suspected Leila had something to do with that. Bev scooted books aside, sat in a melamine circa 1955 office chair, and propped her graying cast on the arm of the chair. "I wanted to ask you something."

Leila doodled in the margin of Conroy's notebook. "The D.A. said I shouldn't to talk to you directly. Only to your lawyer. And not to him."

"It's scientific. Well, medical."

Leila picked up a pen, one of those fat, smeary kinds that Conroy detested, and flipped it over her knuckles. "Okay, what do you want?"

"If Conroy did have rabies, would it have changed *him*, his thoughts?"

Leila's shoulders released. "Behavioral changes are a major symptom of rabies."

"Is that why he got the apartment?"

Leila leaned on Conroy's smothered desk and licked her burgundy-lipsticked lips. "He didn't consult me. It could have been the rabies virus, making him act so weird."

"You didn't want him to move out?"

She shook her head. "I told him he was an idiot."

"Peggy must have wanted him to move out." Bev settled herself farther into the chair.

"Peggy?" Leila frowned. "Is she the slut who left the underwear in his suitcase? Or was it Valerie Lindh who did that? I have a hard time keeping them straight."

Bev smacked the chair's armrest with her right palm. Her left arm lay dead in its leaden cast. "He *was* having an affair with Valerie Lindh." And he'd lied to her about that, too.

"Well, he said he was." Leila flicked the pen into the air, and it turned end over end near the fluorescent light like a tumbling dragonfly. She pinched the falling pen out of the air. "God only knows what was running through his head sometimes."

Bev wanted to poke this little git. "Peggy attended the funeral."

"No!" Leila sounded scandalized. She straightened.

"You did, too."

Leila's lips thinned, and she licked them again. "Dante said it would look worse if I didn't go, because the whole lab went. I tried not to interfere."

"And I barely saw you, but that Peggy introduced herself to me."

Leila shook her head. "Uppity bitch."

"That's what I thought!" Conroy had deceived them both. Consorority sparkled in Bev's heart. "I thought she shouldn't have come."

"Did *she* know," Leila illustrated her question with scooping pen sweeps in the air above the desk between them, "that *you* knew," one more black arc in the air, "who *she* was?"

"I think so. She was so smug."

"Uppity bitch." Leila shook her head.

"Yes," Bev said. "Uppity bitch." She smiled at Leila, tentatively.

Leila grinned an embarrassed half-smile and looked at her lap.

Something tickled in her head. Bev asked, "Do you know Father Dante?" Bev's spine clenched, rounding her shoulders, and she bowed slightly, an inborn posture of raised vestigial hackles. This lithe, smoky, floating cunt pursued every man she sniffed out, flying through the air and sticking on them like a hunting jellyfish, a vaginal man-of-war jellyfish.

"Dr. S. had mentioned him and we googled him. He helped me with some fMRIs." Leila was oblivious that Bev could stab her with that ballpoint pen she was flipping around. "And, I don't know, we just got to talking. I don't have a supervising professor right now, you know."

Bev clutched the arms of the chair as if she were handcuffed to it. "Are you screwing him, too?"

Leila uncapped the pen and clicked the cap back on. "I would never, ever, fuck a priest. It's anathema. It's obscene. Heresy. Sacrilege. And I won't be that kind of *victim*." She dropped the pen into the spine crease of Conroy's open notebook. "Aren't these the questions you should be asking me about your husband?"

Bev's spine arched back and yanked her soft body with it, as if recoiling from a slash.

"Why are you so interested in the priest, Beverly?" Leila closed the notebook on the pen.

"He's *my* priest. You're taking him away from me, too."

"You're screwing him, aren't you?" Leila asked.

"I"—*am not good at lying and I was but I'm not now*—"no." Bev recoiled.

"You're fucking him." Leila stood up and tucked Conroy's notebook under her arm. "I don't give a shit. All that sanctimonious suffering he spouts is just shit." She picked up a thick, red book with papers hanging out like a ragged sandwich, said, "I've got to go write my thesis," and walked out.

Bev breathed through her mouth and tasted whiskey. God, oh God. Now that little bitch knew about her and Dante. She'd tell the prosecutors. There was nothing to do but sell the house and provide for her girls because she was going to jail.

Bev rifled through her purse, found a brown prescription vial, and dry-swallowed two little green pills. *Work*, she commanded them. *Hurry up and work.*

The Daily Hamiltonian:

Witness List for Trial of Alleged Doc-Killing Wife

By Kirin Oberoi

The trial of Mrs. Beverly Sloan, who allegedly stabbed her husband Dr. Conroy Sloan at his recently rented apartment near UNHHC, will be here in New Hamilton.

Dozens of witnesses are expected to testify, but only a few names have been released. Witnesses scheduled to testify for the prosecution include: Leila Sage Faris, 24, a graduate student in the laboratory of the deceased Dr. Sloan; Peggy Anne Strum, 38, a New Hamilton University College of Medicine Department Secretary; Dr. Sridhar Bhupadi, a forensic scientist, and the paramedics who were first on the scene, Carleton Davis and Josef Menz. Witnesses scheduled to testify for the defense include Monsignor Dr. Dante Maria Petrocchi-Bianchi, S.J., M.D., Ph.D., the Sloans' priest, who lives in Rome, Italy and works for the Vatican but is temporarily assigned to the OLPH Catholic Church.

Judge Leonine Washington has threatened a gag order, but none has been imposed.

THE NEXT DAY, Leila sat in Conroy's office in his grimy chair, trying not to tip over his paper stacks, working with his notebooks to figure out how he'd stained those thin sections of mouse brain. His samples looked good but he hadn't written down the names of the antibodies he'd used because he had been hiding that he was working with fucking rabies virus.

Leila must have been as quiet as a sacrificed mouse and entirely hidden behind the city block of paper stacks because Joe and Yuri started talking loudly outside the open door.

"You see morning paper?" Yuri asked. "Why they call Leila to witness? Why not all of us?"

"Thank your lucky stars you don't have to testify, Yuri-go. She and Sloan were friends. Maybe he told her something."

"Do you mean he was sleeping with her?"

"I think she's dating someone else. Maybe it's about his computer. He always had trouble with it and needed her help. God, you remember the red Xs? Maybe because she figured out about the fucking rabies virus."

"Fucking rabies virus. My ass still sore. You think his wife killed him?"

"That's what everyone says, but I don't know. She was so nice at all those Christmas parties. Never thought she'd be a snapper."

"Snapper? Fish?"

"No, Yuri. The fish is a red snapper."

"Is that communist crack?"

"A snapper is someone who *snaps*, goes crazy."

"Yes, Mrs. Sloan did not seem red snapper. I didn't even get Porsche. Capitalist swine."

"Yes, Yuri."

Leila's reputation was safe for the next few months. God or lack thereof willing, she planned to defend her Ph.D. thesis, testify, deposit her thesis, and leave this goddamned town the next day.

The prosecuting attorneys had interviewed her last week, and they'd been pissed when Leila admitted to the affair.

Beverly Sloan had surely told her lawyer that Leila had been screwing Conroy. If she hadn't, that priest had. Leila had thought Dante *liked* talking to her. That priest didn't *like* talking to her. He wasn't staking out the Dublin because she was smart or interesting or because he wanted to talk about the impossibility of a deity in a scientific, logical universe. He had an ulterior motive. He was a stinking hypocrite, screwing Beverly Sloan and probably other women, too. Asshole. Tomcat. Catamite, probably.

DANTE SAT IN HIS LIBRARY, reading yet more literature on the treatment for victims of child sexual abuse, but he still felt like he was blundering in every counseling session.

A knock jostled the library door. "Come in," he said.

The door rattled, hesitated, and slammed open. Leila, glaring at the stubborn door, said, "Sorry. That door sticks." She rattled the knob.

Dante's heart pulled together and rose at seeing her again. "Hello, Leila! It's the humidity. Come in. Sit. You haven't been at the Dublin, lately. Coffee?"

"Just dropping off the first paper. It made it past abstract review at *Nature*. I'll let you know if they want revisions." She held out a few pieces of paper. Leila's hand was on the doorknob, ready to jump backward and slam the door, as if his attack were imminent.

Dante flipped the stack sideways and craned his neck to look at a picture. Neon green and red lines floated in black space. "Nice confocal."

"Yeah."

Her defensive gestures had returned in force. He hadn't shown up, drunk and belligerent, on her doorstep at midnight lately. He touched his Roman collar and realized he was wearing his cassock in the chilly library. "I can take out the collar."

"I should go. If you want your name on the next paper, I'll put it on. Other than that, we probably shouldn't talk. Lawyers, and all that."

LEILA SHIFTED on her feet in the dungeon of an office that Dante evidently inhabited. The wooden door and the stone walls could muffle any scream.

"I don't understand." His dark eyes looked genuinely perplexed.

How calculatingly sweet, like a bright angel, but he was a fallen angel, and the hypocrite had screwed Conroy's wife after caterwauling about searching for something that couldn't be found in a life of debauchery. He'd implied that he'd given up women, the liar. Leila wasn't interested in fallen angels or debauched priests. He wasn't *caged* at all. He prowled. "Oh, you know, the Beverly Sloan thing. The prosecutors told me that I should only talk to her attorney, and I don't have to talk to him if I don't want to, and I really shouldn't discuss that night with anybody else who was a witness. You're testifying for her, aren't you?"

"Both the lawyers have called me. But we can still discuss science."

"Let's just get these papers out. You're going back to Rome soon."

He bent his neck, and his head bobbled left, inviting sympathy, flirting. "It will be years before I return to Roma. I have sublet my apartment."

"So the Inquisition has you by the short and curlies."

"Pardon me?" He scratched at his collar.

"They're running your life."

"Oh, yes. I was thinking, however, when you are ready to submit the second paper, perhaps I should write a response rather than being named as an author."

"The Church's response?"

"No, my own. I think the second paper should have only your name. It's a seminal paper. It's going to change things. If you publish it alone, you could write your own ticket in a university, perhaps go directly to faculty."

"No way." She touched the cool, insulated door behind her back.

"You could. Crick did."

"Crick as in Watson and Crick," Leila said. "As in *DNA*. This is just neuroanatomy." Surely, he was joking.

Dante tapped the molecular manuscript on the coffee table. "You're explaining how we perceive the world, and what areas of the brain cause us to believe the things we do. There is a great deal of support for your ideas, but it's disparate, from many fields. I can tie it up, support your data. I think you could," he licked his lips, "win prizes."

Three little syllables that tripped on the tongue and buzzed at the end had driven Conroy mad.

Dante must still be trying to get her into bed. This fallen angel and debauched priest had invoked that old demon Flattery, that furry apparition that rubbed so softly against your skin.

"I've got to go." She walked out, pulling the door behind her. The swollen door bumped the jamb.

"Leila?"

She trotted out of the church, into the sunny, cold parking lot. The unseasonably cool May wind spun her black hair, and she yanked it out of her eyes with one hand while she fumbled with her car keys in the door with the other.

"Leila!"

"Look," she called across the parking lot, "if there's something you think should be changed, call me, or email, or something."

She got in the car and punched the accelerator.

The Daily Hamiltonian:

Trial Set for Slain Doc's Wife

By Kirin Oberoi

Judge Leonine Washington today announced that the trial of Mrs. Beverly Sloan, accused of stabbing to death her husband Dr. Conroy Sloan last February at his newly acquired apartment near the UNHHC, will begin on July 10. Jury selection will take place on July 6 and 7.

DANTE WROTE, *John's abuse was typical of N's predations, combining sacred Catholic symbolism with perversion. One series of events of which Samual had knowledge occurred a year ago, last May. On fourteen days in succession, N forced John to reenact the Stations of the Cross in the nude, and N sodomized or was fellated by John in each position as was suggested by the pose of the figures in the station, while John recited aloud the prayer for each station (intermittently, in the latter case). Father Samual entered the library on the seventh day (Christ's second fall), while John was on his hands and knees on the floor and N was sodomizing him. S surveyed the situation, turned, and closed the door behind him. John says he distinctly remembers the click of Samual locking the library door. Even if that were the first time that S had evidence of N's abuse, if he had intervened, he would have spared John another consecutive week of abuse and occasional abuse during the following six months until N was removed by the IEA and CDF. The thirteenth station, Christ's death on the cross, still terrifies John and included overtones of autoeroticism and necrophilia.*

Dante closed the folder and locked it in his desk drawer. It was a cool May evening in the middle of a rugged, week-long cold snap, but he decided to change into his jogging clothes in the rectory and run at least seven miles, perhaps ten, and then avail himself of the bottles of liquor in the lower drawer of his nightstand. In the months since that Leila in the bar had pried open his head and asked so innocently, so deviously, *why,* insomnia and nightmares alternately denied him rest. If he didn't dream of viewing the abuse through a stained-glass window that wouldn't yield when he pounded on it, he dreamed of reliving his ordination from above, silently screaming, trying to stop himself.

Dante was crossing the church when he recognized Bev's hourglass figure kneeling before the statue of the Virgin Mary. She sported two free, uncast arms.

It had been twelve weeks, nearly thirteen.

"Hello!" he called. His hoarse voice jarred him.

She looked up from the Rosary that dangled between her palms.

Dante walked over. He held out his hand, palm up. "Let me see."

Bev raised her skinny, withered, wrinkled arm. Dante held her weightless limb. A red, twisted scar snaked around her wrist. He asked, "Does it still hurt?"

"It's okay. I took a pill."

"I suppose you won't get many more of those, now that your arm is out of the cast."

"The orthopedic doctor said to call him if I needed more, if the pain is persistent."

Dante pulled his hand away slowly, and she let her arm drop.

BEV DIDN'T LIKE IT when people inspected her scars, even this new one on her hand. The scar on her wrist stung like a needle scratch when the onyx Rosary beads swept across it.

His long legs twisted as he sat on the floor beside her. "How is it?"

"My hand is weak, clumsy, numb on one side of the pinky finger, but it works." The rosary wound so tightly around her fingers that her nail beds were alternately white and crimson. She loosened her grip.

Dante leaned against the wall that formed the side of the Virgin's niche. He drew his knees up and rested his elbows on them, his side toward Bev, and looked out over the church. "I remember when you ran in here, my first day."

Bev nodded and spilled the Rosary chain from one hand to the other. In her left hand, the beads felt hard and cold and tingled along the side of her palm. Her strong right hand hardly registered their light substance.

"I was so jet-lagged," he said, "and I had been drinking on the plane, trying to sleep, and I was tired. Samual said that he had to leave and would I take confession for him, and I pictured a nice room, a couple of chairs, and he showed me to the antique torture chamber, not used since the Middle

Ages. And then you ran into the confessional."

Bev ducked her head. She must have seemed crazed. Even now, madness howled outside her foggy walls.

"And you said you felt abandoned by God, and I didn't know what you meant, but I did my best, considering that a drunken headache was beating in my brains."

Bev leaned over so her legs curled to the side—her knees groaned as she released her weight—and propped herself up on her strong, right arm. She said, "I wish I could change everything. I never would have unpacked his suitcase. I would have assumed some sort of accident had happened at the airport. Or I would have left him then, taken the girls, hidden, scrubbed toilets to support us." She spun the Rosary beads with her weak hand.

"That sounds like remorse," Dante said. "I think you could confess."

"It's still not right, not time, something," Bev said. "Before, when I've needed to confess, I've known and hated the sin for its own sake. There's a blank smear over that night, like a half-dry oil painting someone scraped a trowel over." Her cheeks warmed, and she cleared her throat.

His long fingers dangled off the ends of his arms, elbows resting on his knees. "How often are you taking the pills?"

"Every four hours or so. The places where the bones are knit together are sore, like the new bone hasn't hardened yet."

"Narcotics can have many effects on the brain."

"I'm not seeing pink elephants."

He inclined his head and tugged at the curls with his fingers, straightening his hair. "Or in your case, perhaps the lack of pink elephants."

Bev looked away, down the long hall of the church. "I don't like that."

"I've been thinking a lot about the brain and the soul, lately, where our soul resides. I think you should wean yourself off the pills. It might not be your soul that can't find God. It might be a psychopharmacological interaction of the drug with your brain."

Bev leaned back on her arm and coiled the Rosary beads around her hand. "And what would that mean for God, if a pill can block the Omnipresent, the Omniscient, the Omnipotent?"

He shrugged. "Maybe that is the reason that most religions have rules about alcohol and other mind-altering drugs. Maybe our connection through our brains with God is tenuous."

"The pills keep me from worrying about things." Bev waved her benumbed fingers in the air, dispersing worrisome thoughts, like nerve damage and murder and prison and widowhood and orphaned children.

"Don't take the pills anymore, please."

Bev dragged her finger through the black rosary beads, dragging them scraping across the floor, into an X or an 8. She swirled them into a vortex. "All right."

Chapter Nineteen

"Ladies and Gentlemen of the Jury." The District Attorney, George Grossberg, turned to face the jury but remained in profile for the blazing lights and cameras behind the rows of spectators. "We are here in this courtroom because Dr. Conroy Robert Sloan was murdered, because a doctor in good standing in this community was fatally stabbed with a knife, and because the forensic evidence supports that his wife, Beverly Maria Sloan, stabbed him.

"Now, she says that she didn't do it, and she might even testify that she didn't, that it was an accident or a mistake, but we don't think it was. She'd been abusing him for years and that night, she killed him. He had bruises on his ribs, his arms, and a fresh bruise on his left eye. One of his elbow ligaments was torn. You're going to hear from the defense that the doctor was cheating on his wife, but we're not here to judge the victim. The fact that he was cheating on her and that he had left her *that very night* was her motive for killing him. She went over to his apartment enraged, intending to kill him, and she hit him in the face and then she took one of the steak knives from the set he'd just bought, and her fingerprints were on that knife, and she stabbed him through the heart with so much anger that one blow killed him. Thank you."

BEV CLASPED HER HANDS together as Heath Sheldon rose from the table and walked over to the jury box. Her healed wrist twinged. She'd been off the pills for a week now, and Dante had said that her liver should metabolize all the chemicals soon. She hadn't managed to quit them in May, or June, but now they were gone, though the fuzziness would have been welcome when the prosecutor said that she went to the apartment intending to kill Conroy. The quiet, glowing presence of God would have been welcome. Hopefully, her liver would hurry up and deconstruct the chemicals so she could hear God again, even though she thought that God's absence didn't have anything to do with those green pills that the orthopedic doctor had so readily dashed off scrips for.

Behind her, in the audience seats, Dante leaned over and rested his hot face on his hands. Because he was to be called as a witness, he shouldn't be in the courtroom, but the court had allowed him to stay because he was Bev's spiritual advisor and because it was assumed that nothing could affect his testimony because he was a priest, and therefore he had some mystical access to absolute truth and possessed perfect morals.

IN THE JURY BOX, four men and eight women watched Heath Sheldon approach them.

To Tom Agosin, the lawyer seemed primped and slick, a superficial man with a shallow case. He hoped Beverly Sloan had more to offer than just this snake oil–selling lawyer.

Gabriela Rossetti couldn't imagine being so angry at someone as to strike them. She had never struck her children, and they were fine, gentle teens now. Even through screaming fights with her ex-husband, she never entertained the thought of hitting him.

Margaux Dominic remembered that her steak knives needed sharpening. She had a dinner party for the members of her husband's law firm, and they were planning to grill steaks for them and portobello mushrooms for the junior partner, the short redheaded woman, the vegan.

HEATH SHELDON SMILED at Margaux, Gabriela, Tom, and the nine other jury members he'd selected during *voir dire*. Potential jurors who'd looked him in the eye and smiled at him, these he'd kept. The prosecutors used their challenges on Catholics and health care workers, probably at the behest of some overpaid, useless jury consultant. No one knew what went on in the jury room, whether the interactions were more closely akin to the gestalt of a hive mind or the sociopathy of a crazed, looting mob. His perfect jury was one who liked him and so might completely ignore the facts.

Heath smiled brilliantly, twinkling through the inadequate defense he was about to put on. If Beverly Sloan hadn't done it, the defense would have been easier. He hoped to mitigate the sentence and not look too idiotic in front of the cameras. No one watched LawTV anyway, except other lawyers and his mother.

If you can argue the law, then you argue the law. If you can argue the facts, then you argue the facts. If you can't argue the law or the facts, you just argue.

He said, "The prosecution has given you a set of facts and constructed a plausible theory around them. Indeed, the prosecution's job is to convict Beverly Sloan, regardless of what happened in that apartment that night. Mr. Grossberg, though he included facts, did not tell you the whole story. I'm here to tell you the whole story.

"Conroy Sloan is dead; there is no mistaking that fact. He died from a knife wound to the left ventricle of his heart. That, too, is not in dispute."

He inhaled, buying time. "His wife, Beverly Sloan, touched the knife that killed him because her fingerprints were on the knife handle, and she went over to his new apartment that night because he had indeed abandoned her and their two daughters. But there's more."

He patted the sides of his blonde hair. "There was a struggle in that apartment, that night. Her blood was also on the knife and on the countertops, and Conroy Sloan's fingerprints were also on the knife.

Remember, he was a lot bigger and stronger than she was.

"The fingerprints on the knife were from her left hand. Her left arm had been so badly broken that night that she required emergency surgery or else she might have bled to death because so many blood vessels—major blood vessels, the ones that people try to cut when they slit their wrists—were torn by the splintered, broken bones ripping her wrist apart from the inside. She has nerve damage from those injuries. She couldn't have stabbed him with her left hand. It was too badly broken. We'll show you X-rays of her smashed wrist and hand.

"Beverly Sloan is a small woman. Conroy Sloan was a tall man. He smashed her arm and hand. She's a pianist, and her hands are her living. He's a doctor. He knew just where to break. Her other hand was sliced open, too.

"As soon as she could, even with her crushed arm, she called 9-1-1. Mrs. Sloan was hysterical. She called because Conroy was hurt. She didn't mention that her own arm was in pieces and she was bleeding internally. That isn't the reaction of a killer.

"And the knife that killed Conroy Sloan was a steak knife that was four and a half inches long." He held his tanned, manicured fingers four inches apart. "Personally, if I was selecting a knife because I was planning to kill a person ten inches taller than I am, who outweighs me by almost a hundred pounds, I'd pick a big knife. In that same carving block, there was a sixteen-inch chopping knife, an eighteen-inch bread knife, and a twenty-inch carving knife.

"A four-and-a-half-inch steak knife? That's a knife you use to cut someone's hand.

"And last, Conroy Sloan had *one* knife wound.

"I've been a criminal defense attorney for a while, and I've seen a lot of homicides committed in a lot of different ways, and here's the thing." Sheldon leaned on the jury box rail. "I've never seen *one* of anything. The prosecution says that Beverly Sloan was *enraged*, so out of control and enraged that she stabbed her husband to death. But the knife went in *once*. *One* time.

"I've compiled a list here of other homicides. These, in backward chronological order, are the last five homicides against which I defended people. I haven't selected these. I haven't left anything out. Won some, lost some." Won four, lost one. His overall record was 87-8. He retrieved a piece of paper from the pocket inside his suit coat.

He consulted the list and spoke to a different juror with each item. To Tom Agosin, "Blunt force trauma to the posterior skull with a cast-iron skillet, at least eighteen blows."

To Margaux Dominic, "Stabbing with a military-style all-purpose tool, like a Swiss army knife but the blades are up to a foot long: twenty-six wounds. There was evidence that he tried to hack her arms and legs off with the 'entrenching tool,' the shovel."

To Hara Carson, "Gunshot wounds: thirteen. That's all the bullets the gun held. Twelve in the clip, one in the chamber. Dents in the gun's hammer showed that the perpetrator kept shooting after the gun was empty, at least three times."

To Chessa Kendrall, "Stabbing with long, sharp scissors: a hundred and twelve stab wounds. Thirty-eight defensive wounds to the hands."

To Kirsta Prestby and Toby Yazee, "Assault with a motor vehicle. She hit her husband once, backed up over him, and ran over him again, for a total of three passes or six axles." That was the case he lost.

He folded the paper in half and tapped it on the jury box. Some jurors, like the man on the left, looked disgusted. "Now this isn't just an exercise to show you how brutal people can be. It's a list to show you how brutal they *are*. When a person kills another person, especially someone they know, especially if they are *enraged*, they don't just kill them. They *overkill* them. They stab or shoot or pound or slash or strangle again and again because they don't just want the person dead, they want them *dead-dead-dead*.

"Now in this case, we have *one* wound. *One* stab. That's not a measure of how angry she was. It's an indication that she *wasn't* enraged and that this *isn't* murder. As a matter of fact, we have an alternate theory, that Conroy Sloan stabbed himself, whether for attention or to actually commit suicide, we don't know.

"Beverly Sloan did not murder her husband, even if he was an adulterous, cheating, conniving bastard."

"Objection!" The prosecutor yelled. "This isn't about the victim."

Sheldon was ready. "Prosecution opened the door, your Honor. His character is part of their theory of motive."

"We already stipulated that he was committing adultery."

Judge Washington tapped her gavel. "Then you won't mind the defense reiterating it, but let's keep the adjectives to a minimum, counselor."

"Thank you, your Honor." Heath Sheldon returned to his seat and touched Bev Sloan's hand. Juries liked to see the defense attorney make physical contact with the client. Even a scum-sucking, bottom-dwelling lawyer wouldn't touch a murderer.

There were too many women on the jury, though. Women weren't forgiving creatures. Women didn't side with wronged wives. They would think that she should have stood up for herself earlier or left him. Too many women meant a hanging jury.

HARA CARSON didn't like the defense lawyer's list of atrocities, but they were valid. Even when she spanked her dog for piddling on the carpet, one swat hardly seemed like enough. She smacked him with the folded newspaper three times, and *three* spanks seemed satisfactory.

Guy Papineau wondered how many weeks of lesson plans he had written for his class's substitute teacher. State-mandated testing was next week, and he just might get out of it.

Chessa Kendrall wondered how many murderers that slick lawyer had set free with his wily arguments.

Judge Leonine Washington masked her irritation and dismissed court for the day. The D.A., George Grossberg, objected to everything. The A.D.A., Georgina Pire, was nervous in front of a jury and sweated through her clothes. Between George and Georgina, the two Georgies, they were going to blow the case. And that defense attorney, Sheldon, plucked every heartstring in the room and was just arguing. Leonine looked at her watch. Damn. She was going to be late picking up Adaya and Adarius from day care, and the day care Nazis were going to assess the twenty dollar late fee again, as if her twins were rented movies. Her husband, a cardiologist, had to work late again. He was far too important to retrieve their children from the baby warehouse.

No wonder Beverly Sloan had snapped.

The Daily Hamiltonian:

Priest, Woman in Apartment with Wife and Dead Doc

By Kirin Oberoi

The prosecution began its case this week in the trial of the State vs. Mrs. Beverly Sloan, accused of fatally stabbing her husband, Dr. Conroy Sloan, last February in his newly rented apartment. The first witnesses to testify for the prosecution were the paramedics, Mr. Carleton Davis and Mr. Josef Menz. Davis testified that four people were present in the apartment when they arrived. One of these was Dr. Conroy Sloan, who was bleeding lightly from a knife wound to the chest. Davis identified the defendant, Mrs. Beverly Sloan, as also being present in the apartment and stated that she had some blood on her hands.

In a shocking revelation, both paramedics agreed that the other two people in the apartment were Monsignor Dr. Dante Petrocchi-Bianchi, S.J., M.D., Ph.D. (the defendant's spiritual advisor who was in the courtroom and identified by the witnesses) and Ms. Leila Sage Faris, a graduate student in Dr. Sloan's lab, listed by the prosecution as an upcoming witness.

BEV KNEELED in front of the Virgin Mary's sunset-lit niche. Touch-up patches of shiny, cobalt blue enamel speckled the Virgin's pale robe and new pink paint like square skin grafts lacquered the abraded places on the Virgin's feet where adorers pressed their hands.

She murmured, "Hail Mary, full of grace, the Lord is with thee." She continued through the Hail Marys and Our Fathers, looping the rosary beads. It was no use. Everything was useless. The worst was that her girls had no father and their mother was so stupid she was going to jail.

Dante genuflected and knelt beside her. His black cassock pooled on the wood floor. He asked, "Are you praying for acquittal?"

"That's not for me to say."

He scratched the hair near his temple. "You're off those pills?"

"Yes." Her rosary beads lay on the wood floor like fat, black ants caught in a loop.

"Can you remember anything about that night, yet?"

Bev shook her head.

Dante's hands condensed into fists. "I had hoped that was the pills."

"I'm afraid it wasn't." God wouldn't be stymied by mere pills. *Sin* repelled Heaven and the Holy Spirit and the Virgin Mary.

"Well, maybe we can do something." Dante rocked onto his feet and was standing.

"What? What could we do?" Her desperate hand gesture flipped the rosary beads out of her hand. They clattered on the wooden floor.

"Let's go to the library." Dante offered Bev his hand, and she grasped his palm with her good hand. Her left hand was still too soft to lift her weight. He tugged, and her body became weightless and flew.

Dante settled into his customary counseling chair and fidgeted to find a comfortable position. His coccyx was bruised from the courtroom's wooden benches. "I'd like to hypnotize you to help you remember."

Bev blinked and shook her head. "*Recovered memories*, aren't those implanted by the therapist or made up?"

Hypnosis. Psychobabble. Gobbledygook. "Hypnosis can be useful."

Bev leaned forward in her chair, her eyes wary. "You aren't hypnotizing the children, the ones who said they were abused, are you?"

"The children don't need hypnosis," Dante said. She still didn't want to believe that Nicolai was a predator. He'd charmed them all. Most child molesters charmed everyone, and the spellbound parents never questioned why this man spent hours in locked bedrooms with their children, or took them on long trips, or bought them extravagant gifts.

She was a doctor's wife. Perhaps a medical explanation would sway her. "Sometimes, neurons have stored the memories, and you can build new synapses to find the memories."

Her eyebrows were up and her head was forward, open.

Placebo effect was his aim, here, so the better his baloney sounded, the better the placebo response. If she believed that she was hypnotized, then she would tell him why she was not able to "feel God," as she put it. He said, "During intense relaxation, endorphins hyperstimulate the hippocampus, allowing neural stem cells in the hippocampus to mitose and form new neural paths to the memory centers, such as the dentate gyrus and posterior cingulate gyrus, creating bridges to neurons involved in short-term and long-term memory." That was industrial-grade hand-waving.

"Oh," Bev said, and her eyebrows arched. "Well, okay then." She laid her head against the back of the chair. "What do I have to do?"

"Relax." Dante leaned over to the wall switch and flipped off the overhead lights, which left only his desk lamp behind him. Soft, diffuse light reflected from Bev's cheekbones and forehead. She looked younger, perhaps twenty-five, not that he'd ever wished her younger.

"Close your eyes," he said. Her eyelashes furred below her eyes, and her rose eyeshadow looked like petals on her lids. This was how she must have looked before Sloan stole her away from the Israeli, impregnated her, and cheated on her.

He said, "I'm going to hypnotize you, which means you will become very relaxed. You will feel relaxed but alert, and you will still be able to act of your own free will. As I count backwards from ten, you will enter a state of hypnosis." That sounded like tripe. He should have invested in spooky music. He counted backward. "Now you are very relaxed. Are you relaxed?"

"Yes." She whispered, as if even her larynx was relaxed.

His incantation for hypnosis must have worked, or the placebo effect did. "You should now think of the night that Conroy Sloan died, but you will be calm. What can you remember?"

"Laura and the girls went to the movies. You and I were having a drink, several drinks, and we went upstairs." Her hand touched her collarbone. "You tried to take off my shirt, and I had to keep pulling it down." She squirmed sideways.

"You are calm and relaxed," Dante said. She had tugged at her shirt when he'd run his hands under her blouse. "Why would you want to keep on your blouse?"

Her shoulders turned sideways. "I thought, after I married Conroy, I'd never have to explain the scars again."

"Scars?" He'd never noticed scars.

Her shoulders turned. Her spine curved, squeezing her into a ball.

"You are hypnotized. You are calm. Your breathing is slow and calm." As a psychiatrist, he should prescribe antidepressants or anti-anxiety medications until these thoughts didn't trouble her. If he were her psychotherapist, he could probe, discover how this memory was causing psychic damage and help her cope. If he were her priest, he should delve just far enough to discern that she was blameless of sin and commend her soul to God. As an exorcist, he should not ask superfluous questions and expel the demon. If he were her friend, he would back off and allow her not to tell him. As her lover, he should have known about scars under her shirt. Dante leaned his forehead against his hand. "You are calm and relaxed. You view these memories as if watching television. Who has made the scars?"

"My mother."

Breath escaped him. The thought of *scars* hung like choking smoke in the air, as if the scars had smoldered for decades on her back. The air in the room had dropped to the floor and lingered there, crawling out the crack under the door. He hadn't known. The bedroom was always dark. He should have noticed that she was hiding something, *scars*.

Dear God. "With what did she do this?"

She shrugged. "Belts. Cigarettes. Spatula. Electric cords."

Oh, God. *Spatula*, a kitchen implement. Dante asked, "Knives?"

Bev's head dropped, and her chin touched her chest. "Knives."

Knives. Bev had been hurt with *knives*.

He'd only tried this stupid hypnosis thing to relax her, to make her believe that she could feel touched by God again. He was a fool. "Bev, is this memory troubling you, such that you believe that you cannot feel God?"

"It was a long time ago."

"All right. Let's go back to that night, the night Sloan died."

"We went upstairs." Bev uncoiled a little. "We found the note."

"Yes." Dante smoothed his hair away from his eyes.

"I went to Conroy's apartment."

He dropped his hand away from his face and watched Bev. "Tell me."

She lay on the chair, half turned sideways, crouched. "The walls were white, and there was a bowl of red wax apples on the coffee table. I wanted to throw an apple at the wall and watch it splatter like paint."

"Yes. You're very relaxed. Tell me what happened."

"And there was a green kitchen countertop, and I stumbled, and I couldn't work the cell phone. My thumbs missed the buttons, and my left thumb wouldn't work at all. I had to set the cell phone on the counter and press the keys with my right hand."

"Do you remember anything about knives?"

Her neck straightened, and she pondered this. "Knives poked me in the back."

Poked? Dante frowned. "Sloan poked you in the back with a knife?"

Her head tipped sideways. "I don't know."

"What else do you remember from that night?"

"Floating, my arm hurting, then nothing. Colors turning to black."

"All right." He rubbed his face, and evening stubble grated his palm. "All right. Was this the night when you stopped feeling the presence of God?"

"No," she whispered again. "Before, too."

"Do you know why you can't feel the presence of God?"

"I don't know, but I must have done something."

Ah, she was inferring that something must have happened because she didn't feel this God presence. He'd thought she knew something happened and so she shouldn't feel the whatever-it-was. He'd mixed the order of cause and effect. Now, he had to explore the other side. "So what does this *presence of God* feel like to you?"

Bev smiled and her legs extended to the floor. "Warm."

"Just warm?" Might be hot flashes. She was young for menopause.

"No, like someone wrapping their arms around you. Like something bad was happening but it stopped. For those few moments, you'll never be lonely again." The wrinkles of worry and stress smoothed out of her face, and her smooth skin reflected the falling lamplight. Her face shone as if she was in love, as if with the light of God he'd heard described. His hand dropped to his worn chair. "Go on."

Bev's hand strayed up to her shoulder, and she smiled. "It's like feeling everything, from the spaces between stars to the surface of the earth to atoms swirling around in your cells, and knowing them all." Her smile drooped. "But I can't feel it anymore."

Dante had stopped breathing, waiting for the end of her recitation. He didn't know if she was manic or schizophrenic or a saint. "How often did you feel that?"

She smiled wistfully. "When I took communion, when I prayed."

He'd never felt what she'd described and was glad he was so benighted because being cut off from that must be torturous. Her bruised knees jutted out below the hem of her black skirt.

It must be psychosomatic, or psychotic. She must be creating this aura or projecting it or else she had soul-level proof of Divinity. "Bev, listen to me." He couldn't say anything to help her because he had never seen what she had. She might be hallucinating. He had no map to help her return to a place he'd never been. "That feeling still exists inside you."

Yet, if her ecstasy was evidence of mania or psychosis or epileptic aura, its absence might mean she was sane or cured. It could not be ethical to return her to that prior state.

But she pined for it, for God. A priest could not deny God to a petitioner.

His first day in America when she had stumbled into the confessional, frantic, he had helped her, and she had found the strength to confront her philandering husband. Her daughters needed her with every milligram of strength she could muster.

And she looked so sad, exhausted. Her grief disheartened him. He said, "When you kneel in church next time, you should relax. God is all around. You believe that God is in the church."

"Yes." She sounded resolute.

"You must open this shell around yourself. It will crack slowly, like an egg hatching, and you will feel glimmers of what you described. The next time you come into the church, bits of the shell will flake away, and you will feel more. The third time you pray, the shell will fall away and you will feel as before, and God will be there for you. Do you understand?"

"Yes," she whispered.

"Do you believe this will happen?"

"Yes?" A definite upnote lilted, questioning. She did not believe. It might work.

"All right. I will count up now, and you will awake," he remembered old movies with staircases and playing cards and spinning spirals, "refreshed and relaxed. You will remember everything we discussed," because he did not imagine otherwise. "When you are ready," just in case hypnosis worked, "your memory of that night will return to you, but you will be calm. Memory is only truth, and it is better to know the truth."

Dante rubbed his forehead. If she was feeling otherworldly phenomena, if she was hearing voices, she might have an insanity defense, though he did not know American law.

But he couldn't talk to her lawyer unless she gave him permission to do so because he was her confessor and her counselor. Before he'd left Roma, he'd had a thorough grounding in American law concerning *privilege* for both doctors and priests.

Her head bobbed. Strands of her gold-flecked hair caught on the chair's dark upholstery.

"Bev, you will wake when I count to ten. One. Two…" At ten, he flicked on the lights.

Bev squinted in the flaring light and rubbed her eyes.

HEATH SHELDON clasped his hands as he approached Dr. Sridhar Bhupadi, who had been enjoying a morning of the prosecution's softball questioning on the witness stand. Bhupadi was an egotistical, self-righteous worm who shaved the truth for the prosecution. The Georgies had already run through his forensic credentials and their scripted testimony that the knife recovered from Conroy Sloan's chest had Beverly's fingerprints and Conroy's blood on it. No surprises, there.

"So, Dr. Bhupadi," *Boop-uh-dee*, Heath said, "You testified that Beverly Sloan's fingerprints were on the handle of the knife."

"Yes," Bhupadi smirked.

"That wasn't a question, Doctor. Please refrain from testifying unless you've been asked a question."

"All right."

"That wasn't a question either." Heath paced the courtroom. "Beverly Sloan's fingerprints were on the knife."

Bhupadi stared stolidly ahead of him. He and Sheldon had squared off five times in court. Sheldon's quibbling to liberate guilty clients irritated the hell out of Bhupadi.

Heath asked, "Which of her hands fingerprinted the knife?"

"The fingerprints were from her left hand."

"Her left arm was badly broken that night, and she had emergency surgery to reconstruct blood vessels in her left arm later that night, right?"

"I wouldn't know about that." Bhupadi smiled slightly, the insolent jerk. Heath hated it when Bhupadi screwed up his patter.

"The blood you recovered from the knife, Dr. Bhupadi, was it a pure sample?"

"No." Bhupadi waited. If Sheldon wanted him not to answer unless directly questioned, he could play that game. Bhupadi had played this game often with Sheldon, that slimy albino.

Heath waited, then tapped his foot impatiently, an excellent bit of stage business to show the state's witness was being recalcitrant and would not be forthcoming with information that could exonerate his client. The railroading plot was central to Heath's story. "Did you find anyone else's blood on that knife, besides Dr. Sloan's?"

Bhupadi, the prim scientist, scowled. "Yes. The defendant's blood was on the knife."

"So she'd been cut with it?"

"She had bled on it." He stared at the seam where the dark paneling met the white ceiling.

Heath played to the jury, raising his gold eyebrows. "And do you know whose hand was on the knife as it went into Conroy Sloan's chest?"

"No I do not."

"Who was the last person to touch the knife?"

"It appeared that the victim's fingerprints were the uppermost ones."

"Was Conroy Sloan trying to pull the knife out?"

"I could not say."

"Yes or no, please, Dr. Bhupadi."

He stared upward, which the jury might see as rude, Heath hoped. "It is unclear from the forensic data."

Heath leaned on the witness box. Damn new shoes were killing his pinky toes.

"Objection!" From behind Heath, D.A. George Grossberg, shouted again. "Objection!"

"What?" Heath turned around, his hands spread apart. That little stickler had already objected a hundred times today.

Judge Washington leaned on her elbows. "Yes, prosecutor. What is it this time?"

"He's encroaching on the witness." Grossberg said.

Judge Washington glanced at Heath, and he thought her eyes rolled as she looked back at Grossberg. Judge Washington said, "Overruled. Proceed, Mr. Sheldon."

"Thank you, your honor." *Score! Score!* Heath turned back to the forensic twerp on the witness stand. "So he might have stabbed himself."

"It is unclear from the forensic data."

"At the autopsy, did the medical examiner state whether the blow was from the victim's own hand or someone else's?"

"The report did not specify."

"So you didn't do those tests."

"I did not perform the postmortem examination. I can only testify as to what's in the report. The report did not state whether such a test had been performed."

"But if it was performed, the results would be on the report."

Bhupadi turned his hands over in his lap. "Yes."

"So the testing for that was not performed."

"It would appear not, but such a test for a knife wound would be impossible to perform. In the case of a gunshot wound, it is easier to discern whether the wound might have been self-inflicted due to the proximity of the weapon when it was fired."

"Objection!" Heath said.

Bhupadi continued, "But in the case of a knife, the weapon is always within the victim's reach. Thus, you can never be certain whether a knife wound was or was not self-inflicted."

"Objection!" Heath said again. "He's lecturing."

Bhupadi continued, "Thus the tests that the defense asks for cannot be performed."

"Objection!" Heath repeated.

Judge Leonine Washington tapped her steepled fingers together and looked down. "Overruled."

"He was lecturing, your honor, not answering the question."

The judge said, "It's 'lecturing' when it gets on *my* nerves. Proceed."

"Yes, your honor." Heath had at least distracted the jury even if he hadn't gotten the testimony thrown out. Well, if it wasn't thrown out, he could use it. "So, Dr. Bhupadi, your testing could not distinguish whether the wound was self-inflicted."

"No we cannot."

"And so you can't say whose hand was holding the knife when it stabbed Conroy Sloan."

"No we cannot."

"Could Conroy Sloan have been holding the knife?"

"It is unlikely."

"Why is it unlikely? His fingerprints were on the knife."

"Yes," Bhupadi conceded.

"And they were the uppermost fingerprints, right? Conroy Sloan's fingerprints weren't smudged by anyone else's?"

"Yes. But he could have tried to pull the knife out of his chest."

Heath nearly fell to his knees and thanked God for that lovely, lovely leading phrase. "Would Dr. Sloan, as a doctor, have tried to pull a knife out of his own chest?"

"Objection!" Behind Heath, George the prosecution lawyer yelled, "Conjecture!"

Heath said, "The witness opened the door."

Judge Washington shifted in her chair. She knew the answer to this. Living with a cardiologist had a few benefits, and a smattering of medical knowledge was one of them. Heath Sheldon might have something. "I'll allow it, but I want to see where this goes."

Heath repeated to Bhupadi, "Would Dr. Sloan, as a doctor, have tried to pull a knife out of his own chest?"

"I did not know Dr. Sloan."

Heath sighed and flipped one hand in the air. "Fine. As a doctor, Dr. Bhupadi, if *you* had an object sticking in *you*, deeply embedded in *your* chest, would *you* pull it out?"

Bhupadi scowled deeper. Slimeball defense lawyers rankled him, especially this Heath Sheldon guy who knew too much science for his own good and bamboozled everyone. "No."

Heath waited for Bhupadi to finish telling the audience, er, jury why he wouldn't remove a knife. And waited. And waited some more. Bhupadi was being obstinate *again*. Heath prodded, "And why not?"

Bhupadi's lip lifted in a repressed snarl. "Ripping an object out of one's heart would cause yet more damage, bleeding, and probably kill the person immediately. A surgeon should remove an embedded object in an operating room under controlled, sterile conditions."

"Would you even touch it?"

"No."

"So, according to your testimony and your forensic data, Conroy Sloan and only Conroy Sloan must have been holding the knife when it went into his chest, since his fingerprints were the uppermost, and since he wouldn't have touched it after it was in there."

"Objection!" Boy Georgie was at it again. "Objection! Conjecture!"

Heath bent over the rail of the witness stand at Bhupadi. "Might Conroy Sloan have been holding the knife when it stabbed him?"

"The witness may answer," Judge Washington said.

Bhupadi's jaw popped. "Yes."

"Oh," Heath said, "one more thing, doctor. In other murder cases where a knife was the murder weapon, on a murder victim's body, have you ever seen only one stab wound?"

"Objection!" Georgie Boy yelled again. "Irrelevant!"

Judge Washington said, "The witness can answer about cases with which he is familiar."

"Dr. Bhupadi?" Heath asked. "Have you ever seen only one stab wound on a murder victim's body?"

Bhupadi shifted in his seat. "No."

Heath smiled for the jury. "Usually more stab wounds than that?"

Bhupadi smiled back at the blonde bamboozler because the prosecution attorneys had told him to. "Yes."

Heath smiled at Bhupadi. "Thank you, doctor." *F.M.G. asshole.*

Bhupadi smiled at Heath Sheldon. "You're welcome." *Whathah rundi.*

BEV STARED AT THE BLANK, yellow notepad in front of her. She didn't want to hear about the knife. She didn't want to hear about the blood. She couldn't deny what all those experts said. Blank spaces like empty gallery frames interrupted the hallway of her memory.

Dante leaned over the railing and touched her shoulder. Bev leaned back and laid her hand on his. Lydia, sitting beside the priest, patted Bev's other shoulder.

Bev wouldn't cry. She wouldn't. Her eyes burned.

Heath returned to the table while the next witness, a forensic technician who had analyzed the blood in the kitchen, was sworn in.

The forensic technician, Mercedes Gonzalez, said that she had been working for the forensic lab for a year since she graduated from college. Her huge, brown eyes glanced around the courtroom, and she kept staring at Bev.

Georgina, the A.D.A., asked, "And what did you analyze in this case?"

"Blood splatters," the girl said, and she drummed her tiny fingers on the rail around the witness stand. "Blood splatters and smears."

Bev's heart clenched around its own supply of blood.

"Please describe the patterns of blood in the apartment, using this diagram of the kitchen to explain." The line-drawing kitchen diagram was two feet high by three feet long, and it looked like the designers' perspective illustrations when Bev had had the kitchen remodeled two years ago. She wished for that fifteen thousand dollars back. That was a year and a half's tuition at OLPH for both girls.

The technician cleared her slim throat and glanced at Bev again. The girl was wearing blue glitter mascara. The tech ducked her head and said, "The small blood pool in the center of the kitchen floor where the deceased's body was found, measuring twenty centimeters in diameter, was the source for the majority of the blood swipes, wipes, and splashes in the kitchen." The girl clicked a laser pointer, and a glowing red dot whirled in the center of the schematic.

A blood pool, Bev hated the idea that Conroy had been lying in a pool of his own blood. He'd gasped, while he was lying on the white linoleum floor, trying to say something, while the knife in his chest quivered with his heartbeat. A tear fell out of Bev's eye and splashed on the yellow paper with Heath's thick, black writing, smearing the word *Bhupadi.*

"Please continue." Georgina crossed her arms and pointed her sharp nose at the diagram.

"This blood pool was predominantly composed of blood from the victim. A splatter of the victim's blood on the upper kitchen cabinets suggests a small spray of blood, perhaps from the initial blade entrance, occurred while he was standing, before he fell." The red dot from her pointer swung over to the upper cabinets and jiggled.

"How can you tell that he was standing when this spray occurred?"

"The blood was a fine spray, perhaps even an aspiration, about six feet above the ground and tightly grouped. Like with a water pistol, if you're standing close to a water pistol, the droplets are close together."

A fine red mist hung in the air and flew past her left eye, and Bev's fingernails scratched the courthouse table. Her left arm was paler than her right and sore in the joints.

Mercedes continued, "A struggle flings blood everywhere, on the walls, on the ceiling, sometimes a hundred feet away. There was no indication of that. Other than the one spray on the countertops, the rest of Conroy Sloan's blood was transferred, probably originating from the pool."

"Transferred?" Georgina looked interested.

"Blood can be picked up by other people, on their hands, shoes, or clothing, and moved to a new place." The Mercedes girl sounded like the smartest kid in class.

"And can you tell that blood was transferred?"

"Yes. Instead of drops, droplets, or sprays, transferred blood is a blot, a swipe, a wipe, a smear, or a print."

Georgina cocked her head to the side. "And were there any of those in the apartment?"

"Lots," the girl said. "One of the paramedics walked through the blood pool and tracked it through the living room and out the front door. The sole of his running shoe matched the print."

Bev smeared the tears on her cheeks and wiped them on her black skirt. That was *Conroy's* blood they were talking about. The paramedic had stepped in *Conroy's* blood and tracked it across the living room carpet, leaving umber footprints burned into the beige carpet.

"Ah. That's interesting," Georgina said. "Could you tell if Beverly Sloan transferred blood anywhere in the apartment?"

The red dot scribbled on the wall telephone in the kitchen perspective drawing. "A bloody palm print on the telephone matched Beverly Sloan's right palm. The fingerprint technician made the palm print identification. Beverly Sloan had blood on her right hand when she picked up the phone receiver."

But the kitchen phone hadn't been hooked up yet. Bev had called the paramedics on her cell phone. The stupid buttons had been so tiny, and her left hand was useless and so heavy that it felt like she was holding a gallon of milk.

"Did Beverly Sloan leave other bloody fingerprints or palm prints in the kitchen?"

"Yes. Here," the laser scratched the black and white kitchen drawing, "on the counter in several places, and on the floor where the victim lay."

When Bev had crouched on the floor beside Conroy, blood leaked down his side from the protruding knife and stained his shirt. Her hand squished on the floor. Was that a memory or imagination?

"Were there other bloody fingerprints or palm prints in the kitchen?"

"We found handprints and fingerprints matching Beverly Sloan's, both the paramedics', Leila Faris's, and Father Dante Petrocchi-Bianchi's."

"What does that tell you?"

"That all of them were in the kitchen some time after the victim was stabbed, and they all touched him while he was bleeding or they touched the blood on the floor."

"Did you find blood anywhere else in the apartment?"

"More blood was found on the doorknob. Partials matched everyone in the apartment."

"Was anyone else's blood found in the apartment?"

"Drops and droplets of Beverly Sloan's blood were found on the kitchen counters, near the spray on the cabinets," the laser pointer touched the diagram again, "and a smear of Beverly Sloan's blood was found on the deceased's hand."

"Is that amount of blood consistent with the wounds that her doctor testified that she had sustained on her right wrist and hand?"

"Yes."

In the kitchen of the apartment, under the glare of the fluorescent bulbs, greasy drops of her blood slid off her wrist and dripped on the green veneer counter. She had been sitting on the counter, something poking her back. Her left hand held a knife. She had cut cold, superficial slices into the accordion folds of her right wrist and palm.

Georgina the prosecutor prompted Mercedes Gonzalez through all the blood evidence, which washed over the apartment in a huge crimson tsunami from the way the tech described it.

Heath stood and adjusted his suit. He reviewed his notes, flipping the pages on the yellow pad. He began his cross-examination with, "When did you sample the blood in the apartment?"

"Sunday, February fourteenth."

"Was that the day you Luminoled the apartment?"

"No, we took samples of visible blood on Sunday, and then we used the Luminol on Monday the fifteenth."

In his cross examination, Heath led the girl back through her testimony, paying particular attention to blood sprays, splatters, droplets, and drops. "You said, Ms. Gonzalez, that the blood on the counter you attribute to Mrs. Sloan was," he consulted his notes, "drops and droplets."

"Yes."

"Did you find Beverly Sloan's blood anywhere else?"

"On Conroy Sloan's hand and on the knife."

"Well," Heath strutted around the courtroom. "How did her blood get on his hand?"

"He must have been nearby when she sustained the wound." The girl enunciated every consonant in the last three words.

Heath asked, "And how did Mrs. Sloan's blood get on the knife?"

"The wounds on Beverly Sloan's right wrist are consistent with the type of knife analyzed." Again, Mercedes's statement was very carefully worded.

"The knife in Conroy Sloan's chest."

"Yes."

"So he cut her hand?"

"That conjecture is beyond the scope of the forensic testing."

"Well, let's stop a minute." Heath walked over to the drawing of the kitchen. "If Beverly Sloan was bleeding from her hand here," he took a red permanent marker out of his pocket and drew red spots on the countertop while the prosecution attorneys muttered about him messing up their drawing, "and Conroy Sloan had her blood on his hand and on the knife, and we know that he was standing here when that fine spray of blood hit the cabinets here," he scribbled red jagged lines on the cabinets, "which is practically just above the drops of Beverly Sloan's blood—"

"Drops *and* droplets," the girl said.

"Then Conroy Sloan was standing over her, holding the knife with her blood on it just before he stabbed himself, wasn't he?"

The girl blinked her blue, glittering eyelashes. "That conjecture is beyond the scope of the forensic testing."

Bev listened for three more days to the tales of blood and gore and the force of the knife ("enough to slice off a chunk off a tough steer steak," said the gruff medical examiner, and pressed his Texan mustache around his lips, and that the deceased had bruises in various stages of healing on the wrist, arm, and left eye, which were consistent with ongoing abuse) and to repetitive analysis by the psychiatrist and the police 9-1-1 operator and yet another forensic technician for the 9-1-1 tape (two minutes of her own coarse voice grabbling, "I think it's his heart. I think it's his heart," and "fifty-one Vita Place, the townhouses by the hospital, number fifty-one, Vita Place,") and the horror of it filled her mind with scarlet and shining steel until she understood why God hated her, because a gentle and loving God could not gaze upon such atrocity and barbarism (the slitting of wrists, the breaking of arms, the stabbing of *hearts*) without turning away in revulsion from everyone who committed such sins, who was even capable of committing such sin. When Bev had found those pink, terrible, pink, horrible pink silk panties, her soul had devoured itself, and she'd changed into an evil, damned creature. That was it. That was why she was forsaken.

Bev endured when that faded auburnette Peggy Anne Strum swore to tell the truth on the Bible and then sat up there on the stand and lied and lied and lied.

IN THE CHURCH'S LIBRARY, Dante sat beside Bev in the counseling chair that he used to think of as *Sloan's* but now was *the other chair* and held Bev's hands. Her delicate fingers trembled like a grasped bird. It had been two days since their hypnosis session.

He asked, "Have you tried praying in the church yet? To see if anything has changed since I hypnotized you?"

Her head dropped forward one defeated notch. "It didn't work. I can't feel anything."

"It could be subtle at first."

She wiped her tears with the backs of her hands. "I must have killed Conroy."

"Bev, if you don't remember, then you don't know."

"I don't know if I remember." Tears, tinged with smoky makeup, fell onto her cheeks and she wiped them on the cuffs of her pink shirt. "All those horrible pictures of the blood and the drops and smears and the knife, and the diagrams of his ribs and his heart and where the knife cut open his heart, I can't get them out of my head. Sometimes I think I might remember something but then it seems like I'm thinking about what they're describing."

The trial was preying on his mind, too. "So you don't remember."

She fanned herself with open fingers and tapped her chest, as if she could air-dry the tears that she couldn't wipe away fast enough. "And Leila Faris testifies next. I don't know what she's going to say. She seems to know everything. Leila told me that Conroy was seeing Valerie Lindh, too."

"Leila *told you?* You talked to Leila?"

"She knows about all his other women, who they were, how many there were." Bev dropped the tissue and her fingers crept into her hairline. "She knows about us, too."

"Did you say Leila *told you?*" he asked.

"I went to Conroy's lab a few months ago. She was there. I think she knew about us, or figured it out from something I said. She'll probably tell the jury."

"Months?" Dante asked. "Two months?"

"Maybe. I think so."

A cramp drove breath out of him. Leila had been dodging him for about two months.

Bev touched her eye with the tissue, and the white tissue sopped up pink, lavender, and black as if the color was draining out of her and soon she would be monochrome, the reverse process of those tinted portraits in his mother's living room that were now in his sister's attic, shell-pink lips and cherubic golden skin. Bev said, "She told the police I was the only one in the apartment. She's going to take the stand tomorrow and tell them I did it."

He stroked her hand. "Don't cry. Don't despair."

"I still don't know what to do with the girls." She snatched up the tissue and rested her face on it. "It's all falling apart. *I'm* falling apart."

"I'll talk to Leila. I'll find out what she will say."

Bev swiveled toward him. The skin under her eyes was greasy with wiped tears. Tears rolled over her lower eye lids and dripped off her soaked lashes. "Please don't go there." She dropped the tissue in her lap and touched his arm. "Not you, too."

"I could find out what she knows, what she's going to say tomorrow. She owes me a favor." He missed talking to her about science, and he missed her long, cool, glances over her cigarette from between the falls of her black hair.

"Not you, too." Bev stumbled out of her chair and Dante shoved himself farther into his chair's upholstery as Bev's soft body landed on his knees. "Don't go."

Her mouth covered his, lips smoothed by lipstick and breath ripe with whiskey—when had she had time to drink? He grabbed her arms and tried to set her away from him, back and off the chair and his legs and lap, but she whipped her arms around and his hands dislodged and she grabbed his collar, expertly unsnapped it, and unbuttoned him to the waist.

His body had acclimated to her soft lips and skin and breasts pushing on him, and rushing blood roared in his ears. He'd been dying without this.

His hands crawled up her shirt and reached around behind her back, tracing the ridges and creases quilted into her skin.

Scars.

LATE IN THE LAB that evening, with Conroy's office door closed, Leila read Conroy's notes, still trying to figure out what his settings had been on the fMRI. She'd had it with the gossip from Yuri and Joe and all the others. They all sucked. Their voices leaked into Conroy's office despite her efforts, and she wanted to scream.

Joe asked, "Did you see LawTV tonight?"

"No. I had gel running. What was wrap-up?"

"Peggy Strum testified." Joe tried to sound casual.

"Our department secretary? What for?" Yuri labeled tiny tubes with a fat marker. His yellow gloves acquired blue stains on the fingertips.

"Sloan was sleeping with her."

The pen flipped out of Yuri's fingers and blotched blue on the waffled paper covering the bench. "Now I know he crazy. Maybe rabies virus make him nuts. Screw secretary slut. Leave the Beverly. Buy new Porsche and not sell old one to loyal postdoc."

AT 1:30 in the godforsaken lukewarm July morning, after finessing her experiments and cell lines and viruses to last for a while because testifying at that asinine trial might take *days*, Leila tripped on the metal floor trim because the elevator had been too tired to haul itself that last inch to flush with the hallway. She grabbed a wiggly wall sconce to catch herself.

A black-cassocked shamble hunched beside her door.

That goddamned batshit priest was once again, *once again*, leaning on her doorjamb and *stalking* her like a black fluttering poltergeist. "What are you doing here?"

He closed his magazine. "Waiting for you."

"Witness tampering. Go away." She jingled her keys.

His head inclined, a resolute, stiff-necked bow, and he studied the hallway's rough carpeting. "I ask this favor because I helped with Danna's parents when you called me."

Bastard, bringing that up. She swayed sideways from one sore foot to the other. Her exasperated hands were too heavy and smacked her legs. "Damn it. Monsignor, if you threaten me, if you try to change what I'm going to say, I swear I'll go to the D.A."

"I have never threatened you. I have only offered to help. I need to ask."

"Fine." She walked past him and unlocked the door. Two different clicks, one high in pitch and raspy, one lower and sharp, echoed in the deserted hallway.

She thumped her purse on the hallway table and flicked light switches until halogen and incandescent light blazed. Owing priests favors was dangerous, but she hadn't had a choice. Danna's parents had needed someone. Still, she was pissed at herself for trusting another hypocritical priest. The question wound up and popped out. "Were you banging Conroy's wife?"

Dante's eyebrow quivered, and his angelic demeanor slipped toward wariness. "Pardon?"

She glared. She knew she was glaring and glared harder. Let the bastard shrink. "Conroy's wife. Were you screwing her before she killed him?"

His lips thinned, drawn inside. His graceful brows dropped. "Yes."

The bastard admitted it. Any less expression and he would have been bragging. She popped her palm against the wall plaster. "I thought you were different."

He shoved his hands through the side slits in the cassock into his pants' pockets.

Meth padded out of the bedroom, and Leila patted his heavy, Labrador head, gave him a soft puppy treat from the silver box on the table, and shooed him over to his nest. She went to the kitchen and brought back a tray with scotch, two glasses, and a bottle of water. Drinking herself to sleep might take a while, so she might as well start. She dripped scotch into one of the glasses and sat in an armchair opposite the couch. "Pour yourself a drink, *Monsignor*."

He leaned forward to pour his drink, a deep one with little water. "Thank you. It's been a rough day. *Salute*."

"Let's get this over with."

Dante sat back. "How many women did Conroy Sloan have?"

She held up one finger. "Peggy Dumbass, the one who wanted to marry him and left her knickers in his suitcase after they went away for the weekend together on the university dime. What an idiot. Everyone was talking about it. People from other labs obliquely told me to warn Conroy to stop being so obvious. And he was fined for it under his contract's morals clause." She added another finger. "Valerie Lindh, a professor from

Paris who's at Cornell now. They're on the same NIH study section." A third finger bound with an opal and silver filigree ring. "Another woman, but I didn't know much about her. Mary something. I got the feeling it was opportunistic, not ongoing."

"And you," he said.

No reason to equivocate now. "And me." Four fingers.

He sipped his scotch and pondered it. "What are you going to say about what happened?"

He meant when that priest-screwing slut bitch killed Conroy. The scotch whiskey scorched her raw throat. "Conroy called me and said he'd rented an apartment. I called him an idiot but went over there anyway."

The priest finished his drink and poured himself another. "You talked about what?"

She sipped. The scotch tickled her calves. "He had some cockamamie idea, since he'd freed himself of Beverly, that I'd shack up with him, that I'd follow him around like a nitwit toy poodle. I told him to go back to his wife."

The priest poured himself a third drink.

She said, "You must have had a rough day."

He touched his temple and sipped the scotch. "Peggy Strum said the same thing, that he had gotten the apartment so they could be together, that they'd set a date to marry."

Leila laughed one syllable, *Phuh*. "Whatever. He told me he broke it off with her. And I didn't see Peggy outside the apartment."

Just-Dante nodded and sipped.

The heavy crystal glass in her hand reflected lamplight into the brown scotch like an iridescent rainbow trout flashing in a murky lake. "I wondered what you were doing there. Didn't even occur to me you were fucking the wife," she said quietly. "I'm a terrible judge of character. Especially priests."

"Oh?" He sipped, waiting for her to spill her guts. He could goddamn wait.

"I was completely taken in by your *pity-me* act at the Dublin." She mocked his sullen, whiney demeanor. "'*I didn't know what was missing in my life.*' I thought you were different. You were trying to get into my pants. You wanted some ass."

"No." He shook his dark head, and his hair swished past his cheekbones. He dragged his hair back with his fingers.

"Motherfucker," she said, buzzed, bordering on dizzy drunk. "You thought you were going to get some ass." She chugged the scotch.

"That's not it at all." The harsh lamplight threw shadows down his cheekbone and jaw. He gingerly touched his temple, a gesture that suggested the nerve that fires into a migraine, the indented collection point for hangover, the soft skin a Russian roulette gun presses. God, that was sexy, that pensive, smoldering darkness, the threatened implosion, suggested secrets and arcane knowledge. If he wasn't a priest, if they had met in a bar, she might have brought him back to her place and explored that darkness. She drank bitter liquid fire.

"Please don't get drunk."

"Do what I want." She sipped again.

He touched his throat. "Should I remove the collar?"

"Leave it. I want to remember what you are."

He set his empty glass on the tray. "That night, what happened after that?"

"While he was arguing, he grabbed my arm again, and I decked him. I left. Beverly Sloan arrived." Her hand flipped back and forth in the air, miming entrances and exits. "Her breath reeked of booze. She stormed up the sidewalk and went inside, and you drove up. We stood outside and listened. I couldn't make out words, just yelling. Could you?"

He shook his head, poured himself another, and slammed the shot. Leila matched it.

"Then Beverly Sloan called your cell and we went inside." Her constricting throat squeezed her voice louder but she could barely hear herself over her resounding heartbeat. "Conroy didn't move." His sudden breaths rattled his chest. She woke at night sometimes, convinced she'd heard Conroy coughing and gasping, but it was only her geriatric dog hacking. "I should have kept trying CPR. If I had done chest compressions, maybe it would have squashed the blood out of his chest and he wouldn't have suffocated. If I'd kept doing artificial respiration, maybe he wouldn't have drowned. It's ridiculous. There are so many ways you can die, and it was just a little knife, one poke, once. It's *ridiculous*."

"It was his left ventricle." His voice was quiet.

Blue and amber slivers of light sparkled in her glass as if the scotch flamed. "I should have cracked his chest and sewn up his heart with fishing line."

"You're not a surgeon."

"I've done mouse surgery. I know my way around a chest."

He pressed his palms together and leaned toward her. "Nothing could have saved him."

Damn priest thought he was counseling her. "The bitch murdered him."

His mandible muscles under his jaw bunched as if he were accustomed to grinding his teeth. "You didn't see that," Dante said softly. "That's speculation."

"Don't tell me what I know. There were two people in that apartment. A knife was in one of their hearts. How do you suppose *that* happened?"

His hands floated apart as if parting the sea and time. "I only know I didn't see."

The aggression in her spine leaned her toward him, and she said right at him, "Your lover killed her husband."

He shook his head. "I didn't mean to have an affair with Bev."

She scoffed, "Did she tie you up? Threaten you with a gun? Tell you that your bishop wouldn't believe you anyway and that it was your little secret?"

"Of course not." Blood vessels in his eyes were beginning to dilate from the scotch. He poured himself another, neat.

She poured one, too. "Is there anything else you want to ask or are you going to leave now?"

The black-cloaked priest sat back on the couch and crossed his arms across his chest. "Were you sleeping with Sloan when he moved out?"

Nothing mattered now. Being coy was stupid, considering that Conroy was dead and the priest knew anyway. "I broke it off a week or so before he moved out."

"Why did he break it off?"

Asshole wasn't even listening. "I dumped *him*. He got possessive, like when he grabbed my arm that time outside your church. He started doing crap like that, thinking he owned me. That wasn't part of the deal."

"What was your deal?"

"You interrogate everybody like this?" Leila sipped her drink. The scotch had undertones of lemon and bronze.

He turned over one hand to expose his pale, vulnerable palm. "In the seminary, one learns to discuss the nature of sin with penitents for confession."

"This isn't confession. You don't even have your goddamn purple stole on. You didn't kiss the cross and mutter over it. It's not confession." Leila shifted her cool glass to her other hand. "It was casual fucking. That's all."

He frowned. "That's a harsh term."

"It's just fucking."

"There is no affection, no love?"

"It was just *ass*. Why make it more complicated, bring *love* into the equation, when it's not there, when it was never meant to be there?"

Dante grounded his glass on the tray. "It's a difficult distinction."

"No it's not. Fucking is friction and sex, fun, kinky. It's a roller coaster. Call it 'friendship with privileges' if you're squeamish. What did you and Beverly call it?"

"Not that." His head turned away, tortured and Byronic again.

"Really?" Leila tapped her glass on the silver tray. "She loved you? She seemed pretty upset when Conroy left her. Didn't seem like she was in love with another guy."

"It's not important." He traced the rim of his glass.

Leila braced her forearms on her knees and leaned over. "Were you in love with her?"

Dante's marble skin flushed rose. He inhaled through his nose, straightened, and crossed his long legs. His face had become academically calm, as if he'd decided she was an interesting specimen. "Were you in love with Conroy?"

Her sarcastic laugh snorted through her nose. "Love is for fools. This has nothing to do with Beverly's trial."

"Yet you have so many lovers."

"They're not 'lovers.' I have friends. I have sex with my friends. I get some ass."

"Not 'make love.'"

"How soggy." Her legs ached from cooking at the lab bench all day.

"You've never been in love," he sipped, "and you've never made love?"

"Sound like you're *projecting* there, Monsignor." Leila's fingernails bit her palms. "Aren't we talking about *you?* Priests exhibit classic narcissism, believing they have a hotline to God."

He cleared his throat. "Do you think you can fall in love?"

"Nope." Leila shot her drink down. If she shocked him enough, he might storm out and leave her alone. She poured another glass of scotch. Her tongue and teeth were numb, and her legs were drifting toward ease. The numbness had to crawl inward to her stomach before she would be able to sleep. "Since I can't make love, I might as well get fucked."

"Is that what you're doing, when you're having sex with the men?"

Leila smiled though her teeth grated on each other like chewing sand. "I didn't say only *men.*"

"Women, too?" His eyebrows rose slightly.

An innocent façade, she was sure. The perv probably liked hearing about lesbian action. "Yep."

"What are you looking for? What are you missing?"

"You're projecting again. You were out of control and destroying yourself. I'm happy with my life." She crossed her arms across her chest and wished that her clingy black top wasn't so low-cut and thin, almost lace. Her throat and sternum were on display. "You're asking me the questions your little old priest asked you. This has nothing to do with the trial tomorrow. Ask relevant questions or we're done."

"I'm trying to help you."

"I don't want your help. I don't want a priest thinking he can help me." Hot scotch swirled in the back of her throat.

He clasped his hands together and paused, licked his plush lips. "You were abused by a priest," he said, "sexually, I'd guess."

Rage drove Leila to her feet and she walked toward the dining room to get away from him. She wanted to smash the highball glass against the wall, but the glass was heavy and the antique plaster was friable, so she dropped her arm. Her hair fell around her face, curtaining her so he couldn't see her face redden. She stared at the glowing Tiffany chandelier above the dining room table and tried to breathe long and low because she was safe here, in her own home, in her own life. "You don't know shit."

"I know a lot about sexual abuse by priests. I could help."

"You don't know *shit*."

"Was it covered up and the offending priest transferred?"

Her hands wound around each other. "Get out."

"I wanted to ask, because it bothers me, where was your mother?"

The chandelier glowed and blue-speckled the walls. She set the empty glass on the dining room table and rubbed her palms together, staying calm. "Busy."

Sandpapering sounds behind her. "I could help you."

The Tiffany chandelier dangled precariously above the table. Rustling behind her like clothes shedding made her wince at the thought of a naked priest in her apartment. She was breathing too fast, like she was going to be sick. She inhaled through her nose, drew in air, and counted to three in her head. "I don't want help."

"I could help you. I'm a doctor."

"You're a *priest*. Some people who have been hurt by a priest don't want to talk to a guy who wears the same uniform. You ever think about that?"

"I removed the collar."

If he was naked when she turned around, if that motherfucker thought he was going to get some ass, she was going to break his neck. She had taken martial arts for seven years. "You're just another hypocritical, ass-grabbing priest."

"No, I'm here to stop the abuse and counsel the victims. That's what the Holy Office does now. We stop the abuse."

"So that's what the Inquisition is doing these day? Abused kids?"

"Pedophile priests. They're defrocked and sent to a Dominican monastery in Italy."

"That's the official story, anyway."

"Yes," he said. "That's what we tell people."

"I don't care, and I don't want to talk about it."

"Have you ever talked about it with someone?"

"That's none of your business."

"You're living as an untreated survivor of abuse. It's hurting you."

"Was that your problem, too?"

He exhaled, and his breath sighed through the apartment, around the columns and plaster crown molding, into her bedroom. "No, I was just a callous ass."

"I don't give a shit. Get out."

"Tell me who he was, and I can send him to the Dominicans in Italy."

"I don't want your help. And you *don't* know shit."

"You're right. I don't know. Tell me."

"Get *out*."

Footsteps. The footsteps on the wooden floor ricocheted off the walls and moldings, and she knew he was coming at her. She braced herself. He wasn't going to touch her. *She wouldn't let him touch her.*

"Leila."

"Get away from me." Her hands curled. Her fingertips retreated into her palms like snakes protecting their heads in their coils.

He said, "I'm counseling children at the parish so they won't hurt like you do. Memory is, as it were, the belly of the soul, and these priests are destroying children's souls." His whisper hissed like an ill wind near her shoulder, funneled around her ear's pinna, slipped inside to her tympanic membrane, vibrated and activated her cochlea, and traveled as neurotransmitters into her brain and she couldn't block him out. Dante the priest was in her head, insistent, whispering, "But I don't know how they feel. They're too young to tell me, and I worry that I'm doing more damage. Tell me."

"Go away." The first knuckle of her left index finger cracked.

He whispered, low and soft, "Tell me what happened to you."

His long, black shadow spread on the floor beside her, thrown from the stronger lamps in the living room. The glittering chandelier cut blue snowflakes out of the shadow's homuncular form, like a shifting demon slithering on her floor and grinning at her, or a black-robed priest lying on her bedroom floor while her oblivious mother slept two rooms down the hall. She said, "Get out of my apartment."

"Tell me what he did to you."

"Get *out*."

The shadow on the wood floor raised its arm, and a black sleeve fluttered on the horizon of Leila's vision.

She whipped around, grabbed that extended black-clothed arm, and crammed it against his back, shoving up hard.

Chapter Twenty

The presses clattered, churning out long sheaves of newsprint.

The Daily Hamiltonian:

Dr. Sloan's Secret Lover Testifies

By Kirin Oberoi

Yesterday, in the Beverly Sloan murder trial, D.A. George Grossberg and A.D.A. Georgina Pire elicited testimony from prosecution witness Peggy Anne Strum that she had been having an affair with Dr. Conroy Sloan, the victim, that continued until his death. Strum also stated that she and the deceased had planned to marry next February after he had divorced his wife, his alleged murderer, Beverly Sloan.

During cross-examination, however, Mr. Heath Sheldon, the defense attorney, produced an email from Dr. Sloan to Strum, in which Dr. Sloan told Strum that he would not see her any more because he planned to remain married, and an email reply from Strum to Dr. Sloan stating that he couldn't "break it off" with her and that she would "do something drastic." Under heavy pressure from the defense attorney and despite repeatedly overruled objections from the prosecution, Peggy Strum admitted Dr. Sloan had seen her only in her professional capacity as department secretary for the two weeks prior to his death.

The refutation of Strum's testimony drastically weakened the prosecution's case. The State alleges that Beverly Sloan's motive for killing her husband was that she was enraged because he was leaving her for another woman and was soon going to divorce her.

PUSHED, Dante fell towards the dark bed. Crimson silk rushed at him out of the dark like a rogue wave. His arm was free, his elbow tendons stretched to their limits. When his hands touched the bedspread, he sprang back, flipped over, and scrambled backward away from her silhouette in the lit doorframe. "Leila, what are you doing?"

She grabbed his ankle and hauled him back over the silk coverlet. "No, Leila, *stop*."

She vaulted, hesitated in the air, and collapsed around him, her arms and knees pinning his arms and legs to his sides. Her whiskey-rancid mouth grabbed his mouth.

He twisted, but the friction of her lithe body twined around him sharpened his senses. His body was already lathered from Bev, but he'd resisted her, the smallest of victories. "Leila, stop," he whispered under her mouth.

"Shhh," she growled near his throat, and he stretched his neck and closed his eyes. Blood gushed through him and swelled in his chest.

"I could shout," he said, but his lungs were waterlogged.

"No one would believe that a big, bad Roman priest like yourself, one with a track record of seducing so many, many women, didn't rape the little college student. Besides," she kicked the door shut with a long lever sweep of her foot, and streetlight glared though the blinds in red slashes on the bed and gilded streaks on the walls, "Six inches of solid plaster are bolted to these walls. No one will hear you."

Heat like the Roman sun reflecting off glazed tile baked his chest where her body rested. "Leila, stop." He held her shoulders and set her back gently.

She twisted and slapped his arms off her. Her knuckle drove between his ribs, grinding interstitial cartilage, and he flinched. His head landed on the pillow. His legs splayed everywhere.

"Leila, you have to stop." He held his hands defensively in front of his chest. He'd provoked her to this. She straddled his waist, and his dick strengthened, filling, and pushed his pants toward her. If she leaned forward, her breasts under that black lace blouse would fill his hands. The image raced along his skin.

Her arms swooped and snagged his wrists, forcing them over his head. The bones in the backs of his hands slapped the heavy ironwork and wood headboard. She held his hands stretched above him and leaned over him, kissing him so hard that she bruised his lips between their teeth.

Grinding clicks squeezed his wrists.

"What are you doing?" He thrashed, and she sat back on his hard dick and pelvis. He strained his neck around to look above him. Handcuffs shone around his wrists in the intermittent light like steel dashes. "What did you do?"

"Don't move," she shushed.

"Stop this." He jerked back, and the short chain between them clinked on the wrought iron interlay in her headboard. "Unlock these!"

"You want this," and her hand ran between her own legs and traced the tip of his shivering dick through his pants and his cassock.

"No, I don't want this." His skin remembered long, humid nights and nights of this in Roma, though he'd been the one outside the handcuffs, whispering *you want this* and barely touching them, until they arched with want, and then ripping into the women. *Nights, them, women,* his memories were in plural.

"Don't say you don't want this," Leila whispered beside his ear, everywhere on his body at once. "He never let me say that I didn't want it. He got angry. Angry was worse."

"Leila." His infernal body arched under her legs. Light streaked her lace blouse, and clusters in the lace or her nipples spotted her torso. If that blouse was off her, he would be able to see her skin, touch her skin. Running away wouldn't drive these images out of his head. He could conceivably kick his way free of her, break the headboard to free his hands, but he might hurt her. "Don't do this."

"You're just like him, you know." Her voice was soft and almost kind near his other ear. "Arrogant, because you think you're different. He was amazingly beautiful, blonde hair and golden skin, angelic, even in Los Angeles where everyone cuts off anything that makes them feel bad. Angels and fallen angels all look alike."

His body stilled. She was telling him about her abuser. He could rationalize his lack of resistance in a thousand ways: that she only felt safe enough to talk with him restrained, that her story would allow him to empathize with the abused parish children, that this was therapy for her, that he would trade a modicum of his shattered priesthood if it helped her. He had already broken his vow of chastity.

But he didn't like being handcuffed. "Leila, let me out. I will leave, or stay, as you want."

Her teeth dragged at the skin on his neck, just below his ear, as if her teeth were pointed. "He liked to be in control, too."

"I only wanted to talk." His attention was focused on that small patch of skin, raw from her nip, that her breath scalded. "Stop."

"Don't say that. Say *yes*."

"No." His throat was tight, and his rasping voice hurt.

She hovered above him, softly lit on one side by the glowing streetlight streaks. Her hair curtained off her face, leaving darkness. A faceless pagan Norse goddess looked like this, a death goddess. She'd looked faceless like this when her hands had covered her face over Conroy's body. Leila whispered, nearly against his lips, "Say *yes*."

He rationalized again that this might help her, that his celibacy was already gone. "Yes."

She whispered, "Have you used handcuffs on women?"

"Yes." There was no reason to lie. The cloth on his shoulders loosened as she untied the cincture around his waist, unhooked the long line of hooks and eyes down his cassock, and unbuttoned his shirt. "Leila, I can't do this. I can't do this to you."

"You've come here in the middle of the night three times, Dante." Her fingernail tickled his chest, and he tried to lie still but he inhaled at the faint scratch. "You've arrived here drunk. You've gotten drunk while you were here. You're drunk now."

"I'm not." But the quick scotch had disconnected his body from his mind, and once she reached his navel with her nails and trailed her way past it, he gasped.

"You know what kind of woman I am." She crawled around him, leaning over his stomach. "You knew what coming here, at night, drunk, to such a woman, meant."

Truth, he had only truth. "I wanted to talk to you."

"You could have called me on the phone to talk." She flicked aside his pants button. Her lips touched his stomach. "You could have waited until daylight." Her breath wafted over the skin on his belly. "Things like this don't happen in daylight. Things like *this* only happen at night."

"That's not why I came over here. The first time, I was drunk."

"Women use that *drunk* excuse all the time to explain why they slept with some guy, why they aren't sluts because they weren't responsible." Her cool lips brushed his belly. "So men use that excuse, too, do they?"

"No, men don't care."

"I like that." Leila wrapped her arm under his waist and lifted his back, and he arched with her arm, complicit. She nipped near his navel.

"But I'm a priest. I can't do this."

She lowered his back to the bed and ran her hands over his legs, rubbing his thighs. "You're not responsible. You're drunk. You're tied up."

"I am responsible. I'm a priest."

"You tried to grab me in the Dublin, drag me over to you. Your head was tilted. Your mouth was opening."

"I didn't mean it that way." He had meant it that way, but he had stopped.

She was back up near his ear again, whispering, "Say you did."

The darkness of the room, the secretiveness, stole into his head. "Yes."

"And you waited for me at the Dublin, stalking me, trying to find me."

"It wasn't like that."

She breathed on that vulnerable hollow of his throat. "Say yes."

"Yes."

"And you've wanted this ever since you gave me your card with your phone numbers, found out where I live and where I work, started coming over here, trying to get to me, trying to provoke me into this so you wouldn't feel guilty about it. You didn't sin if I seduced you."

"Leila, I swear to you, I didn't think that. I wanted to talk."

"Ah, ah. You're arguing again. It's no use saying that you're not like that, that you weren't thinking that." Her lips nuzzled his ear. "You like this." She kissed him.

"Yes," he said on her slick lips.

"And you like this." Her lips dropped to his neck. He turned, ostensibly to crane his neck to look at the handcuffs and see if there was room for his hands to slip out, but his neck elongated to allow room for her to mouth his neck and shoulder. "You like this, don't you?"

"Yes." The tight handcuffs creased his wrists. His hands tingled, falling asleep. He struggled to pull himself closer to the headboard to relieve the pressure.

"You probably thought earlier that you could fight me off if you wanted to, after all, I'm a small, thin woman."

He could hardly breathe.

She nipped his collarbone. "Silence implies consent. Why didn't you?"

"I might have hurt you."

"Then it wasn't because you wanted to fuck me."

"No."

"How altruistic."

In the rectory at night, her face had floated over the memories of other women, and he'd jacked off to her image dozens of times these last months.

Déjà vu surrounded her in the streaked darkness. His skin strained. He'd primed his body for this. He was so stupid. "You've been hurt enough by priests."

"You were afraid you'd hurt me. How childlike. Children are always worried about hurting or disappointing an adult."

His drumming heart stumbled. She had cast him in the part of the child, which meant she was playing the part of the abusing priest, acting out her abuse. The pedophile had used her innocence, her sympathy, to manipulate her, until she had none left and could take the role of the demon. He said, "And you don't fear hurting anyone any more."

"I'm nothing," she said. "I'm a mote. I can't hurt anyone."

God had allowed such a man to do this to a child while he wore a Roman collar, and atheism flowed along Dante's nerves, following the rough scratch of her lace blouse on his chest. He wanted to cradle her, soothe away what that man did to her, but the handcuffs chained his arms above his head. "Leila."

She covered his mouth with her soft hand. "Don't say anything."

"*Leila.*" His voice was husky with testosterone. Her hand trembled and lightened on his face. He kissed her palm, which smelled like scotch, flowery hand lotion, and laboratory gloves.

She jerked away from him and sat up, straddling his waist. Slices of light tiger-striped the left side of her body. "You're enjoying this."

"No."

"Bastard." Her open palm cracked across his face. "Don't make me angry." She towered above him on her knees. "Angry is worse."

Angry is worse. That pedophile had manipulated her, made her an accomplice by threats. His heart vibrated. She slid up him like a rearing cobra. His body craved hers as if she were pressed together out of nicotine and alcohol and caffeine and cocaine. Dante asked, "Did he do this to you? Did he tie you down?"

She murmured "Dante," against the skin of his throat and his body jumped as if he had heard his name in a dark alley. "The first time I saw you, when you were saying Mass," his own fingers holding the communion wafer and lifting his gold-rimmed, gem-studded chalice, the soft vestments on his skin, sunlight beaming in the church full of people looking at him, "I wanted you," she said from the darkness. "Even reading about you on your website," before he'd seen her, when she had been somewhere out there, "seeing your picture, I wanted to know you, talk to you, touch you."

She had been stalking him before he even knew she was there, and vulnerability darkened the world. He asked, "Did that priest say such things to you?"

"It was your soul." She pulled his shirt and long cassock up his arms, past his shoulders, and bunched them around his wrists, restraining him further. The sheet was hot under his back. "I could feel your soul, your pure, beautiful soul, drawing me to you."

He knew she wasn't talking about his damned, rent soul. She was reenacting her abuse, changing his world from innocent to dangerous, showing him how the priest was just innocent background to her, practically foliage, and then, like lightning, *un colpo di fulmine*, he struck her. "Leila, don't do this to yourself."

"You made me want you."

"*Leila.*"

She unzipped his fly and, one-handed, pushed down his pants and pulled them off one leg with his shoe wrapped in the cloth.

"*Leila, don't.*"

She stripped off his underwear. He was naked from his wrists to his feet. His skin was oversensitive as if he had burned off that first layer of callused dermis, leaving him pink and raw. His dick was still so hard it curved back at his belly. She said, "God put this desire for you into my heart and my body."

"That's wrong." His skin was frantic for hers.

"God wants us to be together."

"How can you presume to know the mind of God?"

She shoved her knee between his thighs and cupped his balls. "Don't argue. Don't make me angry. *Angry is worse.*"

His heart battered his lungs. While she held his testicles, he didn't want to say anything to make her angry. This was how fragile she'd felt.

She climbed between his knees, forcing them apart. She said, "It is God's wish for us to be together, so it isn't a sin."

"Don't."

She stroked his dick, gently tugging the membranous foreskin, and shivers crawled on him. Her cool hands massaged him, somehow relaxing and tightening all the muscles from his knees to his shoulders. She bent her head down and whispered, right above his belly, "Say yes."

His body pressed air out his mouth. "Yes."

Her wet lips parted and wrapped around the head of his dick. Electric charge ripped through the bed. His spine arched and he bowed onto his shoulders, which screamed when his arms twisted against the steel cuffs.

Years, it had been years, and his blood roared under his skin. *Ah, un pompino.*

She plunged down, and he wrapped his hands around the iron railings above his head, trying not to shout. Tattered remnants of his restraint fluttered into the dark corners of the room.

Her head bobbed, and streaks of light rolled across her flashing black hair. He closed his eyes. "Oh, God."

She slowed and moved sideways. Cold air slapped his dick. She cat-crawled up his body—lace blouse over her breasts scraping his stomach and chest—and reached for the carved, bulbous nightstand.

He gasped for air. Reason dove into his forehead and he sighed, "Leila, don't."

"You want this." She retreated between his bent knees again and he closed his eyes. His soul concentrated to his sex.

Something cool nudged his ass.

"No!" His body contracted upward, repelled away from her. "What are you doing?" She was not going to cram anything into his ass. That was homosexual, and he wasn't, he'd *never*, and he *wouldn't*. "No!" He held onto the cold wrought iron in the headboard and pulled himself away from her.

She grabbed his ankle and yanked. The whole bedspread with him slid toward her. "You'll like it if you relax."

"No!" Panic whipped though him and he scrambled back, twisting his shoulder and wrenching his rotator cuff as the handcuffs pulled his hands.

She slithered up his body and kissed his lips. He turned his head away from her. A soft, metallic click near his right ear, like a key in a lock, and he opened his eyes.

Stripes of dark air interrupted the blued steel barrel, and trigger, and grip, in Leila's hand.

He jerked away from the flat handgun, but the handcuffs held. His arms and shoulders strained. "*Stop!*" Cool steel nudged his temple. He should have broken away sooner. If he tried to kick her, she might pull the trigger, and the bullet would fracture his skull and cranium shards and chips would slam through his brain. Mortality suffocated him.

"Lie down," she whispered near his shoulder, and her lips touched his skin.

The gun rasped on his hair near his temple. "Leila, put down the gun. Unlock the handcuffs."

The slightest tic of the gun's mechanism lifting the hammer from its rest brushed his ear like her long hair. "Lie back, Dante."

"Did the priest who molested you use a gun? Hold it at your head?"

"Some guns are inside your head."

If he kept talking, she might talk herself out and stop this. "I don't understand."

"You will."

"Leila, don't." The cold gun slid down his temple and rested on his cheekbone. The sharp sight scratched his skin down to his jaw. His heart slammed like repeating gunshots up his neck and into his head. The cardiac clatter cracked with adrenaline and each crash seemed to be the gun detonating and killing him, and he died a hundred times every minute. He was shocked to find himself alive a hundred instances a minute. His dick strained with bursting hypertension.

The gun pressed under his jaw, and her cool fingers wrapped around his testicles, massaging, threatening. "Lie flat."

He slid carefully down until his bound hands were above his head and he lay flat under her. She crawled backward through the light-streaked dark and parted his legs again with her knees. Her hand holding the gun drifted down near his ribs, rubbing muscle and ribs, and the muzzle still pointed inward toward his heart. The only thing he could do was breathe. He wrapped his hands around the iron headboard, and his eyes burned.

The cold gun chilled his belly. In a beam of white light, her finger curled around the trigger. The hammer flinched. The bullet would singe up his chest, enter under his chin, and blow the top of his head off.

Light stripes followed the curve of her cheek as she smiled in the dark. "Don't move."

Her hot mouth was on him again, and he gasped. One of his feet slipped on the silk.

Again, something cool nudged his asshole. "Don't do this. I understand."

Her mouth came off him and cold air clung to his wet dick. "You don't know shit."

The small, cool thing pressed his skin. "He threatened you."

The cool thing wormed into his body. Leila's wet mouth engulfed his cock again. She licked him while he was inside her mouth.

Something besides the heat and shocks of the *pompino* was happening to him. The nerves in his dick were squeezed between her mouth and the small, cool thing, like his dick, extended deeper into his body and it all rubbed.

She stopped and whispered, "I love you," then grabbed him again with her hot mouth.

Sensation drained from his body into his chest and he crashed out. Every spurt sucked his brain, blasted down his spinal cord, and cannoned his soul out of him.

Dante held no illusions that she loved him. The pedophile priest had told her that he loved her.

Telling her that was another abuse. It had ripped love out of her body.

"*Oh, Leila.*"

THE NEXT MORNING in the courtroom, Bev held hands with Mary, Lydia, and Laura, and they prayed before the attorneys arrived. Bev looked over the seats and milling spectators at the camera crew spooling out cable, uneasy because Dante was late. He had been punctual every day.

Mary's hand gripping hers was cool, and Mary said, "We pray to You, Holy of Holies, and we ask You to soften the jurors' hearts so they will acquit Bev."

Telling God what He should do unnerved Bev. Asking for a direct intercession was presumptuous, especially when she had sinned so terribly that God had abandoned her.

Mary patted Bev's shoulder with her long, pale fingers.

Dante still wasn't there. He'd never been late before. Bev should have demanded and stormed and cried and begged him not to go to Leila's apartment.

The lawyers trickled in, their shoes' hard soles sounding like Rosary beads falling on wood, and Heath tapped her shoulder as he sat down. "You okay today?"

Bev nodded.

Leila sat on the hard bench behind the prosecuting attorneys, yawning and sipping a triple shot skinny latte. She'd slept in her red gauze-draped bed for only two hours, from five to seven, before her alarm clock had shrilled and she had stumbled, still drunk, into the shower. Her head buzzed, and the wood rails of the courtroom slanted when she blinked. Her liver chewed through the scotch, processing like a busy computer, somewhere on that slippery metabolic continuum from drunk to hungover. She sneaked a scientific paper out of her oversized black purse and began reading *Six-Dimensional Confocal Microscopy*, though the words shimmied away. Pictures in the article—green and red fluors like neon lights bent into arcane Asian ideograms glowing at midnight—rippled like she was looking at them through a rainy window. Blasted booze.

Dante had been asleep in Leila's bed, unlocked, when she had left to go to court.

The judge called the court to order and started the day's business.

At the back of the courtroom, the television lights ignited. Leila's half-breed hand holding a thin pen above the tube light pictures paled two shades. Her name rang through the courtroom: "Leila Sage Faris!"

She shoved the paper in her purse and hurried up to the witness box.

Dante rounded the door into the courtroom and pressed the double door closed. Leila was walking to the witness box and fussing with some papers. She looked up, beautiful in her crisp white shirt and black skirt, and she saw him in the back of the courtroom with his eyes too wide and full of hope and his lips open.

Beside the door, a camera swung and hot television lights bore down on him.

Leila glanced at Beverly Sloan, who had turned at the defense table and stared at Dante.

Bev's mouth opened, and her jaw shifted forward.

Leila looked back to Dante.

Their eyes pinned him against the courtroom's doors. He ran a hand through his sweaty hair and shook as if they held guns on him. The heavy doors behind him rattled in their frames.

Judge Washington rapped her gavel and said, "Ms. Faris, if you please?" She didn't know what nonsense this was but they had a full day of testimony. She'd already postponed the next trial on her calendar a week because that damned prosecutor felt the need to object to everything and because Heath Sheldon was wasting time playing to the LawTV cameras. She shouldn't have allowed the cameras in her courtroom.

Leila's chest was tight with psychosomatic asthma. Dante's eyes were wide. He blinked and, shoving one hand in his pocket, composed his expression and reduced the volume of his eyes to vulnerable anxiety. Last night, his arms and legs had coiled around her all night long, as if she were a ruined column rife with vines. This morning, when Leila had been dressed and ready to leave her apartment, well-armored in crisp clothes, she'd touched Dante's bare shoulder and he'd jumped and flipped toward her, entangling himself in the red sheets, and his abysmal eyes had been large and black and hungry. He'd said he hadn't slept in weeks and he needed her. She sprinted out of the apartment, nearly tripping over her dog to escape.

The jury fidgeted and watched Leila Sage Faris.

The Georgies conferred together over their lawyerly notes at the prosecution table, their briefcases standing open around them like grammar school books corralled at the desk perimeter, hiding answers from the bully across the aisle who had teased that he would copy exam answers. George Grossberg muttered under his breath until he remembered how to exactly phrase that all-important question near the end of Leila's testimony so that she could produce the equivocal answer they desperately needed.

Leila stepped up to the witness stand. The bailiff swore her in.

When Heath tapped her shoulder, Bev turned to the front of the courtroom and watched Leila, with her shining hair so carefully twisted into a French knot, swear to tell the truth.

Dante found his usual place behind Bev and her lawyer. Bev's friend

Mary removed her satchel from the seat beside her for Dante. He smiled at her, and she bobbled her blonde head to reply. She set the bag at her feet and removed a small embroidery project. The gold and green leafed pattern matched the church's Easter altar cloth. Dante touched Heath Sheldon's shoulder and made writing motions when Sheldon turned. He passed back a thick black felt-tip pen and a legal pad.

"COULD YOU TELL US what happened that night?" George Grossberg asked.

Leila recited the pithy, skeletonized answers that they had agreed on:

Conroy was alone in the apartment when Leila arrived around ten o'clock.

George the avid prosecutor nodded, and his curly brown hair flopped at his hairline cresting the crown of his skull. He checked his notes on the turmeric legal pad.

Leila's fingernails scraped the wooden witness chair. That terrible night, the first thing she'd told Conroy was that he was an idiot. She'd tried to fix his stupid mistakes, leaving his wife, blowing his career. She'd told him what to tell his wife, and yet he couldn't find it in himself to keep his life together, to become the department chair and to receive the grants and prizes and to have his family, as if he'd been happy to throw it all away. He'd turned his face toward Leila, that besotted, sentimental, dear avuncular face, and he'd said he loved her and that he couldn't stand being without her, the tragic idiot. He had written a note for Beverly, Conroy said. A note. Blithering idiot.

Leila recited that she had left the apartment, and Beverly went in.

George glanced toward the jury box and smiled, trying to charm them. His eyes were Ashkenazi-variegated hazel, a green pond rimmed by black. He gazed at Leila and blinked, scrunching his eyes at her, an affectionate gesture and far too intimate. She pushed back into the crusty witness chair, adding inches of airspace between them.

Leila had waited outside and had seen no one else go into the apartment. Monsignor Petrocchi-Bianchi had arrived minutes later and waited with her in the cold February night.

She'd only seen Dante a few times in the two weeks before that terrible night: twice at the church, once at the Dublin, once drunk on her doorstep.

Behind the defense table, Dante braced one arm against the railing that separated the gallery from the court, as if he were ready to vault over it. His forehead crumpled and his lips opened, as if he were watching her burn. Conroy had declared that he was ready to rip apart his entire life for Leila. The priest, last night, had clung to her. She destroyed men.

Leila and Dante entered the apartment, and Leila found Conroy unconscious on the kitchen floor with a knife in his chest.

Conroy's long arms and legs were tossed carelessly on the vinyl linoleum and that knife stuck in his chest, like a child's amateurish mounting of a grasshopper with a silver pin on a white foamcore board, and Leila's throat exploded and she'd screamed. Conroy's breath rattled in his chest, pneumonic. She'd leapt at the floor with her hands and tried to help him breathe because he was suffocating. He might have thought he was in a well or a cave or buried alive. The damned priest had tried to pull her away but *Conroy couldn't breathe.*

The priest had seen what happened to people who loved Leila. He should take that to heart. He shouldn't have said those things this morning.

And this damned George lawyer shouldn't be smiling at her.

Leila wasn't a harmless mote. She was as poisonous as if she'd been weaned on foxglove and nightshade, an apoptosis ligand incarnate. Saving anyone she latched onto was impossible. Apoptosis was her nature.

George Grossberg smiled and pressed down his steel wool hair. They had gotten through the first few questions quickly, as they'd planned.

George reached the end of his questioning and walked back to his desk. As an apparent afterthought, he asked Leila, "And what was your relationship with Conroy Sloan at that time?"

Here was the place for the equivocating answer. *Your relationship* and *at that time* meant that she should answer about what she thought their relationship was on that night, not what he thought and not previously. If the defense raked up other muck, they'd look like they were trying to smear the murder victim. The prosecution had decided to sacrifice Peggy as Conroy's mistress and thus the sole root of Bev's *rage* because they needed Leila to look like an unbiased witness.

But Leila wasn't an unbiased witness. She'd fucked Conroy until he'd ripped apart his whole life, and his wife and his daughters had been caught up in his insanity. It was Conroy's own fault that he'd been entangled, but she was the spider and the web.

It would hinder her professionally when the story slithered out that she had been screwing her professor, but maybe it would warn off any stupid man who thought he should get involved with her, like the Roman-collared Monsignor who had clung to her last night, who now sat behind sad Beverly Sloan. That Leila had liked Dante, that there had been some small tenderness toward him, that she thought of last night as *one perfect night* meant nothing. Her presence and her flesh would destroy Dante, too.

The planned answer was, *He was my mentor for my Ph.D. studies, and we were friends.*

Leila inhaled one last breath and smiled her demure student smile. She said, "Conroy and I had an adulterous, sexual affair for seven months, but I broke it off with him a week before that night. That night, he told me he loved me and he had left his wife to marry me."

"Objection!" George Grossberg yelled.

Judge Leonine Washington licked her teeth and said, "You can't object to your own witness answering your own question."

Leila shouted over their arguing, "I told Conroy that I wouldn't marry him, that I wouldn't sacrifice the work and the science and myself for him, and that I'd sabotage him professionally if he persisted. He tried to grab me, and I hit him in the face, his left eye." She took a deep breath and looked past the A.D.A. Georgina with her frizzy hair, slumped on the desk, past the cameras with the towering, blazing lights, over to the defense table.

Bev had wrapped her Rosary beads around her hands, straining against them, and tears fell from her chin onto the red, swollen areas of hand flesh puffing between the black beads and silver chain. God, another betrayal, but Leila could save her from Conroy's ultimate stupidity.

Dante was half-standing behind Bev, clutching the witness rail.

Heath Sheldon's mouth had fallen apart and his eyes swelled until he looked like he had witnessed a three-hundred-yard hole in one and the winning touchdown and a record-shattering home run and the do-you-believe-in-miracles hockey goal.

Leila said slowly and clearly, and she almost believed it herself, "Conroy punched the wall, and then he threatened to kill himself."

HEATH SHELDON BOBBLED. He was an entire Californian crowd leaping to its feet but dropping back into his chair at the same time because he should have known all about what she was going to say though he hadn't and because he didn't want the jury to see him celebrating *winning the impossible case.* He could do the happy chicken dance when he got back to the office. Sober, he had to look sober and respectable because absolutely literally the jury wasn't out yet. He still had to finagle the jury to make sure they understood that the Leila chica had corroborated his whole cockamamie alternate theory of the crime and that *he had won.*

The courthouse railing was cool under Dante's hands, and the muscles of his palms and along the undersides of his fingers strained against his knuckles and metacarpals, straining to bury his fingertips in the resistant soft wood. Bev, her shoulders a foot in front of his cramping hands, crumpled and wept into her hands. Heath Sheldon plucked tissues from his briefcase and dropped them without looking beside her damp hands and one on her soft brown hair, where it clung like an old-fashioned church veil. Dante unclamped one hand and reached for Bev's soft shoulder. He should comfort Bev, who hadn't loved him and had used him, even while he longed for Leila. Bev reached up to his hand on her shoulder and grasped his fingers.

Leila watched them, especially their intertwining hands, from the witness box.

LAST NIGHT, lying in Leila's dark bedroom with his sprained arms shackled over his head, Dante stared at the red gauze striped with streetlight draping her bed, swallowing rage. "Unlock me," he whispered.

"Why?" Her voice was hoarse and she swiveled, sitting on the edge of the bed next to the striated window.

"I want to leave."

"Maybe I'll keep you here." Her gravelly voice was flat and angry.

"I can break the headboard."

"It's reinforced with wrought iron. Maybe I'll bring home some gay guys to shag the hetero."

His breath caught in his throat and he coughed. "What do you want?"

Metal slid on metal, and a spark jumped in midair. Leila's cigarette lighter glowed brighter than the slatted blinds behind her. "You wanted to know what it's like. Afterward, when your head is full of lies and you hate yourself, you know that it's going to happen again, and again, and there's no way out."

Powerless.

Leila owned a large dog, probably fierce when he was younger, and a gun. She had jabbed that pressure point on his side because she knew where it was, and she'd mentioned punching Conroy when he'd grabbed her. In the church's parking lot, when Conroy had grabbed her, she slipped his grasp and jammed his arm with easy skill. Her walls were reinforced with thick plaster. Even her bed was guarded by veils. She'd created a well-armed fortress because she was powerless, *a mote.*

She smoked in the night, and the tip glowed orange. "He was in my grade school every day, all day, waiting for me to make a mistake so he could haul me off to his office for punishment." Leila unlocked the handcuffs, stood on the opposite side of the bed so she was a dark, lean silhouette against those glaring window slats. "Go home."

Dante dragged the bedsheets over his skin that was still moist from her mouth and rubbed his chafed wrists. "I'm sorry. I'm so, so sorry."

"You don't know shit. I should have used the strap-on and raped you until your ass was bleeding instead of just the Cosmo girl prostate massage with the finger dildo. I should have called the guys and let them pass you around. Go home."

"Leila, I want to help you."

Her breathing rhythm changed to staccato, and her silhouetted hand touched her face. Cigarette smoke streamed toward the ceiling. "I don't want your help."

"He was a monster, Leila. If you tell me who he is, the Dominicans will track him down. If he's still a priest, he will be removed to the monastery. If he isn't, we'll find him anyway."

Her shadow nodded. "He's in New Mexico, still a priest."

"Then the Dominicans can have him. Tell me his name. He will be on a plane for Italy in a few days."

"It's over. I don't want to testify and I don't want to see him."

"There are no courts. You don't have to talk to anyone else. You only have to tell me, once."

She smoked, and her exhaled jet of smoke boiled in the air. "I wouldn't have to tell anyone else?"

"No. Just tell me, only once, tell me the names and places, and that will be all. It will be over. You won't have to think about it ever again."

She paused, considering, and Dante thought that he had her, but she said, "It was a long time ago," and shook her head. "I'm okay, now."

She wasn't okay, and Dante knew she wasn't because she'd shown him her fear and powerlessness and pain, but saying that wouldn't convince her. "Has he hurt anyone else?"

She smoked the cigarette. "In my high school, he had someone else."

"Since then?"

"No. He's not working at a school anymore. He can't get at little girls."

"There are no schools around where he is, or homes, or people?"

Leila tapped the cherry off her cigarette into an ashtray. "But he's not working there."

"He will find more girls. Pedophiles are like rabid dogs. They fight to escape and get to children, like heroin addicts."

The glowing tip of her cigarette trembled in the dark. "My God. He might still be doing it. Oh my God." She coughed. "All right." She took a deep hit off the cigarette and blew it out. "His name is Sean Gelineau."

She talked, and Leila remembered details about those years of her life and the names of other girls who the priest had stalked around the elementary school.

Bedsheets covered Dante's naked body. He wrote notes in the motionless striped streetlight on a pad of paper she tossed him.

Leila wouldn't turn on a lamp. She said, "It's easier in the dark."

She paced, but she didn't cry. She opened the bedroom door, and Meth the dog trundled in and followed his mistress around the bedroom as she paced, a dark hole in the light-striped walls, occasionally resting as if her pacing and ranting were routine, though the black dog eyed Dante warily, his retinas flashing metallic green in street light in cadence with his panting doggy breath, as if the presence of someone else in the room was a variation that must be watched.

"Was there anyone else you told at the time?"

Leila sat on the bed, her back to him. "No one who's alive now." She sniffed once.

He flipped down the pages. His cramped writing, outline and bubbled side notes, filled eight sheets of paper.

"It's why we joined the Coptic church. My mother wouldn't go to a non-Catholic church. So my father, from Florida, talked to my mom one last time, said that it was important that I knew my other roots, so we joined the Coptic Orthodox church, and I changed high schools." Leila sighed. "It's late. I have to be in court tomorrow."

"Leila, I'm so sorry." He hesitated as he reached, because he was a naked man in her bed and she had been a defenseless, fragile, and raped child. He touched the rough lace on her shoulder and braced in case she turned around fighting.

She flinched, but she didn't run, and she didn't punch him.

He stole his arm across her shoulder.

She stiffened.

He draped several folds of the sheet across his lap and wrapped his arms around her.

Her hands jerked, splayed in the air, and then touched his back. Her neck bent. Her lips touched his collarbone, and she started to pull the sheets away from his body.

"No," he said and adjusted her head so her cheek pressed his shoulder.

Her body quaked, but she didn't cry. They slowly descended to the sheets, and he touched his lips to her lace-encrusted shoulder, just once, before he slept.

GEORGE GROSSBERG stumbled back to his chair and said, "The prosecution is finished with this witness." He knew the jury was watching, but his head fell into his hands and he swallowed the chunky sick in his mouth.

Heath Sheldon leapt to his polished loafers.

Judge Leonine Washington wagged a finger at Sheldon. "Oh, I think we all need to break for lunch. And you, counselors," she crooked her finger at the Georgies, "in my chambers, now."

LEILA STRODE THROUGH the courtroom, trying to outrun Dante and Beverly and the lawyers and the people with the cameras and bright lights. Thinking she could outrun them was pretty dumb, since she had to pass them to get out. She trotted. Dante swam over an older lady and jiggled her knitting. Leila was almost to the door, right beside the scruffy guy holding a white notepad in front of the camera resembling a bazooka, when Dante touched her shoulder and she shied out from under his hand as if he had jolted her with a cattle prod. "Leila!"

She ducked through the door as a scruffy guy aimed a smaller camera at her.

Dante caught the door and jumped after her, but she zigzagged through the crowd and ducked into a ladies room.

When Dante's arms had wrapped around her last night, when the priest's naked body had form-fit to hers, she'd thought he wanted to fuck her, but he hadn't tried, and she'd lain awake, waiting for him to roll over and for his hands and mouth to hold her down, but he hadn't, and she didn't know what to do now.

AFTER LUNCH, Leila reaffirmed that she was still under oath and Heath Sheldon cross-examined her, reaffirming the scenario she had volunteered at the end of the prosecution's examination. Dante sat behind Beverly Sloan, his head hanging in his hands, while Beverly Sloan silently fiddled with her Rosary beads. Behind them, spectators scribbled notes, and the three black cameras flanked by blazing light trees swiveled and alternately rested on Leila, the attorneys, Beverly, or the Judge.

Leila had hidden in the ladies' room the whole lunch break, not even venturing outside for a cigarette. Nicotine-hungry worms scurried through her mind while Sheldon phrased his questions so precisely that she only had to say "yes" or "no." Leila was good at not answering too much. The oral defense of the Ph.D. candidacy exam will beat the tendency to expound right out of a person. Anything you say is the basis for another question, so the trick is to answer but say as little as possible.

Dante sat behind Beverly Sloan, his head resting on his arms. The note he'd slipped to Heath Sheldon during the prosecution's disastrous examination read, *Be careful. You resemble someone who hurt her. Don't get too physically close. And she's exhausted.*

Heath frowned and scribbled back, *You didn't threaten her, did you? Bribe her?* Dante shook his head, and Heath blew a long, relieved breath into the middle of the courtroom. While he questioned Leila, he lounged against the defense table, as far away from her as he could get and still be near the jury, and he noted every time she touched her temple or massaged her neck. She *was* exhausted. If that priest had commanded her to lie, if he'd exercised undue authority over her and she was committing perjury, Heath should stop her testimony because he couldn't suborn perjury, even though Leila's testimony was very good for his client. Very, very good. But Heath didn't know what had happened. Could have been anything. Probably was nothing. Probably nothing *illegal.* He asked, "Why did you leave Conroy Sloan alone in that apartment, if you thought he was suicidal?"

Leila said, "Conroy Sloan was becoming more and more unreasonable. I feared he might attack me again. Beverly Sloan was walking toward the door, and I thought that he wouldn't commit suicide with her there. I guess he hurt her arm while they were wrestling for the knife, before he stabbed himself."

Heath gaped but snapped his mouth closed. He waited for the Georgies to object to the blatant speculation, but they didn't. His knees weakened. God loved him.

Bev twisted the Rosary beads into a noose. Leila had said that Conroy wanted to marry her. That horrible Peggy had said the same thing. Conroy wouldn't have lied like that. Maybe he was sick. Maybe it was that terrible rabies virus.

Dante listened to Leila's contralto voice answer the lawyer's questions. Knowing that he'd ripped those memories out of her head last night and now this lawyer was scalpeling precise answers out of her hours later sickened him. She wasn't even weeping. He should be, but his eyes burned hot and dry.

Last night, when her mouth had touched the skin on his shoulder, when she'd tried to pull the sheet off him, his body had cried to leap at her and bury himself in her. Leila was a bundle of nerves he'd scraped raw, and she'd responded to his body that way because that was how she, powerless, responded to priests and to all men because, her words, she *might as well get fucked*. Dante's chest and his lungs were crushed by cardiac tamponade because his heart bled.

Heath Sheldon tossed off his last few questions just out of curiosity while he was circumnavigating the defense table, while he had Leila Faris on the stand and under oath. "Other than yourself and Peggy Strum, do you know if there were any other women with whom Conroy Sloan was carrying on sexual affairs?"

Leila said, "Yes."

Heath stopped, wondering if the jury and his client needed to know yet more. "Would you tell us their names and how you know about them?"

Leila said, "I saw Conroy and Dr. Valerie Lindh together at meetings. When I asked him about it on the night he died, he admitted a long-term, intermittent affair with her. There was also another woman named Mary, whom he mentioned a few times, but I don't know her last name."

Bev turned in her seat to whisper something like *Isn't that odd?* to Mary, but Mary was staring at Leila with horrified eyes and glanced back at Bev, startled. The embroidery project slid off her lap and fell on the dusty courthouse floor.

Bev whispered, "Not you, too?"

Mary whispered, "I'm so sorry. I'm so sorry. It was an accident, several accidents. But I stopped. I'm so sorry."

Bev squeezed her Rosary beads. "You could have told me."

"With everything else? It was easier to bear the guilt than to do that to you. I'm *so sorry*."

Dante listened to the women whispering. If Sloan were here, Dante would punch him in the face. Wrath was leading Dante around again, but Sloan deserved some wrath.

Heath Sheldon watched his client Bev whispering to her pale friend *Mary* and shook his head. He didn't need to *smear* Conroy Sloan. The guy was a slimeball, and when a lawyer thinks someone is a slimeball, that's some serious slime. He should add *Mary* to his witness list.

Heath asked Leila, "Did Conroy also propose to Peggy Strum?"

Judge Leonine Washington glanced at the prosecution table, but they were furtively whispering to each other, probably blaming each other for the fiasco, and so they missed this obvious objection to Leila's speculating or hearsay about Conroy's actions. So be it.

Leila said, "I think it's entirely possible that he proposed to Peggy, and Valerie, and anyone else, and that he was lying to all of us, maybe just to get a reaction."

Heath's chest tightened like a heart attack. He knew he was asking her to try on the glove. "Do you think Conroy Sloan was leaving his wife?"

"I think he had profound emotional problems, likely precipitated by my actions and possibly exacerbated by an infection with a neurotropic, psychotropic virus released in the lab. I think he may have told Beverly Sloan that he was leaving her so that she would beg him to stay. I think he told the women that he wanted to marry them so they would want him."

"Do you know how he got the bruises on his body, besides the one on his left eye, which you testified that you gave him?"

Leila nodded. "He punched the wall, so that's the bruised knuckles. He also grabbed my arm on a previous occasion and I twisted his arm behind his back. And rough sex, of course."

Heath could hardly breathe. He embodied every fictional courtroom lawyer all the way back to Daniel Webster's litigation with the Devil. He wanted to leap onto the defense table and shout his questions with his fists raised in the air. He spun a felt-tip pen on the table lazily and asked, "Do ya think he could have stabbed himself?"

Heath, Leila, and Judge Washington waited three nerve-wracking, fingernail-scratching, teeth-grinding seconds for the objection on the grounds of speculation, but the Georgies were still whispering to each other, oblivious. Leonine rolled her big brown eyes and Heath repressed the spring-loading in his calves that wanted to bounce around the courtroom. "Leila?"

Leila knew she could count on this lawyer to ask the ballsy question, especially since the demoralized prosecution attorneys had abrogated their responsibility. "Conroy Sloan was a medical doctor, and he was arrogant and probably sick with a fatal, dementing viral disease, which he might have known about or which might have been affecting his judgment. He probably thought he could miss all his vital organs with such a tiny knife and that everyone would rush to his bedside, and everyone would forgive him all his indiscretions. Suicide attempts, especially with less lethal means like a small knife, are usually cries for attention. He may have been actually suicidal. I'd just told him that I wouldn't marry him and that I would destroy his career if he didn't leave me alone. Either one of those could have been the reason that he stabbed himself."

IN THE JURY BOX, Tom Agosin was disgusted by the slutty witness and the tomcatting dead doctor. There was nothing to redeem this case, except perhaps the long-suffering widow at the defense table. After word had gotten around Tom's Baptist church that he was on the jury, his pastor had approached him. "There's been a big shakeup over at that Catholic Church, Perpetual Help," his young pastor had said, shaking her head. Her curly, blonde hair bobbed. "Two priests disappeared. I don't mean reassigned. They *disappeared*. Brother Samual was a friend. First, one new priest came, stayed a few weeks, and then he and Sam's assistant pastor Brother Nicolai left one day. Sam was shook up after Brother Nicolai disappeared. Then a new priest arrived at the parish, an Italian guy, an honest-to-God Roman Monsignor, a Jesuit, and Sam was scared of him, wouldn't talk about him and actually spilled his coffee when I asked. Then Sam sent an email that he'd been recalled to Rome and left the next day. We used to discuss theology through email and at coffeehouses, and he hasn't emailed. It's like he fell off the face of the Earth."

Tom Agosin had watched the priest sitting behind Bev with a mixture of superstition and horror ever since, because he was pretty sure that the red piping on the cassock that the man had worn one day last week meant that this guy was indeed the Roman Monsignor who made other priests fall off the face of the Earth.

Gina Salerio had also seen Monsignor Dante Petrocchi-Bianchi sitting behind Beverly Sloan, and she knew exactly who he was. The Monsignor had given Gina communion both times she'd been to church in the last six months, and he was counseling her friend's son, John, though her friend wouldn't say why John needed counseling, just that Monsignor Petrocchi-Bianchi was a good man and a good priest, and she said it with desperate conviction, often.

In the jury room during deliberations, Tom Agosin asked Gina if she knew anything about the Monsignor and told her what his pastor had said, and Gina told him what she knew. They didn't know why the good Monsignor was sitting behind Beverly Sloan or what was going on at the church, but they agreed it was something important.

Tom was less convinced that it was benign. In his experience growing up in New Jersey, Italians plus people disappearing meant Mafia.

HEATH SHELDON admitted that he had no more questions for this witness. Bev sniffled beside him, and he grabbed a wad of dry tissues out of his briefcase and handed them to her.

George Grossberg, standing straight despite the sparking pain in his neck, called Malcolm Hay to the stand.

Heath Sheldon riffled through his documents and found the single mention of Malcolm Hay as a character witness for Leila Faris. Crap. Leila's testimony was fine just as it was.

Malcolm entered the courtroom and saw Leila huddled in the back row and the priest sitting in the front, looking guilty. No one had even deposed him before the trial.

After the usual rigmarole about his being a Scot and a couple of unprovoked, filthy glances from the court reporter who was pissed about trying to transcribe his testimony through his Scottish burr, Malcolm was duly sworn in. Not that he gave a whit about this whole pig circus.

The prosecutor, the blonde lady attorney, asked him if he knew anything about Leila Faris and Dr. Conroy Sloan having an affair.

Malcolm's eyelids rolled up, and his eyebrows dropped. "Och, no, that's slander, t'is. She'd've had none of that. My buddy O'Malley fancied her."

Georgina smiled. "Did you ever see anything about their relationship that suggested it was more than a mentor-mentee relationship?"

"No, never. Och."

Heath Sheldon decided not to ask Malcolm Hay any questions. His not knowing about their relationship didn't mean that it hadn't existed. Leila had admitted it. Shortening his time on the stand would do just as much good as any discrediting he could have pulled off.

Malcolm didn't remember seeing the thin stripe of red Porsche tail lights driving away from Leila that night when Conroy had returned from the NIH study section. Even if he had remembered Conroy's black Porsche, Malcolm wouldn't have ratted Leila out.

That was nobody's business but her own, t'was.

GEORGE GROSSBERG sat at the prosecution table, holding his head in his hands, while Georgina Pire stated for the record that the prosecution rested its case.

Chapter Twenty-One

Bev kneeled before the niche of the Virgin Mary. The clicking of the Rosary beads comforted her. The hollow church was quiet. She had to pick up the girls from Lydia's soon. Christine insisted on knowing what had happened at court, who had testified, what they said, why the judge had upheld or overturned objections. Dinah preferred denial and chittered about cartoons.

The church door clunked open behind her. A swath of light clambered over the blue-robed Virgin.

"Bev? Is that you?" Dante's voice rang through the church.

She twisted around and sat on the floor.

He walked up the center aisle and around to the Virgin's niche. He spun and settled on the floor beside her, leaning against the wall, knees bent. "You finished with the lawyer quickly."

Beverly said, "He was busy. He had papers to file." She fiddled with the black Rosary beads and dribbled them onto the floor.

"There isn't much trial left. I testify, then your medical expert, then you, and that's all."

"And then I go to jail. Laura is in our will as getting the girls if we both died. She's said she'll take them for me, but I can't bear to leave them."

Evening sunlight reflected from the polished pews and touched Dante's face with gold. His skin was the color of the honey oak of the crucified Christ behind the white-draped altar. Both had strong, Mediterranean features. The Christ's face was haggard with suffering. Dante's eyes were gathering similar lines. He said, "If Laura can't take the girls," and his voice held a note of panic, "if something happened, I would take care of them."

This was odd. "That's nice of you."

He glanced up at her. "There are American schools in Roma. My apartment is too big for just me. I have too much money, professor's salary, Monsignor's stipend, family money. They could go to America for university." He looked away, over the church pews. "If they needed me, I would be there for them."

She touched his hair, so silky and black. Damp strands of it fell through her fingers. "You've thought about this."

He tucked his mussed hair into place with his fingers. "If they need someplace, they are welcome. I would, or, it would, or... I don't know." He couldn't seem to finish a sentence. He sank both of his hands into his hair. "They would be taken care of. I would take care of them."

"Don't you travel? Isn't this what you do, go different places, help people?"

His head rested on his crossed forearms. "I don't know what I do."

"You've helped Luke. Laura says so."

"Have I?" His voice wove around his arms and lost itself in the thin air over the pews.

"I'll leave the girls with Laura," she tried saying the words, "when I go to prison," and she didn't choke or vomit. "I think you need to help other people."

Dante covered his face with his hands. His voice was a far-off trumpet. "It's too hard."

She stroked his hair. "Kids like Luke need you."

He nodded, though his hands still covered his face.

ANOTHER INSOMNIAC NIGHT pacing the rectory. The night before, Dante had slept in Leila's bed. That night, he paced with his arms wrapped around his chest, holding his cell phone in case she called. He called her at home and on her cell. His body groaned with loneliness as his footfalls thumped the whitewashed wood of the rectory floor.

That morning, Dante donned his full ecclesiastical regalia—Jesuit black cassock and Monsignor's red-piped cape and stole—and at court swore on the Bible that he would tell the truth, the whole truth, and nothing but the truth, so help him God. No lightning struck.

Heath Sheldon started with a windy explanation to the jury that since Monsignor Dr. Dante Maria Petrocchi-Bianchi, S.J., M.D., Ph.D., was in fact a doctor (and a psychiatrist at that) and a priest (and a Vatican Monsignor and a Jesuit at that) some of his communications were privileged. The judge, a curvaceous black woman, instructed the jury that they shouldn't interpret Dante's refusal to answer any question as being positive or negative, or that he even knew the answer. She smiled at him, and her slim smile reminded him of Nyla, a Parisian college student of Nairobi descent.

Heath Sheldon nearly bowed to Dante. "Dr. Monsignor Petrocchi-Bianchi, what was your relationship with the deceased?"

Heath Sheldon asked many questions about Conroy Sloan, and Dante answered what he could, when he could. Equivocating, meandering Jesuit theology had prepared him to answer such tedium with alacrity and evasion, and it did not require much attention.

Heath Sheldon read questions from his chair beside Bev. She clicked through her beads, praying the Rosary. Fragile skin clung to her skull and slate shadowed her tired eyes.

Sheldon asked, "Do you know if Conroy Sloan was having an affair with Leila Faris?"

Dante settled his hands in his lap. "I could not answer that."

Dante watched the oak double doors behind the gawking spectators and checked his cellular phone for messages during breaks, but Leila didn't call.

The Daily Hamiltonian:

DEAD DOC'S LOVER SAYS SUICIDE
by: Kirin Oberoi

Today in the case of the State vs. Beverly Sloan, in a devastating blow for the prosecution, Leila Sage Faris acknowledged she was one of four mistresses of the deceased Dr. Conroy Robert Sloan and that he had threatened to commit suicide the night he died.

LEILA COLLECTED a few personal effects from the lab that afternoon while the conservators stripped her flat, uninstalled the Parisian plaster, and packed the Tiffany chandelier, the antique furniture, the tapestries and the art in acid-free paper-lined, humidity-controlled cartons. By the time she got home, the only things left would be what she needed to survive the next few days: dog accoutrements, a sleeping bag, and her computer. She would spend her last days in New Hamilton camping out in her apartment, drinking goodbyes, caulking nail holes, and printing her final thesis copy.

The newspaper was lying outside the lab door, innocuous as an empty syringe. She considered ditching it, but that was juvenile.

The paper pile on her desk was two feet high. Conroy's slovenly habits were communicable. She began sorting the pile into keepers and trash.

Joe slapped the newspaper on the table by her desk. The page was open to a short commentary about her testimony. "You and Dr. S.?"

She nodded and tossed academic papers into a huge trash can beside her desk. Technicolor papers swished into the trash bin, evidence of her highlighter habit.

"*Why?*" Joe's deep eyes rolled.

"Just because."

"Then why *me?* I thought we were friends." He scrubbed his eyes with the heels of his hands.

Leila tossed out a sheaf of outdated journal papers. "It just happened. It was nothing."

Joe stared into the lab. "Did he leave Beverly for you?"

Leila resumed trashing paper. "He knew I was graduating this summer. We'd discussed that I wanted to postdoc at Columbia."

"Then *why?*"

In Leila's hands, Conroy's lab notebook fell open to a scan of a gel with random bands like schizophrenic dimmer switches. "His rabies virus test was inconclusive." She pressed his cold notebook to her chest. Chill seeped past her sternum into her lungs. Lies frosted her voice. She said, "Conroy was raving, howling, gibbering, moon-barking *rabid.*"

DANTE DESCENDED the stairs of the Dublin Underground and scanned the room. Leila sat near the pool table in a long booth with Malcolm and Joe. Dante ordered two pitchers, a Guinness and a sweet pilsner, and carried the pitchers over. He edged past the burly, raucous men shooting pool. Joe scooted toward the wall as Dante approached, making room.

"Och." Malcolm reached for the Guinness pitcher. "Beware of Romans bearin' gifts."

"Far more treacherous than the Greeks." Dante slipped in next to Joe. They nodded at each other then resumed staring straight ahead. "*Buona sera*, Leila."

"*Buenos noches*," she said. Both her hands protected her pint glass.

Malcolm poured himself a pint and sipped. His face contorted as if someone had stuck a vacuum up his nose and sucked the skin inward. "The Americans screw up even Guinness. Padre, how is American beer like having sex in a canoe?"

Dante sipped and considered how a priest should answer that question. "I wouldn't know."

"They're both fucking close to water."

Dante watched Leila smile gently and glance at Joe, who glared at his beer as if it had insulted him. She looked down again.

Leila's smooth black hair and dark eyes seemed to alleviate the pain of the world, even if she wouldn't look at Dante and only stared plaintively at her beer.

LEILA SAT WITH THE PRIEST after Joe and Malcolm went home around eleven o'clock. If she had left with Malcolm, he would have interpreted it as a sign that she was finally going to bed him, even though the conservators had disassembled her grand bed that afternoon. If she left with Joe, he would demand they *talk*. Instead, she was alone with the Jesuit who knew things about her that she hated, and she hated his knowing them, and she wanted to run outside into the warm rain alone.

Dante lifted the half-full pitcher of pilsner. "I began the paperwork for the Dominicans."

Leila nodded.

Dante ran his hands through his hair, combing it back with his fingers, an unconsciously sexy move that called attention to the wavy hair that skimmed his earlobes. He probably wasn't aware. "He should be in the Alps within a week." He sipped his dark beer and one of his eyebrows tipped down. "I suppose it is what they deserve." Dante turned his mug so the handle faced his other hand. "Well, it's not my problem. My job is to counsel children and gather evidence. The men are none of my concern."

"Aren't you just keeping them someplace, so they won't mess with kids anymore?" She didn't like the way he was talking.

The priest rotated his mug in his hands again. He didn't usually display nervous tics like that. "That monastery isn't a very nice place."

Worry worked itself into a knot in her chest. "How so?"

Dante's head bobbed side to side. "The Dominicans are a severe sect.

The Dominicans ran the CDF, back in the bad old days. I'm a Jesuit, so I'm an outsider, but I'm their shrink so they tolerate me." He smiled. "They know I don't have political aspirations, so I am harmless."

"Hmmm," Leila said. "More harmlessness."

"Yes, indeed." He chuckled and pressed a hand against the side of his face, embarrassed. "*Harmless*. My poker tell."

"But the Dominicans?"

Dante sat back and rotated his glass between his palms again. "Sometimes I think the men would be better off in an American prison, even though pedophiles are murdered there by other inmates." Dante scratched his eyebrow. "The Dominicans have harsh ideas about curing pedophiles. They believe that abusing children is sin, not disease or crime. This is the Vatican's official opinion, too, and the Dominican brothers are dedicated to stamping out sin. They are industrious about it." Dante frowned. "There have been suicides."

Leila's hand held the beer glass halfway to her mouth when his word *suicides* slipped in her ear and lodged in her throat like a sideways tortilla chip. She reversed the beer's direction and it slopped on her knuckles as the mug thumped the table.

Dante wiped the corner of his mouth with a bar napkin and continued, "I shouldn't be talking like this. I say more than I should, sometimes. It's being away from fellow Jesuits, living alone in the rectory, no family near. It is not like this in Roma. I begin to understand how some priests take companionship anywhere they find it, or at least how they are undiscovered for so long. Not that that excuses them. Not at all."

The worry knot writhed and tightened. "Why would they commit suicide?" Leila asked.

Dante stared at his beer. "The Dominicans' ideas of sin and redemption can be harsh."

Leila's breath fluttered near her throat. "Like, what, torture?"

"I don't think the Dominicans lay a hand on them. It's penance. It's not how I would run a treatment facility, but they did not ask for my opinion. They utilize solitary contemplation, all day, all night, for weeks, if necessary." Dante said.

"Solitary *confinement?*" What had she done?

Dante leaned over his beer, crouching. "They expect the men to be heartily sorry for offending God. They make sure the men are heartily sorry."

Leila's heartbeat sped. "I thought it was just a place to keep them."

Dante shook his head. "It's more like the camp where the Americans housed terrorist prisoners, Guantanamo Bay, but with overtones of conversion. Perhaps 're-education' is a better word."

"The Vatican can't just toss people in a… a *concentration camp.*"

"We're a government and a country and a corporation," Dante said. "The U.S. has camps like this. Many governments do. It shouldn't be shocking that the Vatican does, too."

Hysteria, real hysteria, narrowed her vision. The black-clothed Jesuit across the table leaned back in his seat and frowned as if he had mentioned that the Church was engaged in minor accounting indiscretions. "Sean just won't go. He's too smart for that. He won't go."

"Then they'll convince him. They're very persuasive. He'll probably go willingly. If he doesn't," Dante shrugged, "we just throw them on a Vatican plane and take them. The IEA is getting quite good at that. We enlisted the Mossad to work with us on logistics." Dante shook his head. "One of the men who engineered the Eichmann kidnapping in Argentina has been helping us coordinate. Isn't that ironic, considering we gave Eichmann the passport to get to Argentina in the first place?"

"You're kidnapping them and taking them to *concentration camps?*"

"Lower your voice." He turned his palms up on the bar table, begging holding. "There is only one place. After what that man did to you, what would you think is a just punishment?"

"Not this." Leila's voice rose. "I thought you were just going to put him some place where he can't get at other girls, not some Catholic Auschwitz."

"It is not like the Shoah." Dante glanced at the oblivious horde playing pool next to them, reached into his suit coat, removed his wallet, threw a twenty on the graffitied table and stood. "It is entirely different. Come on."

"Where?"

"Elsewhere." He unfurled his fingers toward her. She took his warm, smooth hand and scooted out of the booth. He held onto her fingers and asked, "Your apartment?"

She shook away his hand. "My apartment is being dismantled. I don't even have chairs."

His brows twitched. "Why is that?"

"I'm moving to New York this weekend."

"You're leaving?" His eyes expanded and his chin swiveled as if watching something rotate very fast.

"I'm depositing my thesis on Friday. My postdoc starts in two weeks. I waited to defend until before I testified so I wouldn't have to come back."

"I didn't know." His fingertips touched his forehead and inched back into his hair. "We could sit in my car."

"No." Leila stepped back. She didn't sit with priests in cars in remote, dark spots, behind mini-malls, in the parking lots of city parks.

"My church is close."

"I'll drive myself." She walked away. She watched the cobbled pedestrian mall sidewalk and rain-fed grout rivulets under her boots. If he was lurking back there, watching her ass jiggle or staring mournfully, she couldn't go to the church, and she needed to know what was going on.

Sean needed to know.

DANTE PACED the church's center aisle, glancing at the wooden icon hanging on the cross where the long arms of the sanctuary crossed the nave. Backlights bounced from the rear wall of the church behind the icon in a fair approximation of a divine nimbus, and a cruciform shadow quadrisected the pews.

She wasn't coming. Almost half an hour had passed. He paced to the communion rail, pivoted, and walked toward the doors. If she didn't show up in five minutes, he was going to her apartment. He tossed his tiny cell phone in the air and caught it behind his back.

The rear doors opened. Leila, a black-clothed sylph, trickled in.

He strode through the church toward her. "You told me the truth, yes?"

"Yes." She stared at her feet.

He reached where she stood. "Then he should go to the Dominicans."

She clasped her hands together in front of her chest. Her elbows clenched tight to her sides, vulnerable. "I can't do that to him. He was my lover for five years."

That word, *lover*, that she had denied existed for her two nights ago, rolled between them. The things that pedophile must have told her when she was ten years old, in the fifth grade, until she was fifteen. "That man was an abuser, not your lover."

Her contralto voice was tiny in the wood and plaster of the church. "I love him."

His grip tightened around the pew. "He is a demon incarnate. I analyzed these men, treated them, medicated them, even exorcised them. No devil possesses them but they are legion among us. I think, *I believe*, that they are not sinners, but they are evil. Their souls are forfeit or twisted. *Evil* is the only word strong enough to describe the way they disregard the damage they inflict."

Leila whipped her head around, dodging those words. Her hair swung sideways. "You're rationalizing to make them less than human so you can treat them however you want. Hitler demonized people, stripped them of their humanity so he could kill them."

"Ah, the Hitler card," Dante countered. "Reductio ad nazium. When something offends you and yet you have no answer for it, compare it to one of Hitler's policies."

"They're human beings. They're not *evil*. It's a disease. Or a predilection. Or a misdirection."

"You've obviously read the literature. There is no cure for pedophilia."

Leila's voice rose, speaking over his. "Or something they have to work through to become fully human."

"That's Nietzsche, that there is no sin but only selves needing to reach the fullness of themselves. It's a lie. It is impossible to reach fullness for oneself while destroying other human beings."

"I'm surprised *you've* read Nietzsche." Her angry voice tore through the church.

"We read him in the seminary. The professors consider it a vaccination against atheism."

"Didn't work for you, did it?"

"It was too late for me." He rubbed the oiled wood of the pew.

"You can't kidnap him." Her voice cracked like an adolescent boy's. Her hand dipped into her purse. "Sean's not going to be 'heartily sorry,' no matter what you do to him."

He wanted to wrap his arms around her because she was hunched over, her arms and elbows clamped, protecting her torso from incoming body blows, but if he approached her, she might run. She might attack. Dante didn't want to restrain her hands. Holding her fists would connote when she resisted that terrible man, *Sean*, when he had held her down and raped her. Sometimes, Leila had said, Father Sean had laughed at her ineffectual attempts to defend her body from him, but he grew angry at resistance, and he enjoyed being angry at her. *Angry was worse.* Submission was less violent.

Dante said, "Sometimes, force must be used in the service of truth." The Inquisition's own words, utilized for centuries, soured on his tongue. He paced faster. "They must be locked up forever, every one of them. They are like rabid dogs or starving lions. They can't stop themselves, especially the primary pedophiles, the ones who prefer children under thirteen and for whom gender is less important than age. They will offend again. They will rape children every chance they get. There is no cure or treatment or penance for it."

"You don't believe in free will. How very Calvinist of you."

"Calvin thought that some souls are predestined to go to Hell. His theories do not apply to psychosexual behavior or psychopaths."

"Bullshit. You're a drug dealer of opium for the masses and you don't even sample your own wares."

He shook his head, but she was right. "Nietzsche, Calvin, and Marx. No wonder you left the Church."

"And Jim Jones. You guys are drinking your own Kool-Aid."

Dante grabbed the back of the pew and squeezed it hard. "I grew up under John Paul II, who was a mystic, but most men in the Vatican are not like him. Vatican politics—how far they rise, what they control and who is in their influence—comprises their whole lives. They have nothing else. These pedophiles threaten the Curia and the Church. They will do anything to protect themselves." And he was in it too deeply to leave.

"You can't have Sean! You can't take him to a place like that just to save your own hides."

Frustration rose. This Sean was just another psychopathic, narcissistic pedophile. Dante had seen too many of them to be sympathetic. "Why would you protect him?"

"I loved him. He was my lover for five years. How can you ask such things?" Her voice choked. "You must never have loved anyone in your whole life."

Ridiculously, horribly true. Dante's breath caught under his rib cage.

He crossed his arms over his chest. "Define love."

She whipped her head around and glared. Tears smeared her dark irises. Her wet cheekbones shone silver. Her hand dipped into her purse, and she blocked her body by holding her purse in front of her, a classic defensive posture. "It's like God. You either feel it or you don't. I loved Sean, and I love science because it fills the void God left when He deserted the world. Any divine spark behind creation wouldn't want to be worshipped. It would want to be understood. Love is being understood at a cellular level. I understand the universe, the stars, and the world and people and cells and viruses and DNA and atoms and quarks and strings, and It understands me back. Science knows the mind of God."

Wonder dropped his jaw. "You aren't an atheist."

"Sure I am. *If* there is a God, *since* there *isn't* a God, I want to understand creation."

Dante's heart tumbled under his palm pressed against his chest. "You've read Newman."

"Yeah, and you've been reading that other Catholic anti-Semite, Hitler." Her breath caught in a sob when she inhaled.

"They aren't death camps," he said. "Hitler killed people. The Dominicans are trying to convert them."

"So it's like Dachau, not Auschwitz."

"I've told you, it's more complicated than that."

"No, it's not." She pulled the blued-steel gun out of her purse.

Ah, he hadn't seen the last of that gun. His heartbeat raced counterpoint to his mortality. Disturbing associations of that gun with her body curving around him lapped his mind. The gun's deep barrel stretched away from him toward infinity. His hands unwove and splayed in front of his chest, as if he had the ecclesiastical power to ward off bullets. "Leila, don't."

Leila held the gun straight out in front of her, her shoulders and arms forming a triangle with her hands and the gun at the apex. Her voice rasped. "I want you to write a letter to the Vatican and tell them to leave

Sean alone. Tell them I lied. Tell them I'm a psychopath. I don't care what you say, just call them off."

"Why didn't you just tell me that you had lied?"

"You wouldn't have believed me."

He nodded.

A tear fell on her cheek. The gun quivered in her shaking hands. She squinted her eyes shut and more tears dripped from her eyelashes. She bowed her head over her outstretched arms.

"How did he manipulate you so?" Even though he knew.

"Stop it. Just stop the psychobabble and write the goddamned letter."

"My computer is in the library, over there." He pointed to the door camouflaged in the rightward wall of the church just before one long arm of the cruciform shadow.

"Let's go." She bobbed the gun muzzle toward the door.

Going to a secluded location with an armed woman might seem foolhardy, but as a priest, he was vow-bound. She was his poisoned communion wine, and he brought the proverbial chalice to his lips. Ah, her lips, her lips on his, and his lips flushed sensitive, remembering.

She said, "Tell me what they're going to do, how they're going to look for him."

"I don't know."

"I'm holding a gun, Dante. The first rule of guns is that you don't point a gun at something unless you intend to destroy it. Tell me how they're going to kidnap him." Her footfalls clacked on the wood floor behind him.

"They'll talk to him first, try to convince him to go willingly."

"It won't work. Sean won't go. He'll have heard something."

"A van will pull up beside him. Someone strong will grab him and throw him in. He'll be sedated. His Church superior will be informed that he was transferred and will not call the police. Someone else will pack his belongings. They'll hold him in a safe house, then put him on a Vatican plane for Roma. From there, vans. With priests, it's easier than you think.

No one asks questions. When Nicolai and Samual disappeared, a few people asked questions, and I said they were transferred. No one reported anything. Nicolai went willingly after Father Domingo discussed it with him. Samual was picked up."

He turned his doorknob and pushed open the door of the library. It was still swollen from the humidity and opened with a crack. "After you?"

She hesitated and watched the door as if something might leap out at her. Her arms holding the gun drooped. "You go first."

He walked inside and sat down in his computer chair. He crossed his legs, resting one ankle on his other knee, an unstable position for lunging.

She followed him into the library and kicked the door closed. It stuck against the frame, and she pushed it with one hand, not enough to latch the mechanism but enough to keep it from creaking open. Her other slim hand held the gun, which listed away from him toward the books.

He touched the laptop's switch, and it whirred and clicked. He asked, "Is there something specific you want me to tell them?"

"Just tell them to leave him alone."

Dante started the word processor and typed a letter to the Vatican detailing the unreliability of the original witness and the recent recanting of her testimony. He concluded that, in the absence of other substantiation, the file should be placed on indefinite hold. He printed the letter and swiveled in the office chair to hold it out. "Is this what you want?"

She advanced, holding the gun low and away, beyond his reach. He held out the letter. The paper didn't quiver in his grasp. She snagged it and stepped back. She read and glanced at him, watching him in case he moved to grab her. Dante leaned back in the office chair and stretched his legs, another unstable position for jumping. "Okay," she said.

Dante found stationery in a desk file drawer, reprinted the letter on the creamy, thick ragstock, and sealed it in an overnight delivery envelope.

Leila said, "I'll mail it." He held it out to her, and she took it from his hand in the halting way that a beaten animal accepts food. She lowered the gun until it pointed at the blue carpeting, though she held it stiffly out from her side and in front of her toes, ready.

Dante dragged his hair out of his eyes. "If you want to talk," he said, "call me."

"After the other night?" She flapped the stiff envelope at the gun. "After *this*?"

Dante's throat closed at the thought of never seeing her again. "Any time."

Tears flipped over her mascara-smudged lower eyelid and slid down the contours of her cheekbones. She stepped over to the door, yanked twice to jerk it open, and was gone. Her sprinting footsteps in the church echoed through the open door.

Dante turned back to the computer and composed an email to the acting head of the CDF, warning him to disregard the express letter about Sean Gelineau and to proceed with forming and extraction team.

Chapter Twenty-Two

"Ladies and gentlemen of the jury." Heath Sheldon leaned on the table beside Beverly Sloan.

Bev flicked through her Rosary beads under the table, hardly registering their movement through her hands, and her tongue and upper palate twitched around the silent syllables inside her mouth. The fingering motions of pinching the beads and progressing to the next decade were comforting, like playing the piano. The positions and attitudes of her fingers corresponded to tones in her head, though there were words instead of pitches. She played the Rosary.

Dante sat behind Bev, his damp forehead resting on his wrists crossed on the rail that separated the spectators from the court. Though his position resembled an attitude of prayer, it was a pose of exhaustion. His eyes burned.

Heath Sheldon said, "At the beginning of this trial, I told you that the evidence and the theory of the crime didn't add up. So why would the prosecution even charge someone in such a case that appears to be an accident or suicide?"

Leila was crowded into the back row near the television crew's hot lights. She'd tied her hair back in a fishwife's knot, as if reining in her hair would make her invisible. She hadn't worn sunglasses or a hat. Such accoutrements would make her more conspicuous than she already was, the mistress of the dead man who had been smeared with his blood and had destroyed his reputation by publishing his atrocious experiments.

Danna's story had worked its way though the undercurrent of the scientific community. Critical letters were published in *Nature*, stating that the scientific community should repudiate Conroy's rabies data because they had been obtained by risking human life and circumventing safety and ethics. Some letters compared the rabies work to the hypothermia and hypoxia studies conducted on prisoners at the Nazi death camps, which are sealed. *Reductio ad nazium.*

No one mentioned that Leila's HIV results were also beyond the scope of the lab's license. Her data suggested a new drug target for HIV-associated dementia, so it was useful. Colombia had called Leila last week to confirm that her quick-promotion fellowship was waiting for her. The whiff of notoriety whetted their interest.

Heath glanced at the yellow notepad he held. "First-degree murder has the most stringent definition for conviction. First-degree murder means that the act was premeditated, that it was committed with malice aforethought, that every action taken was entirely intentional, and that the perpetrator had no remorse and didn't try to save the victim's life.

"That's just not what happened. This incident, from the evidence that we have, doesn't fit any of these definitions." Heath tapped his notepad with a fat black pen. "Now, you should ask yourselves why the prosecution did that.

"One possibility is that they think you folks will convict a ham sandwich if they tell you to, even if they have a shoddy case." Always a good opener to appeal to any mavericks. One contrarian could hang a jury.

Heath continued, "Another possibility is that they didn't interview their witnesses properly. They said Beverly Sloan had abused Conroy Sloan, but it was Leila Faris who defended herself physically from him and testified to leaving the bruises they attributed to Mrs. Sloan. They blew it again when Ms. Faris told you that Conroy Sloan had threatened suicide that very night, and the prosecution objected to their own witness's testimony." Heath shook his palomino head. "That one I'll put in my book someday."

Heath watched the eight women and four men on the jury. "But there are darker possibilities, beyond the prosecution's pride or stupidity.

"Here's one: conviction rates for women who are accused of killing their husbands, even if they didn't do it, even husbands who were abusive, even in direct self-defense of themselves or their children, are preternaturally high. There is still, *still* a sentiment in society that women are the property of their husbands, and *property* shouldn't fight back. When a dog bites its master, even if the guy was beating it at the time, the dog is put down at the vet's or with a rifle." Two of the women in the jury box, the gray-haired woman, Rinpoche, and the Italian Catholic, Salerio, crossed their legs and their eyebrows twitched downward, a microexpression of unease. Good.

"On the other hand, men accused of killing their wives enjoy some of the lowest conviction rates and the lightest sentences in the judicial system. I'm sure we can all think of a famous example or two. And again, that's because women are *still* treated as *property* and a man can dispose of his *property* however he wants to."

Heath crossed the courtroom in front of the jury box, stroking his jaw philosophically. "And that leads us to another possibility: a *man* of high standing in the community is dead, and even if it was an accident or an act of God, someone *here* needs to pay because the world is logical and orderly and things happen for a reason. That's the way we like it: cause and effect, action and reaction. A psychopath was abused as a child and kills people who look like their abusive parent. Terrorists plot a conspiracy, and police or G-men thwart them. A serial killer has a predictable pattern to his crimes and is apprehended.

"A man dies an untimely death, someone is convicted of killing him."

Heath set his yellow legal pad on the blank table in front of Bev, who studied her hands sorting the Rosary beads. He said, "The prosecution is counting on your need to understand the world as an orderly, rational place. But the world isn't an orderly, rational place. Good drivers have traffic accidents. Pedestrians slip and fall on perfectly dry sidewalks. Sometimes, in a struggle over a steak knife, someone gets cut.

"There's one more reason why the prosecution gave you a charge of first-degree murder that they knew they couldn't support: they don't want you to convict Beverly Sloan." Heath drew a deep breath. The prosecution would refute this in its own closing statement, so he had to tread carefully to make their refutation support his argument. "Political pressure can make prosecuting attorneys do strange things. The prosecution may have known that Conroy Sloan either killed himself or died by accident, but they couldn't admit that with" and his long, suit-clad arm swept toward the cameras and supernova lights at the rear of the courtroom, "unusual media exposure. So they gave you a charge that you couldn't convict on." Took care of any prosecution sympathizers.

"Now," Heath said, "let's go through the evidence and discuss why this all adds up to not only reasonable doubt but to trumped-up charges."

In the jury box, seated on office chairs with permanent butt indents, twelve men and women listened to Heath Sheldon list the evidence against the defendant Beverly Sloan and systematically destroy it, like so many sheets of paper blown out a window and falling into a trash bin fire.

Each of the jurors had already decided Bev Sloan was innocent. They pretended to debate for a few days so they didn't look like one of those idiotic California juries with its communal head up its collective ass, but they'd already acquitted her. Bev Sloan would walk away a free woman.

Heath smiled sadly at the jury as he finished his closing arguments. "I'm not sure why the prosecution is dead-set on a first-degree murder charge because it doesn't fit any of the possible scenarios for that night. Beverly Sloan didn't *murder* anybody."

Murder, that word scrambled Bev's mind even more than *prison*. She would be labeled a *murderer*.

Murderess, that quaint word, embodied too many ladylike connotations of old-world femininity to define what had happened that night she'd been holding a knife and it had fallen toward Conroy's chest. The media didn't change their vocabulary if a suicide bomber was female, to *suicidess* or *bomberette*.

Murderer.

Leila held onto her stiff-backed notepad of white paper and took notes because she compulsively took notes. She wasn't entirely sure why she wrote *first-degree murder charge includes premeditation*, but it seemed important. Maybe because the Inquisition's conspiracies would be tried in the Hague or Nuremburg someday, if worldwide crimes were tried anymore.

She wrote, *malice aforethought, guilty conscience, conspiracy.*

Maybe pedophilia came in different degrees, if not legally than morally. Say, a sadistic pedophile who warped his victims' minds might be a first-degree pedophile, or a creepy guy in a park might be committing second-degree child attack, but a man who happens to fall in love with a girl just a few years too young to legally give consent, eight years too young, and if they maintained a relationship that wasn't just about sex but were lovers, maybe that would be different, maybe that would be third-degree pedophilia, or maybe they should have a different word for it, like the difference between *murder* and *manslaughter.*

Leila wrote, *evidence of concealing the crime.*

Mary, Lydia, and Laura sat behind Bev and watched the prosecutor lay out her closing argument. Mary cringed when the prosecutor glossed over Conroy's many affairs, citing them all as immaterial and an attempt to smear the victim, and she tried not to show the cringing. Lydia and Laura hadn't been in court when that little snippet Leila had singled out Mary as another of Conroy's conquests. Lydia and Laura still acted friendly and casual, like they didn't know. Bev must not have told them. If Bev had told anyone, condemnation would have wafted through the church's air and Mary would have had to change churches, perhaps to another county considering the familial and social ties that bind Catholic parishes. Mary was beholden to Bev for not ratting her out, and Mary would have bribed a jury member to hang the jury, or bribed them all to find Bev innocent, or threatened their families, if she had known how.

In her closing argument, Georgina recapitulated Conroy Sloan's death. "Beverly Sloan was holding the steak knife when it stabbed Conroy Sloan.

Her fingerprints were on the knife. The steak knife's serrations scraped one of his ribs and then entered his pericardium, the sac in his chest, and stabbed him in the left ventricle of the heart."

Bev braced her palms on the table. When her lungs expanded, nothing filled them.

"Conroy Sloan bled to death inside his own chest until he finally suffocated from the pressure of cardiac tamponade and died of exsanguination," Georgina said. If only there had been more blood in the reconstruction and the pictures of the kitchen floor. Jury convictions directly correlated with blood volume.

Bev's fingernails bit the table. Those words, *cardiac tamponade* and *exsanguination*, those meant that blood had compressed his beating heart and he bled to death inside. Again, medical vocabulary obscured horror. Leaking blood had strangled his heart and lungs until his own blood anaconda-crushed him.

Georgina stared at the jury as she paced in front of them, reading the autopsy details. Several gazed back, nonplussed. She finished her closing with, "Beverly Sloan was so enraged by her husband's infidelity and his abandonment that she killed him that night. She waited to call 9-1-1 for help until he was unconscious. She *murdered* him. She knew what she was doing when she drove a knife into his chest and into his heart and *she murdered him.*"

Bev's head dropped forward onto her folded arms. The fake wood table blurred an inch from her eyes. *Murder.*

The knife had slipped into Conroy's chest, through his white shirt, just to the right of a pearly shirt button. She timed it like she timed the impact of a golf club whipping through a ball. She could have turned her hand aside, *but she hadn't.*

Bev had *murdered* him. *Murder.*

Murderer.

DANTE LEFT COURT EARLY, had a few drinks at the Dublin, and walked into his church. His black shirt sucked the July sun and fattened with heat.

In one arm of the cruciform church, Bev's hourglass silhouette, kneeling at the Marian niche, shifted.

Dante closed the doors behind him. The air conditioner sprayed chilly cross-streams into the church, fighting the sunlight rolling on the roof and lancing through the stained glass windows, changed in color but not muted in intensity. Floating ochre, green, and purple puddled the warm air he walked through toward Bev.

Dante sat on the floor beside her, resting his tired back against the wall. Arthritic soreness had infested his skeleton for months. Finding a comfortable position on the wood floor was wasted time, so he adjusted for the least torturous. "I could hear your confession, if you want."

"I can't." Her Rosary hung in her fingers like a beaded noose, *sans* corpse. Purple and gold squares of light draped her white blouse like handkerchief ghosts. "I can't feel God anymore."

Dante's own heart clenched in pity or jealousy. "God decides what is to be forgiven."

"God can't hear me. I can't hear Them."

"Who is *Them?*"

"Mary, mostly. Well, I've only really *heard* Mary."

"You *hear* voices?" *Oh, no.*

"Only the once. Other than that, I felt God's presence."

"So you're not hearing voices." The back of Dante's head ground against the plaster wall as he tried to stretch a kink out of his neck.

"Not any more."

Visitations, voices, interventions were all metaphors for the great Mystery that was mysterious because it was intangible, not sensory. "Not hearing voices *any more?*"

"I saw the Virgin Mary once." Bev gestured aimlessly with floating fingers toward the towering porcelain figurine in the niche. "In Chicago."

"The Holy Virgin Mary, the Mother of God, was in Chicago." He adjusted his tailbone on the wood floor. "In a tortilla? Or an oil smear on a window?" Maybe the Blessed Virgin Mother of God was hungry for a Chicago hot dog. No, she would've kept kosher.

Bev said, "No, in the Church of St. Sophia. In Her niche."

Dante rubbed his face in exasperation. "A corporeal visitation."

"Well," Bev's smooth forehead and lineless eyes suggested she was discussing lunch, "the statue didn't come to life. It was more like an image moving over the surface of the statue, like ripples on water."

An atypical anti-psychotic was the first drug an American doctor would prescribe. "Have you had other hallucinations?"

"It wasn't a hallucination. I really saw it."

That was the definition of a hallucination, that they *really saw* it. "And what did the Blessed Virgin say?" Crude incredulity laced his words.

"She said that it was all right if I converted to Judaism for Malachi, that She and God wouldn't leave me."

"Malachi, the Israeli." Another man she didn't love. Her denial of continuing symptoms might mean that there had been only the one hallucination. A mere schizophreniform disorder rather than full-blown schizophrenia was possible. "And you never heard voices again."

"No. I could feel the presence of God, but I didn't ever see or hear Her again."

One schizoid episode did not a schizophrenic make. The feeling of an aura, whether sacred or merely ecstatic, could be a manifestation of any of several physical maladies, from epilepsy to migraines. Dostoevsky had ecstatic epileptic auras of such intensity that psychiatrists still refer to them by his name, though Dostoevsky's auras never offered relationship advice.

His tense lower back spiked from sitting on the hard floor. Resting his forearms on his bent knees stretched his twitchy ligaments. "You don't need a personal intervention from God. The Church provides spiritual intervention by priests. And thus, I can hear your confession, and you can feel the presence of God again because you will be forgiven."

"Sometimes," her head swiveled to look at the towering statue of the Virgin, "some sins are so terrible that they can't be forgiven. Some people can't ever repent enough." Her words were slow and measured. "They're going to Hell, a real Hell, forever."

Dante rubbed his eyes until he saw blue neon streaks. "And you?"

She nodded. "It's kind of liberating, in a way."

"Because you think you are going to Hell, so now you can sin all you want?" He held back his hair with both hands, wanting to rip until black fiber filled his palms.

"What a terrible thought." She held her palm out pensively, and cobalt blue light from the windows filled her hand. "I've been worried all my life about attaining Heaven and dreading and avoiding the pains of Hell. Now, when I do something, I do it because it's the right thing and because it pleases God. There isn't a Heaven cookie dangling in front of me and a Hell stick beating me from behind."

Dante's own soul was damned to hellfire in which he had no belief. Such certainty was a dark comfort and too severe for someone as fragile as Bev. "You aren't going to Hell. Catholicism has all the answers. It's one of the benefits of being Catholic."

She hesitated and bit her lower lip. "It doesn't feel right."

"Maybe you need a doctor."

"It's not that." Air flowed through her voice, as if she couldn't find the strength to vibrate her vocal cords. "Maybe I need a priest."

"How is that?" The cast of the sodium-yellow light on the oak floor resembled the deep glow that suffused Vatican windows.

"Maybe," her soft alto voice dropped to nearly *sotto voce*, "maybe I can't take communion because I know it would burn my tongue, and sometimes I can't remember things about the night Conroy died and then other times it feels like I can remember but it's like it happened to someone else, and there's *rage*, this penetrating *rage*, like that first day you were in the confessional. It's been going on for a long time, and it feels like it's building, and it doesn't feel like *me*."

Resistance to communion, blackouts, alienation, alien emotions, these described possession by demons. "Bev, you're not possessed."

"But what if I am?" Her breath rasped and her hand reached up to her mouth. "What if God didn't send you here to save my marriage? What if God sent me an exorcist?"

Such things, the laity worried about. "How long have you suspected this?"

"Months." Her hands crept over her mouth to her warm brown eyes.

"You're in a church. You're praying to the Virgin Mary. You're holding a Rosary. Did you bless yourself from the font when you entered?"

Her hands covered her whole face. "I couldn't bring myself to touch it. I haven't for months." Her voice shrilled. "I would contaminate the font."

"A bishop has to make a finding of possession before an exorcism can be performed."

"But you examined priests who molested children for signs of possession."

"Yes."

"What if the vision of the Virgin Mary was a demon and it was all a lie? What if there's something else *in* me?" Her fingers curled on her white collar, ready to rip.

Her revulsion for her own flesh was reminiscent of his mother's reaction to her cancer. "You aren't possessed. You can say the name of the Blessed Virgin Mary, the Holy Name of Jesus, and God. You obviously have no aversion to the Church, as you are here and pray every day. Have you spoken any unknown languages?"

"No." Her brown hair swept her face and chin. Strands clung to her moist cheeks.

"Displayed feats of unnatural strength?"

"*I killed my husband.*"

"You're cobbling together what you've heard in the court. It's not a real memory."

"There's something *in* me. I can feel it. Please, *do something.*"

The court case was over. The jury was deliberating. This was not a plea for an insanity defense or manipulation by a canny defendant, as might have been the case with a pedophile.

Yet exorcisms should only be attempted by priests free of sin and strong in belief, and neither of those specifications applied to him. Battling demons with one's own soul mired in a state of mortal sin was suicidal. He was also a little inebriated, surely a disadvantage when confronting the Great Diabolical. Exorcisms could continue for hours or days, and Leila was leaving tomorrow. Tonight was his last chance to talk to her.

God, what an ass he was, scheming about an assignation with Leila while Bev feared her body was afflicted by a devil.

Merda. He had driven Bev to adultery and not saved her from her own fury that he had seen on his first day in this terrible church. *If* he was damned, *since* he was damned, nothing could damn him further. The Rite of Exorcism might ease Bev's mind.

It was, in effect, a placebo exorcism.

There was no one else in the church among the empty pews overlaid with jewel-toned polygons of light. "I need to prepare."

Before an exorcism, a priest should confess his sins and receive communion. There were no other priests left to confess to. The Dominicans had taken them all. Dante could make a confession directly to God and allow the Holy Spirit into his shredded soul.

"Pray," he told Bev, "to the Virgin Mary for strength and guidance."

Bev swiveled on her knees to face the alabaster statue robed in blue and gold stars.

Dante's back and legs complained as he stood and approached the altar. Gold light from the window behind the towering, carved crucifix slanted past him and onto the floor. The exorcism rite proscribed that a crucifix should be present. Dante wore a silver crucifix, of course, but the five-meter colossus of the suffering, dying Christ also filled the role. The Christ's wooden foot was cool in the summer evening light, even though the church was warm.

He prayed, "Come Holy Spirit into my soul. Enlighten me that I may know the sins I ought to confess and grant me Your grace to confess them fully, humbly, with a contrite heart." Dante's chest seized up. Once, even a few months ago, these words meant something to him, back when he'd believed in good as well as evil. If he was to battle demons, *since* he was to battle demons, he needed comfort and grace.

The putative Holy Spirit had been writhing in his soul for months. "Bless me, Lord, for I have sinned. I have had sexual relations with a woman, a vulnerable woman, violating my Holy Orders and her marriage vows. It was my fault. I didn't stop myself, and I hurt her. Please forgive these sins, and all the myriad other ones, wrath against Conroy Sloan, lust for Leila Faris and Bev Sloan, pride when I was so wrong, and envy for Conroy Sloan's family life and Leila's intellectual freedom. Grant me forgiveness so I can say the rite for her, even though she isn't possessed. She's an alcoholic, and confused, and hurt, but not possessed."

The setting sunlight dimmed on the suffering, dying Christ.

The act of contrition rolled from his mouth as facilely as the rest, "and avoid the near occasion of sin, Amen." He pushed his creaking body up from its knees.

In his shadowy library, his surplice and purple stole were in the desk drawer, folded neatly as if for long storage. The stole warmed on his neck. He locked the church doors and walked back to the altar rail. His fingertips dragged on the altar as he passed. The silk caught the crenellations of his fingerprints. "Come over to the altar."

Bev walked to the altar rail and kneeled as if to receive communion.

"Inside the rail, with me."

Her eyes darted sideways and she bit her lip. "All right."

"Lay your hands on the altar." What he still thought of as his side, the priest's side of the altar oversaw the empty pews that furrowed the church. Bev stood on the other side, her back to the church. He flattened his palms on the cool white altar cloth embroidered with itchy gold crosses and blue silk stars. Bev did the same.

This dispelled any lingering superstitions that a demon might reside in Bev's body. Laying one's hands on a consecrated altar encasing the relic of a saint would scald a demon. He'd seen it happen. This was, indeed, a placebo exorcism. "Respond as during the Mass."

Bev nodded.

"Kyrie eleison."

Her brown eyes were solemn. "Kyrie eleison."

Familiarity with the exorcism rite soothed Dante like Sunday Mass invigorates the faithful. Most priests commune with the Divine and seek Grace. Dante was a dark mystic who battled the Diabolical, and thus knew that somewhere, somehow, Light from True Light must exist as the absence of the Darkness.

After the calls to God and the responses asking for mercy, Dante said, "Now we say the Litany of the Saints." She nodded, eyes wide. "Holy Mother of God," Dante said.

"Pray for us."

And so on through the next sixty-some invocations, Dante recalled each saint, and Bev asked for their prayers. The empty church filled with their whispers like spiderwebs unreeling across the pews and kneelers, up to the oiled beams. The repetitive chants lulled him, and the weight of the whiskey tilted his body. Pressing the altar with his forearms steadied him.

Across the stone altar, her cold hands wrapped his fingers. The fading light lit the pale part in her hair. "From all evil," Dante said.

Together, they said, "Deliver us, O Lord."

"From all sin," he continued.

"Deliver us, O Lord."

"From the snares of the Devil."

Bev choked and she turned her head, swallowing, when Dante said, "Deliver us, O Lord. Bev, are you all right?" Her pianist-strong fingers tightened. Pink nail tips poked the skin on the backs of his hands. "Bev? What is it?"

Her head jerked. "Release me," she growled. Her hoarse, cramped voice spun in the waste space above them. Her hands sprung off the altar as if away from fire but his fingers tangled with hers.

Dante held on. Bev struggled against his hands. Battle lust thrummed in his chest. The pinky knuckle on his left hand crackled. "From anger, hatred, and all ill will, deliver us, O Lord."

"Let me go!" That smoky voice rasped from Bev's body. Her tense fingers jerked in his hands.

"Demon or devil, what is your name?" Discovering the diabolical's name is standard exorcism protocol. Encouraging a patient to communicate with auditory hallucinations was not standard psychiatric practice. "Devil or demon, I command you to tell me your name!"

Bev yanked her hands. "Let me go!" Her voice sounded like thirty years of tobacco strata coated her throat. Bev jerked and pulled Dante against the silk-draped altar between them and slapped the air from his whiskey-queasy stomach. His stomach scraped stone.

Dante called, "From lightning and tempest, deliver us, O Lord."

Bev shrilled a cackle. Dante grabbed her wrists. She dragged him against the altar again.

"From plague, famine, and war, deliver us, O Lord. From everlasting death, deliver us, O Lord."

Bev shrieked, "No!"

"Devil or demon, what is your name?"

Bev flung herself sideways but was tethered by Dante's hands. She grated out, *"Murderer."*

He leaned toward her, hunting. "Is that your name, *Murderer?*"

"*Murderer.*"

The trial's graphic, repetitive descriptions of Conroy's death had been too much. She'd internalized the accusations. Dante held her wrists. Her trim hands double-locked over his arms.

Her fingernails spiked his forearms. The struggle, even with an imaginary demon, thrilled him.

Dante edited the Holy Rite of Exorcism. His voice projected over the pews. "I command you, unclean spirit, 'Murderer' or whoever you are, along with all your minions now attacking this servant of God, by the mysteries of the incarnation, passion, resurrection, and ascension of our Lord Jesus Christ, by the descent of the Holy Spirit, by the coming of our Lord for judgment, I command you to obey me to the letter, I who am a minister of God despite my unworthiness."

Bev's head lolled backward and she panted. Her hands trembled but she didn't struggle.

He untangled her fingers from around one of his arms, snared both her wrists with one hand, and reached across the altar to brace himself against her forehead. "They shall lay their hands upon the sick and all will be well with them. May Jesus, Son of Mary, Lord and Savior of the world, through the merits and intercession of His holy apostles Peter and Paul and all His saints, show you favor and mercy. Amen."

"Amen," Bev panted in her normal voice. The muscles of her skull shifted under her hair and his hands.

Dante dipped his fingers in the holy water font beside the altar. "May the blessing of Almighty God," he touched her forehead with damp fingers, "Father," her sternum, "Son," her left shoulder, "and Holy Spirit," right shoulder, "come upon you and remain with you forever."

"Amen," they said.

Dante shouted to the oak domed ceiling far above them. "Almighty Lord, Word of God the Father, Jesus Christ, God and Lord of all creation;

who gave to your holy apostles the power to trample underfoot serpents and scorpions; who along with the other mandates to work miracles was pleased to grant them the authority to say: 'Depart, you devils!' and by whose might Satan was made to fall from heaven like lightning; I humbly call on your holy name in fear and trembling, asking that you grant me, your unworthy servant, pardon for all my sins, steadfast faith, and the power—supported by your mighty arm—to confront with confidence and resolution this cruel demon." Energy grabbed his chest and rattled him. "I ask this through You, Jesus Christ, our Lord and God, who are coming to judge both the living and the dead and the world by fire."

"Amen," Bev said and wiped her damp cheek on her shoulder.

Dante said, "I cast you out, unclean spirit, along with every Satanic power of the Enemy, every spectre from Hell, and all your fell companions; in the name of our Lord Jesus Christ." He genuflected and traced a cross on Bev's grief-wrinkled forehead. "Begone and stay far from this creature of God." Genuflected again. "For it is He who commands you, He who flung you headlong from the heights of Heaven into the depths of Hell. It is He who commands you, He who once stilled the sea and the wind and the storm."

He touched Bev's forehead again. She shook her head as if trying to escape his damp palm and fingers. "Be still, I command thee." Dante pressed her head more firmly. She stilled.

Holding Bev's head, Dante called into the air and glimmering wood above them, "Hearken, therefore, and tremble in fear, Satan, you enemy of the faith, you foe of the human race, you begetter of death, you robber of life, you corrupter of justice, you root of all evil and vice; seducer of men, betrayer of the nations, instigator of envy, font of avarice, fomentor of discord, author of pain and sorrow."

Bev struggled delicately again. Dante restrained her hands.

"Begone, now! Begone, seducer! You might delude man, but God you cannot mock. It is He who casts you out, from whose sight nothing is hidden. It is He who repels you, to whose might all things are subject. It is He who expels you, He who has prepared everlasting hellfire for you and your angels, from whose mouth shall come a sharp sword, who is coming to judge the living and the dead and the world by fire."

"Amen."

"Almighty God, we beg you to keep the evil spirit from further molesting this servant of yours, and to keep him far away, never to return. At your command, O Lord, may the goodness and peace of our Lord Jesus Christ, our Redeemer, take possession of this woman. May we no longer fear any evil since the Lord is with us; who lives and reigns with you, in the unity of the Holy Spirit, God, forever and ever."

Bev said, "Amen," with him. He let go of her hot hands so she could genuflect and wipe the tears off her face. Her palm smudged with pink, black, and gold makeup, and she rested it upward on the white altar cloth, so she would not stain it.

Dante bent to stretch his back, tight from fighting her over the altar. Sweat trickled in his hair. This farce might have exorcised a splinter of a multiple personality generated from her mother's abuse, or it might have indulged her mental illness and imbued it with religious trappings.

"There was something." Bev looked at her hands, spread-eagle on the altar cloth.

There was nothing to do but concede the validity of the rite to maintain its placebo effect. "It appears there was something, but it's gone now."

"How do you know it's gone?" One cheek was pale without its rouge.

"My exorcisms always work." He smiled gently. "It's the one thing I'm good at. Usually, the afflicted takes communion at this point."

She shook her head. A strand of her gold rust hair caught on her wet eyelashes. "I can't."

"If the demon is gone, you can."

"*Murderer.* The demon was named *Murderer.* But I can't take communion. I killed him."

"This suggests that you were not in control. You can confess."

"I don't feel enlightened to unburden my soul. It wouldn't be a real confession."

His facile opinions about confessional validity had come back to haunt him. The laity was too impressionable. Bev was too fragile. "I should make that determination."

"It's all right, you know, that I can't confess, that I can't take communion."

"You can't mean that."

"It's all right. I couldn't really say I had *faith* before, because I'd *seen* the Virgin Mary and I'd *felt* God. I had proof. If I doubted, I prayed or confessed, and God returned, and I had proof. But now, I can't feel that. I have to have faith."

Dante was so empty of soul that his ears whistled through the air as he shook his head. "You can be reconciled with God."

Bev shook her head again. Her hair shimmied over her shoulders in the darkening church. "Not me."

"You don't know that," he said.

"I'm sure. At least, now, I know. Not knowing was worse. Praying and hoping and not knowing and feeling nothing and dying inside and praying again, every time, was worse. Now I know there was a demon, and now it's gone, but the sin is still there. I can feel it."

In the wide, empty church, slants of gem-colored light, oranged by the last of the setting sun, slashed the air.

"Yet you pray so much." He hadn't meant to say it. Watching her pray felt like an alcoholic watching someone savor a smoky, single malt scotch.

"Mostly the Rosary. I like the Rosary, the Hail Marys, the Our Fathers. *Thy* will be done. It reminds me that it is God's will that is important. Conroy was so sarcastic about religion, called it the opium of the masses and that thing about man not being free until the last king was strangled with the entrails of the last priest."

"Marx and Voltaire." Sloan had stolen that quote, like he'd stolen everything in his life. Leila had used the Marx quote. Was the Voltaire from her, too? Whiskey rose in Dante's chest and flushed into his blood.

Light fell from the windows and cast confused rectangles of color, like someone had spilled caskets of bejeweled, metallic Vatican treasure on the rows of pews. He pulled the stole off his shoulders. The cloth abraded the scruff of his neck.

She said, "I like the Lord's Prayer. *Thy will be done.* My will doesn't matter." She smiled. Her silk skin rose on her cheekbones, pulling the slight softness from her jaw.

Dante's skeleton juggled until he was standing. A priest should find comfort in the Church to withstand the pain of being alone in a world of women. A priest should have faith like Bev's that asked for God's will to be done and filled loneliness and absence. A priest, when threatened by guns, should commend his soul to God and, when confronted by the possibility of miraculous intervention or demonic possession, should not diagnose pathology.

"I'll see you on Sunday," he said.

"I'll be here just a little while longer." She walked past the altar rail, over to the blue-robed mannequin with open arms.

Dante walked out of the church. Twilight covered the parking lot and the street beyond that led downtown to the Dublin.

LEILA WAS READING as she lay on a sleeping bag draped over an air bed and absently ruffling Meth's velvet ears while he napped on a blanket.

The printer on the floor cabled to her laptop computer scraped across the paper, printing the final draft of her thesis. A file folder under the laptop held the thesis signature pages with each of the five required signatures in thick, black ink. The new dean of the medical school had signed on Conroy's line, *Dr. Linus Petering, M.D., for Dr. Conroy Sloan, M.D.*

Knocking on the door punctuated the printer's mechanical scratching. Irritated, she pushed herself off the bed and meandered through her bare apartment.

The peephole conferred acromegaly to the priest's features, jutting his jaw, overhanging his brow ridges, and flattening his nose like a pugilist. She'd thrown him out, tied him up and molested him, and threatened him with a gun. He was insane to show up again.

Leila opened her door to the crazy priest.

Without the peephole's fisheye lens, his features resumed their angelic aspects. His empty black collar flopped open two buttons, exposing tan skin and chest fuzz below his collarbones. The top black button dangled from a black thread.

"Why are you here, at midnight, again?"

Blood vessels were a riot of ivy in the whites of his eyes, swollen by alcohol or smoke or emotion. "Can we discuss a matter?" His desolate voice was harsh and his head turned, staring down the hallway, not meeting her eyes.

Leila opened the door wider. "The couch is already gone."

Dante walked past her into her spartan apartment, redolent with fresh paint and wood floor cleaning solution. The wall behind her didn't yield as she flattened herself to avoid touching him. The Tiffany chandelier he'd admired was gone. A rudimentary fixture forged to resemble shaded candles hung in her empty dining area and cast blocks of shadow up her walls and ceiling. The conservators had rolled up the tapestries and boxed the paintings and crated the plaster facades, leaving her white walls dull. He touched the chalky paint and said, "I guess now someone would hear me."

"I'm sorry," not enough air filled her lungs, "for threatening you."

Dante waved his fingers in the air as if dispersing cigarette smoke.

She continued, "I was going to write you a letter to explain, but that's such a cowardly way to do it. I was going to call, but whenever I picked up the phone, I couldn't think straight."

"Yes," Dante said and his black eyes widened. "I can't think straight." He pulled a pillow off her air bed to sit on the floor. He patted the bed beside him to indicate she should sit.

It was less threatening for him to sit beside the bed, not to try to sit on it with her. She sat on the middle of the bed. Its ends ballooned. Meth was asleep, not guarding her like a proper watchdog. She prodded him with her bare toe. He snorted and flopped his head on his paws.

The printer hissed and cobra-spat pages of text.

"How could you love him?" Dante rubbed his fingers into his temples. "He's a monster, a pedophile."

"He was my first lover." Two blunt ribs curved in and prodded her heart.

Dante lowered his hand near Meth's nose, offering. The dog sniffed, whuffed, and closed his eyes. "He *raped* you. He was brutal."

Her fingers trailed over the nylon sleeping bag on her bed. "Dante, stop."

"It's brainwashing, like Stockholm Syndrome. I've seen it before. He told you that he loved you. He told you that he was in love with you, again and again."

It couldn't be brainwashing because she had felt his heart beating under her palm when he'd pressed her hand against his bare chest after they'd made love for the first time and told her that she was the only woman he'd ever loved. Her throat swelled as if she had an anaphylactic allergy to the terrible thought. "*It's complicated.*"

"You were ten years old," Dante said. He touched the floor as if to push himself up. "You probably hadn't yet learned long division. You ran away at the end of the summers to avoid going back to him."

Dante didn't understand and she didn't think she could make him understand. "But sometimes I missed him. Sometimes I called him during the summers to talk to him, but I don't want to see him now. I'm hiding. He doesn't know where I am. He showed up in California a few years ago, before I moved here. Meth cornered him." She ruffled the sleeping dog's ears. He declined to wake but grunted. "You should have seen Meth when he was young. He was magnificent." He was grayer around the muzzle than last week, it seemed.

"But how could you *love* him?"

"I just do." Her pulse patted her wrists. The priest was lounging on her pillow like triumphant Caesar. "Do they already have him?"

"No." The priest looked down and away from her, to the gold fringe on the pillow, hiding something, lying to her.

They were going to take Sean anyway. If he didn't go with them, they were going to throw him in the back of a van and take him away. She couldn't undo it. She couldn't stop it. The vibrations in her heart slowed, but her fingers trembled. "And they aren't going to, right? I sent that letter."

"Correct." Still looking away. Lying again.

"Then why are you here *again?*" She grabbed a pillow off the end of the bed and stuffed it against her abdomen, something to curl around.

The priest leaned back on his hands, his long legs thrust out and crossed at the ankles like an ad for Versace Clerical Wear for the fashionable Vatican wonk. "I just wanted to talk to you."

The printer slid a mostly blank sheet of paper into its tray and started chewing out a new chapter. "It's past midnight, and I have to deposit my thesis tomorrow before I leave for New York, Father."

"Not 'Father.' I'm leaving the priesthood."

"Come on." Her lungs simpered, wanting nicotine. She shook out a cigarette and lit it.

He crossed his ankles the other way. "The only time I feel anything is during an exorcism. I believe in the Devil more than I believe in God. I've seen more evidence for the Great Diabolical than of any Supreme Goodness. A priest should not be excited by battling the unholy. My ordination and Holy Orders will be nullified."

"You're getting an annulment from God."

He scratched a thick eyebrow. "So to speak. 'Laicized' is the term."

"Sorry." Sarcasm was uncalled for with this man who had not contacted the police when she'd threatened him with a gun or when she'd assaulted him, who had offered a friendly ear because he was the only person alive who knew about Sean, and who had wrapped his body around hers that one perfect night that still defied definition in her head.

He smiled. "No one else would joke about my leaving the priesthood. I love your sense of humor."

"God, you like my bitter sense of humor?" Unease wafted around her head. His vocabulary was disconcerting.

His legs bent, and he rested his elbows on his knees as if idly tossing twigs into a campfire. His inhalation was too deep for casual conversation. "It's one of the things I love most about you."

The drifting uneasiness grabbed her scalp and dove under her skin, racing toward her extremities and compacting her flesh. "Stop."

"Leila." He clasped his hands, imploring or praying, but stared at the floor.

"You should go." Her jaw clenched. Her chest followed suit.

"Leila." He touched the bed beside her leg.

Such a small gesture wouldn't have been threatening to someone who didn't have extraordinary intimacy issues and who wanted to run like hell at the sight of his black priest's clothes and blunt, empty Roman collar, open like he'd ripped out the plastic insert. "Don't say anything else."

"Leila, I love you."

"*You don't.*"

"I can talk to you. You understand when I talk about science and religion. I could allude to Voltaire and Watson and Crick in the same breath, and you would understand."

She tried to joke to turn the conversation away from its black-ice skid. "What would that be, modeling the best of all possible, possible replication mechanisms for *Candida albicans*? Or that man won't be free until the last king is strangled with the double helix, B-form DNA of the last priest?"

His lips opened. "That's your phrase. I knew it must be."

"It's Voltaire." She smoked the cigarette, and warmth from the smoke opened her lungs.

"It doesn't matter." He turned his head aside and seemed to be talking to himself. "It doesn't matter."

"What doesn't matter?"

"Did you love Conroy Sloan?"

"No." She puffed the cigarette. Calm, sweet smoke drained into her arms, cooling her. "It was just ass. We were going to break it off when I graduated."

The priest's long fingers floated toward her elbow. "Don't move to New York. Stay with me, here."

Slamming her hands over her ears would block out such vile sentiments, but her body wouldn't move. If he touched her, if he lunged for her, the gun was in the laundry basket behind her, under the potted plants and quart cans of touch-up paint. The hollow-point semi-wadcutter rounds would blow his guts through his back. If the bullets missed, if he still came at her, her hands were strong enough to twist his neck until his spine broke between the C1 and C2 vertebrae. If all else failed, there was a steak knife in the kitchen sink. "You need to leave, now."

"Leila?" He reached out again.

Her arm recoiled and elbowed her own ribs. "Don't touch me."

"When I'm finished with the counseling here, we could go to Roma. The university would give you a professorship. You'd have your own lab, could research whatever you want."

"You're drunk." Leaning back, her hand hovered near the laundry basket. "You're drunk again."

"I have had a few drinks, but I've thought about this lately, often. Leila," he set a knee on the floor and moved over it until he was kneeling in front of her. "Would you marry me?"

She scrambled backward off the air bed and kicked the velvet-napped balloon at him. "I can't. I won't. You're a priest!"

He fended off the airbed and shunted it aside. Meth woke and grunted. Dante said, "I wouldn't be a priest, just another professor. We could collaborate or not."

"No." She spider-crawled backward. The laundry basket bumped her back and plant leaves itched her neck. "No."

"I want a family to belong to, to belong to you." ·

The words expelled as if she'd been punched in the chest. "*You're a priest.*"

"I'm not. Being in America, alone, made me realize how lonely I was as a priest. I'm leaving the priesthood."

"You'll *always* be a priest." In the laundry basket among the plants, her hands found waxy leaves and gritty soil ground under her fingernails. "*Ontologically changed*, that's what you said and you *meant it.*"

"It's James Joyce, not what I think."

"Of course it's what you think." The rough pots scraped her searching hand as she delved farther into the basket, but the towel-wrapped gun eluded her. "It's what all of you believe."

He turned his hands palms up and sat back, gazing at his hands as if inspecting for stigmata. "But I don't *believe.*"

"Pray to God to help you in your unbelief."

Leila's hand was wedged between the plants, amidst the laundry and paint cans, searching for that damned gun that slithered away every time she got a pinky on it.

IT WAS MIDNIGHT, and the presses slammed headlines onto the morning paper rushing underneath the crashing template:

What We Talk About When We Talk About Murder
By: Kirin Oberoi, Syndicated Columnist

After a trial fraught with shockers, the jury is deciding the fate of Beverly Maria Sloan, who allegedly stabbed her husband, Dr. Conroy Robert Sloan, last Valentine's Day. A verdict of not guilty is anticipated, considering the complete breakdown of the prosecution's case.

The sordid case was rife with accusations of the victim's adultery and dueling medical experts, but something about this trial just doesn't add up to a nice, tidy sum. I watched this trial every day, read every analysis, watched LawTV, and I don't have the answers, either. The questions outnumber answers.

I do know this: truth and justice are different entities. The court system will roll through the lives of everyone in this trial, but the point of the trial was not to find the truth. The jury didn't hear the truth; they only heard what the justice system determined to be relevant facts. There was more to this trial than the jury heard.

Here are some of the truths that the jury did not hear:

Conroy Sloan was conducting unauthorized, reckless experiments with rabies virus in his lab. One of his graduate students died. If Sloan were not dead, he would undoubtedly be on trial for murder. He may have been suicidal because he had killed his student and should go to prison for it. In addition, his rabies test was equivocal. If he knew he was infected, he may have killed himself to avoid that painful death.

In the hospital and on heavy narcotics, Beverly Sloan ensured that her husband had received Last Rites before he died, as if she knew he had committed mortal sins and his soul was in danger of damnation. Though she had undergone surgery, she did not ask for Last Rites.

Dr. Leila Sage Faris, whose testimony concerning Dr. Sloan's threatened suicide proved disastrous for the prosecution, published Sloan's rabies virus results and her own data about the HIV virus. Her data suggests that near-death experiences, those friendly tunnels and lights that people attribute to God and Heaven, can be changed or eliminated by the presence of viruses in the brain. HIV brings on vibrant hallucinations in the wake of dying neurons. Rabies virus suppresses such visions. Her conclusions suggest that all religious experiences and thus deities are artifacts of neurology. Her research is being denounced from pulpits as an affront to God. Her previous mentor might not have published his own data in this manner. She has accepted a prestigious fellowship at Colombia University.

If near-death experiences are artifacts of neurology, one wonders what Conroy Sloan saw as he lay dying on that kitchen floor with the knife with his wife's fingerprints in his chest, held by Dr. Faris, his mistress, and Monsignor Dante Petrocchi-Bianchi praying for his soul.

DANTE RAISED his head from his hands. His eyeballs stung where his palms had pressed them. If Holy Orders hadn't branded him, then his soul must be saved for other things, like love. "Leila, I love you. I want to marry you."

"How can you say that?" She paced in the wide, empty apartment behind the air bed and the laundry basket filled with ivy-trailing, potted plants. Her sock-clad footsteps pattered like mouse feet. "Marriage is stupid. I thought that was the *one* thing the Catholic Church understood, why they demand a celibate priesthood."

"Leila, sit down. Let me explain."

"You were looking for some answer that screwing every woman in Rome wasn't satisfying in you. You took Holy Orders and dedicated your life to the Church. I'm not your answer. I'm not anyone's answer."

A priest should not be an empty shell shuffling about in black cloth.

"I'm renouncing it."

"You can't. Life is about desire and pursuit, Dante. It's not about *having*. Marriage is *owning* someone, *owning* as much as a dog piddling on a fencepost. *Marriage* may have been a good deal in the past, when childbearing was dangerous, when a man was willing to lay down all his earnings to *own* a woman who would risk her life so he could reproduce his genes. Marriage may have been best back then because when a woman died giving birth, the man would assume the grub was his and raise it. But it was all just genes. It was all reproduction and bargaining for the chance to replicate DNA."

She dodged back and forth, smoking, jumping toward the plants packed in the laundry basket, hesitating then drifting away but heading right back. "But it doesn't have to be like *that* anymore. It's stupid, wearing matching rings so the world knows you're reproducing together and hoping the little gold talismans repel other sperm donors. Keeping women locked up in harems was a better reproductive strategy."

Her cigarettes and lighter lay on the sleeping bag, so close, and his cells hadn't eaten nicotine for hours. He lit one, holding it the American way between his thumb and two fingers.

She said, "But the Church *understood* that some things are bigger than one person, bigger than reproduction, bigger than your DNA. If you believe in God, then God is one of them. Making the world better is one of them. Understanding mystery, or the Mystery, is one of them. If you harness yourself to a person, you give in to mere reproduction and you can't see beyond that. Celibacy allows you to devote yourself. Don't you see that?"

Dante flicked ash in the metal ashtray. "I would have thought you would be the last person to defend a celibate clergy."

"Celibate means *unmarried*. They're stupid to demand *chastity*, too. The problem is that you let in people who want to be seen as priests, not people who want to be a part of something bigger than themselves." She stood behind the laundry basket, smoking.

His body was dying for her bare skin. Sucking smoke and filthy air from the cigarette mollified his flesh for the moment. "I can't be a priest. I have no faith."

"I'm sorry about that, but I'm not your answer."

"You talk about desire. I want you."

She stepped back and crossed her arms over her red shirt. Her hand that held her cigarette popped out of her knotted limbs, and the smoke climbed past her shoulder and black hair and long, silver earring. "You can't have me."

"Because I'm a priest."

"No, that's why *you* shouldn't want *me*." She picked an ashtray out of the laundry basket and stubbed out her short cigarette. "I'm not that kind of girl, Dante. I'm not the kind you love." Her brown eyes were wide and moist, almost tearful, but no remorse blunted her stare. "Oh, I screw around. Casual fucking is fine, but when men love me, it destroys them. Look what happened to Conroy. Look what happened to Sean. If I latch onto you, you're finished. I'm a walking apoptosis ligand."

"Leila, don't say that."

"It's the best metaphor out there. I must be cardiac tissue specific."

Dante's heart seized as this girl described herself as an inducer of orderly, programmed death of the heart. His cigarette left a long smear of black chalk ash in the ashtray as he stubbed it out. "Who told you this?"

"Nobody had to tell me. In 'Rappaccini's Daughter,' Hawthorne, the girl was permeated with poison because her botanist father had fed it to her since she was a baby, like a Monarch butterfly that eats digitalis and becomes poisonous so birds won't eat it, and she killed people she kissed. The first time I read that, when I was twelve, I wanted to be her, and now I am. I destroy men, every man I get close to."

Twelve years old, after two years of molestation, she had wanted to be poison so she could kill her tormenter, and then she endured several more years of abuse. Intervening years cemented those terrible lessons. That pedophile priest, Sean, had hurt her so much, so very much. *The memory is, as it were, the belly of the soul*, St. Augustine had said, an agnostic comment. With those searing memories, Sean had immolated Leila's soul. If Leila believed that she couldn't love, then it was impossible for Dante to reach her. Damn that man.

Damn him.

Dante's damnations filled with weight as though oil poured into them. The other children, John, Luke, Valerie, Sarah, Zach, and the others, were as spiritually mauled and mangled as she was. Nicolai and Sam and Sean had done this to them. *Damn them all.*

His hands pressed his eyes. Smoke lingering in the air circulated with his breath. There were more pedophiles out there. Even now, they hid within the Church, handing communion to unsuspecting parents while they eyed their children, waiting. Dante had catalogued their predations.

Maybe a girl had few friends and wanted someone to talk to. The priest understood isolation too well, so they felt less lonely around each other, and it seemed only natural to talk about their feelings and longings, and then they touched each other, and he stuck his fingers inside her.

Maybe a boy didn't want to smoke or do steroids like the other kids on the team, the priest understood self-discipline around one's peers, and they talked about how drugs were bad for their bodies, but wrestling and tickling were perfectly fine, and that led to grabbing and rubbing.

A girl didn't want to go home because her parents fought all the time, and the priest listened, and then he hugged her, and then he kissed her, and it seemed like a movie when he took her in his arms, but then it hurt.

Or maybe the priest took a boy to see an R-rated movie that everyone else was seeing though his parents deemed it too sexy, and they went back to the rectory afterward and watched even sexier movies, and then they tried a few things from the porn.

Or a girl wanted to try beer, and the priest taught her what a depth charge is, and then he raped her while she was drunk.

Or a boy wanted to talk about what he needed to do to get on the school soccer team. Fellatio for second string. Anal if he wanted to be a starter.

Damn him.

Beyond his fingers that covered his face, something rustled.

The pedophiles would be ripped out and thrown into the pits of hell, if Dante had the stomach for it. He could avenge Leila, and Luke and John and Valerie, and the rest. He could use the savage resolve of the Church.

Damn that priest who had ripped out Leila's soul and had convinced this beautiful, beautiful girl that she was poison and that she couldn't love, that she killed with love. The soul is the source of love, and memory is the belly of the soul. Damn him and all the others like him.

Damn him. Damning rose out of Dante's stomach and swirled in his chest. The words ceased to be a curse and became an imperative.

If Dante were a priest, *since* Dante was a priest, he could *damn* people. If he became a Vatican politician, took control of the CDF, held the reins of the Inquisition, he could change things. He could make sure that not one of them ever hurt a child again.

His hands slid down his cheeks. Leila was right. For life to have meaning, you must serve something bigger than yourself. Dante could parcel out logical, measured revenge.

She watched him from beyond the laundry basket of foliage.

"I have to go back." He stood.

Leila stood behind the basket, hands on her hips, and squinted. "What?"

She might not understand why, or she might think he was the worst of them. He was contemplating sending them to Hell, becoming Leila's avenger and Bev's demon. "You're right. I'm still one of them. I think like them."

He took a business card out of his wallet and tossed it on her navy blue sleeping bag. The card tumbled through the air and landed carelessly, like a whore's payment. Handing it to her would have been a better gesture.

The white card had landed face-up with the keys and tiara of St. Peter in the top left hand corner. His full name and titles scribbled a black line of minute type in the center. His affiliations were smaller, below his name. "You've entered dangerous territory, religion and science. You might need to discuss something, or an opinion, or protection."

Her hand flopped at her side, indicating everything. "I don't think so."

"Nevertheless, if you want to talk about anything, about science, about Sean, if you need a priest, call."

Her chin notched down. "So you aren't leaving the Church."

"No."

"Good," she said and gazed down at her foot or the floor. Her voice was flat with suppression. There must be a thousand things she wanted to scream at him.

The printer ground out a last page—*light will be thrown upon the origins of religion*—reset itself with a firm clack, and began printing the bibliography.

Darwin, at the end of *The Origin of Species*, had written a similar line about light being thrown upon the origins of man, and Watson and Crick in their seminal DNA paper had referred to that by saying that light would be thrown upon the replication mechanism of DNA. Such lovely allusions floated through her.

"I should go," he said. The door behind him was too close. Which was appropriate for a spurned lover: a kiss, a handshake, a wave, or merely turning and walking out?

"Yeah." She set her burning cigarette in the ashtray and walked around the basket of plants.

Her slight form led him through the smooth, smoky air toward the door. She was leaving tomorrow for New York, and the hurt children here needed counseling, and then he would return to Roma. The door gaped open like a portal to the rest of the world.

A kiss from her would fortify him against his long, cold life ahead. Her body in his arms and his bed seemed like wine and oxygen, but she wasn't the type of woman to be *owned*. She was a more dedicated, celibate priest than he was.

Forcing a kiss would enrage her and she'd slam him against the wall and throw him out the door and burn his card and phone numbers in her metal ashtray. There was no doubt she could inflict physical damage. Conroy's dead, oiled body had borne livid bruises. She'd wrenched Dante's own arm and jabbed pressure points when he'd provoked her. And she had to keep that card. There had to be a chance, however slight, to speak to her again.

Despicable thoughts wormed in his mind. She'd softened in Dante's arms that night in her bed. Balancing gentleness with a hint of anger, a suggestion of *angry was worse*, might manipulate her.

Dante was truly damned if he did that.

At the door, Leila unlocked the several clattering, clicking mechanisms and held her hand between their chests primly for a handshake. "Good-bye, then, Father."

"Just Dante." His hand slid past her fingers, and their palms touched.

An odd softness suffused her voice and her chin tipped up. "Just Dante."

Dante's joints locked like an engine raced without oil. That tip-up was an invitation to press her back against the blank foyer wall and show her that he could do things for her and to her. His head inclined left.

Yet she might be testing his protestation about remaining a priest. If he ducked his head and grabbed her body, she would toss his phone numbers away with the little bits of moving trash in the corners of her sparse apartment, and he would never hear from her again. No one would ever understand his jokes and his science and the world.

But remaining a priest was impossible when his body locked in rigor mortis at the sight of her slim neck arching the slightest bit. Celibacy and chastity were impossible around her.

She moved one foot toward him, an extension with her toe, a balletic tendu. The option of passivity presented itself, of allowing her to come to him, yet this didn't appeal to him in the same way as did crushing her lithe body between his flesh and the wall.

She leaned on the toe and moved closer to his body, rising toward his face. Trembling started in his left leg and crawled up his groin, tightening his skin.

But what of Leila? A few minutes ago, she'd fallen backward off her sleeping bag trying to get away when he'd stretched a few fingers toward her. She'd paced and kept most of the apartment and the laundry basket and airbed as impediments between them. Why on earth would she close her espresso eyes as her face leveled with his? Perhaps she was trying to overcome her aversion to priests. Desensitization therapy.

How altruistic of him to help her.

He was a cad, *un donnaiolo*.

Her hand slipped from his and she touched his shoulder.

Maybe she was testing his resolve.

Maybe it was one last kiss goodbye.

So complicated.

Her lips touched his, and she kissed him slowly. All those nights in Roma, if he had felt like this with a woman, so quiet inside, like he would never be lonely again, he would never have become a priest. His arm slipped around her waist just to steady her, not to control her, and he held the kiss a moment.

He let go with his lips and leaned back.

Her gaze was steady. Her large brown eyes hadn't become drunk with lust nor misty with emotion. She searched for something in his eyes.

His moment of quietus was the sigh of retreating wind before a tornado rips through a house.

His body roared. He whirled with her, slammed the door shut with one hand, pinned her to the wall and kissed her hard, as hard as he could without hurting her. She held him around the neck and lifted herself up, climbing, and her legs clasped around his waist. He buried his face in her neck, perfume and brimstone smoke. Her skin under his mouth was tight, and her black hair swished beside his eyes.

He pushed her hair back from her neck and ears, and his hand came away wet.

He looked at his damp hand and her face. Tears rolled out of her shut eyes, but she didn't gasp, and she didn't tremble.

She touched his neck where he'd torn off the white collar, and her fingers crawled back.

She was *submitting* to him. Even though she had made the first move, it was a feint to draw his inevitable attack and seek some semblance of control. She didn't love him.

He couldn't do this to her again.

"Call me." Hormones and blood thickened his voice and he steadied her on her feet before he released her waist. "If you want to talk, call me. Call me anytime."

He opened the door and stepped into the white hallway.

The door shut behind him, and a thunk sounded through the door, like a body falling against it or a fist driven at the wood.

The empty hall stretched away from him in both directions.

THE EMAIL was distributed from New Hamilton at two in the morning to computers in the Vatican, where it was dawn, and it contained the same message, Rosetta-like, in English, Italian, Spanish, and Latin. The computer tech, a novice from Korea, watched the identical email appear in the email boxes of all the users in the server, including V01, the head honcho, and wondered if it was spam or a virus. He scanned it with anti-virus software, but it didn't read like a malicious program so he let everyone find it the next morning, and the uproar started.

To my Brothers in Christ:

The Enemy is again among us, and It seeks to destroy the Holy Catholic Church by infiltrating us with pedophile priests.

Our lawyers' advice—to deny the abuse, to admit nothing, to cajole or threaten victims to sign away their rights or go away quietly while allowing the abuses to mount by reassigning priests with known pedophilia crimes—has damaged the reputation of the Church and threatens our own souls.

There is talk in America of bishops and cardinals being prosecuted and, if guilty, being sent to prison for not complying with mandatory reporting laws and for facilitating these crimes (accomplice before and after the fact.)

Our policies have also resulted in yet more victims of crimes with stronger civil cases against us. It is estimated that at least 3000 priests have committed crimes against children in the United States. Each pedophile priest victimizes anywhere from a few children to, in the cases of John Geoghan and James Porter, hundreds each. Cases settled out of court cost us $100,000 to $400,000, exclusive of lawyer fees. Losses in court can cost us up to $30 million per case, again exclusive of attorney fees.

The problem of pedophile priests will likely cost the Church two trillion dollars.

If all the abuse stops right now. If there are no further cases.

In addition to legal and financial liabilities we incur by allowing any pedophile priest to continue in any form of ministry, the spiritual ramifications to the victims are extensive. We are risking the victims' souls by allowing them to be exposed to the Adversary and his minions.

Thus, I propose the following reorganizations to the Congregation for the Doctrine of the Faith and the Holy Roman Catholic Church:

1) The Congregation for the Doctrine of the Faith and the Institute for External Affairs must be autonomous, as they were before the reorganization

of the Holy Office in 1908. Sometimes, force must be used in service of the truth. Any means necessary to obtain information from those detained and to ensure that they never offend again must be employed. Information is our weapon in this war against the Great Diabolical among us.

2) Pedophilia stems from carnal lust, which in men, as we all know, is insatiable. Any priest, including bishops and cardinals, accused of any paraphilia must be immediately recalled to the Dominican brothers. Any priest sheltering an accused priest or not forthcoming with information relating to pedophile priests must also be detained.

3) Pedophilia is not merely a sin or a crime; it is also a compulsion and an addiction. Penance, heartfelt sorrow, drugs, electroshock or behavioral modification therapies have no effect. It is incurable. If any of the detained priests ever leave the Dominican monasteries, they will rape more children. It is the nature of the beast that they will sin again, in practice if they can, in their minds if they cannot. They will again betray the grace of ordination. We must give them an opportunity to go and sin no more.

The Sacrament of Reconciliation is a divine gift from God. It allows one who has made a good confession and truly repented to stand again in the good grace of Our Lord and attain salvation. To this end, we should grant the good Dominican brothers full authority to do what they must to extract a good confession and exact proper penance.

As part of the pedophiles' penance, they should be given the option of a method to go and sin no more and avoid all occasion of their sin. We must take care in the context of the penance. It must be presented and accepted as part of the admonition to go and sin no more.

However, if the verifiably guilty pedophile does not accept the penance, we know that he has not made a good and full confession, and the Dominican brothers should invite him to more reflection and self-inquiry until he is fully repentant.

4) The Church was created by Our Lord, Jesus Christ, to save souls, not lives. Pedophiles' sins endanger children's souls. Even if we are wrong

about the nature of reconciliation and the administration of penance and the Divinity does consider the pedophiles to be suicides, we will save the souls of their future victims, perhaps hundreds of souls per pedophile. See the enclosed case studies for details concerning the effects of sexual abuse on victims.

5) We must suspend all operations at all seminaries. Admission standards now are perhaps the most perfectly derived guidelines for rejecting healthy human beings and selecting men who exhibit dangerous personality traits.

CARDINAL PIOTR IVANOVICH recoiled from the description of Luke Dietrich's rape via candelabra and the pedophile's ejaculation into a consecrated communion chalice. He crumpled the paper in his spotted hands, horrified at the heresy that the priest had committed.

Bishop Tomas Aguirre ran from his computer screen and vomited in the bathroom, retching and spitting broth and unchewed pasta, when he read the account of John Williams's obscene reenactment of the Stations of the Cross. His own abuser had raped him in his bedroom while his parents were outside the house, cooling themselves on the porch.

Cardinal Francesco Delfino deleted the email after he read the first few lines. Just another one of those crybabies whining for attention. In ancient Greece it was de rigueur for a man to take a boy or a youth under his wing for mutual amusement.

The Pope, however, liked action plans. When he headed the CDF, he had been stymied by the mystic Pope who wafted within clouds of divine grace but did not understand the reality of cash flow and department politics. To Pope John Paul II, the godless Communists were still the enemy. The current Pope's view was far more pragmatic. He had joined the Hitler Youth as a boy in Germany because it was necessary for him and his family to survive. The Church would survive.

Within a month, thousands of priests including Cardinal Francesco Delfino were jailed with the Dominicans in the Italian Alps and the new witch hunts had begun.

Two months later, the seminaries closed.

Six months later, Dante was in charge of the hunt for pedophiles within the Church.

To some extent, his memorandum was calculated. Churches do not survive for two thousand years if they are threatened by bankruptcy.

The Church would not waste two trillion dollars to protect a few, inconsequential priests.

EVERY TIME Cardinal Dante Petrocchi-Bianchi signed a gold-embossed arrest warrant or a finding of guilt, he checked his phone, hoping that Leila still had his card, that she might call.

Her abuser, Sean, had recanted his sins readily, under moderate pressure.

Her lab's website had listed her email address and lab phone number. She must feel secure to have listed them publicly.

She must know.

In his wallet, a card bore her phone number and email, though he didn't allow himself to pursue her, but holding her phone number in his hand was not pursuit. He'd cut his hair when he returned to Roma in a practical, close-cropped style that attracted less attention from the lithe, lissome Roman women, in whose every step and bend and curve lurked Leila, Leila.

Chapter Twenty-Three: Leila

Leila's forehead thunked against the door as Dante walked away from her apartment. A blue flash popped into her vision, obscured the white-painted door, and spun away. Dante *should* walk away from her, Rappaccini's cloned daughter, a walking apoptosis ligand. He should *run*.

That last-ditch kiss haunted her. She would have fucked a priest.

But he was Just-Dante to her. He wasn't a hypocritical priest who memorized enough Latin to stumble through the Mass and heard your confession and baptized your cousins. He was a scientist and an M.D., and he'd written an essay supporting her when the journals were brimming with brimstone for her.

Like a priest always will, he'd chosen the Church over her.

She leaned against the door. Meth nuzzled his whiskery lips on her palm. The printer, umbilicized to the laptop in the center of the empty floor, grated another page.

Dante had left her. No drunken Jesuit would darken her doorstep ever again. Her chest felt heavy, like a small hole in her right cardiac atrium was leaking blood into her chest cavity. The right atrium is the small, upper chamber that receives blood from the body after the somatic cells have depleted the oxygen, and then the heart passes the blood to the right ventricle, and that pushes the blood up through the lungs to exchange gasses with the fresh, inhaled air. Yes, the right atrium must be her problem, because the wound seemed to be impacting her breathing, too, like she couldn't suck enough air and her body was starving.

She had almost fucked a priest *again*.

She'd wanted to change his mind, to make him fight for her, to make him want her again, but this was better for him. This way, he might live.

During that kiss, she had rationalized that she might as well get fucked because nothing mattered, not working or living or dying. When he'd turned on her, terror rose but she wasn't going to give in to it this time. It was just fucking. Nothing else.

She walked away from the front door and picked up the phone. She scrolled through saved numbers in the phone's memory, selected one, and let it dial. The receiver was cold and hard against her ear, like pressing a revolver to her ear to play Russian roulette.

A click traveled through the phone. Sean's voice whispered the name of his church in her ear, "St. John's Rectory. This is Father Gelineau."

St. John's served as a nursing home for aged priests. His reassignment had been part of the deal with the Church to not go public or press charges after Leila got pregnant. His voice was hoarse from a few more years of smoke settling on his larynx. He'd shared her first cigarette with her. Memories of his smooth voice whispering prayers in her ear raised bile in her throat. "Sean, it's Leila."

Rustling and clattering littered the phone line. "Leila? My Leila? Where are you? I've prayed every day that I'd find you again." His voice was so silky, rehearsed. He'd said the same thing last time, just before Meth chewed his leg half off. He said, "That's an odd area code."

She closed her eyes and rested her hand on Meth's warm head. He slurped his furry lips.

Sean asked, "How old are you now? Eighteen?"

"No." A hot tear squeezed through her closed eyelids, and she rubbed it off her face. When she was fifteen, at the Orthodox church and new high school, the other girls had speculated and gossiped that she'd had an affair with a priest. The rumor was that she'd had an abortion. They were wrong. It had been a miscarriage. Even babies died if she loved them. That had been nine years ago.

Nine years ago: two years of high school, three of undergrad, and four for her Ph.D.

"Ah," he sighed. "You're such a beautiful child." He sounded distracted, distant, like he had sounded on the beach a few blocks from her high school when they'd watched sea lions barking and surfing the glittering waves that pounded the shore, like a Pacific Poseidon was trying to smite Sean and save Leila before they climbed in his Corvette and he took her back to the rectory.

Her mouth was dry. Swallowing creased her throat. "Sean, I want to see you. I've waited for you. Have you been waiting for me?"

He sighed. "I couldn't find you. I couldn't wait for you forever. Would you want me to be lonely?" He sounded pleased with himself. Dante had been right. Sequestering Sean in the desert and surrounding him with old men had not stopped him. Her mistake had been fighting for him, *lying* for him, nine years ago. Leila licked her parched lips. "How old is she?"

"It's too late for us," he said. "I couldn't find you, and now I'm in love with her. She's so sweet."

Sean had told Leila that she was too mature to be called "sweet" anymore when she was thirteen. That day, she'd cried silently all the way through algebra.

Oh, God, she wished that Sean had loved her, but he hadn't. He'd just fucked her. Her frightened heart revved up and shook her body from the inside. "Sean, I talked to someone. I told him. He's a priest, too."

"Another priest? You were with another priest?" Sean asked. "Did you seduce him, too?"

"No." Her throat clamped on sobs. She lay down on the sleeping bag and curled sideways around a pillow.

"Leila, you can't help it. You seduce men because, in women, carnal lust is insatiable. I couldn't stop myself and now you've seduced another priest." His voice sharpened. "Now, who was this other priest you fucked?"

Her chest flapped like a rabid bat in a mousetrap. "He's with the Congregation for the Doctrine of the Faith."

"The Holy Office?" Sean's voice cracked.

"Sean, have you heard what's happening in Italy to priests who," her heart dry-heaved, "mess with kids?"

"*You told the Holy Office?*" Even his voice beat her, cracked her open like a walnut and scraped out flesh. "I'll make you sorry. I'll find you. I'll find you and make you sorry." His voice acquired that raging note, and she coiled more tightly around the beaded pillow and wept with her palm pressed over the phone.

Air rushed into her lungs, breathing for the first time instead of drowning. "They're coming for you."

Dante's business card nudged out from under her arm. Vatican things filled the front, even the long title of Consultor for the Congregation for the Doctrine of the Faith. Leila turned over Dante's business card. On the back, Dante had written in black ink with even, block letters, IF YOU NEED ANYTHING AT ALL, FOR ANY REASON, CALL. Phone numbers with area codes or city and country codes alternated with black lines.

From the phone lying beside her head, Sean said, "No one can run away from the *Vatican*, from the *Inquisition*. They'll find me, no matter where I go, no matter what I do."

She breathed, deeply and evenly, with no terror, no anxiety about who was waiting around the corner, for the first time in so many years. "I know."

She hung up the phone and sobbed until the printer finished grinding out her thesis. When she could breathe, she thumbed Dante's phone numbers into the memory of her cell phone, even though she could never call him. He might answer her call. He might come back, and she couldn't take that chance.

The silence lulled her to sleep, alone, exhausted, though her arms flinched at every pop and groan in the tower of apartments.

THE NEXT DAY, Leila deposited her thesis with the sullen thesis office clerk and drove away from New Hamilton.

Meth the dog sat in the passenger seat, panting and hanging his grizzled head out the passenger side window, flying toward New York.

About the author

T K Kenyon lives near New York City
with her family. She maintains a website
at www.tkkenyon.com.

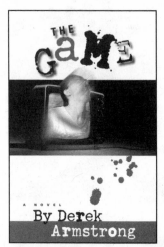

Provocative. Bold. Controversial.

The Game
A thriller by Derek Armstrong

Reality television becomes too real when a killer stalks the cast on America's number one live-broadcast reality show.
■ "A series to watch ... Armstrong injects the trope with new vigor." *Booklist*
US$ 24.95 | Pages 352, cloth hardcover
ISBN 978-1-60164-001-7 | EAN: 9781601640017
LCCN 2006930183

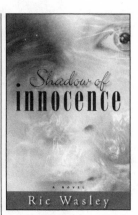

bang BANG
A novel by Lynn Hoffman

In Lynn Hoffman's wickedly funny *bang-BANG*, a waitress crime victim takes on America's obsession with guns and transforms herself in the process. Read along as Paula becomes national hero and villain, enforcer and outlaw, lover and leader. Don't miss Paula Sherman's one-woman quest to change America.
■ "Brilliant"
STARRED REVIEW, *Booklist*
US$ 19.95
Pages 176, cloth hardcover
ISBN 978-1-60164-000-0
EAN 9781601640000
LCCN 2006930182

Whale Song
A novel by Cheryl Kaye Tardif

Whale Song is a haunting tale of change and choice. Cheryl Kaye Tardif's beloved novel—a "wonderful novel that will make a wonderful movie" according to *Writer's Digest*—asks the difficult question, which is the higher morality, love or law?
■ "Crowd-pleasing ... a big hit." *Booklist*
US$ 12.95
Pages 208, UNA trade paper
ISBN 978-1-60164-007-9
EAN 9781601640079
LCCN 2006930188

Shadow of Innocence
A mystery by Ric Wasley

The Thin Man meets *Pulp Fiction* in a unique mystery set amid the drugs-and-music scene of the sixties that touches on all our societal taboos. *Shadow of Innocence* has it all: adventure, sleuthing, drugs, sex, music and a perverse shadowy secret that threatens to tear apart a posh New England town.
US$ 24.95
Pages 304, cloth hardcover
ISBN 978-1-60164-006-2
EAN 9781601640062
LCCN 2006930187

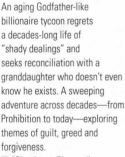